"In late 1944, Richard Matheson joined a combat division at the front as an eighteen-year-old replacement. This savagely realistic novel is the product of that experience. . . . Matheson has managed brilliantly to make all this come alive for the reader."

—*Chicago Tribune*

"Always moving and often funny . . . includes scenes of assaults stunning in their reality and shocking in their violence. It is said that Mr. Matheson waited fifteen years before writing this book. It is well worth the wait."

—*Esquire*

"A first-rate combat novel . . . much more than a superb account of combat. It is an exceptional study of a young American and the catalytic effect of war on the individual."

—*Rocky Mountain News*

"An unusually good war book . . . one of the most distinctive and powerful books to come out of World War II."

—*Oakland Tribune*

THE
BEARDLESS WARRIORS

RICHARD MATHESON

A Tom Doherty Associates Book *New York*

THE BEARDLESS WARRIORS

Copyright © 1960, renewed 1988 by Richard Matheson

This book is printed on acid-free paper.

First published in 1960 by Little, Brown and Company

Design by Jane Adele Regina

A Forge Book
Published by Tom Doherty Associates, LLC
175 Fifth Avenue
New York, NY 10010

www.tor.com

Forge® is a registered trademark of Tom Doherty Associates, LLC.

Library of Congress Cataloging-in-Publication Data

Matheson, Richard.
    The beardless warriors / Richard Matheson.—1st Forge ed.
        p. cm.
    "A Tom Doherty Associates book."
    ISBN 0-312-87831-1 (acid-free paper)
    1. World War, 1939–1945—Germany—Fiction.
    2. Americans—Germany—Fiction. 3. Soldiers—Fiction.
    4. Germany—Fiction.   I. Title.

PS3563.A8355 B4 2001
813'.54—dc21
                                                    2001018782

Printed in the United States of America

0 9 8 7 6 5 4 3 2

With love, for my sons
RICHARD and CHRISTIAN.
May the reading of this story
be the closest they ever come to war.

There never was a war that
was not inward . . .

—MARIANNE MOORE: *In Distrust*
of Merits

FIRST ASSAULT

When Hackermeyer joined the second squad of the third platoon of C Company, the first thing he heard was Sergeant Cooley blowing his top.

Hackermeyer had been sitting in a crowded truck all night and most of the morning and he ached. His legs and arms were stiff. His feet were almost numb. He hobbled to the tent of the company commander who passed him on to Assistant Platoon Sergeant Wadley. Wadley escorted him across the bivouac area, telling him what a rugged outfit he was joining.

"We're fighting men," said Wadley. "We ain't got no room for yellowbellies, understand?"

Hackermeyer grunted.

"*Give 'em hell*'s our motto," Sergeant Wadley said.

"Yeah," said Hackermeyer. Wadley reminded him of his Uncle George; the pretentious authority, the unconvincing bluster.

"Another thing," said Wadley, "I don't want to see you dumping gear, understand? I see you dumping gear, I'll put a bullet through your brain. Understand?"

Hackermeyer sniffed and limped along beside the barrel-chested, long-armed Wadley. Wadley's newly shaven cheeks were red and puffy while Hackermeyer's were colorless and flat. Wadley's helmet liner sat too high on his skull so that his head and helmet formed a giant egg shape. Hackermeyer's helmet rode too low. His inanimate black eyes were shadowed by the rim. Wadley moved in short, swaggering paces, one hand gripping the machine pistol hanging at his side. His expression was alertly grim. Hackermeyer plodded, his right thumb hooked beneath the sling of his rifle, his lean face emptied of expression.

As they neared the hollow where the second squad was, they began to hear the raving voice of Sergeant Cooley, who was talking to another soldier. Cooley saw them approaching and came striding over.

"What's this about leaving our overshoes behind?" he demanded.

Wadley bristled instantly.

"Orders, Cooley," he said in a quietly dangerous voice.

"What idiot would give orders like that?" said Cooley. "Christ's sake, ain't we had enough trench foot? Take away our overshoes and every man in the outfit'll be crawling back to the aid station!"

"I don't give the orders, Cooley!" Wadley shouted. "I just see they get followed out and, by Christ, they'll *get* followed out, understand?"

Cooley turned his head and spat tobacco juice.

"Watch it, Cooley," said Wadley in a threatening voice.

"Watch it yourself!" raged Cooley. "They know damn well it rains two days out of three up here!"

"Cooley!"

"They know damn well we got to walk through water! They know damn well we got to sleep in foxholes filled with rain! They know damn well it's going to snow soon!"

"Goddamn it, Cooley!" bellowed Wadley.

Hackermeyer stood by sleepily while Cooley and Wadley called each other names. He had slept an hour and twenty minutes on the truck and had been taken from the replacement depot two hours after arriving there from a three-day trip across France in a crowded boxcar. He was not interested in what the sergeants were arguing about. Sniffing, he watched them with heavy-lidded eyes.

Cooley appeared to be in his middle-forties. He was a man of medium height, chunky but not oversize. Wadley loomed gorilla-like next to him. Cooley's features were undistinguished except for his eyes which were a livid blue in the grimy, sun- and wind-burned, beard-stubbled leather of his face. He was wearing a

mud-spattered overcoat without stripes. The netting stretched
across his helmet was torn and there was a single, dried-up leaf
under it. Across Cooley's right shoulder hung a carbine.

Suddenly, he turned from Wadley's apoplectic bluster and
looked at Hackermeyer.

"What's this?" he asked.

"What do you think?" sneered Wadley. "A replacement."

Cooley chewed his tobacco reflectively. "How old are you?"
he asked.

"Eighteen," said Hackermeyer.

Cooley spat. "Swell," he said.

He turned to Wadley.

"I ain't running a rifle squad," he said. "I'm running a kindergarten."

"T-S," said Wadley through his protuberant teeth. He turned
away, looking ominous.

"We're not through talking," said Cooley.

Wadley glared across his shoulder. "Maybe you think we're
not through, but we're through, understand?"

"You tell Captain Miller for me—"

"I ain't telling nobody nothing!" Wadley raged. "And, by
Christ, them overshoes better be stacked high before we leave
this area! Understand?"

"Up yours," said Cooley.

Wadley spun around, red cheeks mottling. He looked at Cooley with assassin's eyes.

"Something on your mind?" asked Cooley.

Breath hissed out between Wadley's clenching teeth.

"Watch your step, Cooley," he warned. "Just watch your step,
understand?"

Cooley spat tobacco juice. Wadley glared at him, fingers whitening on the handle of his machine pistol. Then he turned on
his heel and stalked away. After two strides, he looked across his
shoulder.

"Remember what I said!" he ordered. He glowered at Hackermeyer. "You too, soldier!"

Cooley turned to Hackermeyer. "What'd he tell you?"

"Don't dump gear," said Hackermeyer.

"That's up to you," said Cooley. "Just make sure you don't dump that entrenching tool and maybe you'll see Christmas. Where you from?"

"Brooklyn," said Hackermeyer.

"When were you drafted?"

"June."

Cooley exhaled dispiritedly. "And here you are," he said.

"Yeah."

Cooley rubbed his face tiredly. "They must think this is a Boy Scout jamboree," he mumbled, looking around. "Dave!" he called.

The soldier to whom he'd been talking looked up from a book. Cooley beckoned to him and the soldier stood and came walking over. He was tall and well built with a pleasantly handsome face.

"Replacement," said Cooley. "What's your name, son?"

"Hackermeyer."

"This is Corporal Lippincott," said the sergeant. "My name's Cooley."

Hackermeyer nodded twice, his face impassive. Cooley sighed.

"Take him over to Wendt," he said.

"All right." Lippincott looked at Hackermeyer. "Let's go," he said.

"Take over in case anything comes up while I'm gone," said Cooley.

"Where you going?" asked Lippincott.

"To see Miller. This overshoes crap has got to cease."

"Why knock yourself out?" asked Lippincott.

"That dumbass of a colonel has got to see some light," said Cooley, starting off. Lippincott shook his head and smiled without amusement.

"Let's go," he said again.

They started walking.

"Something wrong with your feet?" asked Lippincott, noticing Hackermeyer's limp.

"Cold," said Hackermeyer.

"Better warm them up," said Lippincott.

"Yeah."

"Try to keep your feet dry," Lippincott told him. "Otherwise, you'll wind up getting trench foot. I don't suppose you've had any combat experience."

"No."

"How old are you?"

"Eighteen."

Lippincott nodded gravely.

"How many eighteen-year-olds in the squad?" asked Hackermeyer, remembering Cooley's remark that he was running a kindergarten.

Lippincott thought a moment. "Four including you," he said.

"Out of twelve?"

"Ten," said Lippincott. "We're short."

They walked up to a short soldier who was lying on a spread-out raincoat, head pillowed by his helmet. A cigarette jutted up from his chapped lips and his brown, woolen cap was pulled down over his eyes. His features were stubby, his beard a reddish-blond fuzz. He had a brown towel wrapped around his neck for a scarf.

"Wendt," said Lippincott.

Wendt lifted the edge of his cap from one eye and looked up groggily. "Uh?" he muttered.

"This is Hackmeyer," said Lippincott.

"Hackermeyer."

Lippincott nodded once. "Wendt can tell you most anything you want to know," he said. "We expect to move out tomorrow morning." He patted Hackermeyer's shoulder. "Glad you're with us," he said.

Wendt watched sleepily while Hackermeyer unslung his rifle and pack and sank down with a tired sigh. Hackermeyer blew his nose, then started to take off his overshoes.

"Seen much combat?" asked Wendt.

"No."

"Oh." Wendt blew out smoke which faded into the cold air. While Hackermeyer rubbed his feet, he saw a bazooka and rocket shells beside Wendt. "You a bazooka man?" he asked.

"Yeah," said Wendt. "I got the only one left in the squad. You can lug the shells. I got a buddy did it but they're using him for company messenger." He yawned. "Old Foley," he said.

"He's old?" asked Hackermeyer.

Wendt snickered. "Eighteen," he said. "How old are you?"

"Eighteen."

Wendt snickered cracklingly. "Cooley must have dropped his teeth," he said. "That makes four of us now."

"Why aren't there twelve in the squad?" asked Hackermeyer.

"There was," said Wendt.

"Killed?"

"One was. One was wounded." Wendt coughed. "Hell, we're in good shape," he said. "There's a squad in the second platoon had only one man left."

"What did they do with him?"

Wendt shrugged. "Probably shot him so it came out even," he said.

Hackermeyer nodded.

"You a Jew?" asked Wendt.

"No."

"We got Goldmeyer in the squad and he's a Jew. I thought maybe you were."

"He eighteen?"

"Uh-uh," said Wendt, yawning. "Me, Foley, and Guthrie."

"Guthrie?"

"He's from Los Angeles. He's nuts. His old man writes movies."

"Yeah?"

"You see that movie where the Marine kills off the whole Jap army practically?"

"No."

"Well, he wrote it, Guthrie's old man."

Wendt blew out smoke.

"What a life," he said. "Screwing movie stars and raking in the loot. Boy."

"Why doesn't the sergeant like eighteen-year-olds?" Hackermeyer asked.

"He don't like nineteen-year-olds either," said Wendt.

"Why?"

"He thinks we don't know what we're doing." Wendt yawned prodigiously.

"Who else is in the squad?" asked Hackermeyer.

"There's Guthrie, me, Foley. Goldmeyer. Lazzo. Old Bill Riley—he's really old—thirty-nine. Corporal Lippincott, Schumacher, and the Sarge."

"How old is he?"

"The Sarge?"

"Yeah."

"A hundred and twenty probably. I don't know. Fifty, maybe. I suppose about thirty-eight."

Wendt turned his head slowly and looked at Hackermeyer's gear. "Might as well lighten up," he said.

"Huh?"

"Dump some of that crap. Cut your overcoat to officer length. Get rid of your gas mask—you could use the bag for carrying stuff. Toss out your blankets, shelter half, pegs, rope."

"Sergeant Wadley said—"

"Screw him," said Wendt.

Hackermeyer knew he wouldn't be able to throw away any equipment. It had always been pounded into him by his uncle to take zealous care of everything given to him. Even though he'd hated his uncle, the habit was ingrained. Without thinking about it, he took spiritless care of all possessions and never wasted food.

He glanced at Wendt, who had pulled the woolen cap over his eyes again. Then he looked at the tree a few yards away, its dark twigs reaching upward like charred skeleton fingers. It reminded him of the tree in front of his uncle's house. He thought about the letter he'd gotten from his Cousin Clara, two weeks before, demanding again that he have a monthly pay allotment sent to her and her mother. Clara was just the way Uncle George had been. No matter how poorly they'd treated Hackermeyer, they had always expected gratitude for taking him into their house.

Hackermeyer sniffed tiredly. Well—perhaps it was just as well he'd always been treated lousy. By now, he was used to things being rotten. Maybe combat wouldn't bother him at all.

"What are you doing?" asked Wendt. He had just awakened.

"Changing my socks," said Hackermeyer.

"What for?"

"Keep my feet dry," said Hackermeyer.

Wendt made the snickering noise. It sounded as if he had a congestion in his sinuses.

"Another Schumacher," he said, taking out a cigarette. "He's always changing his socks too. He even changes his underwear."

He shook his head and blew out smoke, tossing the match away.

"Cleans his M1 every day," he said. "Cleans his bayonet. Polishes his mess kit. Even shaves! And you should see his foxholes—they're like two-room apartments! Screwiest nut I ever saw."

"How old is he?"

"Who knows? Thirty, forty."

Hackermeyer put his shoes back on, tied the laces firmly and buckled the legging straps. He started tugging on his overshoes.

"Might as well leave 'em off," said Wendt. "They ain't going to let us keep them."

"I know," said Hackermeyer. He put the overshoes on anyway. He'd take them off when he was ordered.

"You know where we're going?" he asked, after a while.

"Some city, I suppose," said Wendt.

Hackermeyer blew his nose.

"We go alone?" he asked.

"We get tanks sometimes," said Wendt.

"That's good," said Hackermeyer.

"Good, nothing," said Wendt. "You can hear the bastards a mile away. You're near a tank, you get shelled even if the Krauts can't see you."

Wendt stretched his legs, then winced and pressed at his side.

"Lousy bellyache," he said. He relaxed and rubbed gingerly at his side. Then he reached under his pants and scratched his groin.

"Lousy crabs," he said.

"You have crabs?" asked Hackermeyer.

"I got everything," said Wendt. He turned his head and looked at Hackermeyer. "You ever seen a crab?" he asked.

Hackermeyer shook his head.

"If I can find one," said Wendt. His face took on an absorbed expression as he searched. "Wish I was a crab sometimes," he said. "Nice and warm down here. Lots of places for houses too."

Finally he sighed. "Aw, you can't catch them," he said. He grimaced and drew in a quick breath. "Look like real crabs though," he said. "Nearly dropped my teeth the first time I picked one off. I thought it was a scab. Put it on my thumb and the little bastard crawled!"

Hackermeyer wondered if there were any other questions he should ask about combat. He felt he should make some effort to prepare himself.

"Yeah, I got everything," said Wendt. "Had the runs halfway across France. I remember we was in a forty-and-eight, like sardines. It didn't stop very much so Lazzo and Goldmeyer had to hold me out the door." Wendt crossed his arms and shivered.

"Yeah, I got everything," he said. "Probably got the clap too."

He yawned and closed his eyes. Shortly after, bubbly snores began pulsing in his throat.

Hackermeyer took out his crossword puzzle book and started working on the puzzle he'd been doing since early November. He often thought how odd it was that he derived pleasure from crossword puzzles. He'd never cared much for taxing his brain. His report cards had been grotesque. If he hadn't left high school when he did, he'd still be a sophomore. Damn stupid, inattentive bungler; that was what Uncle George had always called him. Well, he'd only gotten bad grades to make Uncle George angry. He wasn't that stupid.

Hackermeyer's eyes drifted out of focus. Not that stupid at all. Actually, sort of shrewd, possessing a cold, calculating sharpness. He imagined himself in combat, moving smoothly, cunningly. He saw himself fling downward on the ground, roll over fast, bullets spitting into the earth nearby, missing him completely. He came up, fast, eyes slitted, rifle barking. One German down, two, then three. They jolted under the impact of his deadly aimed bullets. They plunged over dead. He leaped up, sprinted, weaving, across the field, eluding bullets like an all-star quarterback eluding tacklers; fast and sure and clever. He flung down, jerked out a grenade pin with his teeth, reared up, fired it off like Bobby Feller— right down the gullet of a tank cannon. *Boom!* One Nazi tank kaput. Shouts of flabbergasted surprise from the other members of the squad. *The Congressional Medal of Honor is awarded to Everett Harold Hackermeyer for distinguished . . .*

The sneeze brought him back. Hackermeyer looked around the field, startled, his heart thudding. *I'll show them*, he thought. But he knew it wasn't so. How could he be any good in combat? He'd never been good at anything else.

Hackermeyer sucked in at the cold, damp air. He tried to concentrate on his crossword puzzle but he couldn't. After a while, his thoughts floated into a daydream about capturing a German village singlehanded and meeting a lovely, golden-haired *Fräulein* who had been waiting for him all her lovely life.

"OH, GOD, HERE it comes again," said Wendt.

Raindrops started drumming on their helmets. Hackermeyer sneezed as he got up and unfolded his shelter half, covering himself and his gear. Wendt stared at him.

"Well, Jesus," said Wendt finally. "How about letting a guy sit under there with you?"

"Oh." Hackermeyer looked blank. "You want to?"

"Jesus, what do you think?" Wendt interrupted.

Hackermeyer thought: That's what you get for ditching your shelter half. He grunted and moved over a little to make room.

The rain spattered off the slick surface above them. Wendt took a small book out of his coat pocket and looked at it intently. Hackermeyer, nibbling on half a D-bar, saw that it was a storybook about Mickey Mouse. All the dialogue was in French.

"What do you suppose Mickey's saying?" Wendt asked. He kept looking at the book, confused, then put it away.

"Got any dirty pictures?" he asked.

"No."

"Shoot," said Wendt. He sighed. "I had some good ones in my duffel bag."

Wendt yawned widely, then took out a cigarette and lit it. It was beginning to get dark. Hackermeyer sneezed and blew his nose, wincing at the tenderness.

"You smoke?" asked Wendt.

"No."

"Drink?"

"No."

"Not even beer?"

"No."

Wendt yawned. "Wish this lousy war was over," he said. "I'm sick of sitting in the rain."

"Are the Germans good fighters?" asked Hackermeyer.

"Bet your ass," said Wendt. He bent over, squirming a little. "Lousy bellyache," he muttered. He straightened up, exhaling smoke. "Yeah, I got everything," he said.

The rain was falling more heavily now. Large drops struck the shelter half like hundreds of urgently tapping fingers. Hackermeyer wondered what else he should ask about combat.

"Where'd you get your last lay?" asked Wendt.

"Brooklyn," said Hackermeyer after a few moments.

"Any good?"

"Yeah."

Wendt blew out a cloud of smoke. "Me, I haven't had a thing since Metz," he said.

Hackermeyer listened while Wendt described, in detail, his experience in Metz. When he'd finished, Wendt stared gloomily at the ground.

"Yeah, I been doing it since I was six," he said.

"Six?" Hackermeyer sounded as surprised as he was capable of sounding.

"There was this Southern girl up the block," said Wendt,

brightening. "Twelve years old. I used to go to her house every day."

"Six?"

"She did everything," said Wendt. "It was a real education." He massaged his stomach as he talked. After a while, he lost interest in the story and ended it in the middle of a sentence. "Damn, I wish this lousy rain would stop," he said. "That's all it does here is rain."

Hackermeyer felt around in his pack and found his toothbrush case. He took out the brush and sprinkled some tooth powder on it.

"What are you doing?" asked Wendt.

"Brushing my teeth," said Hackermeyer.

"How come?"

"I always do."

"Shhh-oot." Wendt looked confounded. "You and Schumacher ought to start a club."

Hackermeyer brushed his teeth slowly and carefully and rinsed out his mouth. His canteen was almost empty.

"Where do you get water?" he asked.

"From a shell hole," answered Wendt. "Stick a couple of chlorine tablets in and let it sit awhile."

"Chlorine?"

"Didn't they give you any?"

"No."

"Oh, Christ." Wendt felt around in his pockets and took out a small container. "Here," he said. "Keep 'em. I got another."

Hackermeyer grunted. He supposed he ought to thank Wendt but he couldn't. He'd been forced to say thank you too many times for things that he hadn't been thankful for.

"Wish I had a beer," said Wendt. "You like beer?"

"No." Hackermeyer couldn't stand the smell. It reminded him of his uncle's breath. His father's too. Sweet and gagging.

After a while, he and Wendt lay down back to back. Hackermeyer made sure the shelter half was covering his rifle, then closed his eyes.

He wondered if Wendt had really done all those things with girls. It was hard to believe. But maybe that was because of his own situation. Maybe such things were inconceivable to him because he'd never had a sex experience in his life. He'd never told anyone, of course. He never would. It was easy enough to indicate that you knew more about sex than you did. No one ever asked for details. They were too anxious to tell you about their own experiences.

Hackermeyer sniffed and rubbed at his dripping nostrils. He wondered what it would really be like to get into bed with a naked girl. The only female he'd ever seen naked was his Cousin Clara when he was nine and had walked into the bathroom while she was drying herself. All he could recall was an impression of thick, white flesh and black hair. Hackermeyer made a face. If that was what all girls looked like . . .

He remembered his Uncle George taking him to the cellar that night and whipping him with the razor strop. He remembered crying and saying that it wasn't his fault Clara hadn't locked the bathroom door. Uncle George had beaten him a lot harder after he'd said that.

Hackermeyer opened his eyes and stared at the leaden sky, his chest swelling with breath. Well, that was past. His uncle was dead and no one could make him go back to that house anymore. He was on his own. They might kill him but they couldn't hurt him.

It was strange, he thought. Here he was going into combat in the morning and he hadn't thought about it very much. He supposed that asking Wendt where they were going and if the Germans were good fighters indicated that he *was* thinking about it. Still, he felt no strong emotion. Maybe that wasn't too odd. It had been a long time since he had felt emotional about anything. Even a war couldn't change that. If he was killed, what of it? Nobody would miss him. On the contrary, Clara would be delighted. She and her mother would get a lot of money from his G.I. insurance.

Hackermeyer frowned. It had been stupid to name them as

beneficiaries just for the pleasure of not naming his father. He could have chosen somebody more deserving.

Like Hitler, for instance.

HACKERMEYER OPENED HIS eyes and sneezed. The rain had stopped and it was colder. He heard a sound he couldn't identify. While he was listening to it, he raised his left arm and looked at the radium-lit face of his watch. It was almost ten o'clock.

The sounds grew louder. Suddenly he realized that it was Wendt making tiny vibrating noises in his throat. Hackermeyer pushed up on one elbow and twisted around. Wendt had rolled from under the shelter half and was curled up on the ground, shivering.

"Wendt?"

There was no response. Hackermeyer lay still for a few minutes. Then he struggled to his feet, his bone joints crackling, and shook the water off his shelter half. Lying down, he drew up the collar of his overcoat, pulled down his woolen cap. He felt around for his helmet and withdrew the liner. Putting it on, he lay down again.

Wendt kept making noises in his throat. After a while, he started groaning as if he were in pain. Hackermeyer lay motionless, listening to him. He wondered if Wendt was having a bad dream. Maybe the shock of combat hit you afterward instead of before.

Wendt sobbed. "Momma."

Hackermeyer shuddered. He sat up and felt a cold wind blowing on his cheeks.

"Momma," said Wendt in a pitiful voice.

Hackermeyer swallowed. "Wendt?" he said.

He twitched as Wendt began to cry. "What is it?" he asked.

Wendt kept crying and groaning. Hackermeyer stood up and squatted beside him. He put his hand on Wendt's shoulder.

"Momma?" Wendt sounded as if he were begging. "Momma?"

"What's wrong?" asked Hackermeyer, frowning.

Wendt shuddered violently and drew his legs up further. His

teeth began to chatter. He started making short, breathless sounds of pain. Hackermeyer stood up to get help, then shrank back as a figure loomed from the darkness.

"What's up?" asked Cooley.

"I don't know."

Cooley crouched hastily beside Wendt. "What is it, son?" he asked.

Wendt sobbed and whined. Hackermeyer could hear his shoes kicking fitfully at the ground. He saw Cooley reach down and, suddenly, a cry of agony tore from Wendt's lips. It seemed to fill the night. Hackermeyer jumped.

Cooley straightened up. "Don't let him move," he ordered.

"What's wrong with—"

Cooley was already gone. Hackermeyer turned back to Wendt and looked down blankly at him. Wendt sobbed and whimpered and kept asking for his mother.

Ten minutes later, Cooley returned with a medic and a stretcher. As they lifted the writhing Wendt onto the canvas he screamed in pain and tried to sit up. Cooley pressed his shoulders back.

"Take it easy, son," he said.

Wendt started crying again. He sounded like a frightened little boy. Hackermeyer stood motionless, watching them carry him away. Before they disappeared, he heard the medic use the word "appendicitis."

When they were gone Hackermeyer lay back down on the shelter half. It seemed to be getting colder every minute. Hackermeyer got a blanket from his pack and pulled it over himself. He could feel the uneven surface of the ground beneath him, smell the cold, sour odor of the wet dirt. Far off, he heard a truck climbing a hill in low gear. The grinding of its engine sounded like the howling of some angry beast. Close by, he heard the passing thud of boot falls, the faint, clinking rattle of equipment. He opened his eyes and looked off into the night-hooded distance.

Wendt was lucky to get appendicitis. Now he wouldn't have

to go into combat tomorrow. Of course, he'd already seen action. But he was lucky to miss seeing more of it. He might have gotten killed tomorrow.

Sergeant Cooley probably also thought that it was lucky Wendt had gotten sick. That meant there was one less eighteen-year-old in his squad. Hackermeyer wondered why Cooley objected to teenage soldiers. It seemed, offhand, that they'd be able to adjust to war better than older men. Not having a wife or kids back home, they had less to worry about. And they weren't settled in their ways. They were used to being on the move a lot. They were more independent all the way around. Except, of course, most of them were tied to their mother's apron strings. Like Wendt, for instance. For all his talk, it was his mother he'd cried for in the darkness and the pain. That's where I'm better off, Hackermeyer thought.

He'd heard the voice for several minutes now repeating something. Only as he returned from his thoughts did he realize that what was being repeated was Wendt's name. He pressed up on an elbow and looked around, waiting for the voice to speak again.

"Wendt?" it finally said.

"Over here," said Hackermeyer.

There was a sound of stumbling. A second voice snarled, "Goddamn it, watch it!"

"Gee, I'm sorry," said the first voice timidly. The footsteps drew closer. "Where are you, Artie?"

"I'm not—" Hackermeyer broke off as the figure emerged from the darkness.

"Hi, Artie," said the voice.

"I'm not Wendt," said Hackermeyer.

"Oh. Where is he?"

"He got appendicitis."

"Oh, no," said the voice.

"You Foley?" asked Hackermeyer.

"Yeah." Foley coughed liquidly. "How did you know?"

"Wendt told me."

"Wh-who are you?"

"I joined the squad today."

"Oh." Foley stood there without moving. "Well—did—did Wendt leave a—blanket or anything?"

"No."

"Oh. Gee. I haven't got anything."

Hackermeyer saw Foley's left hand go to his mouth. He heard the faint sound of Foley gnawing on his glove. He closed his eyes for a few moments, then opened them again. Foley was still there. Hackermeyer frowned and pressed his teeth together.

"Well . . . you can—sit on my shelter half, I suppose," he said.

"Gee, thanks." Foley unslung his rifle and drove its bayonet into the ground. He took off his pack and sat down beside Hackermeyer.

"I'm glad to meet you," he said. Hackermeyer felt something nudge against him and realized that it was Foley's hand. He held it for a second, then let go.

"What's your first name?" asked Foley, after Hackermeyer had told him his last.

"Everett."

Foley cleared his throat. "Mine's John," he said, taking out his handkerchief. He blew his nose.

"Just can't get rid of this cold," he said.

Hackermeyer lay down and crossed his arms over his chest. Foley undoubtedly meant he'd had the cold for a few weeks. Not months as it had been with him; and year after year in the wintertime.

"Appendicitis. Poor Artie." Foley sounded unhappy.

Hackermeyer closed his eyes. If he was going into combat tomorrow morning, he'd better get some sleep.

"Did they—serve supper?" asked Foley.

"Yeah."

"Oh. Gee."

Hackermeyer tried to go to sleep.

"I was—delivering a message and didn't get any," said Foley.

Hackermeyer grunted. Tough, he thought. Then, after a few moments, he exhaled irritably, reached into his pocket and drew out what remained of his D-bar. He pushed it against Foley's hand.

"What is it? Oh—gee, I don't want to—" Foley coughed. "You sure you don't want it?"

"No," muttered Hackermeyer. He felt stupid for giving food away.

"Well . . . gee, thanks, Everett."

Hackermeyer heard the crunching sound of Foley eating the hard chocolate. He twisted onto his side with a grunt.

"Boy, this is good," said Foley.

Hackermeyer tried to sleep.

"I sure do thank you," said Foley.

Hackermeyer tensed. Just shut up, he thought.

"Have you been in combat?" Foley asked.

"No," said Hackermeyer curtly.

Foley coughed. "Well," he said awkwardly. "Combat isn't—too bad."

"It isn't?" Hackermeyer opened his eyes in surprise.

"Well, I haven't—really seen much, I guess," amended Foley. "I spend most of my time delivering messages. So—outside of eighty-eights and screaming meemies, I don't see much."

"What's screaming meemies?" asked Hackermeyer.

"German mortar shells," said Foley. "They sound like—banshees or something. I hate them."

"Oh."

"Then there's flak."

"Flak?"

"Antiaircraft shells," said Foley.

Hackermeyer opened his eyes again. "For *us*?" he asked.

"They explode in the air," said Foley. "An air burst can get you in a foxhole."

Hackermeyer swallowed. "You know where we're going?" he asked.

"Some town," said Foley. "It's about—six miles from here, I think they said."

"What's it called?"

"Saar—something."

"Are we in Germany?" asked Hackermeyer.

"Just inside," said Foley.

Hackermeyer felt his fingers twitch.

"Is it a—big town?" he asked.

"I don't know," said Foley. "I really don't know anything about it, Everett."

It was strange hearing his first name. When he was in school, the other boys had always called him Hack. Or Horseface.

Foley finished the D-bar and licked his fingers. "That was sure good," he said. "I thank you again."

Germany, Hackermeyer thought. He'd thought they were somewhere in eastern France.

"Well, I guess we better get some rest," said Foley. He made a sound of rueful amusement. "Big day tomorrow," he said.

Hackermeyer grunted. *Germany*.

Foley lay down beside him on the shelter half and, in a few minutes, began to snore quietly. Hackermeyer lay on his back looking up at the ice-blue stars and thinking about the next day.

After a while he thought again about Wendt crying for his mother. He started to remember the last time he'd cried. It had been over three years before. Uncle George had been so ill that his father—who was Uncle George's brother—had come to stay at the house for a few days. Hackermeyer had been disrespectful to him, avoiding his presence, rarely answering when his father spoke to him and making constant reference to his father's and uncle's drinking.

One afternoon—it had been a Wednesday, Hackermeyer recalled—as he'd risen from the kitchen table without asking to be excused, his father had lost his temper and told him to sit down until they were all finished eating. He'd refused, walking out of the kitchen without a word. Behind, he'd heard the sudden scrape of his father's chair and he'd walked quickly to the front hall stairs. He'd started up the steps, planning to lock himself in his room.

His father had caught him at the head of the staircase and tried to spank him. Hackermeyer had resisted fiercely, kicking and scratching, saliva running down his jaw. Then his father had started slapping him across the face, and he'd lost all fight and slumped to the floor, crying breathlessly. His father had stood over him, breathing hard, glaring down at him. Hackermeyer re-membered how his father's lank black hair had hung in threads across his forehead. *You'll never come to anything*, his father had said. *You'll never come to anything at all. There's nothing but mean-ness in you.*

Then his father had gone back to the kitchen and finished having lunch with Aunt Alice and Cousin Clara. For a long time, Hackermeyer had lain curled up on the cold linoleum-covered floor, unable to stop crying.

He had never cried since. And never would again. There was nothing in this world worth crying for.

December 9, 1944

FOLEY SAT ON the ground, cross-legged and helmetless. He was of medium height and a little plump. His face was roundly pink-ish, resembling that of a young boy. His sandy hair was stuck to his head in clumps. Hackermeyer watched him breathe the lenses of his glasses cloudy, then polish them with a khaki-colored handkerchief. When he was finished, Foley slipped the glasses back on and smiled.

"I think it's ready now," he said.

Hackermeyer picked up his canteen and shook it a little. He unscrewed the cap and sniffed at the contents.

"Try it," said Foley.

Hackermeyer took a sip and moved the water around in his mouth. Gingerly, he swallowed it.

"How do you like it?" asked Foley.

Hackermeyer made a face. "Tastes like a swimming pool," he said.

Foley laughed and clapped his hands. "It does," he said. "It's the chlorine."

Hackermeyer didn't smile. He rarely did.

"Funny, I thought you were about thirty when we were talking last night," said Foley. "I'd have never guessed you were eighteen." He put on his helmet and stood. "Well, I guess I better report to the captain," he said.

Hackermeyer watched him getting on his equipment. Foley seemed completely out of character as a soldier. As if he had been badly miscast for some high school play.

"Maybe I can get to see Artie if I deliver a message far enough back," Foley said. He drew his bayonet out of the ground and looked at the rifle.

"Ooh, it's getting so rusty," he said.

"Clean it."

"I know, I should," said Foley in a distressed voice. "I have so little time, though." He sighed, "Oh, well," and slung the M1 over his right shoulder. He smiled down at Hackermeyer.

"Well," he said, "I guess I'll—see you again."

Hackermeyer grunted.

Foley's smile faltered. "Good luck, Everett," he said and turned away. Hackermeyer watched him walk across the field toward company headquarters.

After Foley had disappeared, Hackermeyer sat on the shelter half, gazing around the field. Everywhere he looked, he could see men talking, reading, writing letters, cleaning rifles, drifting aimlessly. Hackermeyer felt a tightness gathering in his stomach muscles. Soon now, he thought. Combat was getting closer and closer. He noticed that his breath was growing strained and he sucked in a deep lungful of air, letting it waver out between his lips. I'll make it, he thought.

Abruptly, he reached under his overcoat and worked the wallet free from his pocket. He slid out the creased photograph and gazed at it.

She looked so young. When this photograph was taken, she was only a few years older than Hackermeyer was now. He stared at the smiling face of his mother. And, once again, he wondered what it would have been like to know her. She looked so pleasant. Certainly it would have been nicer living with her than with his uncle and aunt and Cousin Clara. Maybe, if she had lived, his father might have liked him too.

Hackermeyer slapped the wallet shut. Well, the hell with that.

He didn't need his father. He didn't need anybody. He was alone and that was the way he liked it.

He heard approaching footsteps and glanced across his shoulder. It was Cooley. Hackermeyer slid the wallet into his overcoat pocket.

"You think you can take over the bazooka?" asked Cooley.

"Yeah," said Hackermeyer.

"You know how it works?" asked Cooley.

"Who'll load it?"

"You if nobody's around," said Cooley.

"I thought you had to have two men."

"This ain't basic training, Hackermeyer," said Cooley. "You know how to aim it?"

"I—think so."

"Oh . . ." Cooley spat tobacco juice, then bent over and picked up the bazooka and the container of shells. "I'll give it to Riley," he said.

He stopped and looked back.

"You know how to fire the M1, don't you?" he asked.

"First you—"

"All right, all right," said Cooley. "Just don't shoot one of us."

"No," said Hackermeyer.

Cooley glanced upward as he walked away. "Kids," he mumbled. He walked five paces, then stopped again and looked across his shoulder.

"Better look to your weapon, son," he said quietly. "We'll be moving out soon."

"I did," said Hackermeyer.

Cooley studied him for several moments, then turned with a sigh and walked away.

IT WAS ODDLY warm for December. Just after eight, sunlight had pierced a rift in the gray pall of clouds, then the clouds had faded. Now the sky was a brassy blue.

The squad crouched in a semicircle around Cooley. It was almost nine.

"We got us a real easy job," said Cooley. "All we got to do is walk across a couple of miles of fields, go through a forest and cross another field to Saarbach."

"Nothing to stop us?" asked Goldmeyer. He was twenty-three, thin, with a worriedly solemn expression.

"Only Krauts," said Cooley.

"No Japanese?" asked Guthrie.

Cooley glanced at him, lips pinched together as though he had just tasted something bitter. He spat to one side, then looked back at the others.

"We're in their territory now," he said. "We'll be up against the West Wall soon. So it'll be slow going. The Krauts ain't running anymore. They're going to fight like hell, so be ready for it."

"You mean we're not reserve squad?" asked Guthrie.

Cooley paid no attention to him.

"This sketch on the ground will give you an idea where we're heading," he said. "This is the hill we're standing on. This is a stream we'll be crossing. It'll be our line of departure. This is a knocked-out town we'll be passing through. Assault position is just the other side of it. Immediate platoon objective is this ridge here. Our squad takes the right side of it. After we take it, we reorganize and keep going for the forest if we can. Here's our route."

Hackermeyer listened carefully, wondering if he should take notes. It seemed like an awful lot to remember. Where they'd be in the platoon column. How they'd change over from squad diamond to skirmish line at the assault position. What they'd do in case of a counterattack. Where the aid station was. Where the company ammo supply would be.

"This ain't going to be no picnic," Cooley warned. "We're up against at least two divisions of Krauts and most of them know exactly what they're doing. They'll be throwing everything at us but Hitler's jock strap. Eighty-eights, machine guns, mortars, grenades, rockets, tanks, the works. Counterattacks are to be expected. So stay on your toes. Figure ahead and keep living. And, at all times, keep your eyes on me. Who hasn't got cotton? Hackermeyer?"

"Huh?"

Cooley took a small box of cotton from his overcoat pocket and tore off a wad. "Put some in your ears before we move out," he said. "Anyone else?" He looked around. "All right, I'll check your gear now."

He started examining their weapons and equipment.

"Now that you know how rough it's going to be, don't brood about it," he said. "I'm not telling you these things to panic you. I'm telling you about them so you'll be ready for whatever comes. Don't start spooking yourselves before it's time. Watch your terrain. When we're shelled—and we will be—try to get behind something—even a rise in the ground. Screen off the concussion. Look for the explosions. Your ears can take it better if you resist the noise."

"Sergeant?" said Hackermeyer.

Cooley turned. "This is Hackermeyer," he said. He looked at Hackermeyer. "Well?" he asked.

"Do we shoot at will?" asked Hackermeyer.

"What?" asked Cooley. The squad members chuckled.

"Do we wait for orders before we shoot?" asked Hackermeyer, tensing.

Cooley stared at him. "I wouldn't if I was you," he said.

Hackermeyer nodded once. So how am I supposed to know? he thought irritably.

"Gawd," muttered Cooley. He shook his head as if recovering from a blow. Then he glanced down at Hackermeyer's feet. "Them overshoes come off," he said.

Hackermeyer nodded.

Cooley turned back to the others.

"You all know what a pile it is for us to leave our overshoes behind," he said. "I saw Captain Miller yesterday and he said there's nothing he can do. It's Colonel Vesey's idea. Makes us more mobile, says the colonel." He spat to the west. "Anyway, the captain says we'll probably get them back after we're in Saarbach."

"What if we don't get in Saarbach?" asked Guthrie.

"Then we'll have cold feet!" snapped Cooley. He hissed out

aggravated breath. "If it turns out we don't get them back right away, try to take care of your feet. Change your socks, dry your shoes . . ." His voice faded off. "Hell," he said, "I know you can't waste time with shoes and socks in combat but—well, do the best you can because we can't spare a man."

He grimaced. "Or a child," he said.

"That's us," said Guthrie.

"Shut your mouth," said Cooley wearily. He looked at the seven of them a moment, then made a clucking sound.

"You'll be fine," he said.

THEY WERE READY to move out. The regiment was spread across the plain, a vast, staggered assembly of soldiers that stretched as far as Hackermeyer could see. He checked his watch. It was nine-forty.

Directly in front of him were Sergeant Cooley and Bill Riley, who carried the bazooka and its shells. To Hackermeyer's left were Lippincott and Goldmeyer, who was assistant BAR man to Lazzo. Schumacher led the diamond. Behind and to the right of him was Lazzo with the Browning automatic rifle. In front of Goldmeyer was Guthrie with the second BAR. Some of them wore combat packs; all carried extra bandoleers of cartridges crisscrossed over their chests. They had three hand grenades each.

Hackermeyer had the impression that he was an impostor, attired in a costume totally unsuited to him. He drew in a long breath and took the M1 off his shoulder. He scratched his leg. He looked at his watch. It was almost nine-forty-five. He made sure the safety lock of his M1 was on. He didn't want the rifle to go off until it was time. He put it back across his shoulder, then unslung it and held it at high port before his chest. He made sure it was loaded. He put it in the crook of his arms, then under one arm, then under the other. Finally, he slung it back on his right shoulder. He checked his watch. It was nine-forty-five.

He twitched a little as one of the platoon officers blew a whistle. Abruptly, he lurched forward, then stopped, seeing that Cooley hadn't moved. Swallowing, he stood watching the Sergeant. After a few minutes, as the men up ahead began to advance, Cooley raised his right arm, gestured once and started walking. Hackermeyer followed him. All he could see ahead was the plain and the endless, drifting mass of troops.

After ten minutes of walking, the plain began to slope downward. Hackermeyer walked more quickly. He could see farther into the distance now. There was no sign of a forest. He felt himself relaxing. He had thought they'd be in sight of Saarbach, even though Foley had said it was six miles away.

At the bottom of the slope was the stream Cooley had mentioned. It was shallow and fast-moving. Hackermeyer hesitated on its bank and looked at the rushing, crystal current. He could see small stones tumbling end over end along the bottom.

He heard a rattling of equipment as Lippincott entered the stream several yards away, his shoes splashing water. Hackermeyer stepped down into the stream, grimacing as the icy water swept across his shoes and soaked the bottoms of his leggings. As he started up the opposite slope, he felt the water squishing around inside his shoes. He'd have to change socks as soon as possible. How long would that be, though? They'd barely started out.

At the top of the slope, they passed through the small, shell-battered town. Every building in it had been reduced to rubble. Hackermeyer wondered where the people had gone. Could the entire population of a town find shelter elsewhere? Maybe they'd all been killed. As he walked, his shoes crunched over the layers of debris on the road. His nostrils became clogged with mortar dust and he sneezed. It sounded very loud. Taking out a handkerchief, he blew his nose as softly as he could.

After five minutes of steady walking, the squad left the town and walked out onto another plain which looked, to Hackermeyer, exactly like the first one—broad, almost treeless with a ground covering of dead, curled-over grass. They were in the assault position now, he thought. The squad began to spread out into a skirmish line.

Hackermeyer wondered how he'd first see the Germans.

Would they be stretched out across the plain, coming in the opposite direction? Would they charge, screaming? Hackermeyer shivered. Suddenly, it seemed as if he couldn't remember how the M1 worked. He concentrated on the process. First you shoved down the clip. Then, either the bolt shot forward by itself or, if it stuck, you pushed it forward manually to insert a cartridge in the chamber. After the clip was emptied—eight shots, wasn't it?—the clip popped out and the bolt stayed back so you could shove down a loaded clip.

Hackermeyer nodded to himself. That was all right. What he might have trouble with was bayoneting. Muscles tensing empathically, he tried to recall how to sidestep and trip an enemy soldier so that he fell on his chest, exposing his back. He tried to remember how to parry and smash in the enemy soldier's face with the steel-edged rifle butt. Absorbed in thought, he stumbled into a rut, almost falling. The jarring rattle of his equipment made Cooley look back. Seeing who it was, Cooley cast his eyes toward heaven.

They were halfway across the plain when the sharp, whistling noises sounded overhead. Hackermeyer stopped and listened, wondering what it was. It sounded as if some unseen giant in the sky were blowing impatiently on his soup.

"Hit it!" shouted Cooley.

Abruptly, a deafening explosion sounded behind them. Hackermeyer wondered how it was possible for him to have gotten down so fast. It seemed as if Cooley's shout still rang in his ears, yet already he was prone, face pressed against his arms. All around him, explosions were crashing. He felt tremors running through the ground and was conscious of the violent pounding of his heart, the shaking of his stomach muscles. Those are eighty-eights, he thought, almost in amazement.

A shell exploded very close and the concussion wave slammed against him, flapping the skirt of his overcoat. The earth leaped spastically beneath him, reared, hung tremulous, then fell away so fast that he smashed down on it. Sight went blurry. Everything around him ran as though he lay beneath water. His ribs began to ache, his eardrums throbbed. He felt as if his insides were expanding. His lungs labored against the fumes of hot explosive.

Abruptly, the shelling stopped.

"Move out!" shouted Cooley. Hackermeyer raised his head and looked around. The other members of the squad were getting up. He struggled to his feet, sucking in a rasping breath. Acrid smoke drifted across the plain. To his right, fifteen yards away, a man was lying crumpled on the ground. He didn't hear, thought Hackermeyer. Only as he started walking did he realize that he was looking at his first casualty.

"Hackermeyer?"

He turned and saw that Cooley was looking back at him. What? he was about to ask when Cooley winked his right eye and turned away. Hackermeyer felt a coagulation in his throat, which he swallowed. He stared at the sergeant's back. What did that mean?

They were almost to the ridge when the shelling started again. Hackermeyer flung himself forward, heartbeat jolting. Overhead, the shells rushed, whistling, fell, exploded, the crashes like that of a giant's fists pounding on the ground.

The shells came in endless clusters. The air was filled with their explosions. Waves of concussion surged across the ground. Shrapnel whizzed like bee swarms. Great clouds of dirt and stone were hurled up high. They spattered down on Hackermeyer's back and rattled on his helmet. A burning odor filled his nostrils. The ground rocked and heaved. Hackermeyer opened his mouth to ease the pain in his ears. He pressed his face as hard as he could against his arms and lay there woodenly, twitching at every explosion. He could smell the reek of dead, winter soil, the odor of his woolen coat, the eye- and nose-smarting pungency of explosive. He closed his eyes and was swallowed by the incredible, maniac din of war.

"Let's go!" Cooley's yell penetrated even the explosions. Hackermeyer raised his head and was surprised to see the Sergeant on his feet, gesturing for them all to advance. Nearby, Lippincott got up, then Schumacher and Lazzo and Guthrie. Swallowing quickly, Hackermeyer lurched up with them and started running through the ground-erupting area.

"Keep moving!" Cooley shouted.

Hackermeyer's breath escaped like steam. His heart pounded faster and faster. He could feel the violent pump of blood through his arms and legs. He kept his eyes fixed on Cooley, his teeth gritted against the endless shattering of explosions.

As they reached the ridge, a wall of explosions blocked their way. Everyone hit the ground. Detonations came so quickly that they seemed part of one continuous, air-splitting roar.

"Dig in!" Cooley howled.

Immediately, the order echoed in a dozen eager voices. "Dig in!" Hackermeyer undid his pack as quickly as he could and, hastily, assembled the pickaxe. Driving it into the dirt, he jerked up a dark, grass-veined clod and flung it aside. The shelling thinned as if the Germans knew that they had halted the advance.

A few inches down, the earth seemed to be composed almost entirely of stone. Hackermeyer had to pull them out by hand. He couldn't get a grip on them until he took his gloves off. Soon his hands were yellow-brown with mud. The sun disappeared behind gray banks of clouds and as the air chilled, the mud began to cake. Hackermeyer felt his wet feet getting cold. As soon as he was finished he'd have to change his socks and—

"Hey!"

Hackermeyer raised his head and saw, several yards in front of him, Cooley and Riley digging a two-man foxhole.

"What are you doing?" demanded Cooley.

"Digging," said Hackermeyer.

Cooley spat.

"And what do you do if the Krauts attack?" he asked. "Shoot Riley and me first?"

Hackermeyer blinked.

"Move over," ordered Cooley.

Hackermeyer grabbed hold of his equipment, crawled about five yards to the right and started digging again. As he pulled away the dark, viscid chunks of earth, he muttered to himself, "How am *I* supposed to know?"

Time fell away. After a while, the shelling ended. Hackermeyer kept cutting deeper, widening the hole, arranging clumps of earth around the top. The ground kept getting rockier and he had to use his bayonet to pry out stones as big as his head. He lifted them one by one, his muscles aching.

"Dig the bottom on a slant," said Cooley.

Hackermeyer glanced up and saw the sergeant looking down at him.

"Water'll run to one end that way," said Cooley.

Hackermeyer kept on digging.

"You all right?" asked Cooley, chewing measuredly.

"Yeah," said Hackermeyer without looking up.

Cooley moved away and Hackermeyer heard him checking on the other members of the squad. They were all right too.

When he finished digging, Hackermeyer lowered himself and his equipment to the bottom of the foxhole and sat down, leaning heavily against the wall. He closed his eyes for several minutes, breathing through an open mouth, his thin chest laboring. Then, sneezing, he undid the bottoms of his leggings and took off his shoes. Wringing out his socks, he put them under his rifle sling to dry. He took a towel out of his pocket and rubbed his feet until they started getting pink. Then he put on another pair of socks. After drying the insides of his shoes as much as possible and sprinkling in foot powder, he put them back on.

He pried loose his helmet and, pouring some water into it, started washing the mud off his hands. While he was doing it, a machine gun started firing in the distance. It didn't sound like an American machine gun.

"Down!" yelled Cooley.

Hackermeyer glanced up and heard bullets whizzing overhead. Abruptly, one of the stones on the rampart of the foxhole spun around, then dropped down on his helmet liner. Hackermeyer grimaced. He took off his helmet liner and rubbed gingerly at the top of his skull. To his right, he heard the rattle of a BAR. He heard a faint vibration in the sky which grew louder and louder until, with a sudden *whoosh*, the shell passed overhead and pulsed off into the distance. Ours, he thought.

Hackermeyer stood and heaved the muddy water from his helmet.

"Trying to drown me?" Cooley's voice inquired sepulchrally.
"I didn't know you were there."

Cooley muttered something.

Hackermeyer put his helmet back over the liner and brushed off the drops of water that fell on his nose. He put his gloves on, crossed his arms and stared impassively at the wall of the foxhole.

Well, he'd seen combat now. Unless it wasn't called combat until you met the Germans face to face. He wondered if that was true. You sure could get killed whether you met them face to face or not. Odd how he'd assumed that the German soldiers would be in sight. Actually, there'd been nothing in sight. The eighty-eight shells had come from nowhere. He'd clung to the ground and waited helplessly. What else could he have done?

Hackermeyer tried to sort out what his feelings had been when the shells were exploding all around him. He had the impression that he hadn't felt anything at all. One thing he knew he hadn't felt was that he couldn't be killed. He'd heard many times that soldiers in battle were convinced that anyone but themselves might be killed. That was a stupid thing to believe. There was no rule that said one soldier would live and another would die. It was all accident. Maybe soldiers forced themselves to believe it because they wanted to think they were special. Hackermeyer had no such delusions about himself. He could get killed as easily as anyone. It was wiser to accept that right away. Then if you survived, it was gravy.

Hackermeyer frowned. One thing still confused him.

Why had Sergeant Cooley winked at him?

"HACKERMEYER."

In the gloom of sunless twilight, he saw Cooley's grizzled face looking down at him.

"Got a job for you," said Cooley.

Hackermeyer stood with a crackling of joints and clambered out of the foxhole. Lippincott was standing nearby.

"Your M1, Hackermeyer," said Cooley.

Hackermeyer reached down and pulled up his rifle. He tugged

the crisply dry socks out of the sling and put them in his pocket.

"That ain't a clothes rack, Hackermeyer," said Cooley.

"I know," said Hackermeyer. The sergeant, mumbling, turned away.

"Let's go," said Lippincott.

The two of them walked across the darkening plain.

"Where we going?" asked Hackermeyer.

"To get coffee and blankets," said Lippincott.

"I have blankets."

"Most of us leave them behind," said Lippincott.

They walked in silence for a while, moving past the dark cavities of foxholes. The helmet of the man in each one looked like a smooth gray rock.

"Well, how did you like it today?" asked Lippincott.

"All right," said Hackermeyer.

Lippincott chuckled. "All right, hanh?" he said.

"How long we going to be here?" asked Hackermeyer.

"God knows," said Lippincott. "It depends on what the rest of the division is doing."

They walked about half a mile and came to a truck parked underneath a tree. As they loaded him up with blankets, Hackermeyer looked around. All he could see, in every direction, was the plain. He was surprised at how far they'd come.

Lippincott got a jug of coffee and some blankets and they walked back to the squad. When they reached the ridge, Hackermeyer had his canteen cup filled with coffee. As he returned to his foxhole, it started raining. He jumped down into the hole and spread his shelter half over the top, weighting down the edges with stones.

Down in the tomblike chill of the hole, he lit a stub of candle and set it on top of his helmet. He sat on his folded blanket, drinking coffee and eating meat and crackers from a K ration. After a while it started to rain harder and he had to keep pushing out the puddle that collected in the center of the shelter half. When he'd finished eating, he took off his shoes and rubbed his feet until they were warm. He put his hand inside the shoes and found them still damp. He held them upside down over the candle flame, wrinkling his nose at the smell of heating leather.

Finally, he put the shoes back on and took out the crossword puzzle book. He remembered the day he'd found his first crossword book in a trash can belonging to the people who'd lived next door to his uncle's house. At first, he'd kept it only for the sake of having a possession. Then, little by little, he'd worked up an interest in the puzzles themselves. He'd never learned to be expert at them but they had helped to educate him a little bit anyway. More than stupid school had, that was certain.

He worked on the puzzle awhile, frowning with concentration. When he started nodding, he put away the book, blew out the candle and lay back in the darkness, listening to the heavy drum of rain overhead. He'd been afraid of heavy rain when he was small. Whenever it had rained hard, he'd lain shivering in bed, face pressed into the pillow so his uncle wouldn't hear him and yell at him for being a crybaby.

Not being afraid to be alone. That's what he had that other eighteen-year-old soldiers didn't have. Wendt had cried for his mother. Probably Foley was wishing he had his mother too. Eighteen-year-old soldiers didn't like to be alone. They needed someone to say it's all right now, sonny boy. Well, he didn't need that. He could get along without anybody. He'd make it all right. He'd show them.

Hackermeyer felt a sudden emptiness inside.

Show whom?

"HACKERMEYER."

He drew back the shelter half and looked at the figure looming above him in the rain-swept darkness.

"Guard duty," said Lippincott.

"Oh." Hackermeyer picked up his rifle and climbed out of the foxhole. He covered the hole with the shelter half, then slung the M1 upside down across his right shoulder and followed Lippincott to his post, listening to his orders.

"You'll be relieved in two hours. Keep your eyes open," said Lippincott, then was gone.

Hackermeyer pulled up the collar of his raincoat and braced

himself on the muddy ground. He didn't know what good he'd be as a guard. Especially since it was impossible to see six feet beyond himself. He squinted to find out if he could identify any nearby objects. He couldn't. He'd have to be careful about shifting position. He might end up guarding the German lines.

He looked at his watch. The radium-lit hands pointed to just past ten o'clock. He lowered his arm, then puckered up his face and sneezed. This Goddamn cold. He'd never get rid of it. As soon as winter came, the cold came with it. Hackermeyer tugged the clotted ball of handkerchief from his overcoat pocket and blew his tender nose. Someday maybe he wouldn't have a cold in the winter. He spat. Sure, and someday Cousin Clara would be Miss America.

It was no wonder he got colds. His uncle's house had always been underheated. At night, the furnace would go out completely, turning the house into an icebox. Uncle George had always said it was a waste of coal to keep the furnace going at night. It had been easy enough for him to say. Between having the heaviest blankets in the house and Aunt Alice lying next to him, there'd been no chance he'd ever get cold. Besides that, he'd always had his gut full of beer. He probably could have slept naked in the alley and never shivered once.

Why was it that his uncle and his father had always drunk so much? Hackermeyer wondered. He couldn't estimate the number of times when, going out for a Sunday afternoon with his father, they'd end up in the dim, cool, musky confines of a bar. There he'd sit on a counter stool, sipping lemonade, nibbling on pretzels or peanuts and wondering when his father was going to take him some place that would be fun. Even the day they'd gone to Coney Island had been spent mostly in a bar.

There had always been those solemn, boring conversations between his father and the bartender or his father and another customer. At some point during those conversations, a few minutes were devoted to him. His father, flaccid-jawed, eyes slightly glazed, would knead his fingers painfully on the back of Hackermeyer's neck and say, "Yes, this is my boy. This is Everett. He's all right. Everett's all right"—the words all slurred and the thick sweetness of his breath clouding into Hackermeyer's lungs, making him ill.

The customer or the bartender would usually ask, "What grade are you in?" or "Do you like baseball?" or some other question he'd have to answer politely or make his father angry. The afternoon would pass and finally his father would say, "I'll take you back to your uncle's now," and there would have been no fun, no laughter. He'd cry when his father left him and he'd cry in his bed that night.

Hackermeyer refocused his eyes and stared coldly into the night. He just wished he hadn't cried all those times, that was all. He hated himself for every single Goddamned time he'd shown his father that he was hurt.

HACKERMEYER WOKE UP with a dull cry as the water-filled shelter half caved in on him. Spluttering and coughing, he struggled to his feet, pulling up the soggy canvas with him. Eyes slitted against the wind-lashed rain, he spread the shelter half across the hole again and weighted it down, propping up its middle with his rifle barrel.

He started to sit down, then twitched in pain and climbed out of the foxhole. Wavering tiredly in the darkness, he opened his pants and urinated. The rain flowed off the edge of his helmet in miniature waterfalls. When he was finished, he got down under the shelter half and turned the blanket over, sitting on the dry side. He sneezed. Wrapping his raincoat around his feet, he leaned back and closed his eyes. Far off, there was a muffled explosion. Hackermeyer listened carefully but there was nothing more. Get some sleep, he thought.

He couldn't sleep. His mind kept dangling in a torpid suspension between consciousness and unconsciousness. Where am I?— he heard himself thinking over and over. Then—Why am I here? . . . Finally—again and again and again—Who am I? . . . Reality sank and faded. His mind rocked slowly in the darkness, seeking to identify itself. *Who am I?* it asked, but there was no answer. He felt alien and disconnected, trapped in some incomprehensible order of events, all without purpose or meaning.

IT WAS VERY still and Hackermeyer heard someone crying. He opened his eyes and sat up, a small puddle on his raincoat spilling to the ground. Grimacing at the tug of cold-stiffened muscles, he stood up slowly and pushed aside the shelter half. A stone fell on his right shoe and made him gasp. The foot felt thick and wooden.

Cooley was leading away Bill Riley, who was walking doubled over. Apparently, Riley had slept all night like that and, now, was unable to straighten up. He had both arms pressed across his stomach like a boy who had eaten too many green apples. Hackermeyer heard him sobbing and saw tears falling from his eyes.

Hackermeyer looked aside and saw Lippincott standing in his foxhole, watching. Lippincott glanced at him and shook his head, a grim smile on his lips. Hackermeyer sat down. Taking off his leggings, shoes, and socks, he rubbed his feet until they tingled. That dumbass of a colonel, he thought.

"Morning," someone said while he was heating a K ration can on a hot box. He looked up and saw Guthrie standing there, a smoke-threading cigarette hanging from a corner of his mouth.

"Sleep well?" asked Guthrie. He was chewing gum too.

Hackermeyer grunted.

"You are Hackermeyer?" said Guthrie.

"Yeah."

"What exciting comestible do you prepare, Hackermeyer?"

"Huh?"

"What's cooking?"

"Pork and egg yolk."

Guthrie blew out smoke. "Baby poo," he said.

Hackermeyer didn't know what Guthrie meant until he glanced down at the contents of the can.

"You've heard about our good Sergeant Wadley?" said Guthrie.

"Was he killed?"

"No such luck," said Guthrie. "He ran off."

"When?"

"Yesterday during Nazi artillery practice."

Hackermeyer frowned. "How come?"

"He was alarmed," said Guthrie. "Threw down his gear and scooted off like Chicken Little. Claimed the sky was falling down."

Hackermeyer didn't understand that.

"He told me if I dumped gear he'd put a bullet in my brain," he said.

"Did he?" said Guthrie, nodding and smiling. "He's a very tough man, Sergeant Wadley."

"Ran away," mused Hackermeyer.

"Like a B-film cliché," said Guthrie.

Hackermeyer didn't understand that either.

"What was that explosion last night?" he asked, starting to eat his pork and egg yolks.

"Some joker blew himself to confetti," said Guthrie.

Hackermeyer stopped chewing. "How come?" he asked.

"Exploded one of his own grenades."

Involuntarily, Hackermeyer looked at the grenades hooked over his cartridge belt.

"I would suggest you use that tape to hold down the arms," Guthrie told him. "Then, if the pin comes loose, you won't. Or you can leave the pins out altogether."

Hackermeyer nodded.

"Well, I must be on my way," said Guthrie. He bowed his head once. "Good cheer, Hackermeyer," he said, turning away. "Happy World War Two."

Still eating, Hackermeyer stood and watched Guthrie walk over to another foxhole.

"Anybody home?" asked Guthrie, tapping his rifle butt twice on a rock.

There was a grunt inside the foxhole.

"Putting in carpeting?" asked Guthrie.

A clean-shaven Schumacher straightened up, holding his shovel. He looked at Guthrie with distaste.

"You should not be walking around," he said.

"Why, is there danger?" asked Guthrie.

"You want to be killed is your business," said Schumacher, frowning. He bent over to dig again.

"I had to make sure your rifle was clean," said Guthrie. "I see it is. And your foxhole is coming along nicely. When do you put on the shake-shingle roof?"

"Go back to your hole," said Schumacher.

"Go back to my hole," echoed Guthrie. "But it's such a cheerless spot, Herr Schumacher. Like sitting in a grave."

"You be in your grave soon you keep walking around," said Schumacher.

"Do you worry about me, Herr Schumacher?"

Schumacher's laugh was a short, humorless bark. "Worry about *you*," he said scornfully. "And stop calling me *Herr*."

"Yes, Herr Schumacher," said Guthrie. "What a loss to the Wehrmacht that you should be on our side."

"You go to hell," said Schumacher.

"But we're already there, Herr Schumacher," said Guthrie. He flipped away his cigarette. "Well," he said, "call me when the van gets here and I'll help you carry in your furniture."

Hackermeyer threw away the empty ration can and, sitting, began to tape down the grenade arms. Wendt was right. Guthrie was a nut. He was beginning to see why Cooley had no taste for eighteen-year-old soldiers.

He thought again about Sergeant Wadley running away. No wonder Wadley had reminded him of Uncle George. That was undoubtedly what Uncle George would have done in the same situation. Bullies were all alike.

"HERE." COOLEY TOSSED down three boxes of K ration and an issue of the *Stars and Stripes*. Hackermeyer picked up the paper and looked at the lead story headline. He scowled.

"What's the matter, Hackermeyer?" inquired Cooley.

"This story," said Hackermeyer, pointing.

"What about it?"

"Senator Says Eighteen-Year-Olds Won't Be Sent Overseas," read Hackermeyer.

"So?"

"There's eighteen-year-olds over here," said Hackermeyer.

"No kidding," said Cooley.

"Why does the Senator . . . ?"

"Write him a letter," said Cooley, turning.

"I don't know his address."

Cooley turned back, one eye squinted suspiciously. Seeing no sign of levity on Hackermeyer's face, he opened the eye.

"They find Sergeant Wadley yet?" asked Hackermeyer.

"Who told you about that?"

"Guthrie."

"He's got a fat mouth," said Cooley.

"Did they?"

"I don't know." The skin tensed across Cooley's cheeks. "If I find him, I'll shove a grenade up his butt," he said.

Something akin to humor showed on Hackermeyer's face.

"You like that," said Cooley.

"Yeah."

Cooley's laugh was a short, explosive burst. "You're a kick, Hackermeyer," he said.

"Why?"

Cooley grunted as if in pain. Then, visibly, he restrained himself. "Look, son," he said. "Ain't no reason you can't make it through in one piece if you use your head."

He squatted down. "Just remember this," he said. "You got only one job—kill the Krauts or capture them. You don't have to worry about anything else. You're all right. I watched you yesterday. You didn't get rattled. You knew what was going on. That's good. One thing I noticed, though. You get up too slow. You're carrying too much gear. Leave your blanket and shelter half, and pack and other crap behind. Supply will bring it up. Just stick your raincoat under your belt. Put your entrenching tool on your belt too. That way you'll move faster. And when you get up—get up fast and at an angle, not straight on. That makes less of a target. Change direction when you run. And get down fast and smooth. Don't telegraph it when you're going to drop. Understand?"

Hackermeyer nodded.

"Good." Cooley spat tobacco juice aside. "Another thing. There wasn't anything to shoot at yesterday; but when there is, keep shooting even if you don't know what it is we're shooting at. Keep moving and keep shooting. And when we move in under artillery, watch for the smoke. The last round'll always have WP in it."

"What's that?"

"White phosphorus," said Cooley. "When you see it, start moving fast and maybe you'll see Christmas."

"What's on Christmas?"

"What's on—" Cooley gaped at him. "What do you mean, what's on Christmas?"

"You said it yesterday too."

"So?"

"I thought maybe—something special happened on Christmas."

Cooley stood up, gritting his teeth.

"It does," he said, "Santa Claus gets his balls shot off." He turned and moved away. "Kids," he growled.

Hackermeyer swallowed and stared up blankly at the spot where Cooley had been. The sergeant didn't like him, that was all. Hackermeyer exhaled raggedly and put the K ration boxes on top of his pack. So what difference did it make whether Cooley liked him or not? He wasn't here to win a popularity contest.

Hackermeyer took a fruit bar out of his pocket and ate it while he read the *Stars and Stripes*. When he was finished, he put down the paper and gazed up at the lead-colored sky. It looked like rain again. That's all it does here is rain, he thought.

He started to think about Cooley giving him instructions on how to run and fall. What was Cooley's reason for doing that? He wasn't interested in Hackermeyer. He couldn't stand teenage soldiers. Hackermeyer thought about it awhile, finally nodding. The answer wasn't hard. Cooley was just protecting his property.

If all the members of the squad got killed or wounded, Cooley wouldn't be a squad leader anymore. No, that wasn't true. He'd just get more replacements. Well, what if Cooley did tell him a few things? That didn't mean he liked Hackermeyer. It didn't mean a thing.

Hackermeyer stared glumly at the wall of the foxhole. Who cares anyway? he thought. He crumpled up the copy of *Stars and Stripes* and bounced it off the muddy wall. Who gave a good Goddamn?

IN THE DISTANCE were muffled sounds of battle: shell explosions and the fire of small arms.

"Hi, Everett."

Hackermeyer looked up from blowing his nose. Foley stood there, smiling awkwardly. Hackermeyer wondered what he wanted.

"How are you?" asked Foley.

"All right."

"Good," said Foley. "I'm glad you're not hurt." He stood there restively, his smile faltering. Abruptly, he looked around. "Well, I—guess I better dig a foxhole," he said.

Hackermeyer grunted. Wasn't Foley a messenger anymore?

"I was told to come back," said Foley.

Suddenly, Hackermeyer realized that Foley wanted to share the foxhole with him. He lowered his gaze. It wasn't very big.

"Well, I—" Foley started, then broke off.

Hackermeyer tightened. It wasn't his concern that Foley had no foxhole. He watched Foley looking around worriedly.

"Well, you might as well sit in here," he heard himself say.

A grateful smile crossed Foley's lips. "Is it big enough?" he asked.

Hackermeyer shrugged.

"I shouldn't crowd you," said Foley.

No, you shouldn't, Hackermeyer thought; but he didn't say anything.

"Well, I sure would appreciate it, Everett," said Foley.

"We'll probably be leaving soon anyway," said Hackermeyer.

"We will?" asked Foley as he lowered himself into the hole.

"We have to go to Saarbach," said Hackermeyer.

"Oh—yes." Foley sat down and leaned his rifle against his shoulder. His eyes were bloodshot and circled with dark hollows. He smiled tiredly at Hackermeyer.

"Where you been?" Hackermeyer asked him.

Foley sighed. "Boy, where haven't I been?" he said. "I've been running around all night."

"You know what that noise is over there?"

"One of the other regiments is in contact with the Germans," Foley said, as if he were quoting from one of the messages he'd carried.

Hackermeyer nodded. He glanced down at Foley's rifle. "Rusty," he said.

Foley yawned and rubbed his cheek. "I know," he said, defeatedly. He took off his glasses and blinked. His eyes looked very weak. If he lost his glasses he probably couldn't see to get around, Hackermeyer thought. He watched Foley polish the lenses and put the glasses back on, then reach into his overcoat pocket and ease out a D-bar.

"Here's to pay you back," said Foley.

"I don't—" Hackermeyer started automatically.

"No, take it," Foley said. "It's not mine anyway."

"Whose is it?"

"Sergeant Jones's."

"He give it to you?"

"They took it off him," Foley said. "He was killed yesterday."

"Oh." Hackermeyer slid the D-bar into his pocket.

Foley closed his eyes and shook his head slowly. "Doesn't make sense," he murmured.

"What?"

"Sergeant Jones being killed," said Foley, sluggishly. "I remember once, in England, he took the platoon for a run. When we were out of breath, he told us 'Take it easy,' till we got our breath. Nice guy." Foley's voice kept slowing down. "He told us—jokes while we walked along. He started singing popular songs and—we sang with him. The people—looked out their windows—when we passed—and . . ."

Foley's face was even more boyish in sleep. He looked like some grimy urchin who had been snatched from backyard play and transferred here. Odd that they were both eighteen yet so different.

Hackermeyer glanced down at Foley's M1. It sure was rusty and dirty. Probably wouldn't even fire. He ran his gaze over the mud-flecked weapon. It was a mess.

Shrugging quickly, he drew out his crossword puzzle book. Well, that wasn't his business. If Foley didn't want to keep his rifle clean, that was his affair. Hackermeyer started working on the puzzle. He has no time, the thought occurred. He's always delivering messages.

Hackermeyer scowled and concentrated on the puzzle. So what? he thought. He wrote down *rye*, then found himself looking at Foley's rifle again. He glanced up quickly at Foley to make sure he wasn't being observed. Foley was asleep. He should make time to clean it, Hackermeyer thought. When you were in combat, you were supposed to keep your weapon clean. Any jerk knew that.

He looked down at his own rifle. It was in good condition. Hackermeyer cleared his throat, then drew in a long breath and let it drift out through his nostrils. He glared at the crossword puzzle book. *Greek letter*, he read. He could never get those damn things.

Casually, he put down the book and picked up Foley's rifle. Taking out the cartridge clip, he pulled off the trigger assembly and removed the stock. He tried to keep his mind blank as he worked.

Suddenly it occurred to him that he wasn't doing Foley a favor after all. Didn't Cooley say that counterattacks could be expected? So by seeing to it that Foley's rifle worked, he was only increasing his own chance of survival. That made sense.

Hackermeyer worked slowly on the rifle, trying to avoid the thought of Foley waking up and finding the rifle clean. He kept visualizing Foley's smiles and thank-yous and gees and gollys and . . .

"Dope," muttered Hackermeyer. He wasn't sure whether he meant Foley or himself.

FOLEY LOOKED UP from the V-mail letter he was writing.

"How come Cooley doesn't like eighteen-year-old soldiers?" repeated Hackermeyer. He'd been thinking about it for some time.

"Doesn't he?" asked Foley, in surprise.

Hackermeyer shook his head. "He thinks we're—kids," he said.

Foley smiled ruefully.

"We were old enough to be drafted," he said. "Except I wasn't drafted, I enlisted—like a nut. I thought it would give me more choice. About where I went, what I did."

"You chose *this?*"

"Of course not," Foley answered. "I enlisted in the A.S.T.P."

"What's that?"

"Army Specialized Training Program. I was taking preengineering studies." Foley shook his head. "I was supposed to be an officer in the Engineers when I finished."

"Why aren't you?"

Foley sighed. "The program folded," he said.

Hackermeyer rubbed at his nose. God, it was tender.

"I was at Cornell University," said Foley. "We took regular college courses—math, physics, English. Plus R.O.T.C., of course. I liked it."

"Why'd it fold?"

Foley gestured vaguely with his hands. "Maybe it was just a ruse to get us in the Infantry," he said. He made a clucking noise. "They didn't seem to worry about us being kids when they made us riflemen," he said.

Hackermeyer nodded. That's right, he thought.

"Oh, well," said Foley. "There's a war to fight. I suppose somebody has to fight it."

"What about . . . ?" Hackermeyer broke off, feeling awkward.

"What?"

Hackermeyer shrugged. "They don't like to be alone," he said.

"Who, eighteen-year-old soldiers?"

"Yeah."

"Who does?" Foley said. "No one likes to be alone, no matter how old he is."

"I don't care," said Hackermeyer, uneasily.

"Sure you do," said Foley.

Hackermeyer tried to look scornful.

"I think eighteen-year-old soldiers are probably just as good as older men," said Foley. "They're in better condition, for one thing."

"They get scared easier," Hackermeyer interrupted.

Foley thought about it.

"What about Sergeant Wadley?" he asked.

Hackermeyer crimped his lips together. "They're careless," he said. "That—that guy who killed himself with his own grenade was eighteen. And Guthrie walks around here like—"

"Taking my name in vain?" said Guthrie.

They both looked up and saw him standing overhead, a packet of mail in his hand.

"Word from the home front," he announced, tossing a V-mail letter down to Foley. "For you, Hackermeyer—nothing. For me, less than nothing; a copy of *Variety*. Carry on." Guthrie walked away.

Foley tore the letter open eagerly. There was a tender smile on his lips as he read it three times, then sighed and put it on his lap.

"From my girl," he said, looking up.

Hackermeyer averted his eyes. He'd been watching Foley read the letter.

"You have a girl?" asked Foley.

"No."

"You get letters from your family, though."

"I don't have any," Hackermeyer said.

Foley looked startled. "What about your mom and dad?"

"They're dead."

Foley looked stricken. "Both of them?" he asked.

"Yeah."

"Gee, I'm sorry, Everett. I had no idea." Foley swallowed. "Doesn't anybody write you?"

"No."

"How—how long have your parents been dead?" Foley asked.

"My mother died when I was born," said Hackermeyer. "My father—" He stopped.

"Gee, Everett, I'm sorry." Foley's expression was distraught. "Your—father raised you by himself?" he asked.

"I lived with my uncle."

Foley cleared his throat. He forced a smile. "Say," he said, "would—you like for—for my girl to"—his smile faltered embarrassedly—"to write to you?" he finished.

Hackermeyer looked at him curiously. "Write to me?" he asked.

"Yes."

"Why?"

"So you could—get mail," said Foley.

Hackermeyer looked confused. "I don't know her," he said.

"Well—" Foley picked up his letter. "If—you want her to, tell me and"—he gestured awkwardly—"I'll tell her."

"That's all right," said Hackermeyer. There was a tension in his stomach muscles that he couldn't account for.

Foley smiled at Hackermeyer, then read his letter again. Hackermeyer looked at him without expression. He didn't understand why Foley had made the offer. Foley's girl didn't know him.

Foley glanced up.

"I saw her the night before we left the States," he said. "We got twelve-hour passes. We were in Camp Kilmer and I live in Vermont. Kilmer's in New Jersey, you know."

Foley made a sound of melancholy amusement.

"All the train schedules were off," he said. "Because of the war, I suppose. It took me almost five hours to get home. All I had was an hour to say good-bye to everybody. My dad drove me all over town and we woke up my aunts and uncles and cousins and I said good-bye to them. I only had about twenty minutes with Jeanie. I sat on the sofa with her in the front room and— her parents went in the kitchen." He smiled. "To make coffee, they said."

He swallowed and glanced down at the letter.

"Jeanie had a robe on over her pajamas," he said. "She looked so pretty. She had a ribbon in her hair. She's blond. She was crying and—" He broke off and released a shaking sigh. "Then I had to go."

Things are tough all over, Hackermeyer thought.

"You want to see her picture?" Foley asked him.

Hackermeyer didn't answer at first. "Yeah," he said then. He wanted to see what she looked like. Foley wasn't much.

Foley struggled up enough to reach beneath his overcoat and take a wallet out of his back trouser pocket. Settling back, he felt around under a leather flap and slid out two glossy photographs.

"This is Mom and Dad," he said.

Hackermeyer looked at the smiling couple. They were sitting on lawn chairs holding dishes of ice cream in their laps. The woman wore a white dress and white shoes and was plumply pretty. The man wore a baseball cap and had on glasses like the ones Foley wore. Hackermeyer stared at Foley's mother and fa- ther. Foley had lived with them all his life. At this moment, they were waiting for Foley to come back to them. It was difficult to comprehend.

He handed back the photograph and Foley handed him the other one.

Jeanie was standing on a porch, leaning back against the rail- ing. She had on a sweater and skirt and saddle shoes. Her blond hair was drawn back into a ponytail. Apparently she was trying to look sexy because she had her shoulders back so that her small breasts pointed upward a little. Hackermeyer felt a vague stirring in his loins. Jeanie was pretty. She was smiling at whoever held the camera. Probably it had been Foley. Hackermeyer swallowed. He wondered if Foley had ever taken off that sweater and the brassiere under it and looked at Jeanie's breasts. Probably not. Foley wasn't the kind. Wendt, now . . .

He handed back the photograph.

"Pretty, isn't she?" asked Foley.

"Yeah."

"You have any pictures?"

Hackermeyer shook his head. He never showed anyone the photograph of his mother. Impulsively, he pulled out his crossword puzzle book and opened it. Foley smiled.

"My father does them," he said. "They're very educational."

Hackermeyer worked on the puzzle for a few minutes. Then the thought that he might be educating himself irritated him and he let his eyes go out of focus. He didn't put the book away because he didn't want Foley to start talking again.

He sat motionless, listening to the sounds of battle in the distance. Why had he said that his father was dead? Did he hate his father so much he didn't even want to consider him among the living? Hackermeyer pressed his teeth together. Well, as far as he was concerned, his father *was* dead.

He remembered the last time he'd seen his father. He'd been on a ten-day pass and, on impulse, since there'd been nothing else to do—he'd seen all the movies around—he'd gone to his father's furnished room on Atlantic Avenue.

His father hadn't even known him at first. Looking a hundred years old, unshaven, bleary-eyed, dressed in a faded blue wrapper, his milk-white calves and blue-veined ankles showing underneath, his feet in torn cloth slippers, his father had stood motionless in the doorway, staring dumbly at Hackermeyer, even saying, "Yes, what can I—" before he recognized him. The hall had smelled of boiled cabbage and grime. Hackermeyer had stood there woodenly, staring at his father. "Hi," he'd said in an expressionless tone, already sorry that he'd come.

The visit had lasted no more than twenty minutes but it had seemed like hours. Hackermeyer remembered sitting on a flimsy wooden chair by the window. Below, the courtyard was littered with rusty cans, bottles, newspapers, garbage, and a rain-soaked mattress. On the other side of the dingy, stale-smelling room, his father had sat, nodding his head, trying to act like a father pleased to see his uniformed son paying a visit. *So tell me about the training*, he'd said and Hackermeyer had mumbled a brief description of hikes and rifle range and K.P. Then silence had fallen and Hackermeyer had sat there stiffly, listening to the faint creak of the chair while he and his father avoided each other's eyes.

After a few minutes, his father had gotten a half-empty bottle of beer from the small wooden icebox and poured it into two filmy glasses. *You're old enough now*, his father had said, showing his bad teeth in a smile. Hackermeyer had felt a twist of anger in himself. He'd wanted to refuse. Instead, he'd sat there, taking sips of the warm, stale beer and listening to his father talk about the Dodgers, about Alice and Cousin Clara. About how difficult it was to find the right kind of work. About a dozen different things, none of which Hackermeyer really heard.

Just before he'd left, his father, with strained familiarity, had asked for the loan of a few dollars. Whatever Hackermeyer could spare without trouble. He'd mail it back in a week. He had some money coming in. Carefully, importantly, his father had written down the address of the army camp even though Hackermeyer knew he'd never get the money back. He'd given his father three dollars, then started to leave. *Wait*, his father had said, walking to the closet and opening the door. Inside, Hackermeyer had seen the suits he remembered so well—most specially the dark serge suit his father had worn for the Sunday visits.

His father had come back with a long, narrow, canvas-wrapped object. It was a fishing rod he'd had for years. He wanted Hackermeyer to have it now. *Good rod, worth plenty in its day—no doubt even more now*. Hackermeyer had tried to say he had no chance to fish but his father wouldn't listen. He'd pushed it into Hackermeyer's hands, insisting. *Certainly have no use for it myself*, his father had said. Hackermeyer had sensed that his father was struggling to maintain some shred of dignity. To give payment for the three dollars which would never be repaid. And he'd resented giving his father the satisfaction, but there'd been no way out.

Good-bye, Everett, his father had said, as gentleman to gentleman. *Come again now. I always like to see you.* For a moment,

Hackermeyer had felt a blinding impulse to smash the rod across his father's face. Then he'd mumbled something—he couldn't remember what—turned around and left. As he'd walked along Atlantic Avenue in the blazing sunlight, he'd flung the fishing rod into a trash can. *You lousy bastard*, he'd muttered to himself. Over and over and over. *You lousy bastard. You lousy bastard!* And, only after a long while—*Papa, why?*

"LET'S GO!" SHOUTED Cooley. "Off your butts!"

Foley's eyes jerked open. "What?"

Hackermeyer pushed to his feet, lifting his gear.

"Are we leaving?" asked Foley. He sounded shocked.

"Guess so," said Hackermeyer.

Foley struggled up and looked around, gnawing on a gloved finger. "I wonder if I'm—supposed to report to the captain," he said.

"He say so?"

Foley kept looking around worriedly. "He said he'd let me know, but—"

Cooley came trotting back with his gear on, his carbine slung across his shoulder.

"Come on, boys, chop chop!" he said.

"Sergeant?" asked Foley.

"What?"

"Am I supposed to report to Captain Miller?"

"Not unless you're ordered," Cooley said. "Get your gear on, son!"

They clipped their belts on hastily, adjusted their helmets, slung their M1s over their shoulders. Hackermeyer pushed the cotton back into his ears.

"Where do you suppose we're going?" asked Foley in a shaky voice.

"Saarbach, I guess," said Hackermeyer.

"Oh. Yeah," said Foley.

A whistle shrilled in the distance. Cooley shouted, "Squad diamond! Move out!" and the squad started north, walking parallel to the edge of the ridge instead of going over it. They'd gone about twenty yards when, up ahead, men started running. Overhead, shells began to flutter northward.

"They're ours!" yelled Cooley. "Keep going! On the double!"

"Oh—gee," said Foley. He started running next to Hackermeyer, who unslung his rifle and held it at high port. "Boy, that's the—army for you—" Foley gasped. "Sit around for—almost a—day, then—run."

In the distance, the American shells began exploding. Hackermeyer shivered as he ran. Ahead of him, he saw Goldmeyer carrying the bazooka and its shells. In the few days he'd been with the squad, it had changed hands three times, it occurred to him.

After they'd run several hundred yards, everyone started slowing down. Hackermeyer and Foley slackened their pace to a trot. "Keep going!" Cooley shouted. They started running again, breath wheezing from their mouths. They crossed a deeply rutted road, clambered over a low stone wall and started down a slope.

"*Look*," gasped Foley.

In the distance, below them, was the border of the forest that led to Saarbach. Hackermeyer felt his heartbeat quicken. The last twenty-four hours had been so completely static that he'd almost forgotten about the Germans. Now, suddenly, he was reminded that sitting was at an end. Remembering and thinking and discussing eighteen-year-old soldiers was at an end. Maybe, in a short while, life itself would be at an end.

Someone shouted. "Hit it!"

For a second, Hackermeyer stood frozen, listening to the sharp, whistling noises overhead. Then, abruptly, he was diving forward, hitting the ground so violently it knocked the breath from him. One shell landed to his right, exploding deafeningly. Another landed to his left. He visualized a third one coming in between, landing right on top of him. It never came. The next shell detonated up ahead, its roar enveloping Hackermeyer. The earth heaved under him. Then the concussion wave was shoving him backward violently, the front edge of his helmet gouging a channel in the mud. Hackermeyer clutched at the ground, his heartbeat pounding. Mud was spattering down on him like rain. Smoke was clouding into his throat and choking him.

"Go!" yelled Cooley. "Go, go, go!"

Hackermeyer turned his head in time to see the sergeant flung aside as if by some invisible hand. Cooley did a half somersault and landed on his side. He's killed! thought Hackermeyer. Another shell exploded near him and he pressed his face into the mud. Now he'd get it. Now. Now. Explosions thundered everywhere. He closed his eyes and waited for the end, blankly, frozenly.

"Names!" yelled Cooley. The sound of his belligerent howl was almost comforting. Goldmeyer's voice was drowned out by the noise. "Lippincott!" "Guthrie!" They shouted simultaneously.

Hackermeyer caught his breath. They were alive too. He yelled his name into the mud. "Lazzo!" "Schumacher!" They were all alive except for—

He looked around for Foley and saw him lying motionless, face buried in his arms. He's killed, he thought. Then Foley called his name out in a choking voice.

"Dig in!" shouted Cooley.

Abruptly, Hackermeyer scrambled over to where Foley was and worked his pickaxe free, grimacing at the heat and deafening noise, twitching as the shrapnel whined and buzzed around them.

"You all right?" gasped Foley.

"Yeah." Hackermeyer flung aside the clods of earth.

They were three feet down when the shelling stopped and, suddenly, machine guns started firing from the woods.

"Down!" yelled Cooley.

Hackermeyer dived into the hole head first, jerking in his legs behind him. Foley fell on top of him. "Look out," he gasped. Hackermeyer twisted free of him and Foley squirmed down further. Above them, inches from the surface, orange tracer bullets skimmed. They could have reached up and touched them.

"Oh . . . God," said Foley.

Hackermeyer swallowed hard. They lay there, motionless, staring at the flashing streamers.

"You—think they'll attack?" asked Foley.

Hackermeyer couldn't speak.

"If they attack," said Foley, "what'll we do?"

"Shoot them," muttered Hackermeyer.

Foley nodded as if Hackermeyer had just made a brilliant observation. Abruptly, then, he made a sound halfway between a giggle and a sob. "What else?" he said. After a moment, he frowned. "What—what if they have tanks, though?" he asked.

Hackermeyer shivered. Cooley had said the Germans would throw tanks at them but he hadn't thought about it.

"What if they do?" he asked.

"Well . . . do we—throw grenades at them or something?" Foley asked.

Hackermeyer sniffed and ran a trembling finger under his nose. "I don't know," he said.

"I guess they'll—shoot the bazooka at them, won't they?" Foley said. He cleared his throat. "Artie used to be bazooka man," he said.

"Yeah."

"He was v-very good," said Foley. "I wonder—how he is."

The tracer bullets kept on flashing overhead like a migration of frenzied lightning bugs.

"Who has the bazooka now?" asked Foley.

"Riley. No, Goldmeyer."

"I hope he—knows h-ow to use it," Foley said.

The moment was, somehow, impossible to believe. Once, he and a boy who'd lived next door to his uncle's house had dug a trench in an empty lot. They had sat in it holding broomstick guns and talking in soft, grim voices about how the "emeny" was going to attack. Looking at Foley and listening to him made it seem as if he were back in that lot again, playing a game of war.

Thrusting the notion aside, Hackermeyer turned his rifle over and checked it to make sure there was a cartridge clip inside. He pushed off the safety lock, then put it on again. He glanced up at the tracer bullets. The Germans must be planning to attack. Otherwise, why would they waste so many bullets?

He looked down and saw that Foley was examining his rifle too.

"I'm—I'm sure glad you cleaned it," Foley said. He swallowed breath and seemed to choke on it. "This is—silly, isn't it?" he said.

Hackermeyer stared at him. Silly?

"I mean . . . it doesn't make sense," said Foley.

Hackermeyer remembered that Foley had also said that Sergeant Jones's death didn't make sense.

"I mean—" said Foley.

His voice broke off as the machine guns stopped firing and a sudden, deathly stillness fell across the field.

"What do you suppose is happening?" whispered Foley.

Hackermeyer shook his head slowly, listening.

"You think they're going to—?"

"Look out!" someone shouted.

Foley twitched violently and made a gagging sound. Across the field, a burst of rifle shots rang out. Hackermeyer struggled to his knees, and raised his head above the level of the ground. He saw men firing toward the edge of the woods and his gaze jumped in that direction. There was a jerking contraction of his stomach muscles. A scattered mass of square-helmeted, blue-gray-coated figures was running out from under the trees, firing their rifles.

"Germans," said Foley. Hackermeyer glanced at him and saw that his face had become as white as chalk.

"Start shooting!" Cooley's yell rang out above the rifle fire. Hackermeyer thought the sergeant was ordering him personally and he grabbed his M1 and tried to aim it at one of the running figures. The rifle felt incredibly heavy. Its barrel end kept sinking. Hackermeyer propped his left arm rigidly. He heard popping noises all around and wondered vaguely what they were. He squinted through the sights and hitched the rifle over until a lumbering, black-booted figure entered his line of fire.

Instantly, the figure vanished. Grimacing, Hackermeyer jerked the barrel over. The figure ran across the sights and, once more, vanished.

"Goddamn it, shoot!" screamed Cooley.

Hackermeyer jammed his lips together. Suddenly, the war telescoped into a private duel between the German and himself. He held his breath. Only his heart pounded unchecked in the fixity of his body as he hitched the barrel over a third time, then a fourth. Abruptly, he gave up trying to track the German soldier. He'd let the German run into his line of fire. Moving the rifle again, he braced it. When the German crossed his sights, he pulled the trigger.

Nothing happened. Hackermeyer jerked the trigger, feeling his head swell out against his helmet liner. It's broke! he thought, then, suddenly, remembered that the safety lock was on. He pushed it off with an indrawn hiss of breath and, aiming quickly at the German, pulled the trigger. The M1 fired with a noise that seemed no louder than the report of a popgun, its jolt against his overcoated shoulder barely noticeable. A gout of dirt jumped up beside the German's moving boots.

Too low. Hackermeyer raised his sights, a churning tremor in his stomach. Get him! someone ordered in his mind. He squeezed the trigger and a second gout of dirt sprayed up across the German's legs. Get him! ordered the unfamiliar voice. Hackermeyer fired a third time but the German kept on running. Hackermeyer shuddered, aimed again, his pupils shrunk to specks in the darkness of his eyes.

Suddenly, the German plunged to his side, his rifle flung away from him. Hackermeyer's mouth fell open. He hadn't even fired. Almost with shock, he remembered that he wasn't alone on the field. Other men were firing too. One of them must have hit the German. The welling of an alien emotion crowded at his body. He was *mine*, he thought, and looked around for another German, his body trembling with a strange excitement.

There weren't any more Germans. A dozen of them were sprawled, lifeless, on the ground. The rest had retreated to the woods. Hackermeyer blinked. It was over so quickly.

Suddenly, the machine guns opened up again, their strident burring ripping at the silence. Hackermeyer dropped below the surface of the ground and, slipping, fell against the foxhole wall.

He looked over at Foley, who was staring at him.

"Wow," said Foley in a trembling voice.

Hackermeyer swallowed.

"Did you—h-hit anything?" asked Foley.

Hackermeyer felt another surge of the odd, disquieting emotion. "No," he said. They shot my German, he thought, indignant.

"Neither did I," said Foley. He sucked in a quavering breath. "I didn't even shoot," he said.

"Why not?"

"I—" Foley gestured shakily with his hands. "I don't know, Everett," he said. He looked as if he were about to cry.

Abruptly, the noise of the machine guns was swallowed by a hideous wailing in the sky. Hackermeyer looked up so fast his helmet almost slipped off.

"Screaming meemies," Foley gasped.

What the hell? thought Hackermeyer. He ducked his head abruptly as the mortar shells exploded and felt a sting on the back of his neck. Gasping, he jerked his hand up to brush away the fleck of burning metal.

Now antiaircraft shells began exploding. Fiery chunks of shrapnel whizzed downward, burying themselves into the ground. One of them bounced off Hackermeyer's helmet with a shriek that made his breath catch. He clutched his drawn-up legs, teeth biting together so hard it drove lines of pain along his jaws. His heart beat like a bludgeon at the tightening wall of his chest. Breath burst from his lips in a choking wheeze. His stomach roiled without control. He felt as if he were about to fill his pants. Cut it out, he thought. He couldn't swallow the saliva that collected and some of it ran dribbling from the corners of his mouth. His clenching teeth slipped suddenly and he bit his lower lip. Cut it out! he wanted to yell. He felt Foley's knees pressed against his and, fleetingly, remembered that he hadn't told Foley to ask his girlfriend to write him a letter.

The shelling seemed to go on endlessly. Hackermeyer's head began to ache and throb. The contents of his body seemed to belly out his flesh as if about to split the seams and spurt from every cavity. The air rocked and leaped with bursts of thunder which seemed to crush him in around the swollen throbbing of his insides. He hunched down lower still, eyes pressed shut, teeth grinding. *Cut it out!*

When the shelling stopped, Hackermeyer didn't believe it at first. Then when there were no explosions for more than half a minute, he raised his head a little, eyes still closed. In the distance was a sound of heavy engines revving. The skin wrinkled around Hackermeyer's closed eyes. What kind of engines would they have here at a time like . . . ?

He sat bolt upright, eyes widened. "Tanks," he said; and, suddenly, froze.

Blood was pouring from the left side of Foley's neck. It gushed across his shoulders as fast as water from a faucet, pouring down his legs and splashing on the ground. Hackermeyer gaped at it. "Foley?" he muttered.

Foley didn't move. He sat hunched over as if asleep.

"Foley?" Hackermeyer's voice was hoarse and wavering. He started reaching out to touch Foley, then pulled back his hand and watched the scarlet blood collecting on the bottom of the hole. It moved around the tips of his shoes as if it were alive.

"Oh," he said faintly. He stared at the blood pulsing from Foley's neck and couldn't understand why it didn't stop. It fascinated him. All he could do was stare at it, forgetting where he was, what he was doing there.

Sergeant Cooley's bellowing voice ended the spell. "Here they come!"

Hackermeyer blinked and shuddered violently. Suddenly, recoiling, he pushed his back up the wall of the foxhole, retreating from the sight of Foley. Across the field, a big gun fired and a shell went screaming overhead. Hackermeyer ducked, then looked across the edge of the foxhole.

His mind did not seem to register what he saw: a gigantic Panther tank grinding out of the forest, its motors roaring. Blankly, Hackermeyer watched the tree-thick barrel of its gun wheeling slowly into position until it seemed to be pointing directly at him. There was a puff of smoke from the muzzle snout,

a belching roar. The shell whistled overhead, exploding somewhere behind him. Hackermeyer straightened up again. He saw
another German tank come crashing through the underbrush
and trundle, squeaking, from the woods. There was a man on its
turret firing a machine gun. Hackermeyer watched in awe as the
dirt-spitting trail of bullets danced across the field. He saw it
pass over a foxhole and saw the soldier in it fling up his arms
and disappear.

Now, as if scales had fallen from his eyes, he noticed figures
moving behind the tanks. He stared incredulously at the German
soldiers, hardly aware of the firing machine gun on the tank, the
crackling of weapons all around him. He twitched a little as, to
his left, his eyes picked up a spurt of flame, his ears the whooshing sound of a bazooka. In the trees, there was a sharp explosion
and the figure of a German soldier crumpled to the ground. A
third tank came lumbering out of the woods like some primeval
beast, more soldiers trailing it.

Suddenly, there was a blinding white-red explosion in front of
the tank and it disappeared behind a cloud of smoke and dirt.
Another explosion crashed nearby, filling the air with thunder.
Hackermeyer looked around dumbly. The sky was filled with
swishing sounds.

"That's ours!" someone shouted.

"Withdraw!" yelled someone else.

Hackermeyer looked around confusedly. All over the field,
men were crying "Withdraw!"—scrambling out of their partially
dug foxholes and running back toward the road. "Get down!"
yelled a voice. "Goddamn it, shoot!" roared Cooley. Men paid
no attention. "Withdraw!" they yelled. "Withdraw!"—as more
and more of them scrabbled from the ground and started running
wildly, leaving weapons and equipment behind. Cooley's furious
shouts were lost beneath the mounting roar of explosions. Hackermeyer saw a man swallowed in a burst of dirt and smoke. He
saw another leap into the air, hands clutching at his blood-
spouting throat. He saw another sprinting, helmetless, his face
deranged with terror. He saw men fleeing, saw the tanks and the

German soldiers and the gouting blossoms of explosions every-where. He watched it all with dumb absorption.

"Get out of there!"

Hackermeyer looked up at Cooley's fury-twisted face.

"Foley's—" he began.

Lunging over, Cooley grabbed Hackermeyer's coat collar and hauled him from the foxhole. "Go!" he yelled.

Hackermeyer found himself running toward the German tanks and wondering what he was going to do when he reached them. Abruptly, Cooley grabbed his arm and spun him violently.

"That way!" Cooley shouted.

Hackermeyer ran again, bullets whizzing past him. He raced between islands of explosions, dirt raining on him, shrapnel buzz-ing past him like fiery hornets. Withdraw! he thought. He glanced around for Cooley but the sergeant had disappeared in the smoky din. He ran around a foxhole, seeing a soldier without a head inside it. Suddenly, he noticed he was carrying his rifle. He must have grabbed it when Cooley pulled him out of the foxhole. He didn't remember doing it.

The stone wall suddenly appeared in front of him. Hacker-meyer rolled across it like a ball and slammed down on the other side. A spatter of machine-gun bullets richocheted off the top of the wall but it did not occur to Hackermeyer that, in falling, he had saved his life. He struggled to his feet and started running again.

Just past the other side of the road, he almost tripped over Goldmeyer, who was lying in a limb-twisted heap, a red-flowered stitching of holes across his back. Without thinking, Hacker-meyer grabbed the fallen bazooka and its container of shells and kept on running. He started up a hill, breath shearing at his lungs like heated knives. Men were running all around him. Every few seconds one of them would cry out and fall or crumple without a sound. Hackermeyer ran mechanically, his face a stolid mask. His legs felt sheathed in lead, but he knew he couldn't stop. He had to keep on running until Cooley told him otherwise.

He was just starting over the ridge when the tank came grind-

ing at him, blotting out the sky. Hackermeyer lunged clumsily
to his left and missed the rasping treads by a yard. He felt the
churning heat of the engine, the noise so loud that he was
ringing-eared deaf for almost a minute after.

As he stumbled on, he glanced back and saw that the tank had
a white star on it. He saw the barrel of its gun recoil, barely
heard the sharp percussion. The tank shuddered, then tilted and
went grinding down the hill. Hackermeyer turned back. He ran
across the plain in crooked, rolling strides. Far to his left, an
American tank was hit. Instantly, the turret was afire and Hackermeyer saw miniature figures tumbling from the smoke. Some
of them were burning. As they ran they looked like moving
torches.

THEY WERE MARCHING along a pitch-black road, their clothes
soaked from the drenching rain which had stopped only minutes
before. It seemed very silent without the heavy falling of the rain.
All Hackermeyer could hear was the faint rattle of equipment
and the sucking sounds of shoes as they sank into the viscid mud,
then pulled loose. The thick slime clung to his shoes, making
them seem a hundred pounds each. Added to that was the weight
of his soggy overcoat, his cartridge belt, canteen and first-aid kit,
the hand grenades, two bandoleers of cartridge clips, his rifle,
and the bazooka with its shells. He still felt a little guilty about
having left his pick near the foxhole. He'd wondered if he was
liable to disciplinary action for deserting government equipment.

"Break!" The call came fluttering through the wet darkness.
Hackermeyer stumbled off the road and sank down on the mucky
ground. He lay back and opened his mouth, breathing slowly,
heavily. Raindrops from overhanging tree limbs spattered on his
face. His hands lay like twisted lumps of bone and flesh, his legs
stretched out like logs of wood. Only his chest had motion, rising
and falling shallowly as he rested.

"Bastards," he heard.

He turned his head a little, one eye opening. Lazzo was lying
next to him. All through the late afternoon and evening Lazzo
had been bitterly disconsolate about Goldmeyer's death. "I hate

the bastards," Lazzo had kept on muttering. "I'll kill every mother one of them."

Hackermeyer was suddenly asleep.

It seemed only an instant before his eyes jerked open, in his ears the sound of a whistle softly blown.

He struggled to his feet and fell in with the rest of the squad. As they started marching again, Hackermeyer thought about Foley sitting dead in the foxhole miles away. He thought about the pretty girl in the sweater and skirt leaning back against the porch rail. It was too bad about her.

Now he'd never get a letter from her.

SECOND ASSAULT

RALPH LINSTROM JOINED the squad at suppertime. Company C was bivouacked in a narrow valley four miles northwest of Saarbach. The troops were spread out at five-yard intervals while the cooks served them from the big, steaming food cans. It had been a damp, chilly day with intermittent drizzles and artillery barrages. Hackermeyer's breath steamed as he shuffled along with the file of men, his mess kit and canteen cup dangling from one gloved hand.

"Hey, Cooley," he heard someone say and looked around. It was one of the sergeants from the first squad. He was gesturing with his head toward a group of approaching soldiers being led by Gaspard, the new assistant platoon sergeant.

"Bet you a fin you get two bottle babies," said the sergeant from the first squad.

Cooley spat tobacco juice. "If I do," he said, "I'm handing in my resignation."

Everyone laughed except Hackermeyer. He wondered if it was possible for a noncom to hand in his resignation. It seemed improbable. Cooley was, likely, not serious.

He watched Gaspard break apart the group of replacements and give two to each squad, except for the third squad, which got one. The two that were brought to Cooley were no more than boys. Hackermeyer saw a glaze of martyrdom in Cooley's eyes as he spoke to the two replacements. Now half the squad was made up of eighteen-year-olds.

Cooley sent one of the replacements over to Schumacher. The other, a slender, good-looking boy, he sent to Hackermeyer.

"Hi," said the boy, smiling nervously. "My name's Linstrom. The sergeant said—"

"Better get your mess kit ready," Hackermeyer told him.

"Oh. Yeah." Linstrom tried to reach around his pack but couldn't manage it. The M1 kept slipping off his shoulder.

"Would you . . . ?" he said, turning his back to Hackermeyer. Hackermeyer took out the mess kit while Linstrom got his canteen cup. They dipped their mess kits and cups in boiling water, then edged past the food cans while the cooks slopped down dark, aromatic beef stew, thick slices of buttered white bread and fruit salad. Their canteen cups were filled with steaming, muddy-colored coffee and they walked away from the sweating, smoke-squinting cooks.

"How about over there?" asked Linstrom, nodding toward a skeletal tree a few yards up the west slope of the valley. Hackermeyer grunted and the two of them walked over to the tree. Hackermeyer sat while Linstrom set down his mess kit and cup and took off his pack. He sat on top of it.

"I catch cold easily," he said.

Hackermeyer sniffled. Not me, he thought. I never catch cold.

"I'm Ralph Linstrom," said Linstrom, extending his hand.

"Hackermeyer." He took Linstrom's hand and squeezed it once without shaking it.

"Where you from?" asked Linstrom, starting to eat.

"Brooklyn."

"No kidding?" Linstrom looked pleased. "I'm from Brooklyn too," he said. "Bay Ridge. What part are you from?"

"Bergen Beach."

"I don't know where that is," said Linstrom.

Hackermeyer nodded. "You eighteen?" he asked.

"Uh-huh. How old are you?"

"Eighteen."

"No kidding?" Linstrom looked at him carefully in the misty gloom. "You look older," he said.

"Yeah." Hackermeyer ate quickly, steadily.

"Where *is* Bergen Beach?" asked Linstrom.

"Near Canarsie."

Linstrom nodded. "Oh. Yeah," he said.

Hackermeyer thought that Linstrom looked a lot like the photographs of his aunt and uncle's son Charles. The same features and hairline, the same sort of smile. He had often wondered if Aunt Alice would have been any nicer to him if Charles hadn't been killed by a car when he was eight. He didn't think it would have made much difference in his uncle's attitude, but Charles had been his mother's idol. His premature death had driven her into a cavern of retreat from which she rarely emerged. Hackermeyer recalled her as a portly woman with a distant sort of smile who drifted about the house, cleaning sporadically, preparing tasteless meals, and offering little if any conversation. Charles was all she ever really spoke about. She had called him *Buddy*. *My Buddy* did this or *My Buddy* did that or *Buddy would have liked* such-and-such. Smiling as she talked about him until, abruptly, her throat would catch, her lips turn under and begin to quiver, her eyes begin to glisten with tears. Then she would get up and walk quickly from the room, no matter who was there.

Hackermeyer put down his canteen cup. He was inclined to believe that it might have been a lot easier for him if Buddy had lived. Not only might his aunt have been more in control of Uncle George but there would have been another boy to talk to. As it happened, he'd been treated more like a boarder than a relative from the time his father had brought him, a month-old baby, to his uncle's house until the day he'd left when he was sixteen.

"What?" he asked, blinking himself free of thought.

"I said is it—rough up here?" asked Linstrom. He spoke as if he sensed that it was a naïve question but had to ask it anyway.

"Depends," Hackermeyer said.

"On what?"

Hackermeyer took a sip of the oversweetened coffee. "On whether you think so," he said.

"Do you?"

Hackermeyer shrugged. "Don't know," he said.

"Oh."

Hackermeyer exhaled and glanced at Linstrom.

"You Swedish?" he asked.

"Half and half," said Linstrom with a smile. "The other half's Norwegian. My mom came from Norway. Christiana. It's called Oslo now."

Hackermeyer grunted.

"That's why we live in Bay Ridge," said Linstrom. "It's a Scandinavian section of Brooklyn."

"Uh-huh." Hackermeyer chewed on a gristly chunk of beef.

"What are you?" asked Linstrom.

"German—Dutch—English," said Hackermeyer.

Linstrom nodded, then drew in a deep breath.

"What are we supposed to do?" he asked.

"Do?"

"I mean . . . what's the objective?"

"To beat the Germans."

Linstrom thought Hackermeyer was being droll and smiled appreciatively. "I know," he said—"but what's the immediate objective?"

"I don't know," said Hackermeyer. He chewed a few moments. "Couple of days ago it was Saarbach."

"What's that?"

"A town."

"How come you—didn't get there?" asked Linstrom as if he were afraid what the answer might be.

"Germans wouldn't let us."

"Oh." Linstrom looked down bleakly at his food. He seemed to have lost his appetite.

"You—think we'll be going back there?" he asked finally. His voice seemed, to Hackermeyer, even thinner than Foley's had been.

"I don't know."

"Do you know when we're moving out?"

"They said in the morning."

"Oh."

Linstrom appeared to have a lump in his throat that he couldn't swallow. He coughed dryly, then took a sip of his coffee, grimacing at the taste. "I just can't get used to coffee," he said. "I always drank milk."

"Mmmm." Hackermeyer started spooning the fruit salad into his mouth. He wasn't used to drinking milk at all. And this coffee, bad as it was, was better than what Aunt Alice had made.

"Are they good fighters?" asked Linstrom.

Hackermeyer remembered asking Wendt the same question the day he'd been a new replacement. Strange how long ago that seemed. He forgot what Wendt had said. He couldn't even remember what Wendt had looked like. Come to think of it, Wendt might have died from appendicitis.

"Are they?" asked Linstrom.

"They're okay," said Hackermeyer. What could he answer anyway? He had no way of judging the German soldier. All he could vouch for was the skill of the German artilleryman.

"I read," said Linstrom, "that, if anything goes wrong, they panic. Is that right?"

Hackermeyer finished off the fruit salad and put his mess kit down. He wiped the back of a glove across his lips.

"I don't know," he said.

"What I mean," continued Linstrom, "is that, you know, they're trained so—so strictly that they're like machines. They can't think for themselves. They have no—no imagination. All they know is what they're taught. I mean they have a certain way of doing things, a certain way of fighting. And—and, if that certain way doesn't work, they get all fouled up and go to pieces."

"May be," said Hackermeyer. It didn't sound very plausible to him. They were the ones who had run away, not the Germans. Whether its soldiers had imagination or not, it was the army that moved forward that won.

He looked at Linstrom. "Where'd you read that?" he asked.

"I don't remember," said Linstrom. "I know my mother read it, though. I remember discussing it with her."

Hackermeyer blew his nose.

"I think it's true," said Linstrom. "That's what makes them so inhuman."

"May be," Hackermeyer said again. He drank down the rest of his coffee and got up.

While he stood on line waiting to wash his mess kit, he thought of what Linstrom had said about the German soldier being a machine. Maybe it was true. Except Linstrom was wrong about it being a bad thing. Machines would make the best soldiers. Nothing could distract them. They could concentrate on killing and not worry about anything else. By that token, he should be a pretty good soldier. He wasn't emotional and the thought of killing didn't bother him. Maybe he was a machine. Why not? Hadn't he been raised like one? They'd kept him running and no more. Maybe he was just the type to be a soldier. Maybe, for once, his usual underestimation of himself was wrong.

Linstrom sat down beside him.

"Some guy over there is keeping a diary," he said incredulously.

Hackermeyer looked over. So what? he thought.

Linstrom's expression grew hard. "How come?" he asked.

"What?"

"How come they let him?"

Hackermeyer shrugged. He had no idea what Linstrom was talking about.

Linstrom glowered for a while. Then he took out a V-mail form and a gold fountain pen and started writing.

"I had a diary," he said after a few moments.

Hackermeyer looked at him.

"I was going to make a book out of it," said Linstrom bitterly. "I even had a title: *The Gateway to War*. I kept it all through basic training and when I went overseas I had almost a hundred and fifty pages. Then this—stupid bastard of a lieutenant tells us we have to hand in all diaries and letters because if the Germans capture them they'll—oh, shit! And I believed him, like a stupid jerk! Almost a hundred and fifty pages."

Linstrom seethed. "Goddamn . . ." he muttered.

Hackermeyer took out his dog-eared crossword puzzle book

and opened it. He was still only half finished with the same puzzle he'd been working on since he joined the squad.

It was quiet for a while. Linstrom finished his V-mail letter and sealed it, his expression a pouting one. Hackermeyer concentrated on the puzzle. It was almost too dark to see.

"Who takes mail?" demanded Linstrom.

"Cooley."

"Who's he?"

"The—" Hackermeyer broke off and looked around. "There," he said, pointing.

Linstrom got up and walked toward Cooley with short, vengeful strides. Hackermeyer watched him go. What a brat Linstrom was. More and more, he was coming to agree with Cooley. Eighteen-year-olds didn't belong in combat. What had they ever experienced that would prepare them for war? They were just kids torn from their well-padded elements, stuck on a battlefield and expected to better seasoned German troops. It didn't make sense.

Hackermeyer remembered Foley saying that. To Foley—a typical eighteen-year-old soldier—none of this had made sense. War had been too alien a crisis for him to understand. It had had no place in his world of parents and school and girlfriend and small-town pleasures. It had been totally beyond him. He had died confused and unaware.

Linstrom returned and sat down on his pack.

"Lousy, stinking army," he said. "Always screwing up."

Hackermeyer put away his crossword puzzle book. It was too dark anyway. He yawned, shuddering as the damp coldness seemed to clutch him for an instant. Then he began to brush his teeth.

"Like before I left the States," said Linstrom. "I got K.P. duty one night in Camp Kilmer."

Hackermeyer remembered Foley talking about Camp Kilmer. About the twelve-hour pass and sitting with his girl for twenty minutes. Now he was dead. Hackermeyer wondered if he were still in that foxhole.

"I didn't do a thing," Linstrom was saying. "Just stood around talking to some guys. One guy, I remember, had flat feet and a punctured eardrum. My brother-in-law has a punctured eardrum and he's 4-F but this poor bastard was going overseas. Just like the army. The physical they gave us was a joke. Stand in front of the doctors, hold up your arms, they look down your throat and that's it. Shit."

Hackermeyer was thinking that he'd never noticed how four-letter words sounded natural in some mouths, strained in others. Cooley, for instance, was a natural swearer. Profanity fell ingenuously from his tongue. With Linstrom it was otherwise. His curse-words sounded forced and studied.

"So I just stood there all night, supposed to be on K.P.," Linstrom was saying. "I went to bed about four. At six they blew reveille. I'd been told—definitely—that I wouldn't have to stand reveille because I'd been on K.P. But, no, this stupid son-of-a-bitch sergeant makes me get up anyway! I just made it. I got mad because some of the other guys weren't there. Then what do I find out but that they got passes the night before! I was in that lousy, stinking kitchen doing nothing! But could I go home? Oh, no! Could I say good-bye to my mother?"

"Don't you have a father?" asked Hackermeyer.

"He left us," said Linstrom distractedly. "So we get our packs on and everything and take a train to the ferry. I could see all the places in New York I've been. The Bear Mountain boat pier and everything. We get to the boat and the—the stupid Red Cross women are running around like jerks giving everybody coffee and doughnuts. Coffee and doughnuts, for Christ's sake! Who wanted them? I felt like—screaming, I was so mad."

Linstrom's breath hissed out and he hit his pack once with a clenched fist.

"To top it all off," he said, "while we were sailing toward the ocean, we went right past where my sister and her husband live in Bay Ridge. I could see the apartment house. I could see the window of their living room!"

Linstrom made a sound of overwhelming bitterness. For a moment, Hackermeyer wondered if he was going to cry.

"Lousy—stinking—army," said Linstrom.

"HACKERMEYER?"

Hackermeyer opened his eyes and saw a dark figure looming over him. "What?" he asked.

"Patrol. Come on," said the figure.

"Patrol?" For a moment, the word had no meaning to Hackermeyer. It was only a sound.

"Come on," said the figure. It was Lippincott.

Hackermeyer sat up, coldly awake. Patrol.

"Take off your helmet and liner," said Lippincott.

Hackermeyer took them off and pulled down his woolen cap. He felt buried in a perplexing dream. Why did he have to take off the helmet and liner? He stood up and stretched his legs.

"Just your M1 and grenades," said Lippincott.

Patrol. Suddenly, the word sprang full-bloom into Hackermeyer's mind. Moving through the night toward German lines. Capturing prisoners. Gunfire in the darkness. Thrown grenades. Hackermeyer swallowed as he started clipping on his belt.

"Leave the belt," said Lippincott. "Stick the grenades and cartridge clips in your pockets."

Hackermeyer did, then slung the M1 over his shoulder. He tried to check the safety lock but couldn't with his glove on. He pulled off the glove.

"What are you doing?" asked Lippincott.

"All right," muttered Hackermeyer. He put his glove back on as he started walking beside Lippincott.

"When we're out there," said Lippincott, "use the corners of your eyes to see with. Keep your eyes moving. Don't stare or you won't see a thing."

Hackermeyer sniffled.

"And blow your nose before we leave," said Lippincott.

They approached a dark figure.

"Are you prepared, Vincent?" asked Lippincott.

"Stupid shit patrol," muttered Lazzo. "What the hell do they think we're going to find out there—Adolph Hitler?"

"Why not?" asked Lippincott.

"Balls," said Lazzo.

Hackermeyer had been, vaguely, aware that reconnaissance patrols had been taking place night and day since he'd joined the company. It had never occurred to him that he might be going on one himself.

"Check your safety locks," said Lippincott.

I did, Hackermeyer almost said before deciding to take off his glove and check again.

"Don't fire unless you absolutely have to," Lippincott reminded them.

"Sure, sure," said Lazzo.

"The password is Lili Marlene," said Lippincott. "Let's go."

Hackermeyer started walking up a slope beside Lazzo. *Don't fire unless you have to*, his mind repeated. *The password is Lili Marlene*. It all sounded very dramatic. Who was going to ask them for the password? The Germans? Were they going to try to penetrate the German lines? Should he try to imitate a German accent when he spoke the password? Hackermeyer felt he should ask Lippincott but he also felt that he was expected to know. The password is Lili Marlene, he told himself.

"Why aren't we wearing our helmets?" he asked softly.

"Noise," answered Lippincott. "No more talking now."

Noise? Hackermeyer squinted. Then he realized what Lippincott meant. Steel helmets might make a noise which would reveal their presence to the Germans. Hackermeyer almost cleared his throat, then decided that he mustn't make the noise. He swallowed laboredly, trying to rid his throat of the obstruction. Lili Marlene, he thought. That was a German song. So it must be the German password. Still, Lippincott hadn't said they were supposed to speak it in a German accent. Hackermeyer took out his handkerchief and blew his nose as softly as he could.

They had reached the top of the slope now and were starting across a level field. It was a starless night. They might have been inside a huge, damp cavern. Hackermeyer wondered how Lippincott knew where he was going. He remembered the night he and the corporal had gone back for coffee and blankets. He had wondered then how Lippincott was able to find the truck so easily. Lippincott must have cat eyes.

"Halt."

Hackermeyer froze at the almost whispered challenge. He felt as if he should whip the M1 off his shoulder but he couldn't move. It hadn't sounded like a German voice, but you could never be sure.

"Lili," said Lippincott.

"Marlene," said the voice. "Who is it?"

"Lippincott. Reconnaissance."

"Okay."

No more talking, thought Hackermeyer. He started walking beside Lazzo and Lippincott again. A dark figure took shape out of the blackness.

"Hi," said the figure.

"Hi," said Lippincott muffledly. "Anything doing?"

"Couldn't prove it by me," said the figure.

Lippincott turned to them. "All right, let's go," he said.

They moved away from the outpost and started across the field again.

"What the hell are we supposed to be looking for?" asked Lazzo.

"Something to tell Miller," said Lippincott.

"Tell him to shove it," said Lazzo. Hackermeyer noticed that he was walking with stiff, wooden movements.

"What's wrong?" he whispered.

"What?"

"The way you're walking."

"Trench foot, trench foot," answered Lazzo sourly.

"No more talking," said Lippincott.

They moved across the field, their shoes sinking into the spongy mud. Ten minutes later, they reached a ridge and started across it. Hackermeyer wondered if it could possibly be the ridge where they'd first dug in. Probably not.

"Keep your eyes open now," whispered Lippincott. "First one who sees Hitler gets a Kewpie doll."

"Balls," said Lazzo.

They began edging down a steep grade. Hackermeyer unslung his rifle and held it in his right hand, bracing his left against the earth. What were they looking for? Maybe they were supposed to see if the Germans were attempting a sneak attack. He'd never thought of it before but using darkness as cover for an attack would be a clever idea. Odd how one assumed that, after dark, everybody went to sleep. Even in a war. He thought about standing guard his first night on the lines. It had never occurred to him that the Germans might attack.

"Down," whispered Lippincott.

Instantly, the three of them crouched. Hackermeyer felt his heart contracting and expanding with convulsive throbs. He looked around but couldn't see anything. Use the corners of your eyes, he thought. He tried but it didn't seem to help.

"All right," whispered Lippincott.

"What are you, seeing things?" whispered Lazzo.

Lippincott didn't answer. They stood and moved forward again. Immediately, Hackermeyer stepped on a rock and thudded down onto his side. Lippincott and Lazzo flung themselves prone.

"What is it?" whispered Lippincott.

"I tripped," Hackermeyer whispered back. Lazzo snickered.

"Oh, for Christ's sake," whispered Lippincott. He pushed to his feet again.

Hackermeyer got up and started walking. His side felt sore where he'd landed. Suddenly, he peeled off his right glove and felt at his grenades to make sure they weren't disarmed. They were all right. He wondered if he would ever use them. Shooting at Germans from a distance was one thing. It was another to—

There was a popping sound overhead. Suddenly the sky was gelatinous with glaring, pink light.

"Hit it!" snapped Lippincott and the three of them dropped. The field seemed, to Hackermeyer, as bright as a lamp-filled room. Pink light shimmered everywhere. He kept waiting for guns to start firing. His stomach walls drew in like steel bands around the churning contents of his stomach. Why didn't they fire? Slowly, he raised his eyes. There was a tree ahead of them. It seemed to dance drunkenly in the wavering glow. Still, there was no firing.

Now the flare, its perimeter of fire contracting, was almost to the ground. It landed, burned to a glowing core, then went out. Darkness flooded into Hackermeyer's eyes so fast it seemed as if he felt its pressure. He closed his eyes tight and saw the dull red glow diminishing. He opened his eyes and it disappeared. There was only the blackness again.

"It wasn't for us," whispered Lippincott.

Hackermeyer thought they were going to go back now but Lippincott kept heading west. His original idea must be correct, Hackermeyer decided. They were going to try to penetrate the German lines. But Lippincott had said not to fire unless they absolutely had to. Wouldn't they absolutely have to if they went behind the German lines?

As if by command, all three of them stopped walking simultaneously. In the distance, Hackermeyer could hear a low-throttled muttering of engines.

"Tanks," whispered Lippincott.

"Bastards," whispered Lazzo. Hackermeyer wondered if Lazzo was thinking about Goldmeyer again. It had been the machine gun on a Panther tank that had killed Goldmeyer.

Hackermeyer started inhaling deeply, then twitched in mid-breath as Lippincott drifted forward into the darkness again. He started after him. What if they ran into a tank? It didn't seem likely that the Germans would risk moving a tank in the darkness. Still, you could never tell.

Abruptly Lippincott and Lazzo ducked down. Hackermeyer followed, heartbeat jolting. He crouched there woodenly, listening so hard that he could feel the tightening of his middle-ear muscles.

There were bootfalls approaching. Hackermeyer felt a chill prickle across his scalp. He held his rifle in a rigid grip. He should push off the safety lock. But in the silence the noise might be too loud.

Someone stumbled in the darkness. "*Verflucht*," muttered a voice, and Hackermeyer realized with sudden shock that it was speaking German. His lower jaw slipped down. Glancing aside, he could just make out the forms of Lazzo and Lippincott. They looked like statues.

Hackermeyer felt a fluttering tremor in his stomach. If the Germans dropped another flare everybody would see everybody else. He visualized hundreds of Germans moving forward in the darkness to make a surprise assault on the American lines. Suddenly it occurred to him that Lippincott might decide they were done for anyway and fire his rifle to warn the others. He tried to swallow but he couldn't. For one horrible moment, he felt the moist tickle of a sneeze starting in his nostrils and he pressed a glove palm across his mouth. The rustle of his coat sounded terribly audible to him.

After a while, the bootfalls faded. Hackermeyer twitched as something ran across his nose. At first he thought it was a bug. Then he realized that it was a drop of sweat and he ran the back of his glove across his forehead and nose. Abruptly he sneezed into the glove.

"Shhh," warned Lippincott.

They rose and started forward again. Weren't they going back? Hackermeyer could visualize them moving deeper and deeper into the German sector until they were killed or captured.

"What'd the Kraut say?" whispered Lazzo.

"Hell," said Lippincott.

They were edging along a narrow draw when another flare popped loudly overhead and filled the sky with quivering pink light. Almost before they'd hit the ground, a German machine gun high on the right slope started firing. Hackermeyer heard bullets whizzing overhead and plowing into the ground on the left slope. Glancing up, he saw bright streaking tracers and the spot up on the slope from where they came. His legs retracted spastically as one of the bullets caromed off a nearby rock and shot up, whining, into the sky.

The flare went out and the machine gun stopped.

"Go," said Lippincott.

They pushed up quickly and ran along the bottom of the draw until they reached the end of it. There, they squatted down in the black shadow of a tree to catch their breath. Hackermeyer sneezed before he could cover his mouth.

"For Christ's sake!" whispered Lazzo.

Hackermeyer blew his nose quietly as they moved on.

"You better stay here, Hackermeyer," Lippincott whispered after they'd gone a little way. "We'll pick you up on the way back. Stay by this rock."

A cold shudder roped down Hackermeyer's spine. What if they couldn't find him on the way back? He was about to ask the question when Lippincott and Lazzo drifted away into the darkness. Hackermeyer shivered. Alone behind the German lines, he thought. Or was he behind them? It didn't seem as if they could have come that far. Still, it also seemed as if they always went farther than he calculated.

He edged back slowly and leaned against the rock. What was he supposed to do until they got back? *If* they got back. He scowled. Was it his fault he had to sneeze? Lippincott knew he had a cold. Hackermeyer inhaled through his mouth and let the air drain slowly. What would Linstrom do if he were left alone like this? Probably start bawling and calling for his mother.

Hackermeyer looked at his watch. It was just past ten. What time was it in Brooklyn? He took a deep breath. What difference did that make?

There was a noise in the darkness.

Hackermeyer went rigid, a prickling sensation on his scalp. Was it a German? Instinctively he pushed off the safety lock of his M1. The clicking noise made him start. He looked around quickly, trying to penetrate the heavy blackness. Use the corners of your eyes! He jammed shut his eyes, then opened them again and tried to see out of the corners.

The noise came again. Hackermeyer's heart seemed to stop. He pushed away from the rock, then stood motionless, not knowing whether to move or stay put. He sucked in breath and clenched his teeth, holding his rifle ready to fire.

In the distance a man coughed. The sound made Hackermeyer twitch so violently that his cap almost fell off.

A mumble of voices began. Hackermeyer turned his head and listened as hard as he could. He couldn't tell what language the voices were speaking. Was it Lippincott and Lazzo?

He took a short step forward, setting his foot down very slowly. The voices kept on. He took another cautious step. Was it his imagination or did the voices already seem closer? It was almost impossible to gauge in the darkness. Hackermeyer swallowed. His throat felt very dry. He needed a sip of water.

He found himself taking another step, then another and another as if the voices were drawing him in hypnotically. He kept moving until, suddenly, he froze.

"Ich bin kranke," said a voice.

A man grunted. *"Was fehlt ihnen?"* he said. It sounded like a second man.

Hackermeyer gritted his teeth, tensing himself for their appearance in the darkness. He'd have to shoot them. He knew that very clearly.

"Ich habe Schmerzen in meinem Brustkasten," said the first voice.

The second man made a faint sound of amusement.

"Sie rauchen zu viel," he said.

"Ha-ha," said the first man.

Hackermeyer realized that the voices were coming up from the ground. Were the Germans lying down or were they in a foxhole? What were they doing here? Was it an outpost? A machine-gun nest, a mortar position? Hackermeyer felt confused and helpless. I should kill them, he thought. Cooley had said that his job was to kill the Krauts or capture them. Could he capture them? No, that would be impossible. But maybe he could . . .

He twitched in reaction as he realized that his finger was tightening on the M1 trigger. What was he trying to do? Suddenly he wished desperately that there was moonlight so that he could see the Germans and shoot them. Could he creep up on them in the darkness and . . . ?

"Hackermeyer?" whispered a voice.

He whirled around, heart pounding. Abruptly he started walking away, certain that the Germans would hear his footsteps but not wanting Lippincott to speak again.

The figures of Lazzo and Lippincott appeared in the darkness.

"I told you to—" Lippincott started.

"There's Germans over there," Hackermeyer whispered.

They all stood rigidly for several moments. Then Lippincott whispered, "Let's go."

"Shouldn't we take them?" Lazzo whispered back.

"You know how many there are?" asked Lippincott.

"No."

"Neither do I. Let's go."

As they moved away, Hackermeyer wondered if the Germans had heard them. Maybe they had and just didn't want to fight. He could have killed them, he thought. He could have killed them easily. Somehow the idea intrigued him. He felt almost regretful for not having tried.

Thirty minutes later, after an uneventful walk, Hackermeyer left Lippincott and started back toward his equipment. Locating it, he sank down on his blanket with a tired groan.

"Where you been?" whispered Linstrom.

"Patrol."

"Was that shooting at you?"

Hackermeyer yawned widely and shivered. "Yeah," he said.

Linstrom was quiet for a while.

"Well . . . what did you find out?" he asked finally.

Hackermeyer stretched out and closed his eyes. He'd found out that he wasn't afraid to shoot Germans, the thought occurred. "Nothing," he said.

He lay there listening to the heartbeat thudding in his ears. *Something's going to happen*, he thought.

He wondered what it was.

DECEMBER 12, 1944

"LET'S GO, BOYS."

Hackermeyer's eyes fluttered open. The ground was covered with a pale, curling mist. He saw Cooley being swallowed by its licking pallor. "Up. Up," Cooley said to someone else.

Hackermeyer raised his left arm and pushed back the mud-flecked sleeve of his overcoat. The watch arms pointed to just past six o'clock.

"You awake?" asked Linstrom.

Hackermeyer looked across his shoulder and saw Linstrom sitting up. He yawned and struggled to his feet, then stretched, grimacing at the soreness on his side. He started gathering up his equipment.

"This is—it, huh?" asked Linstrom.

"Guess so," said Hackermeyer. Abruptly he realized that, the night before, he'd been so absorbed by thoughts of shooting Germans that it hadn't occurred to him he might have been killed himself. And, this morning, he might be killed. Or this afternoon or evening. It could happen any time.

With a shudder, he glanced over at Linstrom, who was putting on his pack.

"Just put your raincoat and shovel on your belt," he said.

"Well . . ." Linstrom stared at him as if debating whether to argue. "Do we just leave the rest here?"

"Supply'll bring them up later."

"Oh." Linstrom stared at Hackermeyer for another few moments. Then, with a sigh, he took off his pack.

"Think we're going back to that—town?" he asked.

"I don't know."

"Well . . . didn't you look around last night? I mean—on that patrol?"

"Not at Saarbach."

Linstrom said no more. Hackermeyer could hear him breathing laboredly as he assembled his gear.

"Coffee and rations down in the hollow," said Cooley, returning. He stopped and gazed down at Linstrom.

"Am—am I all right?" asked Linstrom, gesturing toward his equipment.

"I'll check it later," Cooley said. He looked at Linstrom glumly. "First time in combat," he said. It was not a question.

He started away, then turned.

"Remember one thing, son," he said. "Only a small percentage of guys get wounded. An even smaller percentage get killed. The Krauts ain't aiming at you specially. And, even if you're hit, chances are good it'll only be a wound and you'll be out of it. So don't get all tied up in knots before you start."

"No," said Linstrom.

"Get Hackermeyer here to tell you how to move and fall," said Cooley. "He knows what to do."

Hackermeyer watched Cooley leaving, a sense of mild confusion furrowing his brow. He'd been certain that Cooley lumped him in with the rest of the useless eighteen-year-olds. After a moment, he shrugged. Well, no doubt Cooley did. No doubt he'd only said that to Linstrom to give him a little confidence.

"What about how to move?" asked Linstrom.

Hackermeyer told him briefly how to get up at an angle, move fast, and fall smoothly without telegraphing it. Linstrom nodded gravely. After a while Cooley passed by again and gave Linstrom some cotton. "Let's go, boys," he told them.

"He's a good Joe," said Linstrom after Cooley had gone.

Hackermeyer grunted as he checked his grenades.

"He'll get us through," said Linstrom.

"Yeah." Hackermeyer sensed Linstrom's need for someone to lean on. Cooley was not exactly the father type, but he'd do in a pinch. This, for Linstrom, was definitely a pinch.

As for himself, Hackermeyer tried not to think about it. True, he could not control the slightly thickened pulsing at his wrists. Still, he was not consciously worried. It was obvious that he'd survive if the percentages favored him, be wounded or die if they didn't.

Hackermeyer finished putting on his gear and unclipped his canteen holder. Sliding out the canteen, he worked free the cup, then slid back the canteen and unclipped the handle of the cup. He started toward the hollow.

"Hey, wait," said Linstrom. He sounded alarmed.

Hackermeyer stopped and turned. Linstrom was on his feet, breathing heavily as he buckled on his cartridge belt. Hackermeyer wondered if he should tell Linstrom about taping down the arms of his grenades. The hell with it. He wasn't Linstrom's mother. Let Cooley tell him about the grenades.

Linstrom joined him and they started down into the misted hollow of the valley, the mud pulling at their shoes like wet gum. Below, they could hear the clink and gurgle of canteen cups being filled with coffee, the murmur of voices. Here and there, ghostly figures moved in the mist, appearing for seconds, then disappearing.

"Sure is cold," said Linstrom.

To their right, two figures appeared, moving in the same direction.

"How are they doing?" asked one of them. It was Guthrie.

"The same," said Lazzo. He was limping a little more noticeably, Hackermeyer thought.

"Can't they give you something?" asked Guthrie.

"Sure, they gave me foot powder," said Lazzo.

Guthrie snickered. "And the United States Army Medical Corps marches on," he said.

"Screw 'em," said Lazzo.

"What's wrong with him?" whispered Linstrom.

"Trench foot," said Hackermeyer.

"What's that?"

"Feet get wet, cold. Numb. Swell up."

"Oooh . . ." Linstrom's voice wavered and Hackermeyer wondered if he'd run away like Sergeant Wadley. Maybe not. Wadley had been a bully, hiding his fear beneath a layer of authority. Linstrom's fear wasn't hidden at all. It virtually quivered on the surface. Maybe it was easier to conquer fear when you didn't try to hide it.

He remembered seeing a movie once where a tough sergeant had said to one of the frightened soldiers, "Sure, I'm scared before I go into battle. I'm scared stiff." The frightened soldier had looked wide-eyed with astonishment and said, "You? You're scared?" and had gotten back his courage. Hackermeyer wondered if Guthrie's father had written that crap.

He and Linstrom got in line and Linstrom took out his canteen cup.

"Let's stick together, hanh?" he said to Hackermeyer. "I mean—we can help each other out, okay?"

Hackermeyer made an inconclusive noise. He'd just as soon not be helped by Linstrom. He didn't want some panicked kid on his neck. Still, he was expected to stay with Linstrom, he supposed. That was why Cooley had sent Linstrom to him. Well, he'd do what he could but he wasn't going to watch over Linstrom like a mother hen. Linstrom would have to shift for himself.

"Are there any other—secrets I should know?" asked Linstrom.

Hackermeyer looked at him. "Secrets?"

"You know—tricks? I mean, ways of fighting. There must be some sort of . . ." His voice trailed off.

"There's nothing," said Hackermeyer.

"Oh." Linstrom nodded. "Okay," he said.

They passed the barrel and one of the cooks poured coffee into their cups while another handed them three boxes of K ration each. While they were walking away, the handle on Linstrom's cup came loose and the cup, toppling over, spilled coffee down his overcoat and trousers. Linstrom cried out faintly and dropped his cup and K ration boxes. He jerked off his wet glove and pulled out a handkerchief to blot at the coffee that had dribbled down his wrist.

"Ooh," he murmured. His rifle slipped off his shoulder and he let it drop to the ground.

"Burn yourself?" asked Hackermeyer.

"I don't think so." Linstrom pushed the handkerchief under his coat sleeve, then pulled it out and started patting it hastily against his coat and trousers. Hackermeyer stood there sipping coffee and watching.

"I don't know," said Linstrom. He blotted at the huge coffee stains. "Hot," he said.

Hackermeyer slid the K ration boxes into his overcoat pockets and picked up Linstrom's rifle.

"Maybe I did burn myself," said Linstrom. He straightened

up and looked at Hackermeyer. "You think maybe I should—go to the aid station?"

"I don't know," said Hackermeyer.

"Feels—kind of like I did burn myself," said Linstrom. "Maybe I should." He made a sound of strained amusement. "I wouldn't be much good in combat covered with blisters," he said.

Hackermeyer didn't say anything.

"It's starting to sting a little," said Linstrom. He raised up on his toes and looked around as if trying to see through the mist. "Where is the aid station?" he asked.

Hackermeyer drank his coffee.

"Maybe I—" Linstrom swallowed. "Is there a medic around here?" he asked, raising his voice. No one answered. Linstrom sucked in a trembling breath. "Sure stings," he said.

"Second squad over here," Cooley called out.

"Let's go," said Hackermeyer.

"What about my burn?" asked Linstrom.

"Ask Cooley."

"Oh. Yeah, that's right." Linstrom sounded relieved. He scooped up his K ration boxes and stuffed them negligently into his overcoat pockets. Hackermeyer held out his rifle.

"Maybe you should keep it," said Linstrom. "I mean—maybe somebody will need it after I—"

"It's yours," said Hackermeyer, handing it to him.

"Oh. Well, I'll—" Linstrom didn't finish.

"You want some of my coffee?" Hackermeyer asked.

"No, thank you," said Linstrom politely. "I'm sure I can get some at the aid station."

"Yeah," said Hackermeyer. Well, he wouldn't have to watch over Linstrom.

The squad was assembled around a small boulder. Hackermeyer saw the cleanly shaven Schumacher standing erectly, the bazooka slung over one shoulder. Cooley had almost given it to Hackermeyer, then, at the last moment, had changed his mind. At the time, Hackermeyer had felt a twinge of disappointment. Not that he'd particularly wanted the bazooka. It had just seemed to him that it should have been offered to him after he'd rescued it. Now he didn't care. He was inured to that sort of thing.

"Everybody here?" asked Cooley. He called off the names—Lippincott, Schumacher, Lazzo, Guthrie, Hackermeyer, Linstrom, and Fearfeather, a tall, bony-looking boy with coarse, almost bucolic features.

"I guess you know where we're going," said Cooley, chewing tobacco. "For the two new boys—Linstrom and Fearfeather: We're headed for Saarbach. It's about four miles from here. We'll have to go through the Saarbach forest to get to it." He paused. "This time we're going to make it," he said.

"Sergeant . . . ?" asked Linstrom timidly.

"You two new boys stick to the men I put you with. Ask them anything you want to know if me or Lippincott ain't around. Just—"

"Sergeant?"

Cooley broke off and turned to Linstrom. "What is it, son?" he asked.

"I spilled some coffee on myself."

"That's tough. We ain't got no dry-cleaning service up here, though."

"I don't mean that," said Linstrom.

"C Company goes in first today," said Cooley. "Second platoon leads, we follow. We should make the forest by noon, so watch for booby traps. The Engineers couldn't get close enough to do any sweeping and the woods'll probably be lousy with traps. They're pretty easy to spot if you keep your eyes open. Further in, we can expect pillboxes, machine-gun emplacements, mortar nests, the whole shit and kaboodle. It ain't going to be any vacation."

Hackermeyer saw Linstrom raise his hand to catch Cooley's attention but the sergeant didn't notice.

"Sergeant?" asked Fearfeather. Cooley faced him. "What about our bayonets?" Fearfeather asked. "Do we put them on our rifles?"

"Forget your bayonet," said Cooley. "If we don't use them, the Krauts ain't likely to either and that's the way we like it. Besides—"

"*Sergeant?*" Linstrom's voice was shrill.

"What?"

"I mean I think I burned myself when—"

"On the lukewarm piss they serve for coffee?" Cooley interrupted. Spitting, he turned from Linstrom and went on talking to the squad.

After a while, Hackermeyer shifted his gaze and saw that Linstrom was staring at the sergeant with hurt, uncomprehending eyes. He looked as if he were about to cry. Hackermeyer turned away, feeling embarrassed. Well, he thought after a while, maybe, later on, he'd tell Linstrom about taping down the grenade arms.

Spread out at wide intervals, they moved across the silent plain. Linstrom kept drifting in toward Hackermeyer and, every minute or so, Cooley had to order him away. Hackermeyer walked steadily, breath clouding from his lips and nostrils. In the distance, he saw the forest, so darkly green that it appeared black in the sunless air. Farther off, poking upward like a skeletal finger, he saw the thin white spire of a steeple. They must be attacking from a different direction this time. The terrain looked unfamiliar. There were no landmarks he could recognize.

Still, the countryside was similar to that which he'd seen before. The dead grass, the muddy ground, the occasional hedgerow or barren tree, the pocking of shell holes. To the distant right, he saw a grayish mound and decided that it was a dead cow or horse. To his left, he saw a blackened Sherman tank, its turret half blown off and shredded. His gaze returned to the front. Soon they'd be shelled. The Germans were probably waiting for the entire battalion to come into range before setting off the eighty-eights.

He glanced at Linstrom, wondering how he'd react to the first shelling. Linstrom seemed so much more helpless than Foley had. There had been at least a slight air of competence about Foley. Linstrom seemed like a mama's boy lost in the woods. Hackermeyer grunted to himself and turned his head again. Linstrom would be lost in the woods all right.

Seconds later, the rushing, whistling noises swept across the sky.

"Hit it!" someone shouted.

Hackermeyer dropped instinctively, wincing at the flare of pain in his side. He glanced around and saw that Linstrom was still on his feet.

"Get down!" he yelled.

The first explosion crashed before Linstrom pitched forward and buried his face in his arms. Turning back, Hackermeyer pressed his face against the crook of his left arm and withdrew into the core of himself, hunched against the vibrating earth. It sounds like a thunderstorm, he thought.

He remembered lying in his bed, during summer storms when he was a little boy, when the sky seemed to be exploding with endless thunderclaps and the lightning flashes were like monstrous spotlights flashing off and on—bleaching the night into moments of hideous, artificial day. He used to be so terrified that he couldn't even summon the strength to duck beneath the sheet. Hackermeyer shuddered involuntarily. At night, bombardments would be exactly like what he remembered because the muzzle blasts of the big guns would make lightning flashes in the dark.

"Let's go!" shouted Cooley. Men pushed up and started running. Some of them stayed on the ground. The shelling thinned, then stopped.

"Hey, that wasn't so bad!" Hackermeyer heard Linstrom say. He looked over and saw Linstrom walking several yards to the right, his face animated.

"Is that the way it is all the time?" asked Linstrom. "Is that all there is to it?"

"They didn't come very close," said Hackermeyer.

"They *didn't*?" Linstrom looked like a little boy who had just been informed that Santa Claus is a fraud. "You mean—sometimes they come closer?"

Hackermeyer grunted.

"Well . . ." Linstrom hesitated several moments. "How the hell close can they come?" he asked, failing in his attempt to sound amused.

"They can land right on top of you," said Hackermeyer.

Linstrom said no more. When Hackermeyer looked over a few minutes later, he saw that Linstrom had drifted back and was walking ten yards behind, staring at the ground with brooding eyes.

The company started down a long, gradual slope toward the distant forest. Up ahead, an officer raised his hand and moved it in tiny, rapid circles and Cooley and the other squad leaders broke into a run toward him. Hackermeyer got down on one knee and propped his rifle butt on the ground.

Cooley and the other squad leaders were just starting back when the shelling began again. Hackermeyer dropped forward quickly. This time the explosions were closer. The mud-slimed earth bucked beneath him and he heard the whining buzz of shrapnel all around. Somewhere, to the right, a man cried out in pain.

"Dig in!" Cooley yelled.

Hackermeyer reached back for his pick. The first time they'd started for Saarbach, the same thing had happened. He wondered how they were ever going to reach Saarbach at this rate, much less win the war. Oddly enough, he felt disappointed.

He heard running footsteps and a rattle of equipment. Suddenly, Linstrom was flinging down beside him, gasping, "Let's dig!" Hackermeyer glanced at him and saw how wide Linstrom's eyes were, how strained and white his face had become.

Immediately, they started cutting into the ground. It went quickly with the two of them working together. Hackermeyer tore loose chunks of stone-studded earth and Linstrom shoveled them away. In a short while, the foxhole was deep enough for them to get inside. They dropped down into its chilly interior and kept on digging, their breaths wheezing loudly. The eighty-eight shells kept exploding all around with blasts that shook the earth. Occasional shrapnel buzzed overhead and mud kept spattering on their helmets and shoulders.

When they were finished digging, they sat down and looked at each other.

"Boy," said Linstrom.

Hackermeyer pulled out his canteen and took a drink of chlorine-flavored water. Linstrom took out his canteen. He drank too hastily and coughed, then wiped off his chin.

"Boy, oh boy," said Linstrom. "Was that a close one. I could hear the shrapnel."

Hackermeyer blew his nose.

"Boy," said Linstrom. He shook his head and whistled softly. He looked elated. "Boy, oh boy," he said.

"LET'S BUILD A house," said Linstrom.

Hackermeyer had just awakened from a nap. Cold rain was spattering on his helmet and raincoat. Overhead, shells from the American batteries swished eastward. The distant forest kept erupting with dull, rumbling explosions. Why don't they just set the whole thing on fire? Hackermeyer wondered. Probably because it rained so much that nothing would burn.

"Okay?" asked Linstrom.

"What?"

"Let's build a house. There's some barbed wire down the hill a little way."

Hackermeyer couldn't see how that was going to help them build a house.

"We could cut the poles loose," said Linstrom. "Put them over the hole and stretch one of our raincoats over them. Then we'd have a roof and we could get dry. And if we get shelled, we'll be protected."

"We may leave soon," said Hackermeyer.

"Uh-uh. Some guy said we'd probably be here for a couple of days at least."

"Who?"

"I don't know who he was. Some guy. Anyway, let's build a house."

"I don't know."

Linstrom's face tightened. Irritably he brushed some raindrops from his nose. "Why?" he demanded.

"There may be snipers."

"Oh . . . the hell," said Linstrom. "They couldn't see anything in this rain."

Hackermeyer shrugged. What did it matter to him anyway? He pulled up his collar and hunched down as low as he could. Checking under his raincoat to make sure the M1's safety lock was on, he closed his eyes again. He sneezed. Here we go again, he thought.

After a few moments, he heard Linstrom climbing out of the foxhole. He stood up to see what Linstrom was going to do. Several of the squad were moving around in the rain. Lazzo was stamping his feet as if trying to knock some feeling into them. Fearfeather was pacing back and forth in front of his foxhole, smoking a small corncob pipe and drying his glasses. Beyond them, obscured by the shimmering veil of rain, some soldier was urinating. Hackermeyer wondered where Cooley had gone. He didn't think Cooley would allow them to get out of their foxholes like this if he were around. He glanced at his wristwatch. It was almost ten A.M.

He watched Linstrom walking around as if searching for something. Apparently he found it, because he lay down and reached into an unoccupied foxhole, standing in a few moments with a pair of wire cutters. Hackermeyer wondered who they belonged to as he watched Linstrom start down the slope toward the barbed wire. At one time the wire must have stretched across the entire hillside. Now, only a few yards of it remained.

Hackermeyer reached into a ration box while he watched Linstrom. It wasn't likely Linstrom would get shot at. The rain obscured everything beyond twenty yards or so. The forest was completely hidden from sight. Of course, there might be snipers behind them. Lippincott had told him that German snipers often let enemy troops bypass their positions, then shot them in the back.

Linstrom had reached the barbed wire now. Hackermeyer looked down long enough to open his can of egg yolk and pork. Baby poo, he thought, watching Linstrom while he ate. Linstrom

THE BEARDLESS WARRIORS   *103*

was cutting the wires where they were connected to one of the posts. The wire was old and brittle. The sound of it shearing was a pinging snap like that of a distant shot. The noise made Hackermeyer twitch.

He wondered if he should have kept Linstrom from going down there. He was, presumably, supposed to be watching over him. Still, how could he have stopped Linstrom? He'd mentioned snipers. If that didn't dissuade Linstrom, nothing would.

"Hey!"

Hackermeyer swiveled his head so quickly that it sent electric pricklings up his neck. He saw Cooley standing by the foxhole from which Linstrom had taken the wire clippers. Cooley was looking down at Linstrom angrily.

"Get up here," he said.

Hackermeyer glanced at Linstrom and saw that he was trying to uproot the pole he'd cut free.

"I said get up here!" ordered Cooley.

"Why?" Linstrom's voice was thin. "Can't I—"

"Goddamn it, move!"

Linstrom came up the hill slowly, lips pinched together and quivering.

Cooley snatched the wire cutters from his hand.

"Where do you think you are, on a picnic?" he demanded.

Linstrom swallowed nervously. "I was just getting some— poles," he said.

Cooley made a sound of deep despair.

"Jesus H. Christ," he groaned. "Ain't there enough ways of getting killed already?"

"Just wanted to get dry." Linstrom spoke like a boy afraid of the father who disciplined him yet too childishly stubborn to submit.

Cooley glared at Linstrom, his face hard, his blue eyes fierce. Abruptly he gestured with his right thumb. "Get back to your hole," he said.

"Can't I just—"

"You heard me!"

Hackermeyer sat down and stirred the raindrops into his egg yolk and pork. Linstrom came squishing back across the mushy soil. He lowered himself down into the hole and sat heavily, his face pale with repressed fury, his gloved hands clenched into trembling fists.

"Cheap shit," muttered Linstrom.

Hackermeyer crunched on a biscuit.

"Why shouldn't I get it?" demanded Linstrom in a low, shaking voice. "Why? Was I shot at? Was I?"

Hackermeyer wondered why Linstrom, who had been willing to go to the aid station over some spilled, lukewarm coffee, was also willing to expose himself to possible sniper fire. Probably it wasn't a contradiction. Linstrom had been terrified at the prospect of combat and had been willing to entertain any excuse to avoid combat. Now that he was in the front lines and it seemed innocuous enough to him, he was thinking of making himself comfortable. No, there was no contradiction. Linstrom looked out for Linstrom. That explained his actions. Linstrom didn't know what discipline was.

Hackermeyer's eyes narrowed. Maybe that was why Linstrom said that the Germans panicked when something happened that wasn't covered by their overstrict training. Linstrom resented discipline, therefore tried to make himself believe that discipline weakened the ability to adjust. Hackermeyer felt a flare of satisfaction at having thought of that.

"Stupid bastard," Linstrom muttered.

Hackermeyer recalled Linstrom saying earlier that morning that Cooley was a good Joe. Oh, well. He tossed away his empty ration can and wiped his gloves on his coat. Linstrom was just a kid. What else could you expect from a kid?

COOLEY WALKED PAST the foxhole. "Moving out," he said.

"Oh, for . . . !" Linstrom flung down his bayonet. As soon as the rain had stopped, he'd started hacking out a shelf for his equipment. It was almost finished.

"Lousy, stupid army," he said. "Start to get comfortable, and, right away, they move you out."

Hackermeyer clipped on his cartridge belt while Linstrom got up, groaning, and started pulling his gear together. Suddenly he looked over at Hackermeyer.

"You think we're going into those woods?" he asked.

"I don't know."

Linstrom swallowed. He remained quiet as he put on his equipment and climbed out of the foxhole.

The squad moved parallel to the edge of the woods for twenty minutes, then were told to dig in again. Linstrom didn't say a word. He dug rapidly, glancing toward the forest every few seconds. He kept criticizing Hackermeyer for not digging fast enough.

They were two-thirds finished when they were ordered to move out again.

"What?" said Linstrom. He stood up with his hands on his hips, watching Cooley walk away. Then, with a moan half angry, half afraid, he flung down his spade. "What's the matter with them?" he demanded. "Are they crazy?"

They put on their gear and moved on, parallel to the border of the forest. Linstrom walked in short, flat-footed strides, twisting his shoulders and grunting as if in pain.

"Can't go on much longer," Hackermeyer heard him say.

About three-quarters of a mile northeast of their previous position, the company stopped. Hackermeyer watched Cooley report to the platoon leader, then return.

"Dig in," Cooley told them.

"*Oh*, no," said Linstrom suddenly. He glared around as if looking for someone to argue with. "Oh, no," he repeated. Abruptly he sat down, unhooked his belt, and let it fall back onto the mud. He closed his eyes and, thin-lipped, shook his head as if avoiding the sight of someone who was attempting to get his attention in order to change his mind. "Oh, no, I'm not digging any more Goddamn holes."

Hackermeyer started cutting at the wet ground with his entrenching tool. The muscles of his arms, shoulders, and back ached.

"What the hell are you doing?" asked Linstrom in an aggrieved voice.

Hackermeyer didn't answer.

"How many times are we supposed to—" Linstrom broke off, grimacing, and turned away from Hackermeyer as if from some repugnant sight. He looked at the distant forest, then closed his eyes again, teeth clenched. "Dumb jerks," he said.

Hackermeyer kept driving his pick into the muddy, rock-studded earth. Linstrom would just have to sleep on the ground, he thought.

"Oh . . . shit!" Linstrom blew out breath as if attempting to extinguish a giant candle. Jerking his spade free, he squatted beside Hackermeyer and started digging. "You break my balls," he said.

Hackermeyer felt like telling him to stop cursing until he learned how. He kept pulling apart the oozy ground with weary, methodical movements. Linstrom shoveled away the chunks.

"This is the sergeant's head," he snarled, flinging aside a jagged clod. "Walk, walk, walk. Dig, dig, dig. Sit, sit, sit."

"Oh, shut up," said Hackermeyer.

Linstrom jerked up his head and glared at Hackermeyer. Hackermeyer didn't return the look. He kept picking and, in a few moments, Linstrom resumed his digging. Hackermeyer was surprised at himself. It was the first time in years that anyone but his father had managed to annoy him. That fact annoyed him even more than Linstrom did. It was stupid to let people get in your hair.

When they were about three feet down, Linstrom suddenly drove his spade into the ground.

"I quit," he said.

Hackermeyer stared at him, breathing slowly, heavily.

"Aw, come on," pleaded Linstrom. "Where do you want to dig to, China? We'll probably be moving out in ten minutes anyway."

Hackermeyer thought it over. Then, with a sigh, he put down his pick. Linstrom was, most likely, right. They probably would be moving out soon. If they sat down, the hole would be deep enough for protection against anything but air bursts or a direct hit. That was as much as any foxhole could offer, so what difference did it make?

For a moment, it struck him that the hole was just like the one in which Foley had been killed. Would Foley be alive if the other hole had been deeper? Hackermeyer frowned and put the thought aside. He got down into the hole and sat down, his knees touching Linstrom's. It was starting to get dark. Hackermeyer looked at his watch and saw that it was five-sixteen. We should make the forest by noon, he remembered Cooley saying. Sure, sure.

As they ate their supper, they heard someone laughing hysterically in the distance.

"Who the hell's that?" asked Linstrom irritably.

Hackermeyer shook his head.

"Probably some German," said Linstrom. "He knows how stupid this whole attack is." He made a scoffing sound. "Attack," he said. "Some attack. We've done more digging than attacking. We're going to tunnel our way to Saarbach, for Christ's sake."

Linstrom bit into a biscuit noisily. "Is this what it's like all the time?" he asked.

Hackermeyer shrugged.

"If it is, it's a pain in the ass," said Linstrom.

Hackermeyer was inclined to agree with Linstrom on that.

He glanced down idly at the cracker he was eating. The way it had broken off when he'd bitten it gave it the outline of a crocodile. Hackermeyer stared at it dully. It reminded him of something but he couldn't quite remember what. *Animal crackers*, he thought.

Abruptly it came. That Sunday when he was eight and his father had been so late. All morning and early afternoon, he'd kept going to the living-room window to see if his father had arrived yet. It was hard to understand now why his father's visits had meant so much to him but he knew they had. He distinctly remembered drawing back the living-room curtains so many times that his uncle had yelled at him. He remembered going out onto the porch and looking up and down the street. His father had said he'd be there by ten that morning.

He'd come at three-thirty—and not alone. Hackermeyer still remembered the woman his father had brought. He remembered the egg-white dress she'd worn, her small white hat with the flowers on it. He remembered the two gold teeth that had shown when she smiled. He remembered how shocked he'd been that his father had brought her.

They'd taken him to Coney Island where he'd hardly spoken a word to his father. Shunted from Ferris wheel to Dodgem car to merry-go-round, he'd spent the entire afternoon in isolated motion. He could remember being on the merry-go-round, rising and falling on the wooden horse with the clanging, tinny music in his ears, catching momentary glimpses of his father and the woman sitting on a bench, talking together as if they were alone.

They had bought him frankfurters and orange drink and cotton candy and ice cream and a box of animal crackers. He'd eaten the crackers in the subway that evening, sitting by himself while, behind him, his father and the woman talked and talked. He remembered how the woman giggled and how much he'd hated her.

He'd become cranky and stubborn while they walked him from the trolley station to his uncle's house. He'd kept hanging behind and looking at the sky and his father had gotten angry with him. The woman had tried to put her arm around Hackermeyer, but he'd kept pulling away, which had infuriated his father. They had left him on the front porch and gone. His uncle and aunt and Cousin Clara were at the movies, he remembered. He'd sat there, lips forced together, tears trickling down his sweaty, sun-reddened face, his shoe backs thumping against the steps until, suddenly, with a furious hiss, he'd flung away the box of animal crackers and all the crumbs had spilled across the sidewalk.

"I don't care!" he'd muttered. "I don't care, I don't care, I don't care!"

Shortly after, he had become very ill and thrown up on the lawn.

HACKERMEYER STIRRED AND mumbled in his sleep, his lean nose twitching. He was only vaguely conscious of the nudging at his leg.

"Come on," he murmured.

"Shhh!"

Instantly, Hackermeyer was awake. His eyes popped open, staring sightlessly into the darkness.

"What—"

He broke off as Linstrom nudged his leg again.

"What?" he whispered.

"Look," Linstrom whispered back.

Hackermeyer turned his head and stiffened. There was some kind of animal on the edge of the foxhole. He saw its outline against the sky. He could hear the tiny sniffing sounds it made, the scrape of its claws. A powder of soil was filtering down onto his lap.

"Flashlight?" whispered Linstrom.

"I don't have—"

"I do. Shall I use it?"

"Germans might see it."

"What are we going to do then?" All in the faintest of whispers.

Hackermeyer swallowed. If he grabbed whatever it was, it might bite him. And it might be poisonous or diseased. Nor could he get the M1 into position without startling whatever it was. Startled, it might attack.

A shiver passed through him as he remembered the huge rats that had lived in the foundations near his uncle's house. One of them had run across his feet one day and nipped his ankles bloody. He remembered reading that, during the first World War, great rats had infested the trenches. He swallowed again. If only he could get his bayonet free and stab at it. But there was no chance of that. Slowly, carefully, Hackermeyer drew the blanket off his hands and braced himself. If he could grab it quickly enough, maybe it wouldn't have a chance to bite.

Suddenly a beam of light shot up from where Linstrom was sitting and, transfixed in its brilliance, a small gray rabbit crouched.

"Douse it!" roared a voice just as Hackermeyer grabbed the rabbit. With sudden darkness pulsing at his eyes, he pulled the squealing rabbit down onto his lap and shoved it underneath the blanket. He'd grabbed it out of instinct. Now, instinct told him to prevent its high-pitched squeals from being heard by the Germans. He didn't know why it was necessary. It just seemed the thing to do.

"What the hell's going on?" Cooley's voice demanded.

"It's just a rabbit," said Linstrom.

"A rabbit?" From the night came Cooley's groan of affliction.

"Let me see, let me see," said Linstrom eagerly. He ducked his head under Hackermeyer's blanket and turned the flashlight on again. "Oh, gee, look at him," Hackermeyer heard him say. He felt Linstrom's hands begin to stroke at the rabbit's fur. "He's so cute," said Linstrom.

The rabbit had stopped squealing now and was soundless on Hackermeyer's lap, pulsing with frightened breath. Holding onto it with one hand, Hackermeyer pulled the blanket over his head.

"Sweet little thing," said Linstrom, stroking at the rabbit's ears. "Don't be afraid, little rabbit. We won't hurt you."

Hackermeyer looked at Linstrom's smiling, boyish face. Linstrom's helmet and liner were off and, under the edges of his wool cap, ringlets of golden blond hair were showing. His face was close to beautiful.

"Poor little thing, are you hungry?" Linstrom soothed. He pulled off one glove and stroked the rabbit's furry head. "Are you hungry, little bunny?" he asked. "I wish I had some lettuce for you. Or some carrots. Do you eat carrots, little bunny?"

He glanced up, smiling, at Hackermeyer.

"What shall we do with it?" he asked.

Hackermeyer said the first thing that occurred to him. "Eat it," he said.

A look of absolute horror flooded over Linstrom's face. "What?" he gasped.

Hackermeyer didn't answer. He stared down at the rabbit. It would taste good fried, he thought. But he sensed that he had said it only to bother Linstrom.

"You can't do that," Linstrom said.

"Why?"

"I saw him first," said Linstrom in a shaking voice. "He's mine."

"I caught him," said Hackermeyer. He wasn't enjoying this. Yet he was.

Linstrom's breath faltered. "I wouldn't've told you if I'd thought you wanted to—" He pressed his lips together, looking close to tears. "You can't kill it," he said. "It's just a baby."

So are you, thought Hackermeyer.

"You have no right," said Linstrom. "Why should you eat him?"

"I'm hungry." Hackermeyer wondered why he didn't stop this. It wasn't enjoyable anymore.

"I want him," said Linstrom. There was a glistening in his eyes. If his blond hair had been long, Hackermeyer realized, Linstrom would have looked like a girl about to cry.

"Take him," he said abruptly.

"Yeah." Turning off the flashlight, Linstrom took the rabbit eagerly and sat up with it, pulling away from Hackermeyer's blanket. Hackermeyer heard him whispering to the rabbit.

Kid, he thought. Cooley was right. Linstrom wasn't a soldier. He was a little kid sitting in a hole in the ground playing with a rabbit.

Hackermeyer closed his eyes, pulling the blanket up to his chin. Why did Linstrom annoy him so much? This thing with the rabbit really irritated him.

"Kid," he whispered to himself.

Under his blanket, Linstrom kept murmuring softly and endearingly to the rabbit. Hackermeyer gritted his teeth and tried to sleep. I should have killed it, he thought. He felt his stomach muscles tightening. Goddamn but he wished he'd killed it.

JUST AFTER EIGHT A.M., Company C entered the Saarbach Forest.

Three times, before they reached it, the Germans shelled them. Twice they sweated out the bombardments and, when they were over, stood and kept on moving, leaving behind the dead and wounded. The third time some of the officers and noncoms made them run directly through the zone of explosions. Cooley's squad was into the trees first. Behind them, the barrage increased, slowing up the rest of the advancing battalion.

Hackermeyer and Linstrom walked through the shadowy, rain-soaked woods. Linstrom's face was taut and pale. His gaze kept flicking apprehensively in all directions. Hackermeyer looked around more slowly. His shoes sank into the floor of spongy, wet leaves. Have to look out for booby traps, he thought. Have to look out for machine-gun emplacements. Have to look out for pillboxes. Have to look out for snipers. A long breath shuddered in his chest. There were so many things to look out for.

Far to the right, a BAR chattered briefly, then was still. All Hackermeyer could hear was the noise of shoes moving over leaves and twigs, the sound of bodies brushing past bushes and tree foliage. The American barrage earlier that morning had wrought tremendous damage, toppling the crowns of hundreds of trees and shattering more to scrapwood.

"Where are they?" asked Linstrom in a nervous whisper. It was the first time he'd spoken since he'd discovered that the rabbit had run away during the night.

Hackermeyer's only answer was a grunt. No time for conversation. They had to keep their eyes open. So many things to look for: wires stretched across the ground for them to trip over; booby traps hidden by leaves and bushes; thickly foliaged conifers in which snipers could conceal themselves; clumps of bush and fallen trees behind which might be machine guns and enemy riflemen; dozens of places up ahead where a pillbox might be so camouflaged that you could walk right up to its guns without seeing it. Hackermeyer breathed unevenly. He almost wished the Germans would open fire and be done with it.

He tried to blank his mind to premonitions. Then he realized that he couldn't afford to do that. Better to worry about these things than fall stupid prey to them. He looked ahead and to the sides, both up and down. He even glanced backward at the trees. All around, other members of the squad were doing the same. He caught a momentary glimpse of Guthrie moving among the trees. Guthrie didn't look amused now.

"I thought there were Germans in here," Linstrom whispered.

Hackermeyer sucked at the wet, moldy-smelling air. He started to say something when they both twitched skittishly as a bird went rushing upward from a toppled tree in front of them, its dark wings buffeting the air. Linstrom started to throw up his rifle to fire, then stopped and hunched his shoulders in a convulsive shudder. Hackermeyer paused for several moments, regained his breath, then started on again.

They both ducked automatically as a sharp explosion sounded to their left. There was a momentary splattering of twigs and dirt.

"Watch out for booby traps," Hackermeyer heard Cooley's warning. He looked around but couldn't see Cooley. The woods were too dense. Who had just died? Was it someone in the squad?

"I don't see the sergeant," Linstrom whispered.

Hackermeyer paid no attention. He started to move, then, instantly, stopped again.

"Hold it," he said, and Linstrom froze.

Hackermeyer got down on his knees and crawled cautiously toward a pile of leaves lying on the path between two thick, berry-covered bushes. Bracing himself, he started brushing at the top of the pile with the most delicate touch he could manage. The dead leaves fluttered down its sides. Abruptly, Hackermeyer jerked his fingers back and stared down at what looked like a small flower pot. For one hideous second, he suffered the illusion that he was losing balance and was about to pitch forward on top of it. He lurched backward with a gasp.

"What is it?" Linstrom whispered.

Hackermeyer shook his head. He stood, his legs vibrating. Carefully, he felt around in his pockets until he came across the letter from Cousin Clara. There was a stub of pencil in his wallet. His hand trembling, he lettered BOOBY TRAP on the back of the letter; then, reaching forward gingerly, pressed the paper onto the end of a twig hanging above the German mine.

"Oh," he heard. Glancing back, he saw Linstrom staring at the booby trap.

"Don't step on it," said Hackermeyer.

"Oh, God." Linstrom's voice was barely audible.

They bypassed the booby trap and Hackermeyer looked around to see whether the Germans, anticipating its discovery, had planted another one nearby. That would be just like them. They'd figure that, if the first one was found, the soldier who discovered it would undergo a period of thoughtless relief immediately afterward and be vulnerable to a second booby trap. Hackermeyer stopped walking so abruptly that Linstrom almost rammed into him.

"What is it?" Linstrom sounded angry. As though Hackermeyer were deliberately trying to make him nervous.

"Nothing," Hackermeyer told him. But he couldn't move. His brain was alive with dreads and counter-dreads. There were so many complicated ways in which the Germans could have calculated the planting of their booby traps. They might not have placed a second one near the first, figuring that the man who found the first would be on the lookout for a second. Then, when he didn't find it, he'd relax and be vulnerable to a booby trap a little farther on. For that matter, the ground could be peppered with them. They might have walked past dozens already.

Hackermeyer gritted his teeth. The brain could get so tangled up with fears it kept a person from doing anything at all. Willfully he moved himself, walking like a blind man on an egg-covered floor. Just keep going, he told himself. The worst that can happen is . . .

There was a sudden wailing vibration in the sky.

"What's that?" Linstrom cried out.

"Hit it!" snapped Hackermeyer, dropping. From the corners of his eyes, he saw Linstrom pitch across a small bush.

The German mortar shells detonated as they struck the tree crowns. Six explosions crashed in succession, shaking the air with multiple thunder. Jagged, smoking chunks of shrapnel shot in all directions, shearing away twigs and branches, ricocheting off the trunks with ringing screeches, furrowing deep into the mucky ground.

More shells exploded. Hackermeyer felt as if the deafening bursts would crush his skull in. Suddenly, he realized that the cotton had fallen from his right ear. He looked around for it, then gave up and jammed the end of a gloved finger into his ear instead. Overhead, the mortar shells screamed shrilly as they fluttered downward. Infrequently, one of them passed through the latticework of boughs and exploded on the ground, disgorging cascades of wet, leaf-strewn soil. The air swarmed with shrapnel. A jagged shard of it bounded off Hackermeyer's helmet with a shrieking resonance. Another sliced open the right arm of his overcoat. Another raked a gash across the heel of his left shoe. Hackermeyer jammed his teeth together, then gaped his mouth again, gagging at the dark, acrid smoke that was spreading through the forest like a creeping night.

Off to the right, there was a sudden, rattling blast of automatic fire. Hackermeyer couldn't tell from which direction it was coming.

"There's your target! Fire!" Cooley's yell grew audible between the bursts of detonation. Hackermeyer turned his head and saw tracer bullets flying out into the woods.

"Fire! There's your target!" Cooley shouted.

To the left, a mortar team came running forward, setting up their weapon in a clearing. Hackermeyer watched one of them tear open the taped shell canisters, thumb off the safety wires and start dropping the shells into the tube as fast as possible, falling to the ground whenever explosions came too close. He heard the booming cough of the fired shells; heard, up ahead, their cracking detonations. Abruptly, bullets started flashing overhead, snapping at the branches, ricocheting off tree trunks with a whining shrillness. Heart pounding, Hackermeyer hugged the ground again. There was no question where these bullets were coming from.

Cooley kept on shouting. "Keep firing!" he said. "Fire! Use your weapons! Shoot! Fire! There's your target!"

Hackermeyer grew conscious of the BAR to his right and, glancing in that direction, saw Guthrie firing in long, clip-emptying bursts. He wasn't able to see what Guthrie was firing at but he pulled up his rifle and pressed it to his shoulder. He found himself aiming at a tree a few yards ahead of him and hastily moved the barrel. A bullet skidded clangingly across the crown of his helmet and he dropped again. Reaching up gingerly he ran a finger along the narrow groove in the steel. That was close.

He twisted around and looked to see if Linstrom had been hit. For a moment, he thought Linstrom was dead, he looked so still. Then he saw that Linstrom's lips were moving. He's praying, Hackermeyer thought. It seemed so incongruous.

He twitched as, up ahead, a sharp explosion flared. Abruptly, the German machine gun stopped firing.

"Second squad, let's go!" Cooley's shout came from up ahead. Hackermeyer was startled at how far ahead. He hesitated a moment, feeling as if he were glued to the ground. Then, numbly, he pushed to his feet and trudged forward. He glanced back and saw Linstrom still on the ground even though the German mortar fire had drifted to their right.

"You hurt?" he asked.

Linstrom didn't budge. Hackermeyer felt a sudden weariness dragging at him. Was Linstrom dead already? He walked back slowly.

Linstrom wasn't dead. He lay, face down, trembling like a man in fever.

"Let's go," said Hackermeyer.

Linstrom turned his head and stared up dumbly. His mouth hung open, a silver thread of spittle running from one side of it. There was a smear of black dirt on his right cheek, a soggy leaf clinging to his chin. All the blood seemed to have drained from his face. It was the color of pale wax.

"Come on," said Hackermeyer.

Linstrom seemed to look right through him.

"You coming?"

Linstrom blinked dazedly. "I mean . . . yes," he murmured. "I thought—"

Up ahead, Cooley shouted, "Second squad, let's go! On the double!"

Linstrom got up very slowly. He barely looked at Hackermeyer. Brushing off his coat with the feeble motions of an old man, he started walking.

"This way," said Hackermeyer. He remembered how he'd started running toward the German tanks and Cooley had turned him in the right direction. It seemed so long ago.

Linstrom stopped and looked around. He grunted faintly, then turned and walked past Hackermeyer.

"Your rifle," Hackermeyer said.

"What?"

"Your rifle."

"Oh. Yeah." Linstrom picked it up lethargically.

Thirty yards ahead, the squad was assembled around a fallen tree. Hackermeyer and Linstrom joined them.

"Where the hell have you been?" Cooley asked them.

"Back there," Hackermeyer said, pointing. He glanced across the tree trunk, then gaped. There were three dead Germans lying near a shattered machine gun. All of them were bleeding profusely from shrapnel wounds. One of them had, for a face, what looked like oozing hamburger.

There was a gagging wheeze beside him and he turned to see Linstrom, doubled over, start to vomit.

"Get it out of your system, son," Cooley told Linstrom.

"You'll learn soon enough this is one of the prettiest sights you're ever going to see."

Hackermeyer stared at the dead German soldiers. He couldn't take his eyes away, he was so fascinated by the bloody mangle of them.

THE SQUAD MOVED slowly through a patch of open woods. Up ahead, there was a sound of swirling waters and Hackermeyer visualized a deep, torrential river. How were they going to cross it without rafts? He frowned as he moved across the soggy, leaf-thick ground. Cooley hadn't said anything about a river.

Suddenly, behind him, the sharp crack of a rifle sounded. Hackermeyer whirled to see Linstrom clap a hand to his right temple and drop to his knees, the M1 slipping from his shoulder.

The sudden, chattering blast of an automatic weapon made Hackermeyer jerk his head up. Twenty yards away, he saw Cooley shooting upward, the carbine jolting in his hands. Hackermeyer's gaze leaped in time to see the bulky figure of a German soldier topple from a high, foliage-shadowed branch. The figure turned a clumsy somersault in the air, bounced off a limb, turned another somersault, and landed on its side. Cooley started running toward the figure as Hackermeyer turned to Linstrom.

Linstrom was still on his knees, staring dumbly, his gloved hand pressed against his temple. Hackermeyer trotted over to him.

"You hit?" he asked.

There was a clicking sound in Linstrom's throat as he turned his face up. He looked like a little boy who, never knowing punishment, had just been struck across the face by his mother.

"Let's see," said Hackermeyer, bending over.

Linstrom didn't move. His lips began to quiver.

"I don't see any blood," said Hackermeyer. He turned as Cooley came hurrying up to them.

"Where'd it get you, son?" asked Cooley.

"I'm hit," said Linstrom in a hollow voice.

Cooley pulled away Linstrom's fingers. There was a discolored bruise on Linstrom's temple.

"You're not hit," Cooley told him.

Linstrom shuddered.

"I am," he said.

"The skin ain't even broke," said Cooley. "The slug bounced something off your skull is all."

"I'm hurt," insisted Linstrom. "I ha-ave to go to the aid station."

Cooley looked down dispassionately.

"Get up, son," he said.

"I'm hurt."

"You're not. Get up."

"I am!"

Cooley grabbed Linstrom under one arm and hauled him to his feet. Linstrom wouldn't stiffen his legs. His weight hung on Cooley.

"Get up, damn it," Cooley ordered.

"I won't! I'm hurt!"

Cooley let go and Linstrom flopped onto the ground, sobbing.

"Stay there, then," said Cooley.

"You don't care," said Linstrom. "I could—" He broke off as Cooley turned away from him.

"Let's go, Hackermeyer," said Cooley.

Hackermeyer opened his mouth to speak, then shut it and started after Cooley. He saw Lippincott come over and speak to the sergeant. Cooley shook his head. "Goddamn kids," he said, and there was a break in his voice.

Hackermeyer looked back and saw Linstrom sitting on the ground, crying. He saw Guthrie move past him and say something but Linstrom didn't seem to hear.

Hackermeyer twitched around with a start as up ahead a German machine gun started firing. As he dove forward, his helmet and liner fell off. Grabbing it, he jammed it back on and hooked the chin strap. Glancing up, he saw Cooley and Lippincott behind a fallen tree about fifteen yards ahead. Cooley was crawling past the edge of the tree.

Hackermeyer twisted around and saw Linstrom lying, face downward, on the ground. Now he's really shot, he thought.

Then he noticed that Linstrom's body was tremulous with sobs. Hackermeyer turned away and saw Cooley gesturing rapidly with his arm. He thought Cooley meant for him to come forward and he outlined the word *Me?* with his lips.

Cooley didn't seem to notice. He kept gesturing and Hackermeyer caught a flash of movement to his right. Glancing over, he saw Lazzo dash between two trees and fling himself to the ground. Setting down the bipod legs of his BAR, Lazzo started firing rapidly.

Hackermeyer looked back at Cooley. The sergeant was pulling a grenade off his belt, tearing off the yellow tape, then rearing up fast to hurl the grenade like a pitcher throwing a baseball. Cooley fell again and, in a moment, the explosion roared. There was a whine of flying shrapnel and the machine gun stopped firing. Cooley raised up cautiously to look. Abruptly the firing began again and Cooley dropped. He's hit! thought Hackermeyer. Then he saw that Cooley was crawling back to Lippincott, and Lippincott was separating from him. The machine gun was silent again and Lazzo had stopped firing the BAR. Hackermeyer wondered why the grenade hadn't worked. Maybe the German position was too well protected.

He looked back again. Linstrom was standing with sluggish movements, an expression of bitter solemnity on his face. He picked up his rifle and slung it over his shoulder. Slowly he walked over to where Hackermeyer was and stood beside a tree.

"Better get down," said Hackermeyer.

Linstrom shrugged apathetically. He looked bored.

"What's the difference?" he said.

There was a loud, whooshing noise to their right. Linstrom jolted as if he'd been kicked and they both looked in that direction. The backfire of bazooka flame was just dissipating. In a second, the deafening explosion came. For several moments they heard the agonized screaming of a man. Then it was silent.

Cooley rose to a wary crouch and looked off toward the sound of water. There was no firing. He straightened up and walked to the edge of the clump of trees. There was still no firing. After a moment's hesitation, he looked back and raised his arm, signaling for them to come ahead. Hackermeyer looked at Linstrom as he stood.

"Let's go," he said.

Linstrom blew out weary breath.

"Sure," he said. "Why not?" A dead expression on his face, he started trudging toward the river, which turned out to be a stream no wider than a tank. On its far side, behind a smoking framework of fallen trees, were the dead Germans.

COOLEY CAME BACK in a crouching run and squatted beside Lippincott. He gestured and the squad members started toward him, most of them wolfing down rations. It was the first chance they'd had to eat since they'd entered the forest. Hackermeyer had just begun to heat a cup of coffee and it tasted so awful that he dumped it out. Glancing back, he saw Linstrom sitting motionless against a tree, gazing ahead with lifeless eyes.

As he joined them, Hackermeyer looked at the members of the squad. They all slouched wearily, their faces grimed, their coats, trousers, leggings, and shoes coated with the sticky, leafage-clotted mud. Even Schumacher looked tired and dirty. Guthrie had a scabbed-over scratch on his neck. Lazzo's left cheek was purplish-red with a bruise. Cooley's right trouser leg was torn open and Hackermeyer could see a blood-oozing scrape on Cooley's kneecap. Hackermeyer wondered vaguely what he looked like as he sank down cross-legged on the ground.

"Here we are, Robin Hood's merry band," croaked Guthrie. Nobody paid attention except Fearfeather, who looked at Guthrie curiously.

Cooley noticed the absence of Linstrom and looked around until he saw him. His lips flared back from gritted teeth as he glanced at Lippincott. "Get him," he muttered. Lippincott stood and walked away.

"Up to now we ain't seen anything but scattered Kraut positions," Cooley told them. "Now we're up against a real line—" He pointed across his shoulder. "About a hundred yards ahead."

Hackermeyer glanced around. Linstrom was pushing slowly to his feet, the look of boredom on his face again. He moved stolidly toward the squad. Lippincott said something to him and Linstrom half closed his eyes, exhaling wearily.

". . . Slope about fifty yards to the peak, couple of hundred yards wide," Cooley's voice flared again. "The Krauts have picked it bone-clean. There ain't a thing to hide behind. On top of the slope is a major entrenchment. It won't be easy."

Linstrom moved into the group and sat down, staring into space as if meditating. Cooley glanced at him and began to say something, then changed his mind and went on talking to the squad.

"The engineers are cleaning the slope right now," he said. "As good as they can, anyway."

Hackermeyer glanced ahead and heard, between the volleys of German machine-gun fire, the slamming detonation of rifle-grenade attachments firing explosive cords up the slope. Major entrenchment, he thought. It was difficult to appreciate that all they'd gone through so far was a series of minor engagements. What was a real defense line like?

"As soon as the Engineers pull back, artillery will open up," Cooley was saying. "Between the two, they should pretty well clear out the mines and concertina wire, but don't count on it. Watch your step." He spat to one side. "We move in right after the White Phosphorus."

While Cooley was telling them where each of them would be positioned in the assault line, Hackermeyer looked at Linstrom again. Linstrom returned his look, then turned away with a cheek-puffing exhalation. It seemed as if he were trying to detach himself from the situation. As if he felt it was beneath him. It seemed a total reversal of mood, functionless dread to oblivious apathy. Had Linstrom given up completely, resigned himself to the worst? Or had he reached the point where he just didn't care anymore? Either way, he seemed to have transcended fear. Hackermeyer didn't understand that.

He started as up ahead there was a violent explosion. All the squad members looked in that direction.

"Artillery should start any second now," Cooley told them. "Get yourself into place and wait for the signal. And stay awake."

The squad stretched out into a line and everyone crouched down, waiting. Lazzo and Guthrie, with their BARs, were on each end of the line. To Hackermeyer's right was Fearfeather; to his left, Schumacher. Cooley had positioned Linstrom just behind the line, between himself and Lippincott. Linstrom stood like a statue, the M1 slung across his back. He seemed miles away. Hackermeyer turned back front with a dry swallow. Never mind Linstrom. He tried to see through the woods ahead but couldn't.

He twitched as the Engineers started running back. Easy enough for them, he thought; then realized that they'd been fired on every second they were clearing the slope of mines. One of the men had a wounded arm that spurted blood as he hurried by. Another man was being carried and looked dead.

Hackermeyer glanced upward. A rapid, fluttering *whoosh* of shells had filled the sky. He lowered his head and hunched down tensely, waiting.

Explosions tore away the silence. Hackermeyer bit his teeth together and stared fixedly at the ground. Ahead, the mass of shells plunged into the slope, detonating with blasts of shaking thunder. Even from where he was, Hackermeyer could hear the fluting wail and buzz of shrapnel. I hope they aim right, he thought, remembering how American shells had exploded in their midst during the German counterattack that day. He opened his mouth and crouched down lower still. He felt engulfed by the deafening noise. The earth kept shuddering and bucking under him. It seemed as if the trees were quivering in the ground.

When the silence came, it came explosively, pulsing hard against his ears. He heard a whistle and glanced up. Men were moving forward at a rapid trot. He struggled up, began advancing.

"Go!"

Cooley's voice knifed through the ringing in his ears and Hackermeyer started running, staring at the wall of smoke ahead. Machine-gun fire started. He kept on running. Trees drifted by him, bushes floated past. The jarring of his weight along the ground seemed to echo in his skull. He felt unreal as the swirling smoke came closer and closer, then swallowed him. He felt it curling up his nostrils, stinging his eyes. He kept on running. The silence was completely broken now, yet he had been unconscious of its disappearance. There was a strident rattling of machine-gun fire; to his right, the sharp explosions of mortar shells. Hackermeyer kept running. He was on the slope now. Something buzzed, snapping, past his ear. He stumbled to the side and almost fell.

"Fire!" Cooley's shout lashed out from somewhere. Hackermeyer raised the M1 to his shoulder and fired into the smoke. The butt jarred against his flesh as he fired, running clumsily. There were more explosions to his right. They seemed to be coming closer. Suddenly they were all around and he was falling. To his left, the earth blew away in a geyser of mud. A fountain of burning steel shot upward.

"Go!" roared Cooley. "Go, go, go!"

Hackermeyer pushed up, then went sprawling on his side as a bullet raked across his helmet. He rolled onto his chest just before a cataract of muddy verdure showered down on him. The earth rocked beneath his body. It heaved as if alive. Hackermeyer felt his head and eyes expanding. He couldn't seem to breathe. Bullets popped around him. Nearby, someone screamed. A shell exploded up ahead, the wave of its concussion rushing over him. Machine guns chattered everywhere. Rifles barked. Hackermeyer pressed his face against his coat sleeve, drooling muddy spit. He couldn't think.

"Keep moving!" someone yelled. Hackermeyer wasn't sure if it was Cooley or not. He struggled erect and started up the slope again, rolling drunkenly. To his right, a soldier appeared. Something blasted underneath the soldier, erupting in a gout of earth and flame. The soldier was flung backward without a sound. Hackermeyer kept on moving. He couldn't seem to run. His legs felt caked with iron. He raised his rifle jerkily and fired again, again. The clip popped out and arced across his shoulder. That wasn't eight, he thought.

Suddenly, the earth was gone. With a startled cry, Hackermeyer plunged down into the shell hole, landing on a soldier. The soldier thrashed away and looked at him. It was Guthrie. For a moment Guthrie stared at him as if he'd never seen him before. Then, with a clumsy movement, he patted Hackermeyer's arm and shoved forward on his chest again.

The explosions kept on blasting everywhere. Hackermeyer began to feel a rise of nausea in his stomach. He started gagging, sucking at the air with strangling noises. He clung to the sloping wall of the hole, face buried in his arms. "Go!" he thought he heard Cooley shouting. He couldn't move. Eyes pressed shut, he lay in the throbbing pit and wondered when he was going to be killed.

As the German mortar barrage shifted to the left, Hackermeyer grew conscious of a weight against his right side and glanced over. It was Linstrom, lying face down. Hackermeyer couldn't tell if he was alive or dead.

"Bugler, blow the charge!" he heard Guthrie muttering hoarsely.

"Go!" Cooley's shout cut through the crash of gunfire and explosions.

"Go, he says!" said Guthrie. He pushed up and started across the edge of the shell hole, then came crashing back as machine-gun fire raked above. He landed in a heap and made a noise in his throat that sounded like the whinny of a distant horse. "Go, go, go," he said in the voice of Donald Duck.

Hackermeyer looked up. The machine-gun fire was almost sweeping the ground. If they tried to climb out of the hole, the bullets would shear off their heads. He swallowed, shuddering, then filled his lungs with the reek of wet earth and explosive.

After a minute, the machine-gun fire shifted to their left. Hackermeyer heard a rapid, clicking noise and turned his head. Linstrom's teeth were chattering. He was staring upward with wide, unblinking eyes, his skin the pallor of chalk. His teeth kept chattering as if they moved independently of his will. Hackermeyer stared at him. He had never seen anyone so frightened in his life. Linstrom seemed devoured by terror. His entire body shook. The flesh beneath the skin of his face seemed to quiver.

"Who's got a deck of cards?" asked Guthrie in a hollow voice. "We'll play War."

Suddenly, with an indrawn hiss, Linstrom scrabbled up the side of the shell hole. The machine-gun fire came sweeping back and almost caught him just before he dropped. He started looking around wildly for another way to escape. Hackermeyer became aware of the smell. Fear had driven Linstrom beyond the control of his body.

"You better stay," said Guthrie.

With a sucking whine, Linstrom started up again. Guthrie lunged across Hackermeyer and grabbed Linstrom's ankle. Linstrom froze at the top of the hole and lay there on his back, teeth clenched, breath hissing from his lips like steam, jaws running with saliva. The machine-gun bullets whistled inches from his face.

"Get down!" yelled Guthrie.

With one wrenching motion, Linstrom ripped a grenade off his belt and jerked out the pin. Twisting around to his knees, he threw it as hard as he could, screaming at the top of his lungs. The grenade exploded and, suddenly, the machine gun stopped.

"Don't tell me he hit it," said Guthrie.

"Go!" Cooley's shout broke over them. Suddenly, he was standing at the edge of the shell hole, looking down at Linstrom.

"You got him, son!" he said.

Linstrom stared up dumbly.

"Let's go!" Cooley reached down, grabbed Linstrom's wrist and started hauling him up. Linstrom cried out, aghast. As Hackermeyer clambered from the hole, he saw Linstrom wrenching himself free of Cooley's grip and stumbling away with a sob. He saw Cooley's face go blank, then tighten as he realized that Linstrom hadn't known what he was doing and didn't care now that it was done.

JUST AFTER FOUR o'clock, Hackermeyer and Linstrom plodded across a small meadow which Cooley told them was almost halfway to Saarbach. In the middle of the meadow was the rubble of a shelled farmhouse. Nearby were the ruins of a small barn, and part of a haystack. Painted on the listing barnside were the words: *Ein Volk, Ein Reich, Ein Führer.*

"Sit in the haystack," Linstrom murmured.

"May be booby-trapped," said Hackermeyer. Linstrom didn't argue.

They were almost across the meadow when they passed a deep shell hole. Pieces of equipment lay strewn in all directions and, down in the hole, on his back, was a German soldier. He had been dead a long time. His skin was almost green and, all around the hole hung an aura of sweet, gaseous putrefaction.

Linstrom gagged and staggered off to vomit up what little food was left in him. Hackermeyer couldn't move. He stood by the edge of the shell hole looking down. Maggots were wriggling across the open eyes of the German soldier. Hackermeyer blinked unconsciously and belched. Good thing he had a cold and couldn't really smell the German, it occurred to him.

Abruptly he turned away and walked over to where Linstrom was sitting. Linstrom looked up with haunted eyes.

"Better go," said Hackermeyer.

Linstrom didn't budge. Hackermeyer looked around and saw that men were sitting all over the meadow. Hackermeyer settled down with a tired grunt. He'd rest until Cooley told him to get up. Slipping his canteen free, he took a sip of water. For a moment, he got another whiff of the dead German soldier. It smelled like cheap cosmetic powder. His stomach gurgled. It had been a hideous sight. Still, there had been a certain satisfaction in it and in the sight of the other dead Germans that day. They reminded him that the Germans were, after all, only human, and could be killed just as easily as anyone else. During his first days in combat, the failure to observe any Germans at all had seemed to endow them with exaggerated menace.

Yawning, Hackermeyer put his canteen back in place. It had been a long day. So long that, after a while, even the constant threat of death had become monotonous.

While he blew his nose he looked at Linstrom, who was sitting with his knees drawn up, arms and head resting on them. Odd that he'd been deceived by Linstrom's pretense of apathy. It should have been obvious to him that it had been only an attempt to escape. Hackermeyer had the feeling that Linstrom had practiced this sort of self-evasion all his life, adjusting to distress either by blinding himself to its existence or by deluding himself into the belief that he didn't care about it. Both approaches meant surrender and were worthless in moments of pressure. The proof of that had been Linstrom's instant re-descent into terror as soon as he was faced with death again. He had become so frightened then that he'd risked his life to end the source of fear rather than confront the fear itself. Lack of discipline. It always came back to that. You learned to roll with the punches or you crumbled before them. You sure as hell couldn't pretend they weren't there.

"Hackermeyer."

He looked around and saw Cooley walking toward him.

"Off your butt," said Cooley. "This ain't no place to settle down."

Hackermeyer was just starting to rise when the wailing shriek dropped down at them. What, again? he thought as he thudded onto his side, seeing Linstrom straighten up, a look of dumbfounded shock on his face.

The first shell landed in the center of the meadow, followed by five others. Explosions crashed in the air, their flashes sharp and blinding. There was a moment's silence and Hackermeyer heard a rising whine in Linstrom's throat. Glancing over, he saw Linstrom lying on his side, knees drawn up to his chest, helmet fallen off. Then the second cluster of shells exploded and Hackermeyer ducked. Shrapnel whined around them. Close by, a man screamed out, "My leg!" and started howling in pain. Hackermeyer clenched his teeth and swallowed. When was all this going to stop?

"Go!" yelled Cooley. "Get out of here!"

Hackermeyer clutched at his rifle and, shoving to his feet, ran headlong toward the woods. He lost his balance and went sprawling to the ground, gasping at the burst of pain in his right wrist. He looked around. Linstrom was still lying with his knees drawn high. Overhead, more shells came fluttering downward with the noise of grinding gears.

Hackermeyer started to shout at Linstrom when a piece of shrapnel raked off his helmet. He gasped and, jumping up, sprinted into the woods. Somehow, it seemed safer underneath the canopy of trees. He stopped and looked back. Cooley was bending over Linstrom, yelling at him, but Linstrom wouldn't move. His eyes were shut and he was trembling violently. In front of his face, his gloved hands were like shaking talons.

Abruptly, Cooley grabbed Linstrom by his cartridge belt and started dragging him toward the trees. Whirling, Hackermeyer plunged into the woods, almost falling across the body of a dead German soldier. Only after he'd jumped over it and run on for several yards did he realize that it had been only the upper half of the soldier's body. The lower half was gone, lopped away as if by some giant cleaver.

HE REMEMBERED STANDING like this once before. It was when he was seven and had gone on a picnic with his father, uncle, aunt, and Cousin Clara. The car his father had borrowed for the day had broken down and his father hadn't been able to get a tow truck until ten o'clock that night. Hackermeyer remembered leaving the car in the darkness. He remembered shivering as he urinated against a tree, the woods chilly and alive with sound.

These woods were three times as chilly but there were no sounds. A heavy silence covered everything. Hackermeyer buttoned up his pants. Somewhere a man stumbled and fell, cursing furiously. Another man ordered him to keep quiet. A third man laughed. A fourth man sneezed ringingly and the third man laughed even harder. Someone said, "Jesus, what a way to fight a war." "Shhh!" said someone else. Then it was quiet again. Hackermeyer stifled a sneeze of his own.

He returned to the foxhole beneath the shadow of a thick-boled pine tree. Linstrom was asleep, snoring bubblingly. Hackermeyer could still see, in his mind, the tear-streaked face, the quivering lips. He could still hear the chest-wracking sobs. Linstrom hadn't done any of the digging and it had been hard work cutting away the tangle of roots. The further Hackermeyer had gone down, the thicker the roots had become. The hole wasn't very deep.

Hackermeyer let himself down and sat with a tired groan. He wondered how much longer Linstrom was going to last. It was strange how, after surviving the first few shellings, Linstrom had broken down so rapidly. As if he'd geared himself to take so much and no more. There was just no endurance in him. Maybe that was the trouble with teenage soldiers. They weren't able to—

Hackermeyer twisted his head around so fast it sent an electric shock along the muscles of his neck. Someone was moving toward the foxhole. Hackermeyer grabbed his rifle and fingered off the safety lock. It made a clicking noise in the stillness.

"Don't shoot, boys," said a baritone voice.

"Who's there?" asked Hackermeyer.

"Chaplain," said a voice.

Hackermeyer blinked. For several moments, all he could think was that, for some incomprehensible reason, Charlie Chaplin had come to the woods to entertain them. It seemed incredible but what else could it be? Only when the heavyset form emerged from the surrounding darkness did he realize that it couldn't be Charlie Chaplin.

The figure squatted by the foxhole.

"Chaplain Wingate," said the man. "How's it going, boys?"

"He's asleep," said Hackermeyer.

"Oh. Of course." The chaplain nodded. "We'll speak very softly, then," he whispered. "What's your name, soldier?"

"Hackermeyer."

A gloved hand fumbled at his shoulder, then squeezed it once. "Glad to meet you, Hackeminer," said the chaplain.

Hackermeyer started to repeat his name.

"How old are you?" inquired the chaplain.

"Eighteen."

The chaplain groaned softly and made a sad, clucking noise. "You boys shouldn't be in combat," he said.

Hackermeyer grimaced. What are we doing here, then? he thought.

"How old's your buddy?" whispered the chaplain.

He's not my buddy, Hackermeyer thought. "Eighteen," he answered.

"Oh, dear Lord," the chaplain whispered. Then his voice brightened noticeably. "Well, how's it gone, Hackeminer?"

"Hackermeyer."

"Of course. I'm sorry."

Hackermeyer didn't know what to answer. If he said it had gone fine, it would be a lie. If he said it had gone awful it would sound as if he were being sorry for himself. There was no percentage in that.

"All right," he said.

"How's your health?" asked the chaplain.

Hackermeyer thought about it. His nose was still running and his stomach was on edge. His side was still sore and his wrist ached from his fall that afternoon. Also, his feet were cold. The chaplain wouldn't be interested in any of that, though.

"All right," he said.

"Good," whispered the chaplain. "Where are you from?"

"Brooklyn."

"Good. Nice place. Have a friend there. Pastor Neeby of the Second Lutheran Church."

"I don't know him."

"No, of course not," whispered the chaplain. "Big place, Brooklyn."

Hackermeyer nodded.

"Mom and Dad living, are they?" asked the chaplain.

"No."

"Sorry to hear that. One of them passed away?"

"Both."

"Oh." The chaplain cleared his throat. "Sorry to hear that, boy," he said.

Hackermeyer was silent. Funny thing. The more people he told that his father was dead, the more real it seemed to him.

"Live with relatives, do you?" whispered the chaplain.

"No."

"Where, then?"

"With the army."

"I mean before," whispered the chaplain.

"My uncle."

"How long?"

"Since I was born."

"I see." The chaplain was silent a moment. "How's your spiritual health, Hackermeyer?" he asked then.

Hackermeyer thought about it.

"I don't know," he said.

The chaplain chuckled softly. "Don't, eh?" he whispered. "What's your church?"

"I don't have any," Hackermeyer whispered back.

"You don't belong to a church?"

"No."

"Didn't your uncle belong?"

"Yes."

"Didn't you attend with him?"

"When he went," said Hackermeyer. He wondered if he should mention that his uncle was usually hung-over on Sunday mornings.

"Well, then, you belong," said the chaplain. "What church was it?"

"I don't remember."

"Protestant, I assume."

"I don't know."

"Did you enjoy it?"

Hackermeyer shrugged.

"I guess," he said.

There was a dead silence. Hackermeyer could hear the chaplain's heavy breath. "I see, uh-huh," the chaplain finally whispered. He reached for Hackermeyer's shoulder and patted his helmet instead. His voice grew more cheerful. "Do you ever pray?" he asked.

"No," said Hackermeyer.

"You don't feel the need?"

"No."

"I see," the chaplain whispered. "You might find com—"

"He prays," Hackermeyer broke in, pointing toward Linstrom.

"He does?" whispered the chaplain.

"Yeah."

"And don't you think he finds comfort in it?"

"I don't think so," said Hackermeyer.

"Well . . ." There was another rustling sound and something bumped against Hackermeyer's helmet. He reached up. "Here," said the chaplain.

Hackermeyer took what the chaplain was holding out. It was small and rectangular, hard.

"Browse through it now and again," whispered the chaplain. "I think you'll find there's comfort in it." He straightened up with a grunt of deep exertion and Hackermeyer heard his joints crackling.

"What is it?" Hackermeyer started to say when there was a loud, popping noise overhead. Instantly the forest was illuminated by a brilliant pale-pink flare which floated downward slowly. In the distance, a German machine gun started firing, its tracer bullets skimming above the earth like orange beads. Hackermeyer ducked his head down and heard the crashing sound the chaplain made as he fell. He wondered if the chaplain had been hit. He sat there, looking at the small book in his right hand. The light from the flare was so intense that he could easily read the words HOLY BIBLE printed on the cover. He should have known.

There was a slight movement. Looking up, Hackermeyer saw that Linstrom was awake and staring at him, mouth agape. Linstrom didn't blink. He seemed to be looking right through Hackermeyer.

Abruptly the flare went out and darkness swallowed everything. Hackermeyer closed his eyes, then opened them. The machine gun stopped firing. In the distance, a thickly Germanic voice began to shout.

"Enjoy your rest, swine! You will all be dead by morning!"

"You say it but you don't mean it!" someone shouted back. Hackermeyer recognized Guthrie's voice. Guthrie sure was a weird one.

"Up your ass, Kraut!" snarled another voice—Lazzo's. There was a short burst of BAR fire, then Cooley yelled, "Stop wasting ammo!" and it was silent again. Somewhere in the night, a man cackled. "San Antone," he said, pipingly.

"What time is it?" murmured Linstrom.

Hackermeyer looked at his watch.

"Nine-fifteen," he said.

"Oh," said Linstrom.

Hackermeyer stood and squinted into the darkness.

"You hurt?" he asked.

"No," said the chaplain. "I'm—quite all right. Thank you for asking."

Hackermeyer sat back down. He heard the grunting noises the chaplain made as he struggled to his feet and moved off in the darkness.

"Who was that?" asked Linstrom.

"A chaplain."

"Oh."

Linstrom was silent for a while. Then he asked, "What did he want?"

"Nothing."

"What's he doing up here?"

"I don't know."

Linstrom drew in a long breath and let it waver from his lips.

"At least he doesn't have to stay here," he said.

Hackermeyer grunted.

"I wish I was a chaplain," said Linstrom somberly. So do I wish you were, thought Hackermeyer. He started to toss away the Bible, then changed his mind and slid it into his overcoat pocket. Maybe he could trade it for rations or something.

Hackermeyer settled back with a sigh. One thing certain, he wasn't going to read the damn thing. He remembered the huge, thick Bible in his uncle's living room and how his Cousin Clara used to read aloud from it at night sometimes. He remembered how stern and righteous Uncle George used to look sitting in church, his thick lips pursed, nodding his head at various things the minister said. Acting as if he were a God-fearing Christian instead of a beer-guzzling bully who couldn't believe he wasn't a first mate on the boats anymore.

Hackermeyer opened his eyes. "What?" he asked irritably.

"You think—God is watching over us?" Linstrom repeated in a childlike voice.

Hackermeyer hissed out scornful breath. "Not over me," he said.

DECEMBER 14, 1944

HACKERMEYER SAT UP with a start as he realized that Linstrom wasn't in the foxhole with him. He stood quickly, wincing at the pull of stiffened muscles in his thighs and groin.

Linstrom was sitting against a tree a few yards away, holding something in his hands. When Hackermeyer popped up from the hole, Linstrom raised his eyes and smiled a little.

"Hi," he murmured.

Hackermeyer didn't answer. Hastily he glanced around. There was a milk-white mist curling along the floor of the woods and lying in the trees like wool.

He looked back at Linstrom. "You better get down here," he said.

"I'm all right," said Linstrom.

Hackermeyer sneezed. While he blew his nose he noticed Linstrom's hands.

"What have you got?" he asked.

"A bird."

Hackermeyer grimaced.

"It's dead," said Linstrom. He sounded apologetic.

Hackermeyer shuddered as the stabbing pain hit his kidneys. He climbed out of the hole and urinated. When he turned back, Linstrom was stroking the dead bird.

"I saw it when I woke up," Linstrom said.

Hackermeyer jumped back into the foxhole, grunting at the impact. His feet felt as if they were made of wood.

"What do you think killed it?" Linstrom asked.

Hackermeyer shrugged as he drew off his shoes. "Shrapnel," he said.

"No. There isn't any mark on it."

Hackermeyer pulled off his right shoe and started massaging the foot, gasping at the sting to his almost numbed flesh. Gritting his teeth, he rubbed harder.

"What do you think?" asked Linstrom.

"Concussion," said Hackermeyer. He was surprised at how calm Linstrom sounded.

"I don't think so," said Linstrom.

"You better get down here," said Hackermeyer, still rubbing his foot.

"It died of fright," said Linstrom. He smiled down sadly at the bird. "It was frightened to death by the noise, poor thing."

Hackermeyer wriggled the tingling toes of his foot. He didn't have trench foot yet. He pulled his sock back on.

"You better get down here," he said.

Linstrom drew in a quick breath. "Yeah," he said. He put the bird down gently and, pulling aside a clot of damp leaves, scraped out a small hollow in the soil. He laid the bird's stiff body in the hollow and covered it up, piling leaves over the grave. He looked around a moment, then leaned over and picked up a twig. He pushed it into the ground as a marker.

"Go to sleep, little bird," he said. He started to get up.

Suddenly he fell against the tree, looking up so quickly that his helmet fell off and thudded on the ground. Overhead, the harsh, whistling noises were beginning.

"No," said Linstrom.

"Get down," said Hackermeyer.

Linstrom didn't seem to hear. "No," he said again. There were tears in his eyes.

"Get down!" said Hackermeyer.

Linstrom remained against the tree, looking upward, his breath coming faster and faster.

Suddenly he raged at the sky, "No!"

The first explosion flung him to the ground. Hackermeyer ducked into the foxhole and heard the hissing whiz of shrapnel overhead. A second shell exploded in the trees, a third. The fourth one reached the ground. The air was filled with deafening thunderclaps, with the buzz of shrapnel, the crack and thrashing fall of boughs, the spattering of dirt and stones and leaves descending in a dark rain.

Linstrom's scream of agony pierced it all. Jerking up his head, Hackermeyer looked at him. Linstrom was struggling to his feet, blood pulsing from his shoulder. He looked down at the wound, his expression one of incredulity. He stumbled sideways against the tree and almost fell. Then, twisting around with a shriek, he started running toward the German lines.

"Linstrom!"

Hackermeyer started from the foxhole when a second cluster of shells began to fall and he jerked back down. The last he saw of Linstrom was his slender figure lurching into the forest, his shrill screams wavering in the air.

Then shells exploded everywhere and a flood of ear-crushing thunder drove Hackermeyer deep into the hole. A heavy limb came crashing down above him, its foliage blotting out the light. The earth around him rocked convulsively, dirt spilling from the foxhole walls and trickling under the neck of his coat. His head seemed to be expanding against the helmet liner. He gasped and clapped both hands over his ears, feeling engorged with din.

When the explosions stopped, Hackermeyer sat down limply, ears ringing, hands twitching weakly on his lap. After half a minute, he looked at the limb overhead and, reaching up, tried to push it aside. It wouldn't move.

He jumped as German machine guns started firing. Bullets

zipped above him, ricocheting off the trees with rasping whines. Hackermeyer raised up cautiously and pushed at the limb with his shoulders. It slid away. Just above, the air was thick with mist and shell smoke and flying bullets.

The line of German fire drifted to his left. Without thinking, Hackermeyer clambered from the hole and started crawling in the direction Linstrom had gone. He tried to listen for Linstrom's voice but his ears rang too much.

"Linstrom?" he called. His voice was thick, unrecognizable. He crawled around a smoking shell hole. "Linstrom?" He wondered, vaguely, what he was doing.

He found the flashlight in a clearing. A violent explosion had taken place there. The ground was one vast hollow. The bark of trees was hacked and gouged as if by butcher knives. Saplings had been toppled by the detonation. Hackermeyer looked around the mangled area. Where was Linstrom? He couldn't have gotten much farther than this in such a bombardment.

Now he noticed the colorless slime that was dripping from the lacerated tree trunks. As if many men had blown their noses on them. Hackermeyer's gaze moved dumbly from tree to tree. He couldn't stop because he knew that he was looking at all that remained of Linstrom. His stomach started heaving as nausea bubbled in him. Abruptly he remembered what he'd said when Linstrom had asked how close the shells could come.

He didn't remember crawling back to the foxhole. The first thing he was conscious of was sitting in it, the bitter taste of vomit in his mouth. Numbly he held up his hand. The flashlight was still clutched in his fingers. He stared at it, remembering how Linstrom had used it to see the rabbit. As he let it fall, he saw his right shoe and realized that he hadn't put it back on after he'd rubbed his foot. He pulled it on with shaking fingers and fumbled with the laces and the legging strap. The sight of Foley and the Germans had been bad enough but, at least, they'd been in one piece. Of Linstrom, there had been only that pale viscous . . .

Someone shouted hoarsely, "Here they come!"

Gasping, Hackermeyer grabbed his M1 and lurched up dizzily,

laying the rifle across the rampart of the hole. He looked toward the German lines, his heart jolting painfully. All he could see was the stand of trees, the bushes, and, everywhere, the thickly curling mist. He searched the woods intently. Here they come! his mind cried out. He swallowed quickly, pushed off the safety lock. He checked the chamber. There was a clip in it. The bolt handle slipped off his glove and snapped shut loudly. Hackermeyer swallowed again. Here they come, he thought. But where?

Something landed with a thud in front of him. For a second, Hackermeyer gaped at the object. It looked like a potato masher—the impression came just before instinct drove him below the ground. The grenade exploded sharply, shooting leaves and dirt across the hole. Shrapnel bounced off the trees, one of the smoking fragments thudding against his coat and falling to the bottom of the hole. Hackermeyer gulped and jerked upright.

There was something moving in the mist. Hackermeyer squinted hard. He ducked, gasping, as the rifle shot rang out, the bullet cutting up a swath of leafy dirt in front of him. He crouched a moment, panting, then reared up again.

A blue-gray-coated figure was charging at him, firing from the hip. Get him! cried a voice in his mind. Freezing, Hackermeyer aimed and squeezed the trigger twice. The M1 jolted in his grip, the figure pitched forward, thudding to the ground. Something exploded deep in Hackermeyer. For an instant there was a crimson-edged haze before his eyes.

A shot rang out close by, the bullet popping near his ear. Grunting in surprise, Hackermeyer fell against the foxhole wall, twisting his head to the left. A burly German soldier was rushing toward him, blotting out the sky. Hackermeyer could see his face distinctly.

Suddenly the M1 jarred in his hands as if firing by itself and, magically, a hole appeared in the German's forehead. The German cried out hoarsely and dove to one side, landing on his shoulder. He thrashed on the leaves, trying to raise his rifle. Hackermeyer fired again and heard the bullet thudding in. The German stiffened. Hackermeyer stared at him. Abruptly he fired two more bullets into the German's body. There!

"Fire!" Cooley yelled somewhere. "Shoot! Yell! Use your weapons!"

With a hollow, animal-like cry, Hackermeyer whirled, looking for more Germans, conscious, for the first time, of the rapid crackling of gunfire all around him. He raised his rifle eagerly but there was no one to use it on.

Hackermeyer gasped. Suddenly his legs began to vibrate as he realized that he'd just killed two Germans. Something hot expanded in his chest and stomach. He couldn't seem to breathe. He'd killed them. They were dead. It was miraculous.

There was a sudden crashing in the underbrush and Hackermeyer spun, jerking up his rifle to fire.

"Let's go, boy!" said Cooley. "We're moving in!"

"Yeah." Hackermeyer started clambering from the foxhole. As he stood, he saw Cooley looking at the dead German.

"That yours?" asked Cooley in surprise.

Hackermeyer pointed shakily at the other German lying half-obscured by ground mist. "Him too," he gasped.

There was a tensing of skin across Cooley's leathery cheeks. Something glinted in his eyes. Suddenly he clapped Hackermeyer on the shoulder.

"Come on, Hack!" he said, and turned away.

Hackermeyer ran into the forest after Sergeant Cooley. There was something so exciting deep inside him that, without noticing it, he raced directly through the clearing where Linstrom had been killed. Inexplicably he felt like cheering wildly.

Ten minutes before, the mortar barrage had lifted, a whistle had shrilled to the right, and Cooley had shouted, "Here we go!" Hackermeyer had jumped up from behind an overturned tree, vaulted across its shrapnel- and bullet-pocked surface, and started jogging through the shadowy forest. Up ahead, rifle fire started.

He was trotting past a thicket of bushes when the bullet popped beside his ear and ripped up dirt behind him. Instinctively he jumped behind a tree in time to elude a second bullet, which ricocheted off the trunk and shot off, whistling, into the woods.

Hackermeyer pressed against the tree. He glanced around but saw no one. Apparently the squad was all ahead of him. He shifted and a third shot rang out, the bullet tearing into the ground in front of him. All of them were going into the ground, he realized. That meant that they were coming from above. Hackermeyer caught his breath.

Sniper.

He licked his lips, remembering how Cooley had fired his carbine into the trees and the figure had come toppling down. He swallowed again—his throat unusually dry, it seemed. Inchingly, he raised the M1 until he held it vertically before his chest. He fingered at the safety lock. It was off. He checked the cartridge chamber; loaded. Unconsciously he dragged his lower teeth down across his upper lip.

Now!

He lunged out from behind the tree and fell to one knee, rifle raised, eyes darting upward. The German's Schmeisser barked out in the stillness, the bullet caroming across the top of Hackermeyer's helmet with a ringing whine. Hackermeyer dived behind the tree. The German fired again, the slug burrowing into the earth beside his right shoe. Hackermeyer jerked his legs in and pushed up to a trembling stance, his heart thudding so gigantically that it seemed to rock his body. The woods faded and a tide of darkness flooded toward him.

Instantly he closed his eyes and leaned against the tree to regain his equilibrium. He started to gag on the saliva gathering in his throat and had to cough explosively. Opening his mouth wide, he sucked at the cold, damp air, then raised his eyelids. Things had fallen into place once more. He found himself yawning and shuddering at the same time.

He looked around again. There must be something he could do. He frowned with concentration. Jumping out was worthless. The German wasn't to be caught by surprise. What was more, the bullet had nicked his helmet so quickly that he'd ducked before getting a chance to see where the sniper was hidden.

Slowly, Hackermeyer raised his hand and ran a finger along the groove in his helmet. It ran at almost a right angle to the furrow that the piece of shrapnel had dug there earlier that morning. Hackermeyer inhaled and let the breath fall fluttering from his lips. He felt his hands begin to shake and clenched them on his rifle. He stiffened as the German fired again, the bullet rebounding off the trunk, spitting bark. Hackermeyer pressed against the tree. He had to kill the German, that was all. There was no other possibility.

His gaze moved around hastily and settled on a clump of bushes to his right. It was so thick he couldn't see beyond its surface. Was it possible that he could run to it and get inside? It would offer scant protection from the German's fire, but it would hide him. Moving around within the bushes he might avoid the bullets and, at the same time, locate the sniper's hiding place. He pulled in a long, agitated breath. Should he try? Or would that just be asking for it? He shook his head jerkily. It didn't matter. That was the only thing he could do.

Impulsively, he stuck his rifle out and the silence was shattered by the crack of the German's rifle, the whistling passage of the bullet, the dull thud of it against the ground. Hackermeyer pulled the rifle back and closed his eyes. What did that prove? Except that the German was a patient man, prepared to wait it out. Well, what else could he do? He was behind American lines now. Either he surrendered or he went on fighting. Clearly, this one wasn't thinking of surrender.

For the first time since the sniper had fired at him, Hackermeyer felt conscious of fear. It was an odd sensation; one he hadn't felt for years. Almost irritably, he clenched his teeth. He had to act. It was stupid to stand here waiting. Nobody was going to get him out of this. He got himself out or he stayed until dark.

He consulted his watch. Just past ten in the morning. It would be more than seven hours before dark. He could, conceivably, wait that long; but if he did, the squad might be miles ahead by then. He might never find them. No, that was ridiculous. He had to get the German now.

Hackermeyer looked downward at the hand grenades hooked across his cartridge belt. He stared at them a moment, calculating, then jerked one free and peeled off the tape.

He hadn't thrown a hand grenade since basic training. Now he ran a finger over its cold, knurled surface. Why was it made like that? He shook his head. What did that matter anyway?

Easing down his rifle, he leaned it against the tree and held the grenade in both hands. He pulled out the pin and held the arm down for several moments. Then, impulsively, he let the arm pop out and fly away. Drawing back his arm, he pitched the grenade as hard as he could in the direction that the shots were coming from. The Schmeisser barked and he jerked his arm back, grabbing up his M1, waiting.

The grenade exploded with a deafening roar, firing shrapnel in all directions. Catching his breath, Hackermeyer lunged away from the tree and sprinted for the bushes. His feet felt as if they were shod with lead. It seemed impossible that he could be running so slowly. The German began firing and bullets whistled past him. What if the bushes are booby-trapped? The thought exploded suddenly in his mind. He tried to swerve aside but he was going too fast. Plunging into the bushes, he flung himself to the right.

Twisting around, he squinted upward. The German was pumping bullets into the bushes as fast as he could fire. They buzzed past Hackermeyer's body like hornets as his gaze jerked searchingly from tree to tree. There! He saw the muzzle blast, the drift of powder smoke. Muscles twitching, Hackermeyer propped the M1, aimed, and squeezed the trigger. The rifle bucked against his shoulder. He fired again, shooting at the German's muzzle blast. He kept on shooting until the empty cartridge clip popped upward from its chamber.

The sniper had stopped firing. Hackermeyer sucked in fitful gasps of breath. Had he hit his target? Or was the German playing dead, waiting for him to stand? Hackermeyer swallowed. Wouldn't the German have fallen if he was hit? The sniper Cooley had shot had tumbled to the ground. Hackermeyer grimaced, looking fixedly at the tree. It was like a cave up there, the foliage shaded it so darkly. Why should the German have stopped firing if he was still alive? Unless he was running out of ammunition and wanted a clear target before expending more. Hackermeyer held his breath and listened. It was very still now. The sounds of battle had drifted so far ahead as to be almost inaudible. He tightened suddenly. There *was* a noise. Like something falling or—dripping.

Hackermeyer stood and walked over to the tree. There was a gathering splotch of bright red blood on the leafy ground. He stood there, transfixed, watching the blood arc down in endless, heavy drops. It was so vividly red and glistening. Hackermeyer stared dumbly at it. His gaze lifted slowly, trailing its crimson descent.

High above, the dead German sagged outward from a bough, the rifle dangling from a strap around his neck, his arms swinging loosely. He was belted to the tree. His body swayed back and forth as if a breeze were moving him.

Abruptly Hackermeyer turned and started running in the direction the squad had gone. There was a tingling lightness in his body as though he'd been drinking. He seemed to float across the ground in effortless strides, moving as in a dream. Nothing could stop him. Nothing.

Sixteen minutes later he reached the clearing. There were dead American soldiers lying all over it. Hackermeyer started out among them, looking to see if any were from the squad. It was the first time he'd seen so many dead at once. There must have been a terrible battle here. That sniper might have saved his life, it occurred to him. It was strange to think of being singled out for fortune. That sort of thing never happened to him. Still, if he hadn't been held back . . .

He was halfway across the clearing when, overhead, the fluttering rush of shells began. Hackermeyer staggered to a halt and looked up quickly. For the fragment of a second he felt a sense of angry justification. This was more suitable to the pattern— that he should survive the attacks of three Germans and miss this battle only to be personally assaulted by eighty-eights. Before the idea had flared more than a moment in his consciousness, he flung himself to the ground and hid his face.

The shells exploded in the trees behind him. Hackermeyer

jerked his legs in as the air was filled with billowing thunder. The zing of shrapnel sounded overhead.

"Hackermeyer!"

Instinctively he raised his head and looked around, then pulled it down again as the second flurry of shells exploded in the trees.

"In front of you!"

Hackermeyer looked up again but saw nothing ahead except a rise in the ground, a clump of trees and bushes at its peak. He dropped his head again and a third cluster of shells exploded crashingly. He gasped as the pressure waves gushed over him, pounding at his flesh.

"It's Cooley! Run!" the voice roared down at him.

Automatically Hackermeyer pushed to his feet and started running forward, sensing with his legs, rather than his eyes, the incline he was scaling. He still saw nothing but the trees and bushes.

"Keep coming!" Cooley's voice boomed down at him.

Suddenly a shell exploded close behind and, like an ocean breaker, the concussion wave lifted Hackermeyer off his feet and flung him to the ground, knocking out his breath. Another blast ripped at the air, driving spikes of pain into his head. The earth leaped under him, then dropped away, giving him the sensation of being thrown to the ground. Dazed, he watched the muddy cloud of smoke rush over him, filling his eyes and nose and mouth with clogging fumes. He tried to rise but couldn't. His legs went rubbery under him and he bumped down onto his side.

Someone grabbed him underneath the left arm. He looked up dizzily and saw Cooley's bearded face wavering above him in the smoke.

"Come on, son!" Cooley's shout seemed to reach him from a distance. He felt himself being hauled to his feet. Suddenly he was running next to Cooley, barely conscious of the ground beneath him. He began to sag and Cooley jerked him up again.

"Keep running!" he yelled in Hackermeyer's ear. This time the shout was like a knife-point jabbed against his brain. Hackermeyer winced and kept on running. They were almost to the clump of trees now. Thunder blasted all around them, shrapnel fragments wailed and moaned, skimming by their bodies. Hackermeyer felt the wind of one piece rushing past his cheek.

Now Cooley dragged him by the clump of trees and bushes and Hackermeyer caught a glimpse of curving stone like the top of some ancient ruin. He crossed the peak and instantly was skidding down an incline beside a giant concrete structure. A narrow doorway loomed before him. Cooley shoved him through, he tripped and sprawled inside, tumbling down into a dim-lit chamber.

Lippincott helped him up. "Greetings, Hackermeyer," he said.

Hackermeyer looked around the cold, cement-walled room, which was illuminated by daylight coming through the wall slits and by a single candle on a wooden table. Outside, the explosions sounded muffled.

"What's this?" he asked. His tongue felt swollen in his mouth.

"Pillbox," said Lippincott.

"Oh." Hackermeyer gaped at him. Lippincott seemed to be rising rapidly off the floor.

"Easy." Cooley's face appeared beside him once again, his strong grip under Hackermeyer's arm. Hackermeyer's shoes scraped on the cement floor as Cooley led him to a tier of three bunks on the wall and sat him on the bottom one. "There we go," said Cooley, taking away his rifle.

Hackermeyer sat groggily as Cooley squatted down in front of him.

"You all right?" Cooley asked.

"Yeah."

Cooley grinned at him. "That's the old stuff," he said. "Where you been?"

Hackermeyer ran a sluggish tongue across his lips and inhaled the dankly sour air.

"Sniper," he said.

Cooley stopped chewing. "Pin you down?" he asked.

Hackermeyer nodded slowly. It hurt his head.

"What'd you do?" asked Cooley.

Hackermeyer coughed weakly. "Shot 'im," he mumbled.

Cooley clucked. "We got us a tiger, boys," he said. Hacker-meyer raised his eyes, blinking, and saw that, in addition to Lip-pincott and Cooley, Schumacher and Fearfeather were also there. Schumacher was methodically stripping down his rifle on the middle of the three bunks across the small room.

"What happened to Linstrom?" Cooley asked.

"Hit," said Hackermeyer thickly.

"With what?"

"Shell." Hackermeyer cleared his throat viscidly. "Was— nothing left."

"Oh, Christ." Cooley patted his shoulder. "Lie down now," he said. "We'll be here awhile."

Hackermeyer tried to lift his legs but couldn't. Cooley picked them up and Hackermeyer fell back on the bunk, closing his eyes. Then, laboriously, he sat up again and fumbled for his canteen. As he drank, he watched Cooley talking to Lippincott. In a few moments, Cooley went outside.

"Where's 'e going?" he asked. He could hardly recognize his voice.

"Checking on Guthrie and Lazzo," said Lippincott.

Hackermeyer slid the canteen back into its canvas sheath and fumbled at the clips. He couldn't close them. Painstakingly he inched his gloves off and pushed the clips shut. Then he took off his belt and helmet and slipped back onto the bunk, won-dering what happened to the Germans who had manned the pillbox.

The smell was getting stronger now; a thick, consuming stench that he could almost taste. It was the smell of locker rooms, sub-way toilets, ill-kept kitchens, firing ranges. Acid smells, sweet smells, stale smells; the reek of dirt and grease and smoke and un-washed bodies. It seemed to ooze down his throat when he swal-lowed.

Hackermeyer stared up dizzily at the crisscross of ropes on the bunk above. It reminded him of the bunks on the ship he'd taken overseas. Except that they had had canvas bottoms. He turned his head and looked at the crude, unfinished cement of the walls. There were drops of water trickling down it. It looked like the wall in the cellar of his uncle's house. Used to whip me there, he thought. Bastard. Powerless, he slipped away.

HACKERMEYER OPENED HIS eyes. For a moment, he forgot where he was and sat up so quickly that his head struck the rope webbing overhead and bounced him back.

"Low bridge," he heard someone say. Turning his head, he saw Cooley and Lippincott sitting at the table playing cards. It was Lippincott who had spoken.

Hackermeyer eased himself to a sitting position on the edge of the bunk and looked around with sleep-dulled eyes.

"How do you feel?" asked Cooley without looking over. His jaws worked rhythmically with tobacco-chewing.

"Okay." Hackermeyer looked across the room and saw that Schumacher was reading on the middle bunk. His rifle, glinting with fresh oil, leaned against the wall, its barrel protected by a clean sock, its bolt assembly by a piece of oilskin. That's a good idea, Hackermeyer thought. It was important to take care of your weapon.

Hackermeyer closed his eyes and felt a twinge of pain on his right cheek. Opening his eyes, he touched the cheek with his fingers. There was a crusty thread of blood running outward from beneath his eye. He raked at it with a nail and winced. Reaching into his inside coat pocket, he slid free his steel mirror.

It was a shock to see his face ingrained with dirt, eyes bloodshot, lips chapped, a jagged scratch across his cheek. Picking up his helmet, he poured some canteen water into it. He got a scrap of soap and the damp washcloth from his web belt and cleaned off his face, grimacing at the sting on his cheek. As he washed, then brushed his teeth lethargically, he became conscious of the whispering flutter of shells overhead, the muffled rumble of explosions in the distance. The Americans must be shelling Saarbach.

He realized that he needed to empty his bowels and kidneys and, pushing to his feet, he started for the doorway.

"Where you going?" Cooley asked without turning from his cards.

"Bathroom," Hackermeyer answered.

"There's a room in back," said Cooley.

Lippincott groaned faintly. "Isn't this place enough of a toilet already?"

"No point in getting his ass blown off," said Cooley.

Lippincott grunted. "Oh, well," he said, "I guess it can't smell any worse."

"Hell, man, this is home," said Cooley.

"Sure it is." Lippincott played a card. "How they could live in this stench for months is beyond me," he said.

"I would, personally, prefer an outhouse," said Fearfeather.

"I'm with you," said Lippincott.

Hackermeyer found the cement corridor and edged along its dark length, grunting in surprise as the floor dropped away and he jarred down into a small, dungeon-like room that smelled of burned food and grease. Gritting his teeth, he opened up his coat and pulled his pants down.

When he was through, he came back into the main room and walked over to one of the rectangular slits through which daylight was passing. Bending over, he looked outside and saw the slope that he and Cooley had come running up. It was a perfect spot for ambush. No wonder there had been so many bodies in the clearing. Hackermeyer blinked. There weren't any bodies. Had they been taken away? Or had he only imagined them?

Returning to the bunk, Hackermeyer sat down with a sigh. He opened a box of K rations and slumped there chewing on the biscuits. He could hear the crunching in his head as he ate, causing miniature tremors through his skull. I'll clean my rifle soon, he told himself. It was important.

"Hackermeyer?"

He raised his eyes.

"How come Linstrom got it and you didn't?" Cooley asked. "Weren't you together?"

Hackermeyer coughed on a piece of biscuit. It was strange, but he'd completely forgotten about Linstrom until that moment. Already it seemed days since Linstrom had been killed.

"He ran away," he said.

"Oh—great." Cooley slapped down a card. "And the government keeps sending them over," he said. "Why the Goddamn hell don't they use their brains?"

"Teenagers are all right," said Lippincott.

"Not as soldiers," Cooley said. "I got nothing against them personally, for Christ's sake. I got one at home, ain't I? And there was Jimmy."

Hackermeyer looked at Cooley as the sergeant played cards. He remembered thinking that Cooley wasn't the father type. Now he found out that Cooley had a son. Who was Jimmy?

"They're all right for helping cooks or working in supply or—oh, hell, they're just no good for combat, that's all."

"They're fast," said Lippincott, looking at his cards.

"So they're fast," said Cooley. "What good is that if they don't think? And they don't. They're used to being in a group, thinking like the group."

"You mean that's not the secret of being a good soldier?" Lippincott asked wryly.

"You know better than that," said Cooley. "I'll take a man over a teenager any day. Ain't no guarantee, but he's more likely to think for himself than a kid is."

"Maybe not," said Lippincott. "A teenager has more independence. He hasn't been forced into line yet."

"It's knowing how to operate while you're *in* line that counts," said Cooley.

"Could be," said Lippincott, yawning.

"Don't get me wrong," said Cooley. "I ain't saying that just because a guy is older, he's automatically on the ball. I'm just saying he's had more time to get on the ball. A teenager don't bring anything to war but himself. The only training he has is what the army gave him and, Christ knows, that's not much."

Lippincott clucked. "Fine talk from a noncom," he said.

Cooley spat tobacco juice to one side.

"Trainees get taught every damn thing but what they need the most," he said. "The details of what it's like to be in combat. Look at Linstrom. If basic training was what it should be, he'd have been rooted out, not sent over here. Now he's dead and what the hell does it prove?"

Hackermeyer sat looking intently at Cooley. He'd never seen him so talkative before.

"I'll tell you one flaw in the way guys are trained," said Cooley. "Nobody ever tries to find out who's going to fire his weapon."

Cooley nooded at Lippincott's curious expression.

"Yeah," he said. "Yeah. Obvious? Hell, it couldn't be more obvious. But do they try to find out? The hell they do. Even after a man gets in combat, they don't try to find out."

Hackermeyer noticed that Schumacher had lowered his book and was looking at Cooley.

"Nobody ever tries to find out the most basic fact of all about a soldier," Cooley said. "Does he shoot his weapon or doesn't he?"

"Don't follow you," said Lippincott.

Cooley played a card.

"Take our squad," he said. "We're not so bad, but we don't even make thirty percent fire. I won't name names—but more than half our guys never fired a shot. Simple as that. And why?"

"Inadequate drilling," said Schumacher.

Cooley glanced at him.

"That's only part of it, Bernie," he said, shaking his head. "A small part of it. Not enough to explain why seventy-five percent of soldiers won't fire their weapons. Oh, sure, they'll face the enemy but, Goddamn it, they won't fire their weapons at him!"

He pointed a finger at Lippincott.

"Nobody says a word about it," he said, "but, when the chips are down, seventy-five percent of soldiers are conscientious objectors. They won't shoot and they won't kill."

I will, Hackermeyer almost said aloud.

"A question of discipline and drilling," said Schumacher.

"No, Bernie." Cooley shook his head again. "A question of human nature. If a soldier can't stomach killing you can't make him stomach it by teaching him how a rifle works. And how do you beat your enemy unless you fire your weapon at him? You fire and you advance—hell, that's combat, that's it. And it don't matter if you got anything to shoot at either. It's mass fire that counts, not accuracy."

Hackermeyer understood now why Cooley always kept yelling for them to fire their weapons even when there was no visible target.

"I agree with you one hundred percent, of course," said Schumacher, nodding. "Fire superiority is of the essence. The relating of each weapon to the ground for maximum firepower. This is, however, a matter of drill and discipline."

"Nope." Cooley shook his head once more. "I'll tell you what you got to relate, and it ain't weapons to the ground. It's one guy to another guy. You got to teach a man what he can expect from his buddies in combat. If he knows that, it don't matter if the ground ain't worth anything or if his weapon don't even work. He'll still know what the score is."

Cooley picked up his new hand.

"How do you teach soldiers human nature?" asked Lippincott.

"I don't know, but that's what we need," said Cooley. "Especially for teenagers. They got to have something to lean on besides themselves. All they got is—fast legs and titmilk ideals. You got to make up for that."

"If a grown man's ideals are more established, won't it be even harder for him to kill?" asked Lippincott.

"Maybe so," said Cooley. "Except he's more likely to know why he *has* to kill. And less likely to be affected by killing, too."

He grunted. "Crazy thing," he said. "A soldier fires his weapon and everybody thinks he's doing what comes naturally. Hell, he's practically a hero just for doing that."

Hackermeyer felt surprised. He hadn't thought of himself as a hero for shooting his rifle. Then he recalled that he'd never seen Foley shoot his rifle. Or Linstrom. Or Fearfeather. Or Bill Riley or Goldmeyer, either. Cooley must be right.

"One good thing about a teenager," said Cooley. "They're more used to team pepper than an older guy. If they're not scared shitless, they're more likely to talk it up in combat."

He put down his cards again.

"Which is another thing they don't mention in training," he said. "That you got to keep in touch, let every other man know where you are. That means a lot in combat. Why do I keep telling you guys to shout out your names? So you'll know you're not alone, that's why."

He spat tobacco juice to the side. "War ain't guns against guns," he said. "It's men against men. And the men that have the most confidence are going to win. That's one reason Americans make out in the long run. They're more full of piss than anyone else. But there'd sure be a lot of lives saved if they were given the right kind of training too."

Schumacher made a dubious sound. "I still say discipline or lack of discipline is the key," he said. He reminded Hackermeyer of his uncle. Uncle George was always raving about discipline too. Until now, Hackermeyer had assumed that, even though he'd hated his uncle's guts, he was inclined to think in that direction too. Now, oddly enough, he found himself tending toward Cooley's point of view. Maybe discipline had its limitations.

"Discipline ain't the key," Cooley said as if reading Hackermeyer's mind. "And drilling ain't the key. Combat breakdowns ain't breakdowns of discipline or drilling. They're human breakdowns. Or human break*throughs*!" he said, pointing at Schumacher. "Some of the best soldiers are guys who've been nothing all their lives. When it counts is when they prove themselves. And, by God, you never know who it's going to be."

Hackermeyer stared at Cooley. It was as if the sergeant were addressing him personally. Was it possible that every lack and failure in his life could be, somehow, compensated for in combat? Hackermeyer shivered with a sudden, strange excitement.

"Except, when your best soldiers show up," said Cooley, "it ain't likely they're going to be eighteen-year-olds."

IT WAS ALMOST one-thirty in the afternoon. Cooley and Lippincott had left the pillbox and Hackermeyer was sitting at the table cleaning his M1.

While he worked, he started thinking about Linstrom. It was pretty obvious why Linstrom had broken. He'd always gotten everything he wanted for the asking. He didn't know what it was to be set back. That was why he'd given up almost immediately. He'd had no discipline. The kind you got during childhood. Instead, he'd been hopelessly spoiled. As far as he'd been concerned, he was number one.

Frowning, Hackermeyer drew an oily patch through the rifle barrel. Except why had Linstrom gotten so upset when he thought the rabbit was going to be eaten? It had seemed more than just wanting his own way. Why had he been so sad about the dead bird?

Hackermeyer shrugged it away. It was unimportant. Linstrom had been weak, period. He hadn't been able to adjust himself to unpleasant experiences. Hackermeyer grunted to himself. Linstrom should have spent a few years at Uncle George's house.

Hackermeyer pointed the barrel at the candle flame and sighted through it. It occurred to him that bullets had been fired through it which had killed three different men. It occurred to him that the first time Cooley had really taken note of him was after he'd shot two Germans. He could remember vividly Cooley's look of approval, the hearty clap of Cooley's hand on his shoulder, the way Cooley had called him Hack. He remembered, too, the fierce satisfaction he'd felt after he'd killed the Germans. The momentary surge of release. He wondered what it had been. Relief that he had proved himself a soldier?

"Hackermeyer?"

He looked up and saw the new replacement, Fearfeather, standing by the table.

"The sergeant suggested, before, that, since your partner was killed, you and I might stay together temporarily," said Fearfeather. He spoke in a leisurely drawl.

Hackermeyer didn't reply as Fearfeather sat down at the table and extended his hand. "Leonard Fearfeather," he introduced himself.

Hackermeyer held out his hand. Fearfeather gripped it firmly and shook it twice. "Most pleased to meet you," he said. "You are—Hackermeyer?"

"Yeah."

Fearfeather nodded. "Where are you from, Hackermeyer?" he asked.

"Brooklyn."

"Is that correct? I'm from Columbia, Missouri, myself. That's a university town. My daddy runs a funeral parlor there."

"For the university?"

"No, no, for anyone who dies," said Fearfeather. "And whose survivors choose to patronize us. I was my daddy's assistant."

Fearfeather crossed his legs. "You know," he said, "it is downright tragic how few people appreciate the fact that embalming is a demanding craft."

Hackermeyer made a noise as he started working on the bolt. He remembered how Uncle George had looked in his casket. Like a pink-cheeked wax dummy. That was craft?

"Most folks think of us as merely butchers if they think of us at all," declared Fearfeather. "They don't appreciate the art involved. They think as far as we're concerned it's only meat we're handling. Well, that's not so, Hackermeyer."

"Uh-huh," said Hackermeyer. This Fearfeather was a weird one, too. Not as weird as Guthrie, but pretty weird.

"Folks just don't appreciate the skill it takes to pretty up a cadaver," said Fearfeather, taking off his steel-rimmed glasses.

Hackermeyer blew his nose. It hurt his head a little.

"Well, I'd just like to see them take the kind of mangled ree-mains that we get sometimes and make them something fitting for the box," said Fearfeather. "That's an art—and my daddy is an artist of the highest caliber.

"Why, I remember one particular project of his—an old gentleman who had fallen beneath the wheels of an onrushing truck. Well, I tell you, Hackermeyer, I would defy the best of undertakers to produce from that old gentleman's ree-mains a cadaver which could be shown at services. Mangled? Hoo-eee, he was a pulp, Hackermeyer, a regular, grade-A pulp. I mean every bone in his head was practically mashed to a jelly, you know what I mean?"

"Yeah," said Hackermeyer. Like that German in the entrenchment yesterday morning.

"The front wheel had run directly across of his skull, for the Lord's sake," Fearfeather said, holding his glasses to the candle-light. "Now tell me of a less likely project for the undertaker's craft than that."

Hackermeyer nodded.

"Well, sir," said Fearfeather; he put his glasses back on. "My daddy stayed up nights remodeling that old gentleman's head—and body; it was a mess too. He put into that project, Hacker-meyer, every single iota of skill which he could summon to his fingertips. But I mean, he was calling on resources I would not have even suspected him of po-ssessing. Little tricks *his* daddy taught him. Ways to fashion out the cheeks, firm the chin, re-hang the ears, build up the nose; which was a blob, I'll tell you.

"Any yet he did it, Hackermeyer. Yes, sir, unstinting and with-out complaint, he worked on that old gentleman; and, by the thunder of the Lord, what he produced was art! I mean it was a work of art. Naturally, it didn't look too much like the old gen-tleman as he had appeared in life, but—well, shoot, it was a dang phenomenon he looked like anything at all! I mean he was mashed, Hackermeyer. It was a miracle he looked human! My daddy had, in my humble opinion, wrought a miracle, yes sir. You would have been inspired to see that old gentleman in his box, Hackermeyer. He looked so natural and at peace. I mean there was a glow of health in his cheeks!"

Hackermeyer nodded, started to reassemble his rifle. He wished he had a piece of oilskin for the bolt assembly.

"My father is a top, first-class, grade-A craftsman, Hacker-meyer," said Fearfeather. "And I humbly pray that, someday, I will begin to even approach his level of dexterity."

Fearfeather stretched and yawned. "Oh, well, shoot," he said. He took out his small corncob pipe and began stuffing in to-bacco.

"You know something interesting?" he said. "The sergeant seems to hold the opinion that this squad has been singled out by the authorities as an experiment to see how a squad made up entirely of eighteen-year-olds would make out in combat."

"When did he say that?" asked Hackermeyer.

"While you were asleep," said Fearfeather. "You think it's true?"

"I don't know," said Hackermeyer.

"Myself, I doubt it," said Fearfeather. "Anyway, I don't know as I agree with the sergeant's turn of mind. I mean, what has age got to do with it? I'm eighteen and so are you and I don't count us as children by a country mile. We know what we're doing, don't we?"

"I guess," said Hackermeyer.

"Sure we do," said Fearfeather. "I grant the men that there are eighteen-year-olds who are inadequate as soldiers. I mean like that boy you were with. That good-looking blond boy that got his self blown to bits. What was his name?"

"Linstrom."

"Linstrom. Well, I could see right off he wouldn't fit," said Fearfeather. "I mean, he might have been eighteen in years but, mentally, he was just a child wet behind the ears. Do you agree with that?"

Hackermeyer nodded. Funny how much older than either Foley or Linstrom this Fearfeather seemed, weird or not.

"Well, shoot, what does it matter?" Fearfeather said. "The sergeant is entitled to his opinions as we are entitled to ours."

Sighing, he reached into his overcoat pocket, drew out a small book, and opened it. Hackermeyer saw the words HOLY BIBLE on the cover.

"Chaplain give you that?" he asked.

"Chaplain?"

"He gave me one."

"Oh, I see," said Fearfeather. "No, my daddy gave this to me when I entered the service." He nodded to himself. "My daddy is a most religious person," he said. "He says that working with the departed gives a man great insight into the circumstances of mortality and immortality."

"You think it helps?" asked Hackermeyer.

"Being an undertaker?"

"No, the Bible."

"Well, it surely does, Hackermeyer. It most surely does. I defy you to open up the book at random and fail to find a word of consolation."

Hackermeyer grunted.

"Here, try," said Fearfeather, holding out his Bible.

Hackermeyer took it and looked down at the cover.

"Go on," said Fearfeather. "See for yourself."

Hackermeyer opened the book and leafed through it.

"What does it say?" asked Fearfeather.

"And they committed whoredoms in Egypt," Hackermeyer read; *"they committed whoredoms in their youth: there were their breasts pressed, and—"*

"Now, Hackermeyer," chided Fearfeather. "You know you picked that out on purpose."

Hackermeyer handed the Bible back to Fearfeather, the hint of a smile tugging up the corners of his mouth.

"You didn't think you'd fool me with that old chestnut, did you?" said Fearfeather amiably.

Hackermeyer was surprised at how easy it was to talk to Fearfeather.

"I tell you, Hackermeyer, there are a thousand passages in this book which are a comfort to the mind of one who faces death in the field of battle," said Fearfeather. He puffed measuredly on his pipe. "To have the fear of death cast out," he said, "is of prime importance to a soldier, don't you agree?"

"You don't fear it?" asked Hackermeyer.

"Well, I do in the sense that I would hate to leave this life at such an early age. I mean, I'm looking forward to the day when my Daddy and I are partners in the mortuary together. Still, I know that, if for some unseeable reason, I do get taken, well, there's all my kin waiting to greet me on the other side."

Hackermeyer stared at him.

"Don't you accept survival after death?" asked Fearfeather in surprise.

Hackermeyer shrugged. "Don't know," he said. He hadn't let himself think about it much since he was small, when the thought of dying had terrified him.

"Well, I do know," said Fearfeather. "And I accept and am

comforted by that acceptance, Hackermeyer. I mean, to think of dying and not believe that anything at all is waiting—well, there's a terror for you. Brrr." He shuddered. "Hoo-ee, I couldn't face that for a moment."

"Yeah," said Hackermeyer, vaguely.

"I mean, don't you believe that you will survive?" asked Fearfeather.

Hackermeyer swallowed. "No," he said.

"Why not?"

Hackermeyer didn't answer right away. Why should I survive? he thought. Why should anybody?

"I don't know," he finally said.

"Well, believe me, Hackermeyer, you will survive. If, God forbid, this war should take you from this plane, you will be greeted on the other side by your loved ones. Are your mother and daddy still alive?"

"No."

"Then they are waiting for you on the other side," said Fearfeather confidently. "They are watching you and they are waiting to greet you with open arms."

Hackermeyer stared at Fearfeather, a gnawing distress inside him. He didn't know his mother at all. If what Fearfeather said was true, what could he say to her when they met? And damned if he'd want to see his father anymore. And Uncle George? The hell with that! No, it was all malarkey.

Fearfeather began to read his Bible now, lips moving slightly. Hackermeyer watched him awhile, then took out his crossword puzzle book and started working on it.

After a few minutes, the puzzle blurred before his eyes. It gave him a strange, uneasy feeling to think about the possibility of his mother still existing somewhere. Making sure that Fearfeather was absorbed in his Bible, Hackermeyer took the photograph from his wallet and palmed it in his lap where Fearfeather couldn't see. He sat quietly and stared at it for a long time.

Cooley came stepping through the concrete doorway.

"Here we go," he said.

Several minutes later, the members of the squad were assembled underneath a tree, the raindrops spattering off their helmets.

"All right, here's the scoop," said Cooley. "This next stretch should do it. We move down this slope and through a patch of woods till we come to another slope, a steep one. When we reach that, you'll see a road below—it crosses a bridge. We go down the slope and cross the bridge. Beyond that, there's one more field before Saarbach.

"Everything holds the same. We've blown hell out of the Krauts but they've still got plenty of positions. Plus all the rest—snipers, booby traps, the works. I won't remind you to keep your eyes open. You will or you won't see Christmas." He spat out tobacco juice. "Questions?" he asked.

"How far from the town are we?" asked Schumacher.

"I'd say less than two miles," said Cooley. "Anything else?" No one spoke.

"All right, let's go, then. Keep your eyes on me."

They spread out and started moving through the steady rain. Hackermeyer pulled up the collar of his raincoat and buttoned it at his neck. It was hard to do with his overcoat underneath. He glanced down at his rifle and reassured himself that it was hanging muzzle-down. Then he put the cotton in his ears.

He looked around. To his right, Schumacher was walking in steady strides. Behind their steel-rimmed glasses, his gray eyes moved searchingly. Hackermeyer noticed that he'd shaved. It was remarkable how neat and calm Schumacher was. He seemed almost unaffected by the war.

To his left was Fearfeather. The Missouri boy moved easily, looking straight ahead. Hackermeyer wondered what he was thinking about. Survival after death? Or some masterful embalming feat his daddy had performed? Hackermeyer's gaze shifted. There were Guthrie and Lippincott walking together, chatting quietly. Ahead of them hobbled Lazzo, looking, as always, sour and tense. In the center of the group, apparently tireless, strode Sergeant Cooley. Hackermeyer was surprised by a sudden rush of affection for the squad. For a moment, they all seemed very close to him.

He blinked his eyes and looked ahead. Keep your eyes open,

Cooley had said, and already he was daydreaming. He stiffened and concentrated on the terrain. It was himself he had to depend on, not the squad.

The forest seemed very still. The only sound Hackermeyer could hear was the drumming of raindrops on his helmet. He squinted up at the sky and saw that it was uniformly gray, hanging low and ponderous above the trees. It all seemed very restful: the dark-foliaged trees swaying slightly, the soughing murmur of the rain. Hackermeyer lowered his face and rubbed the wetness off.

He caught himself again. He wasn't keeping his eyes open. Frowning, he crimped his lips together. Damn it, why was he doing what Cooley told him not to do? He'd come this far without serious injury. He wasn't going to get killed now by behaving like some careless kid. Teeth clenched, he searched the woods around him. They were off the slope now, moving on a level. The figures of the other squad members appeared and disappeared among the thickening trees.

Far to his left, a sharp explosion sounded, freezing him. A man began to scream, "My foot! Oh, God, my foot!"

"Keep on moving," Cooley's voice came drifting back. "And watch out for booby traps."

Hackermeyer started walking again. Someone hadn't kept his eyes open. He wondered who it was. The screaming was too distant for it to be anyone in the squad.

He began to wonder why they had to capture Saarbach. What made the higher-ups decide that any one particular place had to be taken? Lots of towns were bypassed, probably cities too. Why didn't they just bypass all of them and go straight to Berlin, cleaning out the isolated pockets of resistance later? He couldn't see how taking Saarbach was going to do anything for—Damn it, he was doing it again! Gritting his teeth, he hissed out breath. He had to pay attention! They might be seeing Germans soon. He couldn't avoid a sense of enjoyable anticipation. He wanted to see Germans.

Up ahead, Guthrie and Lippincott had stopped now. Hackermeyer and the others joined them and looked down over the edge of the ridge. It was almost like a cliff, it fell away so precipitously. Far below, Hackermeyer saw the road Cooley had mentioned; a gray ribbon winding snakelike through the dark forest. His eyes shifted to the gray stone bridge which spanned a deep gorge. Along the bottom of the gorge, a crystal torrent of waters was running. Hackermeyer could see the flecks of foam jumping on its surface. His gaze kept moving. Now, across the plain, he could see the outskirts of Saarbach. They were almost there.

"Let's go," said Cooley. "Spread out thin."

The squad broke up again and, one by one, moved over the ridge. The steep angle of the slope reminded Hackermeyer of the one Lazzo, Lippincott, and he had clambered down during the patrol. It was impossible to walk. He had to lean in toward the sharply pitched earth, holding on to roots and bushes as his shoes plowed furrows in the wet black earth. He kept looking at the opposite slope, wondering if there were Germans marking their laborious descent. It was a perfect field of fire. Excluding the sporadic growth of trees there was virtually no cover at all. Was this the only way they could have gone?

Fearfeather moved by a few yards away.

"How you doing, Hackermeyer?" he asked amiably.

"Okay."

"That's the ticket," said Fearfeather.

They were halfway down the slope when the shelling began.

There were no whistlings overhead. Below them, on the opposite slope, the air was shattered by gun blasts and, almost instantly, explosions roared around them, casting gouts of mucky soil in all directions. Hackermeyer twisted back against the ground and pressed his face against an arm. Detonations thundered everywhere. Flame shot upward at the sky. Trees crashed over, rolling and skidding down the incline with thrashings of dark foliage.

"Withdraw!" Someone's shouting flared between the volleys of tremendous blasts. Hackermeyer pushed up and started clambering for the ridge. He slipped and fell and felt the wind of a shrapnel fragment rushing over him with a sirening wail. He clung to the muddy ground with trembling fingers. Thick smoke poured across him, choking him. Tears sprang from his eyes.

Coughing helplessly, he struggled to his feet and lurched upward once more. A geyser of earth leaped up before him. He dropped and closed his eyes as dirt and stone poured down on him. His coughing turned to gagging. Gasping, blinded by tears, he wavered to his feet and started moving once again.

The hillside seemed to erupt as a deafening roar enveloped him. He felt himself flung upward and around, legs whipping. Landing hard, he bounced across the ground like a rag doll, then started somersaulting down the slope. His rifle butt jammed against a bush and stopped his wild descent. For a second, he was standing upright. Then he pitched forward, skidding on his chest, rolling and twisting down the incline, faster and faster, bouncing off bushes, scraping over rocks. Blood came gushing from his nostrils, spattering across his face, into his eyes. Blinded, he plummeted down the hillside, landing with a brutal jolt.

Then everything was painful blackness.

SOMEWHERE, IN THE distance, was a rumble of exploding shells. Hackermeyer opened his eyes and saw the muddy ground beneath him. He could feel his temples pulsing, driving waves of pain into his head. There was mud in his mouth. Slowly he spit it out. His heart was still thumping heavily, his body trembling. He tried to sit up, groaning at the wave of nausea that flooded over him. He lay down again and closed his eyes. They felt as if they were ignited in their sockets. There was a greasy taste of burned powder in his mouth. Bile rose, gagging, in his throat and he spat it out, pale and greenish and flecked with mud. He rubbed at his burning eyes. Then, slowly, waveringly, he sat up.

The ground looked watery beneath him. He closed his eyes, opened them, closed them again. He pressed both hands against his temples, trying to stop the throbbing. After several minutes, he opened his eyes and looked down at himself. Apparently no bones were broken even though his entire body ached. If he hadn't been wrapped in such a cocoon of winter clothes it would have been much worse. I've got to get up, he thought.

It wasn't until he looked around that he saw the German.

His legs and arms jerked in spastically and he gasped in shock. The German was propped against a bush looking at him fixedly. Only after several seconds did Hackermeyer realize he was dead.

The German's face had an expression of solemn detachment on it. Hackermeyer couldn't take his eyes off him. There was no blood, no sign of wounds. The German's helmet had fallen off and was lying beside him on the ground. His hair was pale blond, as Linstrom's had been. It fluttered in the cold breeze, threads of it quivering against his forehead. The German's eyes were brightly blue.

Hackermeyer looked around. He was in a clump of bushes with the German. He must have landed there after tumbling down the hill. He closed his burning eyes again and bent over, gasping at the damp, cold air. If only he could vomit. His stomach roiled and heaved but nothing came up. Abruptly, Hackermeyer became conscious that his pants were wet. He felt beneath his coat with dull surprise. At first he thought it was from the rain, then he realized that he had done it himself. He gritted his teeth as the throbbing flared inside his head again. That shell must have exploded right under him. How come he wasn't dead?

He tried not to think. He sucked fitfully at the air, waiting for the nausea to subside. His eyes kept throbbing like heated jelly. He pressed both hands over them. He remembered then that his nose had been bleeding and he sniffed experimentally. It wasn't bleeding now, but there was a taste of blood in his throat mingled with the sour flavor of bile and mud and smoke.

He opened his eyes and glanced at the German. Then he worked himself carefully to his knees. The exertion caused his head to pound as though with hammer blows. He was sure his brains were going to spurt out of his ears like gruel. He bent over, panting, trying to regain his balance. After a while, he straightened up and opened his eyes. Gasping, he fell into a prone position, his heart leaping so hard that he could feel it striking at the ground.

The slope was crowded with German soldiers climbing for the ridge.

Hackermeyer couldn't seem to breathe. He looked around dizzily for his rifle. It was nowhere to be seen. He lay staring at the muddy ground and trying to think. He was caught in the middle of a German counterattack. He closed his eyes and felt his lips begin to quiver. What was he supposed to do?

Raising up a bit, he drew aside the bush in front of him. He hadn't rolled all the way down the slope, he saw. There were Germans about twenty yards below him, moving upward steadily, their rifles at high port. He looked at the face of one of them. It looked very grim and determined. Sort of like Schumacher's. Hackermeyer eased the bush back into position. He couldn't surrender. They'd kill him.

He glanced down at his belt, blinking dizzily. Two grenades left. Not nearly enough. There were dozens of Germans coming up the slope. Breath staggered in his lungs, making his chest hitch on the ground. His hands began to shake. What was he supposed to do? He couldn't just lie there. Even if the Germans didn't spot him he'd have to pass through them later in order to get back to the American lines. He closed his eyes and lay there shivering. Do something, he told himself. Goddamn it, do something!

He found himself staring at the dead German. Was it possible? It seemed so stupidly melodramatic. He pressed his shaking lips together. What else was there, though? Impulsively he crawled over to the German's body and tried to unbutton the man's coat. His fingers felt like sausages. He jerked off his gloves, feeling as if his head were expanding and contracting like a bellows. Fingers trembling, he unbuttoned the German's overcoat and peeled it off him. The German's body seemed to be made of iron.

Now Hackermeyer took off his web belt, unclipped his raincoat and slipped it off, then removed his overcoat with shaking haste. Shivering, he pulled on the German's coat and buttoned it to his neck, buckled on the German's belt. It won't work, he thought. It can't work. Even as he thought it, he slipped the two grenades into the pockets of the coat, then reached for the German's rifle and picked it up. Now he'd wait until the troops had passed him. Then, he'd stand and move up the slope among them, to to lose them in the woods above. No, don't, he thought. You're crazy. He braced himself to rise.

The helmet! Hackermeyer jerked his head back down and almost fainted from the wave of shocked dizziness. He pulled thirstily at the air. It's all right, he kept telling himself. It's all right, you'll make it. He fumbled at the chin-straps of his helmet and slipped it off. As he put on the German's helmet it occurred to him, inanely, that it looked like a coal scuttle. He fastened the chin-strap, making a faint sound in his throat as he realized that he could be shot for a spy if he were caught. He forced back the rise of numbing dread. It's all right, he thought.

He stiffened as, yards away, the first of the German soldiers passed him. He crouched there woodenly, every pounding impulse of his heart driving spikes of pain into his head, clouding his eyes over with hot darkness. He closed them tightly. You have to stand, he told himself. You'll go up the slope with them. You'll—

His body acted faster than his will. He found himself erect and stumbling from the bushes. Glancing around nervously, he saw that no one had noticed. It was fortunate that he was on a slope. The men behind him, who might have observed his sudden appearance in a level area, were too occupied with their climbing to notice him here.

Each breath shaking in his lungs, Hackermeyer moved up the slope in the midst of the German soldiers. How far would he have to go to reach the squad? What would he do if any of the Germans spoke to him? How was he going to separate himself from them? Questions jammed his mind. He tried to ignore them and concentrate on the present moment. He felt dazed and numb, as if it were all a dream. What was he supposed to do when he reached the woods above? Even if he lost the Germans, how would he know in which direction to go? He shuddered and kept on climbing. There was no stopping now.

He began to pass dead American soldiers. Twisted into frozen postures, they littered the slope. Some of them were minus limbs, one was without a head. All were torn and raked, their insides exposed, their veins and arteries hanging bluely, their bone ends white and splintered, poking out through flesh, their blood turning purple on the muddy ground beneath them.

Hackermeyer clenched his teeth and moved among them dazedly, feeling as if he were going to topple over any moment. Bodies seemed to be everywhere. The hillside had been ripped apart methodically. Evenly spaced across it were shell holes and a debris of dirt, stone, vegetation, and equipment. The Germans must have had the entire slope zeroed in yard by yard. He wondered if any of the squad were left alive. Maybe they were all dead. Maybe he was the only American left alive in the entire forest. The idea shook him.

Suddenly he stopped and gaped down at one of the soldiers. It was Lazzo and his eyes were open, staring up at Hackermeyer with a bright, pain-sharpened intentness. Hackermeyer felt his stomach muscles tightening. Lazzo had both hands pressed against his chest. Blood was slowly pumping out between his gloved fingers.

"Will you . . . ?" said Lazzo in a hoarse, dry whisper.

Hackermeyer shuddered and glanced around. Other German soldiers were looking at the American dead too, some of them rifling their pockets. To his right, he saw two Germans talking together. One of them threw back his head and laughed. Hastily he turned to Lazzo and stared down at him. For no reason, he noticed how thick and black Lazzo's eyebrows were, the way they grew together.

"Water . . ." Lazzo whispered.

Automatically, Hackermeyer reached around for his canteen, then realized that he'd left it in the bushes. He twitched as, below, a voice yelled something angrily in German. Hackermeyer lurched away from Lazzo, heart pounding, head athrob. Any moment now a bullet would be fired into his back. He climbed a few feet, then glanced across his shoulder involuntarily. He saw, below, a German officer waving his arms. He wasn't looking at Hackermeyer. He must have been telling some other soldiers to leave the dead Americans alone and move on. Hackermeyer kept ascending the slope, almost blindly now, his head pulsing, dark spots dancing before his eyes. He shouldn't have left Lazzo like that. Yet what else could he have done? He wondered if Lazzo had recognized him in the German uniform. It would be awful if Lazzo had recognized him.

He started as a shot rang out behind him. Twisting around, he saw the German officer standing over Lazzo, a smoke-curling Luger in his hand. Something roiled stabbingly in Hackermeyer's stomach. For a moment, he thought he was going to whirl and fire on the German officer. Then, with a shock, he realized that he couldn't do it even if he were willing to die because he didn't know how to operate the German rifle. He swallowed with a clicking noise and moved on heavily. Lazzo couldn't have known him. How could he have recognized him in a German coat and helmet?

A minute later, he clambered across the top of the slope and moved into the woods. He walked steadily and without thought, weaving in and out among the trees, through patches of dark shadow and grayish daylight. Suddenly he became conscious of his leggings and mud-splotched shoes. Even though the coat hung below his calves, someone might notice that he wasn't wearing black boots. Trying to breathe normally, Hackermeyer kept on walking, barely conscious of his feet on the ground, drifting aimlessly among the trees as though without intent or destination. He kept waiting for the Germans to shoot him.

Now, slowly, he began to move to his right, crossing the paths of several German soldiers. Once, he walked directly in front of one, expecting to be noticed for his lack of boots and shot. The German said nothing and Hackermeyer kept on moving until he was alone in the forest. He quickened his footsteps, hoping that he was headed in the right direction. He must be. The Germans had to be going toward the American lines. All he had to do was move in the same direction.

It was very still around him. All he heard besides the thud and suck of his shoes was the moan of the wind high overhead, the stirring of the trees, the drip of rain-soaked foliage. He started walking faster, then slowed down, trembling, remembering that the woods were still booby-trapped. Wearing part of a German uniform did not immunize him against that danger. Swallowing with effort, he lowered his gaze and moved on warily. After all this, it would be hideous to be killed by a booby trap.

To his left, a counterpoint of rifle and machine-gun fire shattered the silence. The Germans must have run into resistance. He hesitated, wondering what to do. If he kept on going dressed like this, he might be fired on by American soldiers. He grimaced, a weight of indecision on him. Then, glancing around nervously, he started forward again. He couldn't stay here either, or the Germans would catch up. If he was fired on, he'd yell that he was an American soldier, that was all. Except—the thought came crushingly—the first shots might kill him. He licked his drying lips and kept on moving. Uncle George was right, he thought distractedly; I don't know what I'm doing.

When he saw the carbine lying on the ground, his immediate thought was—*Cooley's dead*. Breath held, he looked around until he saw the body, half-obscured by bushes. Slowly, legs vibrating, he walked over to the body and looked down at it. He began to tremble and thought that he was going to fall. It was a sergeant, but it wasn't Cooley.

Impulsively, Hackermeyer took off the German belt, overcoat, and helmet and put on the American's helmet, twitching at the warmth of it. He tried not to look down at the dead man, who had no right leg, only a stump of hashlike meat. Hackermeyer realized that he wouldn't be able to remove the man's blood-spattered coat and, grabbing the carbine, he started off.

Suddenly, he remembered the grenades and, turning back, slid them from the German overcoat pocket and put them in the pockets of his field jacket. He shivered. Already he was cold. He couldn't go very long without an overcoat. Hastily he checked the carbine, fumbling with the clip. It slipped out finally and he looked inside. It was empty. Hissing, he squatted by the body of the sergeant until he located a full clip. Just before he straightened up, he covered the dead man's face with the German overcoat.

The gunfire was slackening now, punctuated more by mortar explosions. Hackermeyer moved at a wary crouch through the dim, shadowy woods, trying to watch out for Germans and booby traps at the same time. Ahead, he saw an open area. He'd better skirt that.

Suddenly he froze, hearing a mumble of voices speaking in German. Holding his breath, he edged forward, eased behind a tree, and, after closing his eyes hard for a moment, peeked into the clearing.

In a hollow below, he saw a German mortar team. He watched them dropping shells endlessly into the tube, heard the sharp bang, the upward rush, then, ahead, the flat crumping of explosions. He saw the German noncom listening to a field telephone and passing orders to his crew who made adjustments on the inclination of the tubes.

The grenade was in Hackermeyer's hand before he realized what he was doing. His head felt numb; everything seemed unreal. Heartbeat racing, he unpeeled the yellow tape and jerked the pin free. After a moment, he let the arm pop away and took a deep breath, then lobbed the grenade down at the Germans.

It landed right beside the noncom and rolled against the mortar base. Hackermeyer fell to the ground as it exploded. He waited several seconds, then pushed up waveringly to one knee, the carbine readied. His eyes came into focus. Below, the Germans sprawled motionless on the ground, their weapon lying on its side yards away from them. Got 'em! the voice exulted in his mind.

A shot rang out to his left, the bullet whistled past his ear. Dropping to the ground, Hackermeyer looked in that direction and saw the muzzle blasts of rifles in the woods. Hitching the carbine to his shoulder, he pulled the trigger. The automatic firing of it startled him and he tightened his grip on the bucking weapon; he'd had no idea it had been filed. The carbine seemed to empty itself almost immediately. Hackermeyer struggled up dizzily and started running in the direction the mortar team had been firing. Bullets followed him, snapping past as he ran, ricocheting off tree trunks. He saw a fallen tree ahead and, bracing himself, leaped across it. He cried out hoarsely as he failed to land and started skidding down a steep incline, ending on his side with a breathless grunt.

A German soldier stared down at him, open-mouthed. For a moment, the two of them were statues. Then Hackermeyer jerked up the carbine.

"*Ach, Gott!*" cried the German. He flung his rifle down and threw his hands into the air. "*Nein*, don't—*don't*—" he begged hoarsely.

Hackermeyer started to pull the trigger of the carbine, then, with a jolt of stomach-wrenching shock, realized it wasn't loaded. He stared dumbly at the German. There was a cut on the German's left temple and blood was running from it, soaking into his eyebrow, trickling down his cheek in zigzag ribbons and dripping from his chin. He had no helmet on and looked dazed and helpless.

Hackermeyer glanced around. Another German lay dead nearby. This must have been one of their defensive positions. He looked back at the wounded German. Well, they couldn't just stay here like this. He drew in a shaking breath and pointed toward the opposite side of the trench. The German grunted eagerly and nodded. He started clambering up the incline, Hackermeyer behind him.

Machine-gun fire drove them back. The German tumbled to the bottom of the trench. Hackermeyer stared at him a moment, then yelled, "Hey!" The machine-gun fire drowned him out. He waited for it to stop.

"Hey!" he shouted then. "I'm American!"

"Sure you are, Kraut," said a voice.

"I am!" yelled Hackermeyer. "I'm in the second squad! Sergeant Cooley's!"

There was a pause.

"Come out, then," said the voice suspiciously.

Hackermeyer started up, then hesitated. "You going to shoot?" he asked.

"Come out, damn it!"

"I have a German!" said Hackermeyer. "Don't shoot because you see him!"

"Both of you come out, hands up!" ordered the voice.

"Okay!" Hackermeyer nudged the German and pointed at the

trench wall. The two of them climbed up across the edge. Hack-ermeyer pushed aside the carbine and stood, hands raised. Rifle fire started from the German side and he dropped to the ground.

"You better run!" said the voice.

Bracing himself, Hackermeyer jumped up and sprinted weav-ingly toward a clump of trees ahead of him. He was surprised to find the German right beside him. Bullets popped and whistled all around them as they ran. They lunged beneath the cover of the trees and hit the ground together.

Hackermeyer crouched, panting, in the group of American soldiers while the German was searched. One of them took the grenade out of Hackermeyer's field jacket.

"What's your name, boy?" asked a sergeant.

"Hackermeyer."

"Got your dog tag?"

"Yeah." Hackermeyer dug it out from under his T-shirt and the sergeant examined it briefly, then dropped it.

"Where's your overcoat?" he asked.

"I lost it," Hackermeyer answered. He was afraid to tell the sergeant what had really happened. He was sure the sergeant would never believe it. "Where's the second squad?" he asked.

"Second squad of what?"

Hackermeyer blinked. "Oh, Third Platoon," he said. "Gas-par's the—"

"This is First," the sergeant interrupted. "Third is over that way."

Hackermeyer nodded. The sergeant looked at him a moment longer, then shrugged.

"Well, hell," he said. "Even if you are a Kraut, I don't see what good it'll do you."

"Me?" said Hackermeyer, frowning. "I'm not a Kraut."

"Well . . . don't suppose you are. Go on. Take your prisoner back."

"Yeah." Hackermeyer started up, then crouched again. "I don't have any gun," he said.

"That's your problem, boy," said the sergeant. "We don't have one to spare."

Hackermeyer stared at him. "What about my grenade?" he asked.

"We'll invest it for you," said the sergeant. "Take off."

Hackermeyer shrugged and stood. Instantly, the German stood too. He had been looking frightenedly at the American soldiers and seemed anxious to leave them. Hackermeyer glanced at him irritably, then started off. The German moved right beside him. After they had gone about ten yards, Hackermeyer looked back and saw that the Americans were watching them leave. Did they really think he was a Kraut, for God's sake?

"SERGEANT COOLEY!"

Halfway up the tree-hooded slope, the sergeant stopped walking and turned around. Hackermeyer saw a surprised smile appear on Cooley's lips and, suddenly, he felt an overwhelming urge to laugh. A guttural sound trembled in his throat as he started up the slope beside the German. He barely restrained himself from waving.

Cooley waited, hands fisted on his hips, smiling and nodding. "Well, I'll be damned," he said as Hackermeyer reached him.

"Hi," said Hackermeyer.

Cooley glanced over at the German, then back again. "You do get around, don't you?" he said.

The ends of Hackermeyer's lips twitched upward in a nervous smile. "I got a Krau—a German," he said.

"Caught him yourself?"

Hackermeyer nodded quickly. "Yeah."

"Has he been searched?"

"Yeah, some—some sergeant did."

Cooley smiled at him again and shook his head. "Hackermeyer," he said.

Hackermeyer swallowed. "Yeah?"

Cooley slapped his shoulder. "Glad to see you, son," he said.

Hackermeyer couldn't loosen the stricture in his throat. He looked at Cooley intently, wanting to tell the sergeant how glad he was to be back. Cooley was looking around the slope.

"Why don't you dig in behind that fallen tree over there?" said Cooley, turning back. "You'll be alone, I'm afraid. Fearfeather's already dug in with Guthrie and I'm with Bernie."

Hackermeyer felt an added swell of pleasure.

"Where are they?" he asked. He was pleased to know they were alive.

"The boys are over there," said Cooley, pointing.

Hackermeyer saw, beneath the shadow of a pine tree, two helmeted heads just above the ground surface. Good old Fearfeather, he thought. Good old Guthrie. How marvelous that they were still alive.

He turned back as Cooley patted his arm. "Better get to it, son," Cooley told him.

"How come we're—digging in here?" Hackermeyer asked. He felt as if he wanted to talk and talk with Cooley.

"We're expecting an attack," said Cooley. "We don't know when it's coming but we're sure it will. You better get your gear."

Hackermeyer shivered. "Oh," he said. "Well—" He stared blankly at the sergeant.

"What's wrong?"

"I—I—I don't have any," said Hackermeyer. "I mean—"

"Nothing?"

Hackermeyer swallowed hard. "Well," he said, "I had to—see, I had to leave it." He felt his stomach churning. "See, I was—"

"Okay, okay." Cooley patted his arm. "Don't get rattled. It happens to the best of them. I'll scrape up something for you. You can use Lippincott's M1."

Hackermeyer's mouth opened. "Oh," he said faintly. "Is—is he—?"

"No, just wounded. Come on, we'd better get you his rifle now. You'll be needing it. The rest, I'll get later." Cooley gestured once and the German nodded.

They started up the slope, the German ahead of them. Everywhere Hackermeyer looked, men were digging in.

"Expecting an attack, hanh?" he said.

"It'll come," said Cooley. "Tonight. Tomorrow morning."

Hackermeyer nodded, conscious of a mounting disappointment. He'd gone through so much. Yet nothing was changed, nothing was improved.

"The Kraut came with you even though you didn't have a gun?" asked Cooley.

Hackermeyer cleared his throat. "Yeah," he said. "He was— glad to come." He could feel the exhilaration fading rapidly now. It was like a light going dim.

"Where you been?" asked Cooley.

"Oh, I—fell down that hill," Hackermeyer answered. He exhaled tiredly. "What happened anyway?" he asked.

"The bastards had tanks down there," said Cooley.

"Why didn't we see them?"

"Camouflage."

"Oh." Hackermeyer nodded and looked around. Another lull before another storm. . . . The impression struck him forcibly. No matter how much he'd survived, he'd have to face a lot more.

"Where'd you get the Kraut?" asked Cooley.

"Some—trench."

"Wasn't he armed?"

"Yeah, but—" Hackermeyer shrugged. "He threw it away." He felt suddenly envious of the German. The German had survived the war permanently now.

"Threw it away," echoed Cooley, then grunted with amusement. "You're just made of luck, aren't you?"

Hackermeyer frowned. Sure, luck, he thought. Out of the frying pan into the fire.

"So what happened after you fell down that slope?" asked Cooley.

"I came back up." It occurred to him that Cooley might ask him if he'd seen Lazzo. The thought chilled him. He didn't want Cooley or anyone to know about that.

"Have any trouble finding us?" asked Cooley.

"No." He didn't feel like talking now. The old depression was rushing back on him and he wanted to be alone. There was no point in seeking pleasure. It always backfired on you.

Cooley stopped just beyond the peak of the slope. "Dave," he said.

Hackermeyer blinked and looked around. Under a nearby tree, he saw Lippincott sitting, helmetless, his head slumped forward on his chest. Wrapped in clumsy turns around his left arm was a blood-soaked bandage. Hackermeyer stared at him broodingly. Suddenly he realized how many of the original squad were gone: Wendt, Riley, Foley, Goldmeyer, Linstrom, Lazzo, now Lippincott. Soon they'd all be gone. Hackermeyer felt a sudden urge to curse. All of it to take some lousy little town. And they hadn't even gotten near it yet.

"Dave." Cooley was squatting down in front of Lippincott now. He patted Lippincott's cheek and the corporal's head twitched up. His eyes looked very dark in the bloodless pallor of his face.

"Time to go back," said Cooley.

"No," muttered Lippincott.

Cooley took hold of Lippincott's right arm. "Come on, Dave, let's go."

"Not leaving."

"Well, you're no damn good to us this way," said Cooley, smiling.

Lippincott looked stubborn. "Not hurt that bad," he said.

"Oh, horse shit," said Cooley mildly. "You can't even stand up."

"I can."

"What are you bitching about?" asked Cooley. "That's a million-dollar wound, buddy."

"You can't—" Lippincott's teeth grated together and he shut his eyes. "You can't get by with only four—"

"Five," said Cooley, interrupting. "Hackermeyer's back." He helped Lippincott to his feet. "See Hackermeyer?" he said to Lippincott. "We don't need you anymore. I'll take you to the aid station."

"No."

Cooley picked up Lippincott's M1 and handed it to Hackermeyer.

"Cooley, damn it—" Lippincott's voice broke. He sobbed with pain.

"Shut up, Dave," said Cooley. "You're going back."

"Going to—"

"Knock it off," said Cooley. "That ain't a splinter in your arm, it's a slug." He glanced at Hackermeyer. "Go dig in, son," he said. "You have your entrenching tool?"

"No."

Cooley turned to Lippincott. "Where's your shovel, Dave?"

Lippincott blinked dizzily and looked around. "I—I don't know," he said thickly. "It must be—"

"All right, skip it." Cooley looked back at Hackermeyer. "Get Bernie's or mine," he said. "We're just to the right of where I told you to dig in. Don't forget to camouflage the hole. I'll bring you a coat and some gear soon as I can."

Hackermeyer nodded once and turned away. As he started across the ridge, he looked across his shoulder and saw that Lippincott was still arguing. The German stood nearby, head lowered, as if trying to be as unobtrusive as he could. Hackermeyer turned his head, scowling. The German annoyed him. He seemed so grateful to be a prisoner. It was better to think of Germans as faceless enemies; not as individuals who spoke and hurt and were afraid. Hackermeyer's cheeks puffed as he blew out dispirited breath. He shivered, sneezed. Oh, great! he thought. Now his cold would really get bad.

"Hey there, Hackermeyer."

He stopped and looked to his left. He hadn't noticed that he was passing by the foxhole Guthrie and Fearfeather shared.

"Come here," said Fearfeather.

Hackermeyer walked under the tree and looked down at them. Fearfeather's face was smeared with mud but he appeared unhurt. Guthrie looked tired and glum. There was no sign of drollery in his eyes.

"Where on earth have you been?" asked Fearfeather.

Hackermeyer gestured vaguely toward the German lines.

"Not hurt, are you?" asked Fearfeather.

"No."

"Good," said Fearfeather. His smile disappeared. "But where's your overcoat?" he asked. "Your raincoat?"

"I—lost them." Hackermeyer realized suddenly how thirsty he was. "Could I—" he began.

"Sir?"

"You got enough—water to—"

"Of course," said Fearfeather. In a moment he handed up his canteen. Hackermeyer unscrewed the cap and took a sip of the cold, chlorinated water.

"You see Lazzo by any chance?" asked Guthrie.

Hackermeyer coughed as some water entered his windpipe. He handed back the canteen. "No," he said. He didn't return Guthrie's look.

Guthrie's face tightened. "He's still back there then," he said. He stared toward the German lines. "I tried to get him up," he murmured.

"You did what you could, Guthrie," Fearfeather assured him. "You need have no regrets on that score."

"Sure." Guthrie turned away.

Fearfeather looked at Hackermeyer and shook his head solemnly. Then he frowned. "Hackermeyer, I'm going to give you my raincoat," he said.

Hackermeyer stared at him. As Fearfeather began opening the buckles on his raincoat, he said hurriedly, "You don't have to—"

"Nonsense," interrupted Fearfeather. "Why on earth should I have an overcoat *and* a raincoat and you have nothing? We weren't put on earth for that kind of discrimination." He peeled off the raincoat with grunting effort and handed it up to Hackermeyer. "It's pretty muddy, I'm afraid," he said. "And it's no overcoat, Lord knows. But maybe it will help to take off some of the chill."

Hackermeyer stared at him, holding the raincoat in his hands. He didn't know what to say. He cleared his throat nervously. "Thanks," he muttered. It seemed to come out accidentally.

"You're more than welcome, Hackermeyer," said Fearfeather. "I only wish I had some whiskey I could offer you. That would really take off the chill."

"Yeah." Hackermeyer nodded, then looked around. "Well, I—better dig my hole," he said.

"What are you going to dig it with?" asked Fearfeather.

"I'm supposed to—"

"Here, we're finished," said Fearfeather. "Take my spade. And, here, I think you'll need a pick for the roots; they're nasty. That's all right, isn't it, Guthrie?"

Guthrie didn't answer.

"I'll bring them back," said Hackermeyer, turning away. He couldn't bring himself to say thank you a second time. He trudged over to the fallen tree and leaned the M1 against it. As he donned the raincoat, he looked around. It was a good spot Cooley had given him, he saw. The tree would act as a barricade between him and the German bullets. He wouldn't have to dig as deep either.

With a sigh, he started cutting into the ground. Just below the leaf-clotted surface, the ground oozed with mud. Hackermeyer started breathing through his mouth. He hadn't realized how tired he was. He groaned softly, visualizing the knotted tangle of roots he'd uncover shortly. If only he could lie down and take a nap. His head began to throb. His body still ached from the long, scraping fall down the slope. For a moment, he wondered if he were hurt enough to go to the aid station. He grunted. Why bother? He was doomed anyway. He might as well stay.

"Hackermeyer?"

He looked up, blinking. The figure wavered darkly before his eyes.

"Let me help you get established here," said Fearfeather.

Hackermeyer sniffled, then spat out watery phlegm. "That's all right," he muttered.

"Nonsense, Hackermeyer. I have nothing else to do. Let me help you. Lord knows you look as if you could use a little assistance right now."

Hackermeyer was too tired to argue. If Fearfeather wanted to sweat, let him.

They worked in silence for a while, Fearfeather chopping energetically at the gnarled roots.

"I expect the sergeant—told you that—soon as we're—established here—the forward units are—pulling back," Fearfeather said as he chopped. "They foresee a—general attack by the—Germans."

Hackermeyer grunted.

"Oh, those Germans," said Fearfeather. "They're a Godless—fanatical people. Why on earth they—don't surrender—I surely don't know. My Lord, the—writing is surely—on the wall for them. Yet they go on—battling like—Lord knows what all."

He straightened up and sucked at the air.

"You remember that pillbox we were in?" he asked.

"Yeah."

"Well, by the time we passed it, coming back from that slope," said Fearfeather, "some of those crazy Germans had reoccupied it and were firing at us from inside."

Hackermeyer grunted again.

"Oh, well." Fearfeather bent over to chop again. "It's always been that way, I guess. One crusade—after another. The Godless versus the—God-fearing. Guess the—Germans just don't—know any better."

"Yeah." Hackermeyer kept digging slowly. He tried not to think about how indebted he'd become to Fearfeather.

When the hole was deep enough, Fearfeather helped camouflage it. Then he walked several yards up the slope to examine the effect with one eye shut. "Yes, I think that will do," he said. Returning, he laid a dead-leafed twig across a corner of the hole. "There," he said. He smiled at Hackermeyer.

Hackermeyer braced himself. "Thanks," he said stiffly.

"You're entirely welcome," said Fearfeather. He picked up the spade and pick. "Well, I guess I'll be getting back to the foxhole," he said. "If you need anything, just let me know, hear?"

Hackermeyer nodded. He was surprised and annoyed to find that Fearfeather's departure bothered him. He turned away and grabbed the M1. He wanted to be alone. He sank down and leaned the rifle against the foxhole wall. Christ, it was slimy in there. He spit at the wall, then sat staring at it. Got to sleep, he thought. He closed his eyes. Almost immediately they sprang open. Well, that was great, just great. He was exhausted and he couldn't sleep. That was all he needed.

He inhaled the fetid air inside the hole. God, but he felt miserable. Things seemed worse now than they'd ever been. What was wrong? He couldn't have combat fatigue already, could he? He hadn't even been with the squad a week yet.

The realization startled him. Not even a week? How could so much happen in such a short time? It seemed as if more things had gone on these past six days than had occurred in his entire life. He had been plunged into a nightmare of events; been exposed to more people than he'd ever known before. And they irritated him, all of them. Fearfeather with his lousy generosity— the raincoat, the water, the spade, the help in digging. Foley with his lousy offer to have his girlfriend write. Cooley's lousy winking, calling him Hack, patting him on the shoulder, smiling at him, telling him he was made of luck, telling him he'd get him another overcoat, giving him this good spot behind the tree. Even Guthrie had told him about taping down the grenade arms. Even Wendt had given him chlorine tablets.

Why the hell didn't they leave him alone?

Hackermeyer twisted uncomfortably. There was a stub of root gouging at his back. He turned himself with a muffled curse and glared at the root. He kicked it. Lousy, stupid root! And that prisoner, damn him. Nodding and fawning and—screw him! He was glad he'd killed those other Germans. How many had there been? Six. Good. Good!

Hackermeyer shuddered. He tried to close his eyes but couldn't. Six. He'd killed six men. Six of them. Jesus God, six! He kicked at the foxhole wall. So what? It was his job, wasn't it? Didn't Cooley say so? The hell with Cooley! The hell with all of them! Why the hell couldn't he sleep, Goddamn it!

Hackermeyer jolted up with a hiss and drove his fist against the wall of the foxhole. Die! screamed his mind. He sat there shivering, whimpering at the pain in his hand and wrist, feeling his jawbone quiver. Something was festering inside him. His

brain was in a turmoil. Dreads and furies tumbled over one another. Every thought seemed covered with a sticky web of anxiety. If only he knew what was wrong. Yet he didn't want to know.
Something huge and dark was looming all around him, waiting
to destroy him. He wanted to identify it but was afraid to try.
He felt, somehow, as if he were a prisoner being offered release
after long, unquestioned detention. The dark cell's limited con-
finement was, now, unendurable. Still, it represented comfort of
a sort; adjustment.

Outside lay only the relentless terrors of complexity.

THIRD ASSAULT

"EVERYBODY UP."

Somewhere in the clinging darkness, Hackermeyer heard a voice and faltered up from sleep.

"They're coming. Everybody up. Get ready."

Hackermeyer swallowed watery mucus and woke with an explosive cough, the rifle barrel slipping from his shoulder. He clutched at it with deadened fingers, then looked around torpidly. He felt a moist tickling creep into his nostrils and behind his eyes. His face contorted. Suddenly, he sneezed.

"Hack."

He looked up. Cooley was leaning across the tree trunk. Hackermeyer couldn't make out Cooley's features in the gloom.

"Get ready, son. They're coming."

Hackermeyer sneezed again and Cooley vanished. With slow, constrained movements, Hackermeyer drew his crumpled handkerchief from the raincoat pocket and blew his nose. He yawned widely, shuddered, still yawning, then shuddered again, rubbing at his eyes with the cold, scratchy tips of his glove fingers. Cautiously, he wriggled his toes. He could barely feel them.

Easing off the gloves, he undid his leggings and untied the lace of his left shoe. The lace on his right was knotted. He clamped his teeth together, trying to undo it. This would be just like it, he thought: to be sitting in his foxhole trying to untie a shoelace when the Germans attacked. His fingers, chilled and wooden, fumbled with the hard knot. Suddenly, with a gasping inhalation, he worked his fingers underneath the lace and jerked at it until it broke. Fingers sore, he tugged off both shoes and rubbed at his feet until they ached and tingled. Why did he bother? he wondered. Why didn't he just get trench foot and be done with it?

Pulling on his shoes, he retied the laces. On the eighth attempt, shaking with fury, he managed to knot the broken lace ends. He pushed up with a groan and stretched his muscles as he looked around. Except for a tinge of grayness in the sky, it was still night as far as he could tell. All around, he heard the sound of men preparing themselves: shuffling, clicking, rattling noises, the sporadic murmur of voices. Hackermeyer sucked at the cold, damp air. He wondered if it was going to rain again. It wouldn't surprise him.

He clambered from the hole and relieved the burning pressure in his kidneys. This would be even more like it: the attack coming while he was relieving himself. He contracted muscles and finished as quickly as he could, then lowered himself into the hole again. God, it was cold. There was a chilled emptiness in his stomach. A cup of hot coffee would taste good. He stretched again, yawning and shivering. Where were the Germans? Who had seen them coming? He began to wonder if he'd dreamed the entire thing.

"Everybody up? Grab yourself something to eat. Take a crap. Have a smoke. Do whatever you have to, now. They're on their way."

Hackermeyer looked around, flesh prickling. He couldn't see Cooley but the sergeant's voice certainly wasn't dreamlike. The Germans were coming all right. Just as Cooley had said they would. Hackermeyer swallowed and picked up the M1. It was loaded. A good thing it had belonged to Lippincott. At least he wouldn't have to worry about its being dirty. He set it down and peered across the tree trunk. He couldn't see more than ten feet down the slope. If the Germans were to attack now . . .

What time was it? He drew back his sleeve end. *Two-fifteen?* He looked at the watch incredulously. It must be later than that! He held the watch to his ear.

"Oh, for—"

He dropped his arm in disgust. A swell time for that to happen; the first time since basic training he'd forgotten to wind it. He blew out heavy breath and reached into his raincoat pocket for the box of K ration. Taking out some wrapped crackers, he tore open the paper, looking around. It was getting lighter now. At least the Germans weren't going to attack in the dark.

Hackermeyer made a face. The cracker tasted like wood. He spit it out and reached for the bottom of the hole. Pulling up two loaded bandoliers, he began slipping out the cartridge clips and propping them along the front edge of the foxhole. As he did, he took a sip of water from his new canteen. He'd certainly be in trouble if Cooley hadn't gotten him all this gear last night.

"Hackermeyer."

He turned around.

"Here." Schumacher handed him three small boxes and departed. Opening them, Hackermeyer set the grenades to the right of the cartridge clips. Should he tape down the arms? He considered it as he dropped the boxes and pressed them flat with his shoes. No, there wasn't any point to it. It wasn't likely he'd be carrying the grenades anywhere.

Hackermeyer shivered fitfully. Maybe today, the thought came. Maybe in less than an hour he'd be dead. The cold void in his stomach seemed to expand. He clenched his teeth. If that was the way it had to be, okay.

The bitter acceptance was of little satisfaction to him. It seemed unfair that he might be killed after everything he'd been through. Like yesterday, for example; had it been only yesterday? Walking among all those Germans. In retrospect, it seemed more like a fantastic dream than reality. Yet he had survived it.

He shook himself free. It was stupid to brood. He had to stay alert, it was his only chance. Hackermeyer scowled. Why hadn't he asked Schumacher for the time? He'd bet Schumacher never forgot to wind his watch.

He turned around to see if he could make out any of the others. In that direction were Fearfeather and Guthrie. Over there were Cooley and Schumacher. Five of them left. Lippincott gone. Riley and Wendt gone. Lindstrom and Foley and Lazzo and Goldmeyer all dead. Hackermeyer felt a sudden weight on his shoulders as if a mantle of lead had been laid across them. How could he even think of surviving? The percentages were bound to get him. In his case, they were overdue.

He sneezed and blew his nose. Lousy, Goddamn cold. He stared grimly across the tree trunk. Somewhere out there, in the stone-colored dawn, the Germans were readying their attack. How many of them were there? Did they have tanks? Would the slope be shelled before the attack was launched? He felt sure it would. If anything was standard in the combat he'd seen, it was the artillery barrage prior to assault.

Hackermeyer looked up. He had no tree overhead to protect him. Then again, if he had, there would be tree bursts to worry about. Why were most of the foxholes dug beneath trees, then? He shook his head. What difference did it make? It was six of one, half a dozen of the other.

He closed his eyes and tried to blank his mind. He wouldn't let himself think about it. If he died, he died. There wasn't a thing he could do to avoid it, so why bother thinking about it?

Abruptly, Hackermeyer worked the wallet from his back trouser pocket. Opening it, he held it close to his eyes and squinted at the photo of his mother. Was Fearfeather right? Could he, possibly, be right? If death came this morning, would he see his mother? Hackermeyer shut the wallet quickly and put it away. Don't be such a jerk! a voice told him. He looked down the slope with hardened eyes. Just don't be so stupid. Turning, he picked up the M1 and fingered off the safety lock. There; he was ready.

Suddenly it occurred to him that he could avoid it all by pointing the M1 at his head and pulling the trigger. For several moments it seemed the most brilliant idea he'd ever had. He looked at the rifle fixedly. So simple, he thought. With a shudder, he put the rifle down and stared across the tree trunk again. That's what he'd like, he thought. Only after a while did he realize that he was thinking of his father. He pressed his teeth together angrily. Come on, he thought. Come on, damn it, I'm waiting for you.

As if in answer, there was a machine-like grinding in the distance. Hackermeyer stiffened. It sounded like motors. Yet it was so incredibly loud. He looked down the slope, his eyes searching in all directions. The noise was getting louder. What was it? There was enough light to see that there were no tanks or vehicles anywhere in sight.

Someone shouted behind him and he whirled.

"They're using loudspeakers!" Cooley yelled. "Relax! It doesn't mean a thing! They're just trying to scare us!"

Hackermeyer turned back, shivering. Bastards, he thought. It was just like the Germans to pull a trick like that.

Yet knowing it was a trick did not prevent his heart from pumping faster, his hands from twitching. It was as if they were surrounded by tanks; as if there were tanks coming down at them from the sky. The grinding roar of their engines pounded at his ears. It was a terrifying sensation. All that clanking, howling din and not a thing in sight but the gloom-shrouded woods, the iron-gray sky above. Hackermeyer closed his eyes. That made it worse; he opened them quickly. "Bastards." He said it aloud but couldn't hear his voice. It occurred to him then that, if it were deafening here, it must be even worse for the Germans. That made him feel a little better.

He was fingering the cotton into his ears when the bombardment started.

Instantly the air was swollen with the shriek of incoming shells, the fiery blast of their detonations, the crashing roll of trees, the wail and hiss of shrapnel—all above the endless clangor of the unseen tanks. Hackermeyer had a moment's pang about the grenades and cartridge clips he'd stacked exposed. Then he was constricted to the core of brainless rigidity that, alone, could survive these moments.

Shells came in endless waves. The slope jerked and shuddered. Earth was torn apart—soil, roots, rocks, and grass spraying up in dark fountains. Waves of concussion flooded across the ground in turbulent coils. A suffocating pall of smoke began to cover everything like night returning, dry and reeking of ammoniac cordite. For sixteen everlasting minutes the slope was a leaping, choking, deafening inferno.

Then sudden, pressing silence . . . Gray smoke drifting over

Hackermeyer's foxhole . . . Behind him, someone crying out in agony, "Medic! Medic!" Abruptly, Cooley's voice commanding them: "Get ready." Immediately thereafter, the wildfire crackle of machine guns, the barks of rifle fire . . .

Hackermeyer lurched dizzily to his feet and looked across the tree trunk. Below, the smoke-fogged clearing swarmed with Germans shooting their weapons as they ran, while from the bordering woods came a deluge of enfilading fire support. Hackermeyer stared a moment, stupefied. Then, with a gasp, he grabbed his rifle and propped it on the tree.

"Fire!" ordered Cooley.

Hackermeyer began to aim. Abruptly, a mud-gouting trail of machine-gun bullets angled up the slope toward him and he ducked. Bullets ripped across the tree trunk, spraying bark scraps everywhere, then swept on toward Cooley's foxhole. Hackermeyer bobbed up, aimed, and fired.

The German soldier kept on coming. Hackermeyer aimed again, teeth clenched, body frozen. He squeezed the trigger. The German didn't stop. Hackermeyer shuddered and began to aim again. Suddenly the German foundered. Hackermeyer's gaze jumped startledly. The entire line of Germans was crumpling. He watched them fall, saw the geysering stitch of machine-gun bullets pass behind them.

Cooley shouted, "Fire! Fire!"

Hackermeyer slid the M1 barrel to the left and sighted on another gray-blue figure. Something cracked against the tree trunk, spitting flecks of wood into his face. He jerked down, rubbing at his eyes. A grenade exploded on the slope. "Fire!" shouted Cooley. Hackermeyer shoved up again. The first of the Germans were starting up the slope. He could see the pallor of their faces.

"Grenades!" yelled Cooley. "Get 'em!"

Hackermeyer dropped his rifle. Clutching at a grenade, he jerked out the pin and let the arm spring free. He pitched the grenade as hard as he could. It exploded in the air without effect. The Germans kept advancing. Hackermeyer grabbed his rifle, aimed at one of them, and fired.

A braying outcry jerked his lips back as the German staggered, gaped up the slope as if to find the hiding place of his assailant, then dropped into a humpbacked mound. Hackermeyer sucked in wheezing breath. He didn't notice the dribble of saliva from his mouth. "Fire!" Cooley ordered. Hackermeyer aimed. The rifle jarred against his flesh. The German soldier stopped but didn't fall. Hackermeyer fired again. The German sprawled across the ground. A trumpeting noise tore up through Hackermeyer's throat.

Cooley kept on yelling. "Fire! Use your weapons! Fire! Fire!"

Hackermeyer singled out another target. Then a spray of dirt across his face plunged him down in time to miss a flooding of machine-gun bullets. He slipped and fell clumsily to his side. "Sonofa—!" His voice was feeble, hoarse. He glared up at the flashing tracers. The moment they were gone, he lunged up, face distended.

"Fire!" Cooley yelled.

"I am!" gasped Hackermeyer. His gaze leaped searchingly around the slope. Still the Germans came. He fired at them indiscriminately. The clip popped out. Before it passed his shoulder, he was clawing for another, knocking three of them into the foxhole. He grabbed a clip and rammed it down into the rifle. The closing bolt pinned the tip of his glove thumb. Savagely, he jerked it free. He aimed, retracting as a bullet snapped past his ear.

"Fire!" Cooley shouted. "Fire, fire, fire!"

With a frenzied gasp, Hackermeyer aimed again and fired. The German kept on running. Hackermeyer whined. He aimed with rigid precision, withholding fire until his stomach seemed to swell. He pulled the trigger. The M1 jolted in his grip; the German fell. Again, the brainless cry wrenched upward in his throat. Something trickled on his cheek. He brushed it off, thinking it was sweat.

He fired off another clip, reloaded, fired the rifle empty; reloaded, fired; reloaded, fired. There was nothing in the world but German soldiers moving at him, the rifle in his hands that made them fall, the endless cries of Cooley ordering him to kill.

Hackermeyer's heart rocked and hammered. His breath spilled out in bolting gasps. His lips began to shake. His features grew distorted as aggression, raw and murderous, flooded out of him. He couldn't miss! Every shot resulted in a fallen enemy. The earth was littered with his prey. There were no comrades on the slope; just him and all his enemies, offering themselves as targets. He sank and sank into a blood-filmed haze. The slope became the landscape of a dream, amorphous, misted over. The bloated figures drifted toward him in an endless horde, falling, executed at his hands, to be replaced by more who, in their turn, fell to silent and submissive death.

The explosion brought him back.

A moment past, there was the slope and the attacking Germans. Now the earth in front of him erupted with a crimson flash. A giant blade of shrapnel hit the fallen tree so hard it shifted toward him. Hackermeyer collapsed into the hole, the rifle banging on his helmet. Half a dozen cartridge clips bounced off his back and shoulders. A typhoon of noise surrounded him as a second shell exploded, then a third. He looked up dazedly and saw birds flying overhead in lunatic zigzags. Another shell went off. A litter of earth cascaded down on him. He spat out slime, his body shaking uncontrollably. He started whimpering, partly from involuntary fear, partly from a residue of excitement. With a rattling whine, he pulled himself erect and looked across the lacerated trunk.

The German assault had stopped. Everywhere he looked, the troops were lying prone. Eyes slitted against the battering whirlwind of sound, Hackermeyer's gaze traversed the clearing. At the border of the distant woods, a staggered line of tanks were firing at the slope. A glint of recollection crossed his mind; this was similar to what had happened on that other slope. The memory was instantly eclipsed by the screaming of a shell, its detonation in the trees behind him. Hackermeyer jerked down reflexively. He heard the hissing scorch of a bazooka being fired. He crouched there stiffly, staring at his rifle, feeling as though his insides were about to rupture.

Suddenly, compelled, he reared up, emptying his rifle blindly down the slope. Pulling down, he squatted, trembling violently. After several minutes, he picked up one of the fallen cartridge clips and shoved it down into the M1. He waited, waited. Then his face turned up.

The shelling had ceased.

"Fire!" Cooley shouted.

Hackermeyer pushed up and scraped the M1 barrel across the tree. He clenched his teeth and started firing. He kept on firing until his barrel scorched the bark . . . until he shook so hard that he could barely aim. He didn't know that he was screaming.

TITANIC SILENCE HUNG across the slope and clearing. Minutes earlier, a spectral snow had begun to cloak the widespread congestion of bodies. There was not a stir of air. The large, pale flakes floated downward in unruffled curtains. Hackermeyer felt them on his neck like the touch of icy fingers. He stood motionless, staring at the scene below.

The Germans were removing their dead and wounded. All across the clearing, shadowy figures of men were moving, soundless and efficient. They examined bodies, carried off the wounded, and administered to those requiring immediate care. Shortly before, at the commencement of the truce, the Americans had carried off their own killed and injured.

It was a situation Hackermeyer could not understand. A little while ago, each side had done its lethal best to decimate the other. Now, the guns and cannons temporarily stilled, each carried off the victims of their contest. To Hackermeyer it was a brutal ambiguity; the condition of war at its most unfathomable. He looked at the Germans with hostile eyes. Why were they doing this? Why had they come with a white flag and, in polite conference, arranged to forestall the war until the battlefield was tidied? He grated his teeth. Bastards, he thought. He'd like to pick them off one by one.

He felt a constricting sensation in his chest and stomach and looked uneasily across his shoulder. Cooley wasn't around. He'd gone to company headquarters taking Guthrie with him. Corporal Schumacher, now the assistant squad-leader, was in his foxhole cleaning his M1. Hackermeyer's gaze shifted. Only Fearfeather watched the spectacle below, his expression one of pained solemnity.

Hackermeyer picked up his rifle and held it in the crook of his right arm. He gazed down steadily at the Germans. The pendulum swing of his heartbeat seemed to mount. He began to swallow mucus, then coughed and spat it away. He felt a throbbing at his temples. With a careless motion, he leaned forward and slid the M1 across the tree trunk. He rested on his elbows for a while.

Then, casually, he aimed at the figure of a medic who was squatting by a wounded soldier. He held the grayish coat back in his sights, his finger easing, by degrees, inside the trigger guard.

Hackermeyer shivered. He closed his eyes and took a deep breath. When he opened his eyes, the German was still there, in the same position. Hackermeyer's finger tensed back slowly on the trigger curve. How easy it would be. He kept the front sight centered on the medic's back, shifting it minutely as the German stirred. The stillness rang in his ears. He felt the frosty brush of snowflakes on his neck.

Hackermeyer pulled the trigger. The hammer snapped against the empty chamber and he felt his heart jolt painfully. Straightening with a deep, uneven breath, he put down the M1 and turned his back on the clearing. He shuddered. How easy it would have been.

Hackermeyer sat down and stared at the foxhole wall. He wondered what had made him aim at the German medic. He wondered if he'd really known that the rifle was unloaded.

He wondered what was happening to him—or if it had, already, happened.

"No," said Cooley.

Hackermeyer glanced up, chewing on a slice of buttered bread. Several yards away, Cooley and Schumacher were looking across the small hollow in which the squad was eating. Hackermeyer turned his head and saw Platoon Sergeant Gaspar coming toward them with three soldiers. Two of them were teenagers.

"Jesus H. Christ," groaned Cooley.

Hackermeyer looked at him. The sergeant's teeth were gritted.

"A nursery they give me," Cooley muttered. "Twenty-five's old age in this man's army. Thirty, you're senile. Me, I'm thirty-eight, I'm ready for a fuggin' wheelchair. Jesus!"

"One of them looks older," said Schumacher.

"They'll put him in another squad," said Cooley, standing. "We're strictly the Boy Scout Brigade." With a weary sigh, he plodded up the slope to meet his replacements.

Guthrie spat out gristle. "Our supporter," he growled. He pushed to his feet and started toward the wash barrels.

"Poor Guthrie," said Fearfeather. "He's still upset about Lazzo. And him always trying to make out as being such a clown."

Hackermeyer grunted. He hadn't thought of that but maybe it was true. He was beginning to get the impression that everybody masked their real feelings. Mostly with bravado or profanity or a combination of the two like with Wadley; Wendt; Linstrom. Maybe with Guthrie it was done with screwball humor. Hackermeyer nodded slightly to himself, then, suddenly, frowned. And with what did he hide his own feelings?

He stood up as if to avoid the question.

"See you, Hackermeyer," said Fearfeather.

"Yeah."

Hackermeyer looked down at his feet as he walked toward the wash barrels. The new overshoes felt strange and cumbersome. But, at least, his feet were almost warm for a change.

Guthrie passed him without a word, heading for the slope. Hackermeyer wondered how Guthrie would react if told about Lazzo. Would it make him feel better or worse? Hackermeyer put it from his mind. What difference did it make? He had no intention of telling Guthrie. He dumped his foodless mess kit and empty cup into the barrel of steaming, soapy water. In the distance, the rumble of explosions grew momentarily louder, then diminished again. It had been going on continuously since midafternoon.

As Hackermeyer started back toward the slope, he looked at the two teenage replacements who were standing in the chow line. The first one was gaunt, his face and neck thickly freckled, steel-rimmed glasses perched on his oversize nose. The second was broadly tall and close to handsome. He had removed his helmet, liner, and cap and was scratching at his scalp through curly, brown hair. There was a threadlike, ivory-colored scar on his chin.

Hackermeyer walked across the peak of the ridge and started down the slope. The sky was darkening. He glanced at his watch and saw that it was after five o'clock. How long were they going to stay here? he wondered. Was a second attack expected? If it was, certainly there would be tighter security measures. As far as he could tell, the Germans had been thrown back very hard. It was unlikely they were in any condition to repeat their attempt. In that case, however, why weren't they taking advantage of the Germans' disunion and moving in? Well, the hell with it. Hackermeyer jumped into his foxhole. It wasn't his responsibility. All he had to do was kill Germans. Cooley had said so.

He looked across the tree trunk at the slope. Strange. Already, the attack seemed ancient history. Time was all distorted in war. This time, a week ago, he'd been—what? It was difficult to recall. Oh, yes; sitting in the rain with Wendt and wondering what combat was going to be like. Now he was here and the period of transition had been so crowded with alien faces and experiences that it was impossible to recollect. It was startling how narrow his life had been before he'd entered the army. He'd never really been aware of it until now. Since he'd been drafted and, more particularly, since he'd joined the squad, he'd seen more different kinds of men and boys than he'd dreamed existed. It was odd to think about. The more he did, the more restricted his former life seemed to have been.

Hackermeyer gazed around the shadowy clearing. There was not a single body left. He felt the sensation he'd had looking through the pillbox slit that day and seeing that other slope empty after being positive that it was covered with dead soldiers. The clearing of this area seemed just as magical, even though he'd watched it being done. It was as if no Germans at all had died that morning.

How many did I kill? he wondered. It was odd, but he couldn't remember a single one. There might have been dozens or there might have been—none? Hackermeyer frowned. No, that was impossible. He was certain there had been a lot of them. Only there seemed no way of recalling them. It was like trying to remember the particulars of a muddled dream. Already the details of the attack had faded so much he felt inclined to believe that it had never really taken place. Yet he knew it had. He knew that he had stood in this very spot shooting Germans. Hadn't he? The memory of it was so clouded that he felt displaced and tenuous; as though it had been some other person standing here during the assault. Someone different; estranged.

"Hackermeyer?"

He turned quickly and saw Schumacher with a letter in his hand. "For you," said Schumacher, tossing it down.

They both started as a bullet whistled overhead, followed, in a moment, by the distant crack of a rifle. Hackermeyer jerked around and looked across the clearing. There were no Germans in sight.

"Damn sniper," said Schumacher. He turned away with a disgusted hiss.

Hackermeyer leaned against the foxhole wall, looking at the envelope. It was almost too dark to see it. He made out the return address as that of Cousin Clara. What was she writing for? The allotment probably. She never gave up. Hackermeyer removed a glove and tore open the envelope. He squinted at the small, crabbed writing.

Everett, the letter began, *your father has died.*

A WHILE BEFORE, he'd left the foxhole to relieve himself. Then, instead of returning to the hole, he'd sat down on the fallen tree. Now he was staring into the darkness with sightless eyes, annoyed that he couldn't sleep. He tried to make himself believe he didn't care, but he knew it wasn't so. His body ached with weariness. Even so, he wished they were going into combat now.

He felt a need to be absorbed in fast, mechanical activity.

He shifted on the tree trunk with an irritable moan. *It's the letter*, he thought. He made a brief attempt to pretend that the thought hadn't occurred. Then he pounced on it angrily. Why should the letter keep him awake? It didn't mean a thing to him that his father was dead.

He died this morning in the hospital with pneumonia. We are going to have to stand the costs of the funeral from our own pockets and we think it is only common decency for you to get that allotment sent to us right away. After all, Everett . . .

Hackermeyer shook his head as if to dislodge the words. But they were scored indelibly on his mind. Why should I care? he insisted to himself. As far as he was concerned, his father had been dead for years. This letter only made it official. Hadn't he, already, told others that his father was dead? Why should it disturb him, then? He bit his teeth together until his jaws began to ache. Bastard, he thought. Even dead, his father was making trouble for him.

Hackermeyer pushed up with a restless murmur and looked around. He felt like taking a long walk. He hissed in scornful amusement. Sure, great place for walking, he thought. Abruptly, he wondered if any patrols were being run that night. Maybe he could go on one. Maybe—

His breath was cut off as a startled cry billowed in the night. He jerked around and tried to see up the slope. Somewhere in the darkness above, a man was groaning. The sound seemed very close.

Hackermeyer heard a sound of overshoes moving in the mud.

"What's wrong?" asked Cooley's voice.

"I—I fell," replied the groaning man.

"Yeah, right on top of me," said someone. It sounded like Guthrie.

"I'm sorry. I—" The man began to whimper in pain. "Ooh, ooh, my leg," he said.

"Who is that? Horton?" Cooley asked.

"Yes," said Horton tensely. He started to whine.

"What did you do, break your leg?" Cooley sounded flabbergasted.

"I—I think so," answered Horton.

"I don't believe it," said Cooley.

Minutes later, stretcher bearers carried Horton off into the night.

"What's up, Cooley?" someone asked.

Cooley made a weak, incredulous sound. "One of my replacements," he said, almost dazedly, "fell in a foxhole. Broke his leg."

Hackermeyer thought, at first, the other man was sobbing. Then he realized that the noise he heard was one of stifled hilarity.

"Don't tell me," squeaked the man, "it was the old guy."

"Oh, shut your face," said Cooley gloomily.

The man began to splutter.

"Will you shut up?" said Cooley.

"I can't," gasped the man. "The one guy you g-get that ain't a-a-a—" He exploded into hysterical cackling.

"Quiet, down there!" ordered a voice.

The man, apparently, covered his mouth. Hackermeyer heard him stumbling off into the darkness, snorting apoplectically. "F-fell in a f-f-fuggin' foxhole!" chirruped the man.

Hackermeyer turned and looked toward the clearing again. He wondered what it would be like to have a broken leg and be carried away from the war. He couldn't imagine. He knew that such an escape would never be his. He wouldn't get away from the war until it destroyed him.

DECEMBER 16, 1944

NOW THE OOZING mist had covered everything in sight and the last of the sniper fire had ceased. Hackermeyer sat clumped inside his foxhole, staring upward at the glutinous swirls that looked like thick, coagulating smoke. The sight of it enfeebled him. He could not imagine ever standing up again, much less facing combat. He had an eerie conviction that the squad would never leave the slope but would remain here, passively, until they all were dead. They were, already, two-thirds buried. A few deft shovelfuls of dirt for each of them would finish the interment. He visualized the honeycomb of foxholes filled in and covered; the squad, platoon, and company entombed and silent.

He blinked and looked around as if awakening. This God-damn war, he thought. Its pace was so uneven; violent excitement alternating with absolute stagnation. There was no way of adjusting to it. Each phase dominated the mind—electrifying it one moment, stultifying it the next.

Hackermeyer closed his eyes. He pulled in a long, slow breath and let it empty from his lungs. He shifted and tried to sleep. That would be the best solution; to rest, unconscious, through these periods of deadness.

Moments later, he opened his eyes. No use. He couldn't sleep. His mind refused to turn off. It was filled with these alien voices. They asked questions and they answered questions and, only rarely, did the voices seem to be his own. Like the one that had screamed at him during the counterattack. It hadn't been his own voice, he was certain of that. He didn't lose his temper like that.

Hackermeyer groaned and shifted position again. He felt like a loaded bomb, primed and waiting for explosion. It was similar to the feeling he had during artillery barrages. A rigid bracing against shock; a constant tension of readiness. But readiness for what? It was still the same war. Nothing new was going to happen unless it was his death and that didn't matter. Except that, now, it did matter. Incongruously, as life became more and more plaguing to him, less and less did he wish to surrender it.

"Say . . ."

Hackermeyer glanced up quickly. Hovering overhead, as if he floated in the vaporous mist, was the thin, freckled replacement. He was looking down fearfully at Hackermeyer, his brown eyes magnified behind the thick lenses of his glasses.

"Could you . . ." The boy broke off and bit his lower lip.

"What?"

"Well . . ." The replacement pointed shakily. "The—the man I was with," he said. "The sergeant."

Hackermeyer stiffened. "What about him?"

"He's—" The boy shivered. "I think he's dead," he answered.

Hackermeyer gaped at him. The boy's face wavered phantom-like in the mist. *I think he's dead*, his voice repeated in Hackermeyer's mind.

"Could you . . ."

The boy broke off as Hackermeyer shoved to his feet and climbed from the foxhole.

"Where?" Hackermeyer asked.

"Over . . . there." The boy pointed uncertainly, then started moving up the slope. Hackermeyer walked beside him, a tight pain starting in his chest. No, that's impossible, he thought.

"I—guess a sniper got him or—" The replacement cleared his throat nervously. "I'm—I'm Tremont," he said.

"You were with him?"

"Yeah, I—" Tremont stopped walking and looked around worriedly. "I . . . thought it was this way," he said.

"Well, where is he?" demanded Hackermeyer.

"Over here." Fearfeather's solemn voice came from the mist to Hackermeyer's right. He pushed past Tremont brusquely and moved across the muddy incline. He wanted to run; yet, at the same time, he wanted to turn away and flee. Cooley dead? It was inconceivable.

Guthrie and Fearfeather were squatting beside the foxhole. When he saw them, Hackermeyer's breath cut off so sharply that he made a noise like a guttural sob. Legs trembling, he walked up beside Guthrie and dropped heavily to his knees, wincing at the pain. He leaned forward and squinted down into the foxhole. Abruptly he closed his eyes.

"That's not the sergeant," he muttered.

"Oh," said Tremont faintly, "I—thought he was a sergeant."

Hackermeyer clenched his teeth and shuddered. Jerk! he thought. He felt like hitting Tremont. Opening his eyes, he looked into the foxhole again.

Schumacher had been cleaning his rifle when it happened. He was sitting erectly, the trigger assembly in his lap. His eyes were open, looking straight ahead. There was no blood, no visible wound. Schumacher appeared less dead than frozen into a posture of calm alertness. He seemed to be listening to someone, waiting for an opportunity to refute their words with incontestable logic.

"Jesus Christ." It was Guthrie, awed. "He even died neat."

"MOVE YOUR LEGS," said Cooley.

Hackermeyer drew in his legs and Cooley lowered himself into the foxhole.

"You know Schumacher's dead," he said.

Hackermeyer nodded. "Yeah."

"So I need another assistant," Cooley said. "You're it."

Hackermeyer's brain refused to register the words. He stared at Cooley vacantly. Then the words struck home and his mouth slipped open.

"You're the only one I can trust," said Cooley.

Hackermeyer's lips stirred but no sound emerged. He was trying to remember who else was in the squad.

"Well . . . what about—Guthrie?" he managed.

Cooley shook his head. "Can't depend on him," he said. "He knows his job all right but he don't give a damn."

"Well, there's—there's—"

"No, you're it, Hack," Cooley interrupted. "You're the only one I can ask. Don't let me down now."

Hackermeyer swallowed hard. His head was beginning to feel numb.

" 'Kay," he murmured.

Cooley patted his leg, a brief smile flexing back his lips. "That's the stuff," he said. He looked up with a sigh. "If this soup hangs on, we're going on patrol soon," he said. "Keep your gear ready."

Hackermeyer nodded mutely. Cooley looked at him a few moments longer. Then he patted Hackermeyer's leg again and pushed to his feet. "You'll do," he said.

For minutes after Cooley had gone, Hackermeyer stared at the spot where the sergeant had crouched. Assistant squad-leader, he kept thinking. Corporal Hackermeyer, the assistant squad-leader. It had the flavor of a daydream. Corporal Hackermeyer . . . A position of authority second only to Cooley. It was impossible to grasp.

Hackermeyer blew his nose absently. It seemed as if, only yesterday, he'd joined the squad—a private, a replacement, a nothing. Now he was assistant squad-leader. Instinctively, he sought to minimize the promotion by thinking that it had been given to him only because he'd outlived every other possible assistant squad-leader. Even that couldn't dull the edge of wonder. He was in the position Lippincott had been in. He recalled walking across that field with Lippincott, going for blankets and coffee. Would he be taking one of the new replacements across some field for blankets and coffee? He shook his head, incredulous. And he'd be passing out hand grenades. And having talks with Cooley!

"Assistant squad-leader . . ." The words seemed vested with some mysterious significance. He spoke them again and again. Cooley had chosen him—*him*—to help lead the squad. Hackermeyer felt himself swelling with a hungry exultation. Everything faded but the burning awareness of his elevation.

"Wow," he murmured, spellbound. His body tingled as if he had been plugged into some vivifying circuit. "Wow," he said.

ON HIS ELEVENTH birthday, his father had given him a copy of Jules Verne's *Twenty Thousand Leagues Under the Sea*. There had been colored illustrations in it, and the one Hackermeyer remembered best had depicted Captain Nemo conducting an underseas funeral. He recalled the deep blue-green of the water, the figures in their helmets and protective suits.

This moment reminded him of that illustration. Not that the mist was blue-green. It had, though, the apparent density of liquid. As the patrol diamond moved across the clearing, it was as if they were walking on the bottom of a murky sea. The mist drifted slowly across the ground, twining with an aqueous slug-

gishness around trees and bushes. Unconscious of it, Hackermeyer leaned forward slightly as though resisting tidal pressure.

Around him, the six other members of the patrol appeared
and disappeared like shadows. Only Cooley, to his right, remained in sight continuously, and even he looked insubstantial
at times as though seen through shifting layers of water. The
ground itself was not unlike the oozy surface of an ocean bottom,
Hackermeyer imagined. Finally, there was no sound except for
the sucking noises made by overshoes pulling free of glutinous
mud. It was obvious why the Germans had not attempted to
move their tanks across the clearing. Had they tried, the tanks
would still be here, hopelessly bogged.

Hackermeyer frowned and broke his stride. The mist had a
hypnotic effect that made alertness difficult. He tensed himself
against it. He couldn't afford to sink into reveries anymore. He
twisted around, looking in all directions; frowned again. What
in hell could anybody see in this dingy cream cheese anyway?
He was beginning to think that reconnaissance patrols were self-
defeating. The only time they were run was in the dead of night
or in a mist like this—precisely when visibility was nil. Hackermeyer glanced at Cooley guiltily. It wasn't his place to question
orders. His job was to help carry them out.

He stopped walking as a form appeared in front of him. He
raised his M1 automatically, then lowered it, recognizing the man
as a member of the patrol. He glanced toward Cooley, shrinking
back as the sergeant loomed up beside him.

"Woods," whispered Cooley. "Single file."

Hackermeyer nodded, swallowing. Ahead of him, the man
looked back and gestured with his arm. Hackermeyer nodded
again. After several moments, the man moved forward into the
mist and Hackermeyer followed him. Shortly, he became aware
of entering the woods even though the mist obscured the trees
from sight. He glanced back. Cooley followed several yards behind. The sight of him gave Hackermeyer a momentary satisfaction. He realized that he was not at all worried about moving
into German-held territory as long as Cooley was with him.

The satisfaction faded as he grew increasingly conscious of

the sergeant moving behind him. He wondered if he looked all right to Cooley. He hoped he wouldn't make some stupid blunder. Face tight with strained attention, he moved on cautiously. He had to do the right thing. The knowledge was a mounting tension in him. He mustn't let Cooley down.

What was that? He jerked his head aside, certain that he'd seen a flicker of movement. Stopping, the M1 raised, he stared to his left. There was a sound behind him and he whirled. Grimacing, Cooley pushed aside the rifle barrel pointed at him. "What's the matter?" he whispered.

"Thought I saw something," Hackermeyer whispered back.

"We're falling behind," said Cooley.

Hackermeyer started off again, moving with a skittish distraction. He heard Cooley's words repeating in his mind and tried to evaluate their tone. Cooley was angry with him, he decided. There was a tightening in his chest. He clenched his teeth and walked a little faster, trying to catch up with the man ahead. Abruptly, he remembered booby traps and froze in his tracks. Don't stop! he thought. He willed himself on, his legs beginning to shake. Could Cooley see that he was getting rattled?

Now, he saw the man ahead and slowed his pace, looking around nervously. He felt as if he were surrounded by Germans. He must be losing his grip. He'd heard about that happening to soldiers after they'd been in combat too long. But he'd only been in combat for a week, so it couldn't be that. Maybe it was being made assistant squad-leader. Maybe he just wasn't up to it.

Or maybe it was his mind, the thought came, chillingly. He recalled the great dark welling of anxiety he'd experienced just after he'd made his way back to the squad. The intense pleasure he'd felt at being warmly received by Cooley had, almost instantly, withered, leaving him emotionally off-balance. Maybe that lack of balance had never left him. God knew, his feelings were unstable enough lately. Even the pleasure of being made assistant squad-leader was dissipating now. All he could think of was making mistakes in front of Cooley.

Hackermeyer sucked in fitfully at the air. If only he could stop thinking. But his mind seemed to have acquired a direction of its own. Thoughts kept flashing across his consciousness so rapidly that he could barely catch hold of them. Now he was thinking of Foley, recalling how abrupt and curt he'd been to Foley. Remembering that the only regret he'd felt at Foley's death was that Foley's girl wouldn't be able to write him a letter. Now he was thinking of Linstrom. Had he been too harsh with Linstrom? Would Linstrom have survived if he'd been treated nicer? Now it was Fearfeather. Had he been ungrateful to Fearfeather? Indifferent to Lippincott and Guthrie? Uncooperative with Cooley? Guilty of leaving Lazzo to die?

The unexpected gunfire made him drop so rapidly he landed on his left elbow. Eyes pressed shut, teeth clenched, he writhed on the ground, gasping at the fiery pain in his arm.

Someone shouted, "Back! Back!"

Hackermeyer's eyes jerked open. Rolling over, he squinted hard into the mist, his legs retracting as a grenade exploded up ahead. Someone screamed in agony. A man yelled, "Over there!" Hackermeyer caught his breath and tried to see the Germans. The din of gunfire seemed to envelop him.

Cooley's shout burst in his ears.

"To your left, Hack!"

Hackermeyer turned so fast it sent a shock of pain along his neck muscles. He heard the rattling blast of Cooley's carbine just before he saw two German soldiers rushing at them. Jerking up his rifle, he flicked off the safety catch, aimed, and fired. The M1 jarred against his shoulder and the German skidded on the mucky ground, sat down, looking dazed, then slumped back without a sound. The other German reeled against the impact of Cooley's bullets and crashed down on his side. Hackermeyer lay rigid, waiting.

Cooley sprinted over. "Go," he said, then dove to one side, firing his carbine empty. Hackermeyer whirled and saw another German soldier drop his rifle, stagger forward several feet, then fall into a heap, his helmet rolling off.

"Come on, son," said Cooley, pushing up, eyes searching swiftly as he worked another cartridge clip from the holder strapped around his carbine stock. Hackermeyer started to his feet. "Get him!" Cooley ordered, dropping to his knees as a bullet whistled past him.

Hackermeyer spun and saw a German soldier falling to the ground. Flinging up his rifle, he fired twice. The German cried out, then raised unevenly to one knee, a grenade elevated in his right hand. Hackermeyer fired again. The soldier toppled forward.

"Duck!" gasped Cooley. Hackermeyer flopped on his chest as the grenade went off. Shrapnel buzzed across him.

Cooley grabbed his arm and hauled him up. "Go!" he said. They rushed between the mist-veiled trees, bullets snapping past them with the sound of whip-ends cracking. Hackermeyer tried to watch both Cooley and the ground ahead. He winced as a bullet ricocheted off a nearby tree, howling off into the mist.

"Down!" said Cooley, diving forward. Hackermeyer flung himself prone and heard the hissing rip of machine-gun bullets just above him. "Go," said Cooley. Glancing up, Hackermeyer saw the sergeant crawling rapidly across the ground. He started wriggling after Cooley, hissing at the pain each time his elbow struck the earth.

"Go!" snapped Cooley, lurching up into a run. Hackermeyer angled to his feet and started after him. Abruptly, Cooley's form was swallowed by the earth. Hackermeyer's heart leaped wildly, but he kept on running. Then he saw the bank ahead and, tensing, leaped across the edge.

He landed in ankle-deep water, gasping as an icy geyser of it splashed across his face. Off-balance, he staggered drunkenly along the loose-stoned bottom of the stream until he fell.

Cooley hauled him up. "Run," he ordered. They started dashing along the right bank of the stream, overshoes crunching loudly on the stones. Hackermeyer felt the knife-thrust of a stitch beginning in his left side.

Abruptly, Cooley jarred to a halt and fired upward to their left. Hackermeyer's gaze leaped in time to see a German soldier topple off the high bank and crash, face down, into the stream, casting up a gout of water. Then they were running again, the mist like swirling smoke around them.

Hackermeyer would have passed the opening. He almost fell as Cooley jerked him back. Flailing around, he saw the sergeant pointing at the branch of a pine tree sagging down across the bank. Cooley grabbed the end of it and, pulling it aside, revealed a narrow cave mouth.

"In," gasped Cooley, shoving Hackermeyer toward the opening.

For a long time they crouched together in the cold, wet darkness. Hackermeyer rubbed his elbow, sucking at the cold, slightly fetid air of the cave. Several times, darkness welled across his mind and he thought he'd faint. In the distance, the gunfire faded. Finally it stopped.

Cooley muttered, "Christ."

Hackermeyer swallowed. His throat felt raw. "What happened?" he asked.

Cooley coughed a little. "Most likely—ran into a—Kraut patrol," he answered, breathing hard. "A big one."

Hackermeyer nodded. He opened his eyes and looked toward the cave entrance. The tree branch covered most of it.

He turned back as Cooley pushed something against his arm. "Take a slug," Cooley told him.

Hackermeyer reached up and felt a small bottle in Cooley's hand. He took it away and raised it to his lips. A sharply sweet odor curled up his nostrils, making him start. He took a sip and felt the liquid trickle like a thread of fire down his throat. He began coughing and almost dropped the bottle. Cooley grabbed it and patted his back. Hackermeyer could feel a core of hotness expanding in his stomach. He wiped away the tears. "What's that?" he whispered hoarsely.

"Brandy."

Hackermeyer nodded, still laboring for breath. "Good," he gasped.

Cooley grunted in amusement and patted Hackermeyer's back again. Hackermeyer's eyes were almost adjusted to the darkness now. He could just make out Cooley's form beside him. The sergeant was taking a long swallow of the brandy, then lowering the bottle. "Some more?" asked Cooley.

Hackermeyer was about to say no when he thought that it might offend Cooley. "Yeah," he said. He swallowed. "Thanks."

"Kill it," muttered Cooley, passing the bottle.

Hackermeyer didn't know what Cooley meant at first. Then, as he tilted the bottle to his lips, he realized that Cooley meant for him to finish off the brandy. He took a long swallow, gasping as the brandy scorched its way into his stomach. He wiped away the tears. "Wow," he gasped.

"Gone?" asked Cooley.

Hackermeyer turned the bottle upside down above his open mouth. "Gone," he answered gutturally.

"Rest in peace," murmured Cooley.

Hackermeyer sat down slowly, groaning. "We staying here?" he asked.

"For a while," said Cooley. "Too many Krauts around."

Hackermeyer nodded. He wondered what had happened to the rest of the patrol. They might all be dead. So might he if it hadn't been for Cooley, he realized.

Cooley settled himself with a sigh. "Oh, man," he said. Turning his head, he spat. Hackermeyer heard a rustling sound, then smelled the aromatic pungency of Cooley's chewing tobacco. Cooley bit off a chunk.

"Chaw?" he asked.

Hackermeyer sneezed. "No, thanks," he said, feeling for his handkerchief. He blew his nose as softly as he could. "How long you—think we'll be here?" he asked.

"We'll check outside in a while," said Cooley. "See if things have calmed down."

Hackermeyer nodded. He looked around the cramped interior of the cave. The air was wet and heavy on his lungs. It had a faint, nostril-tickling odor he could not identify. The cave must have been some animal's lair at one time, he thought disinterestedly.

Cooley yawned and stretched. "You're from Brooklyn," he said.

"Yeah."

Cooley belched softly. "Folks alive?" he asked.

"No."

"Both dead?"

"Yeah. My—mother died when I was—born."

"Oh. Jesus." Cooley grunted as he stretched out his legs and leaned back on his elbows. "What about your old man?" he asked.

Hackermeyer swallowed. "He just died," he said. "A couple of weeks ago."

"Oh. Jesus, that's too bad," said Cooley.

"Yeah."

"Same kind of thing with me," said Cooley. "My folks was killed in a car wreck when I was four."

"Yeah?" Hackermeyer looked at Cooley in surprise. "Where'd you live?"

"In Taos with my uncle," answered Cooley. "That's where I live now." He grunted wryly. "That is, I'll live there if this damn war ever ends."

"I lived with my uncle too," said Hackermeyer. He was fascinated to learn that he and Cooley had been raised under comparable conditions.

"Oh, yeah?" said Cooley. "Where was that, in Brooklyn?"

Hackermeyer nodded. "Yeah."

"Funny," Cooley said.

"You like your uncle?" asked Hackermeyer.

Cooley was silent and Hackermeyer wondered if he'd said the wrong thing.

"He was all right, I guess," Cooley finally answered. "A little rough at the edges. Not bad, though."

"Oh." Hackermeyer felt disappointed. It would have been more satisfying if Cooley had hated his uncle.

"Didn't get along with your uncle?" Cooley asked.

Hackermeyer twitched in surprise. How did Cooley know that? "Not much," he said.

"Mean?"

"He was a rat," said Hackermeyer.

"A rat, huh?" Cooley sounded amused.

Hackermeyer shuddered. Maybe he shouldn't have said that.

"Well, he was always—drinking," he said. He shivered. What if Cooley liked drinking? "I mean, he was a—he'd been a first mate on different boats and he was—you know, used to bossing guys around so—" He broke off, afraid that Cooley might think he meant that it was bad for one man to be in charge of others. He didn't feel that way about Cooley.

"How come you didn't live with your old man?" Cooley asked him.

Hackermeyer swallowed. He was beginning to feel dizzy and numb; he couldn't understand why. "Well," he said, "I—guess he figured I was—you know, just a baby. My aunt could do—better with me."

"She nice?"

"Yeah, she was all right." Hackermeyer blinked and shook his head a little. "Except she had a boy who died; Buddy. She was always . . . you know—" He couldn't think of the word.

"Mourning him?"

"Yeah." Hackermeyer's nods were wobbly. "You know."

Cooley sighed. "I know," he said.

"You have a son, don't you?" said Hackermeyer.

"I had two," said Cooley.

"Two?"

"One of them was killed on Guadalcanal."

Hackermeyer stared dizzily at the dark figure beside him. He didn't know what to say.

"His name was Jimmy," said Cooley, after a moment. "He was your age."

Is that why you don't like us? The question flared in Hackermeyer's mind. He almost repeated it aloud. He felt as if he had just come upon an amazing revelation: Cooley didn't like to see teenage boys in combat because his own teenage son had been killed in combat.

"Yeah," he said.

"What?"

Hackermeyer started. He glanced over nervously at Cooley. "I—I mean—I'm sorry."

"For what?"

Hackermeyer wasn't sure. "About . . ." He closed his eyes and concentrated for several moments. "About Jimmy," he said.

"Oh." Cooley nodded. "Thank you, son," he said.

"Yeah." Hackermeyer stared into the gelatinous blackness, trying to think of something else to say.

"How long did you live with your uncle?" Cooley asked him.

"Till I was sixteen," Hackermeyer answered. "How long did you stay?"

"Till I was twelve."

"Oh, yeah?" Hackermeyer rubbed at his dripping nose. "What did you do then?"

"Got me a job on a ranch."

"Out West?"

"Yeah. New Mexico; Taos."

"Oh." Hackermeyer hadn't realized that Taos was out West. "Do you have a ranch?" he asked.

"Small one."

Hackermeyer nodded. He didn't want the conversation to end but he couldn't think of anything to say. His mind felt so fuzzy. "How, uh—old's your other boy?" he asked.

"Fourteen," said Cooley. He made a clucking noise. "And God help his mother if the war lasts so long he gets in it."

Hackermeyer nodded. "What's his name?" he asked.

"Robert; Bob."

"Oh; yeah." Hackermeyer kept nodding. "What's—"

"Hmmm?"

Hackermeyer felt shocked to realize that he'd been about to ask what Cooley's first name was. Suddenly he realized that the brandy must have made him drunk. Except for the beer his father had given him that day, it was the first time in his life he'd had liquor.

"So your uncle was strict, huh?" Cooley said.

"Yeah. He was like a—" Hackermeyer gritted his teeth. He'd been about to say that his Uncle George had been like a sergeant. He thought hard. "He—he was like a first mate," he said.

"And you was a crew member, huh?"

"Yeah." There was a crinkling of skin around Hackermeyer's

eyes. "Yeah, that's right. He ran the place like it was a—a boat or something. He was drunk a lot too."

"Yeah, my uncle was a real boozer too," said Cooley. "He wasn't mean, though. Just a little stupid. Always expected you to know how to do things without him teaching you. Nearly broke my ass learning to ride a horse by myself. Uncle Harry, he figured I already knew how."

"Yeah, my uncle always thought I ought to know everything at school." Hackermeyer frowned confusedly. That wasn't quite the same, he thought. A school had teachers. "I mean—"

He broke off as Cooley rose to a crouch and moved to the cave entrance. The sergeant looked outside for several moments, then returned.

"Guess we can leave soon," he said.

Hackermeyer felt a pang of disappointment. He felt like staying here and talking with Cooley for a long time.

"Sarge?" he said, impulsively.

"What?"

"I saw Lazzo that day."

"What day?"

"That I fell down that—hill," said Hackermeyer. "While I was coming back up, I—saw him."

"Dead?"

Hackermeyer swallowed. Already he was sorry that he'd mentioned it.

"No," he murmured.

"Wounded bad?"

"Yeah." Lazzo had been, hadn't he?

Cooley grunted. "Poor Vince," he said. "You talk to him?"

"I couldn't."

"Why not?"

Hackermeyer drew in a nervous breath. "Well, there was—all these Germans and—"

"Germans?"

"Yeah. I was—" Hackermeyer shrugged. "I was walking with them."

"*What?*"

Hackermeyer shivered. Why hadn't he just kept his big mouth shut?

"What happened, Hack?" asked Cooley.

Hackermeyer told him.

"Jesus H. Christ," said Cooley when the story was done. Hackermeyer was aware of the sergeant staring at him and felt relieved that it was dark in the cave.

"Why didn't you tell somebody?" Cooley asked him.

"Well . . ." Hackermeyer gestured feebly. "I—I couldn't . . . you know, help—"

"Help what?"

"Help . . . Lazzo. So—"

"You mean you felt *guilty* about it?" asked Cooley.

"Well . . ."

Cooley made a sound that was half amusement, half amazement.

"What?" asked Hackermeyer timidly.

"You go through all that and the only thing you feel is guilt for not—" Cooley broke off with a groan. "Jesus, Hack," he said.

"What's wrong?"

Hackermeyer felt the sergeant's hand on his shoulder. "Look, Hack," said Cooley, "I don't know what makes you tick but— believe me, son, you ain't got a thing to feel guilty about. My God, you—" Cooley stopped, incredulous again. "What in hell could you have done for Lazzo when there were Krauts all around?"

Hackermeyer had no answer. He felt that he must look ridiculous in Cooley's eyes.

"So what else happened?" asked Cooley. "Did you knock out any pillboxes? Stop any tanks? Shoot down any airplanes?"

"No," said Hackermeyer. He wondered what Cooley was driving at.

Cooley snorted and patted Hackermeyer's leg. "Oh, boy," he said.

"Well," began Hackermeyer.

"You mean there *was* something else?" asked Cooley.

Hackermeyer cleared his throat. Was Cooley making fun of him?

"There was a—a—some Germans with a mortar gun," he said.

"Mortar gun?"

"I mean a mortar."

"Yeah?"

"So, I—" Hackermeyer cleared his throat again. "I threw a grenade at them," he said.

"And?"

Hackermeyer shrugged. "And they were dead," he said.

"Hackermeyer," Cooley said. Hackermeyer thought he saw the sergeant shaking his head in the darkness and he felt completely foolish. What a jerk Cooley must think he was.

"You know that, if somebody had seen you do that," Cooley said, "you'd probably be getting the Bronze Star about now."

"The what?"

"A medal, son, a medal."

"Me?"

Cooley groaned. "And to think I wouldn't have bet two cents on you when you joined the squad," he said.

Hackermeyer stared at him. A medal?

"What's your first name, Hack?" asked Cooley.

"Everett. What's your—" Hackermeyer stopped and bit his lip.

"Promise you won't tell nobody," Cooley said.

Hackermeyer opened his mouth to speak but couldn't find the words.

"I'll blast you if you do," said Cooley.

"I—"

"My old lady was reading Shakespeare while she was lugging me around," said Cooley. "She got real impressed by *Hamlet*. So Uncle Harry told me, anyway."

"Is that your name?"

"What, Hamlet?" Cooley chuckled. "No, no. I'd settle for it, though. No, the old lady thought Horatio was a great name."

"Horatio."

"You tell anybody and you're a dead hero," said Cooley.

"I won't," said Hackermeyer seriously.

"Good deal." Cooley pushed up again and moved to the cave opening. He slipped outside and disappeared. Hackermeyer strained forward worriedly, then settled back; Cooley hadn't ordered him to leave. He sat there tensely, expecting at any moment to hear a blast of gunfire. Come back, he thought.

He twitched as Cooley appeared at the mouth of the cave and signaled to him. Grabbing his rifle, Hackermeyer worked his way outside and stood beside the sergeant. "Let's go," Cooley murmured.

They started along the bank of the stream. Cooley leaned over as they walked. "Incidentally, son," he whispered, "if you haven't any place better to go when the war's over, come on out to Taos. We've got plenty of room."

Hackermeyer glanced at him, startled. Cooley smiled and patted him on the shoulder. Hackermeyer tried, in vain, to return the smile. Turning back to the front, he moved on beside Sergeant Cooley, his eyes staring sightlessly into the coiling mist.

HE WAS MOVING down the slope when he saw Guthrie leaning on the rampart of a foxhole, left hand propped beneath his chin.

"Hullo, Hackermeyer," said Guthrie in a sepulchral voice.

"Hi." Hackermeyer passed the foxhole, then stopped and stood there indecisively.

"Forget something?" Guthrie asked.

Hackermeyer kept his back to Guthrie, thinking. Impulsively, then, he turned and walked back to the foxhole. Overhead, American shells were fluttering toward Saarbach, the sound of their explosions like a roll of distant timpani.

"What can I do you for?" asked Guthrie, yawning. The bitterness and rancor seemed absent from his voice today. He sounded as casual as ever.

Hackermeyer ran his tongue across his upper teeth. Abruptly, he drew in breath and blurted out the words. "I saw Lazzo the day I was lost. He was on that slope but I couldn't help him because there were Germans all around me."

He stared down defiantly at Guthrie. Guthrie returned the stare, his face devoid of expression. Then, after a while, Guthrie stepped back and gestured toward the foxhole. Hackermeyer remained motionless.

"Come on in," said Guthrie. "The water's fine."

Hackermeyer let out a sighing breath. Bending over, he jumped down into the foxhole.

They stood looking at each other. Finally, Guthrie smiled.

"Why didn't you tell me before?" he asked.

Hackermeyer swallowed. "Because you'd be mad I didn't help him," he said.

"Mad?" Guthrie made a faint sound. "When there were Germans all around you? How'd that happen anyway?"

Hackermeyer told him.

"I'll be damned," said Guthrie. He shook his head slowly. "No, I—don't suppose you could have helped him." He winced a little. "Was he—in pain?"

"I guess," said Hackermeyer. "Except—"

"What?"

Hackermeyer cleared his throat. "A German officer shot him," he said.

"Oh." Guthrie seemed only mildly shocked by the information.

"Well, that's it," said Hackermeyer, turning.

"Where you going?"

"Back to my—foxhole."

"Might as well stay here," said Guthrie. "You have no partner and I have no partner."

"I thought—" Hackermeyer looked around. "What about Fearfeather?" he asked.

"He's with MacFarland."

"Who?"

"One of the replacements. I was with Horton—the character who broke his leg last night."

"Oh. Yeah, I heard."

Guthrie grunted in amusement. "It's just as well," he said. "I doubt if Horton would have lasted very long anyway."

"Yeah."

"So . . ." Guthrie gestured, palms up. "Make yourself to home, if you like."

Hackermeyer nodded vaguely, looking at Guthrie. After a few moments, he sat down and pried open the metal plate on his rifle butt. The oil and thong case and combination tool slipped out into his lap. He started cleaning the M1 as Guthrie settled down across from him and lit a cigarette.

"How was ye patrol?" asked Guthrie.

"We got caught."

"Did?"

"We ran into a—German patrol." He couldn't say Kraut the way Cooley did.

"Anybody hurt?" asked Guthrie.

"Don't know. Sergeant Cooley and I got—separated from the rest."

"Ah." Guthrie blew up smoke. "I presume, then, that our dear sergeant has come to no harm."

Hackermeyer felt himself tightening. Guthrie better not say anything against Cooley.

"Hear tell you're our new assistant squad-leader," said Guthrie.

Hackermeyer tensed further. "Yeah?" he said, unable to keep the belligerence from his voice.

"Oh, I'm all for it," said Guthrie. He picked the cigarette from his lips and flicked away ash. "Except there's not much squad left to assist in leading," he said. "Only us Goddamn kids."

Hackermeyer pulled the oily brush through the rifle barrel. He wasn't going to tell Guthrie why Cooley was against teenage soldiers. It was his secret.

"The Kiddy Killers," said Guthrie. "You loved them in *War Can Be Fun*. You laughed with them in—"

He stopped as Hackermeyer looked at him. Grimacing, he blew a veil of smoke across his face. "Sorry," he said.

Hackermeyer went back to work. "Your father writes movies, doesn't he?" he said.

"That he does, yes," said Guthrie. "He is making the world safe for mediocracy."

Hackermeyer grunted. There was no point in talking to Guthrie; he just didn't make sense. He pulled the wire brush through the barrel again, thinking about Cooley's invitation. It was hard to believe that Cooley meant it. It must have been an impulse, a whim. If he were to show up at Cooley's house after the war, Cooley would, probably, be embarrassed. He'd probably forgotten the whole thing already. Why should he want me in his house? thought Hackermeyer. He pressed his lips together tensely. Then why'd he say it? he demanded of himself.

"Thanks for telling me about Lazzo," said Guthrie.

Hackermeyer glanced up coldly, then lowered his eyes again as he saw that Guthrie wasn't trying to be humorous.

"At least he's not out there suffering," said Guthrie. He blew out breath and smoke together. "The poor, growling Sicilian," he murmured.

"Boys."

They looked up.

"We're moving out in twenty minutes," Cooley told them. "Get yourselves ready. Hack, can you manage this?" He held out the bazooka.

"Yeah." Hackermeyer reached up and took hold of it.

"You two staying together?" asked Cooley.

Hackermeyer glanced at Guthrie. "Sure," said Guthrie.

Cooley handed down the bag of rocket shells. "Keep these here for now," he said. "I'll have one of the others carry them when we move out."

Hackermeyer nodded and, standing, Cooley walked away. Hackermeyer stared at the spot where the sergeant had been. Had Cooley really meant it? he wondered.

"He moves on, triumphant," said Guthrie.

"He's all right." Hackermeyer was startled at the vehemence in his voice.

Guthrie shrank back in mock alarm. "Hackermeyer," he said.

"Never mind."

"All right, he's all right," said Guthrie. "It's just that he and I do not—"

"He only bawls you out because—" Hackermeyer pressed his lips together. He wasn't going to say.

"Because . . . ?" inquired Guthrie.

"Nothing." Hackermeyer scowled at his disassembled M1.

"Because, because, because, because, be-*cause*," Guthrie half-sang. "Because of the wonderful things he does. Doodle-dee-doodle-dee-do."

Hackermeyer cleaned the rifle with tight, angry movements. He wished he hadn't gotten into the foxhole with Guthrie. He was sorry he'd mentioned Lazzo.

"Let me put it this way," said Guthrie. "If dear old Daddy were to write Cooley as a character in a war film, the producer would red-pencil said character as an impossible cliché—the tough, grizzled, tobacco-chewing, expectorating sergeant with the heart of gold." He made a faint, whooping noise. "Impossible," he said.

"He's not," snapped Hackermeyer.

Guthrie looked at him, curiously. Then he raised his hands as though Hackermeyer were pointing a gun at him.

"*Kamerad*," he said. "I'll say no more." He yawned widely and leaned back, closing his eyes. "Wake me in Chicago, porter," he mumbled.

Hackermeyer continued working on the rifle. As soon as he could, he was ditching Guthrie, that was for sure. He didn't like Guthrie. He sat tensely, glowering at the rifle parts as he cleaned them. He was glad they were moving out in twenty minutes.

He wanted to see some Germans.

THE TWENTY MINUTES had extended into forty-five. Cooley and the squad—Hackermeyer, Guthrie, Fearfeather, Tremont, and MacFarland—were gathered beneath a tree waiting for the order to move out. The shelling of Saarbach and its environs had grown intense in the past half hour. There was a constant rumbling in the distance like that of thunder. The mist had thinned a little but visibility was still restricted to less than a hundred feet.

Cooley was checking their equipment, paying closest attention to that of the two replacements. Hackermeyer watched him giving tufts of cotton to Tremont and MacFarland; talking to them quietly. He could not repress a twinge of jealousy at the sight. More and more, he was acquiring a strange possessiveness toward Cooley. The more he tried to control it the stronger it became. He stared glumly at Tremont, watching him nod, his brown eyes fearful behind the heavy lenses of their glasses. In attitude, he seemed a composite of Linstrom and Fearfeather—terrified yet polite. He'd have to keep an eye on Tremont.

MacFarland, on the other hand, seemed more like Guthrie, although deriving less apparent hilarity from life. Except for the thin, ivory scar on his chin, he was better-looking than Guthrie, though not as femininely striking as Linstrom had been. MacFarland's was very much a male face. He was listening to Cooley's instructions, nodding infrequently, not speaking. If he was afraid, it was well beneath the surface. Hackermeyer grunted to himself. He'd keep an eye on MacFarland too.

Scowling, he turned away. Guthrie was right about one thing. There wasn't much of a squad left. *Only us Goddamn kids*— Guthrie's phrase returned to vex him. How in hell Guthrie had lasted so long was beyond understanding. He'd better keep an eye on Guthrie too—see what kept him going. Maybe he was efficient in combat; Cooley had said that Guthrie knew his job. Then, again, maybe Guthrie just hugged the ground and told jokes to himself. Hackermeyer's breath grew labored. There was sure a lot of responsibility being assistant squad-leader.

He blinked his eyes into focus as Cooley squatted down in front of him.

"You and Guthrie will lead out," Cooley told him. "I'll stay between the two new boys and keep an eye on them. Fearfeather'll ride drag."

Hackermeyer nodded, wondering what "ride drag" meant.

"Don't worry about the squad now," Cooley said. "Your main

job is, still, knocking off Krauts." He repressed a grin. "You're too good at that to waste time playing shepherd. Let me do the noodling, right?"

Hackermeyer nodded again, feeling, vaguely, troubled. It was disquieting to hear Cooley talk about his ability at killing. Not that it was a secret. Still, it was something he didn't allow himself to think about, much less mention openly. Not that it embarrassed him, he thought, watching Cooley move away. It was just that, somehow, it seemed a little intimate for discussion.

Anyway, why had Cooley said what he had? Was Cooley sorry he'd made him the assistant squad-leader? Was he, already, withdrawing authority? Hackermeyer felt a tightness gathering in his chest. He wanted to ask Cooley if he'd done something wrong, yet he knew he couldn't.

He twitched as, somewhere in the mist, a whistle shrilled. Cooley looked across the teenage remnants of his squad, his expression solemn.

"Well," he said. He sighed reluctantly. "*Come* on, children."

They did not dismount the slope as the patrol had done. Instead, they straggled along the steeply pitched bank until trees appeared at its base. Gradually, they angled downward until they reached the woods and entered it in a tight squad column. To Hackermeyer's right and slightly in advance of him was Guthrie, the BAR level at his waist. Directly behind Hackermeyer was MacFarland, carrying, in addition to his own gear, the rocket shells. Cooley moved in the center of the column, behind MacFarland and nearly parallel with Tremont, who carried Guthrie's extra ammunition. Fearfeather brought up the rear. Hackermeyer felt, despite his tension, a sense of gratification. The squad was well disposed. The order of it pleased him; its free containment moving through the woods. For a moment, the war seemed orderly and explicable.

Then he saw the deer. It was lying to his left, its small dun body crumpled in an open patch of ground. Its right rear leg was gone, its flank a mash of gore. Hackermeyer stared at the deer's head. Its eyes were open, glazed and staring. Its jaws were parted so that Hackermeyer could see its tongue and teeth. It must have died in agony, he saw.

The satisfaction was gone now. Turning away from the deer did not dispel the turbulence within him. He stared ahead bleakly. Cooley didn't like him, that was all. He'd acted stupidly on the patrol and Cooley planned to ease him out as assistant squad-leader; there was no other explanation. Would Guthrie be made corporal? Fearfeather? Hackermeyer clenched his teeth. The hell with the deer, he thought. What was he supposed to do, cry about it like Linstrom?

A pang of guilt knifed through him for holding the dead in contempt. Suddenly, irrationally, he wondered what he'd do if Linstrom were to rise up from behind that fallen tree ahead and move toward him. He shuddered fitfully. What would he do if his father were to appear and come walking toward him? *I always like to see you*, he heard the ghostly echo of his father's voice. He made a faint noise in his throat, his fingers gripping at the rifle until they ached. It was as if, for the first time, he really understood that his father was dead and he was alone in the world. Completely alone.

He walked on, tense. The trees were thinning out into a clearing and he saw the other squads drifting to the right, following the curving line of woods. He moved in that direction, thinking that the Germans probably had all the open areas zeroed in by now.

Why were the Germans putting up such a fierce resistance anyway? Was it only because they were defending their own soil? The Allied sweep across France had been so incredibly rapid. Now this: slogging through the mud by, relatively, inches. Retreating, then advancing, only to retreat again—an endless time-and man-consuming stalemate.

Hackermeyer grew conscious of fury boiling up in him. Goddamn the Germans anyway! He shivered, trying to force away the blinding rage. It wasn't like him to lose his temper. What was wrong with him? So Cooley didn't like him, so what? So his father was dead; who the hell cared? Hadn't he always been alone? Why start bitching about it now?

He stopped as an explosion flared in the distance. A second explosion followed, then a third; abruptly, the strident buzz-sawing of a German machine gun. Good! he thought. He wanted to fight.

"Keep going," Cooley told them.

"Yeah." Hackermeyer advanced quickly toward the din ahead—the battering of shellbursts, the ripping burr of automatic guns, the flat reports of rifle fire. He flicked off the safety on his rifle, raising it to high port. To his right, he saw Guthrie slip on a patch of slimy moss and fall to one knee.

"Whole damn country's mildewed," Guthrie said to no one in particular.

The squad kept moving toward the sounds of battle. What was going on out there? Hackermeyer wondered. Nobody had bothered to tell them. That was just like the Goddamn army. Ahead, the trees were thinning out again and he could make out a shadowy figure gesturing with his arms. After walking on several yards, he recognized one of the platoon lieutenants waving soldiers out of the woods and ordering them to "Go! On the double!"

"Let's move!" yelled Cooley. "Hackermeyer and MacFarland first! Go!"

Hackermeyer lurched into a run.

"On the double!" yelled the officer, waving both arms simultaneously.

Hackermeyer scuttled across the open ground, his overshoes squishing in the mud. The explosions and small-arms fire were very close now. He could hear the thud of bullets landing all around him. He glanced back quickly. MacFarland followed close behind, face taut, lips drawn back from gritted teeth.

"Come on!" snapped Hackermeyer. He felt the bazooka bouncing on his back.

"Kraut defense-line dead ahead!" Cooley yelled behind them. A smile twitched on Hackermeyer's lips. Cooley had seen to it that they knew what they were up against. He kept on running, the mist drifting past him. To his right, he saw the red flash of a shell exploding. The machine-gun fire was heavier, the crack of rifles getting very sharp. He lunged across the ground in choppy strides, feeling the impact of his weight inside his skull. He glanced back again. MacFarland was still there.

A savage, whistling noise made Hackermeyer dive forward automatically. The shell exploded yards ahead of him, spouting up a fountain of mud that sprayed across his back. Another shell went off, another. Hackermeyer felt shock waves tearing hotly at his clothes. Mud splattered into his eyes and he rubbed at them frantically, gagging on the smoke.

"Go!" yelled Cooley.

Hackermeyer pushed up dizzily and started running. There was another screaming whistle and he plunged to the ground, skidding forward on the mud. The shell exploded to his left, its concussion flipping him onto his back. He rolled back onto his chest, coughing and spitting. Pushing to his elbows, he looked ahead through slitted eyes but saw nothing. The mist clung stubbornly, pierced only by the scarlet flashes.

Machine-gun fire started ripping close above and Hackermeyer scrabbled for the nearest shell hole. MacFarland followed.

"What the hell is happening?" raged MacFarland.

Hackermeyer started to reply when a body came crashing down on top of them.

"Sorry, men!" said Guthrie, scrambling off them. He saluted with his left hand, his face contorted, smeared with mud. "It is a good war, men, a true war!"

"Go screw yourself!" MacFarland shouted at him.

"It is an ill-advised project, father!" Guthrie shouted back.

They threw themselves forward as a shell exploded ahead of them, cascading an ocean breaker of mud across their bodies. They reared up, spluttering. "Jesus!" cried MacFarland.

"He won't answer!" Guthrie shouted.

"Let's go!" yelled Cooley.

They turned and saw him running toward them, followed by a wild-eyed Tremont. The three of them struggled up and left the foxhole. "Stay with me!" yelled Guthrie. Hackermeyer, running, saw that he was yelling at Tremont. Tremont started after him, skidded to one knee, then shoved up again and ran on, drunk with terror. The entire squad rushed forward, moving up a gradual rise. Hackermeyer almost tripped across the body of a soldier. Leaping over it, he caught a momentary glimpse of flesh and gushing blood. He kept on running blindly through the explosion-blasted area.

The piercing whistle sent him to the ground again. The shell exploded just ahead of him, its concussion shoving up his helmet so hard that he could feel the metal clasp gouge into his chin. He tried to rise and toppled over dizzily. Something wet and cold sprayed across his face. He stared up dumbly for a moment before he realized that it was starting to rain. Twisting onto his stomach, he looked ahead but couldn't penetrate the mist. Glancing aside, he saw MacFarland lying nearby, face pressed against his arms. He saw MacFarland reach up cautiously to push the cotton deeper into his ears.

The rain grew heavier and, beneath its icy cleansing, patches of the mist began to disappear. Hackermeyer saw American soldiers sprawled across the shell-erupting slope. He raised his eyes and looked toward the source of German fire. Through a rain-torn fissure in the mist, he saw the parapet of an entrenchment, the muzzle blasts of rifles and machine guns. Sitting on the peak of the slope was a Panther tank, its cannon barrel jerking as it fired. He watched the turret grinding back and forth in small arcs, the cannon firing at the end of every movement. Mortar bursts around the tank had no effect.

On impulse, Hackermeyer pulled the bazooka off his back and sighted through it. "MacFarland!" he shouted.

"What?"

"Load it!"

From the corner of his eyes, Hackermeyer saw MacFarland wriggling over, pulling a rocket shell from its container. Hackermeyer refocused on the tank. The tank kept fading behind showering mud and clouds of smoke.

MacFarland shouted something that was drowned out by a shell explosion.

"What?" yelled Hackermeyer.

"Don't shoot while I'm behind you!"

"Is it ready?"

"No!"

"Hurry!"

Hackermeyer lay waiting, squinting through the sight. The rain was drumming on his helmet, splattering coldly on his neck. "Well?" he shouted.

MacFarland snaked beside him. "Go ahead!"

Hackermeyer drew back on the trigger, braced for the roaring backlash of fire.

Nothing happened. He jerked around, face hardening. "You did it wrong!" he screamed.

"I did not!"

They dropped together as a shell exploded close by, showering mud across them. Hackermeyer felt the shock wave push him against MacFarland's side.

"Take it out!" he roared.

"What?"

"Take it out!"

"Oh, hell!" MacFarland started pushing back when, suddenly, the barrage was lifted. Darting his gaze up the slope, Hackermeyer was startled to see American soldiers running on the rain-swept peak, throwing grenades and firing down into the entrenchment. He saw a man scramble up onto the tank, pull open the hatch and drop a grenade inside, then slam down the cover and leap for the ground. A bullet caught him as he dropped and he kept on falling, sprawling in a heap.

Suddenly, Hackermeyer noticed German soldiers popping up from the entrenchment and, shoving aside the bazooka, he grabbed his rifle. As he aimed, he had the momentary impression that the M1 was part of his arm. Then the fancy vanished as he started firing at the Germans, growing more and more distracted as he picked them off like targets in a shooting gallery.

OUTSIDE, IN THE sleet-riven night, the sharp reports of mortar shells being fired had gone on so long now that Hackermeyer was barely conscious of it as he started reassembling his M1. The flickering of the candle flame made it seem as if the rifle parts were wavering in his hands. Guthrie had acquired a blanket somewhere and suspended it across the cave opening so that they could clean their weapons in some light.

Hackermeyer worked slowly, sniffling. He had been depressed all evening; bothered by the fact that he'd derived so little satisfaction from shooting those Germans in the entrenchment. The excitement had dissolved so quickly that he was beginning to doubt it had existed at all.

Guthrie put aside his BAR and looked up, blinking sleepily. "I don't know," he said, "I just don't know." He yawned. "And that's not all," he said. "I don't even know what it is I don't know. How's that?"

Hackermeyer didn't speak or look at him.

"Hackermeyer, blow your nose," said Guthrie.

Hackermeyer pinched his lips together. He hadn't wanted to be with Guthrie. It had worked out that way because he hadn't made a point of avoiding it. Next time, he'd know better. Maybe he could get to stay with Fearfeather.

"You look distraught, Hackermeyer."

Go to hell, thought Hackermeyer.

"You must emulate me, Hackermeyer, and hide behind a breastwork of jocularity."

"What?" He squinted irritably at Guthrie.

"You must be a joker, Hackermeyer. A clown."

"Yeah, like you." Hackermeyer slipped on the stock and reached for the trigger assembly.

"Actually, you will find it is much easier to adjust to war than to peace," said Guthrie.

Hackermeyer tried to breathe through his nose, swallowed some mucus and coughed. Goddamn son-of-a-bitch cold!

"You know, you intrigue me, Hackermeyer," said Guthrie. "You are the original Great Stone Face."

Hackermeyer tugged the sock over the barrel, remembering that he'd wanted to get a piece of oilskin to protect the bolt assembly. He could have taken Schumacher's, it occurred to him. Leaning the M1 against the cave wall, he rubbed his eyes and yawned. God, he was tired.

As he blew his nose, he looked at Guthrie, who was tearing open a small, blue envelope with a scallop-edged flap. Guthrie glanced at him. "Since you are incommunicado," he said, "I will read my mail."

Hackermeyer thought about the letter in his pocket. Should he send the money to Clara for the funeral? His face hardened. Sure, he thought, I'll run right down to the post office.

Guthrie snickered as he read. "Oh, me," he said. He looked at Hackermeyer. "Here I sit in a cave in Germany in a sleet storm with a Hackermeyer," he said. "And this silly bitch wants me to arrange for her to meet a producer. How's that for the testicle smasher of the week?"

"Your father knows lots of big people," said Hackermeyer. It was not a question.

"Scads," said Guthrie. "Why, you want a screen test, Hackermeyer?"

The skin grew taut across Hackermeyer's cheekbones. "How come you aren't an officer, then?" he asked.

"Because I've seen too many of dear old daddy's war films," answered Guthrie. "I know that joining the Infantry and getting killed is the only decent thing a hero can do."

"Yeah, sure."

Guthrie smiled wanly. "You really want to know, Hackermeyer?"

Hackermeyer didn't answer. Guthrie yawned and picked up his pack of cigarettes, picking one free. "I could have gotten a commission in the Signal Corps," he said, lighting the cigarette.

"So why didn't you?"

"Oh . . . I guess I just didn't want dear old daddy to do anything else for me," said Guthrie. "Or to me." He stared at the cigarette for a moment, then stuck it between his lips and puffed out his cheeks. "There, you see?" he said. "The buffoon doffs his cap and bells only to reveal his shabby soul."

Hackermeyer lowered his eyes. What was the use? You never knew what Guthrie was talking about.

"Tell you what," said Guthrie. "I'll get this starlet to write to you. I'll tell her you're a big producer, you're only over here to get background for a war epic. How's that?"

Hackermeyer grunted. He thought about Foley's offer to have his girlfriend write. He wondered what it would have been like to get a letter from her—what was her name? He thought about the photograph of her. He wished he had it to look at.

"You have a girl, Hackermeyer?" Guthrie asked.

Hackermeyer focused his eyes on Guthrie's face. He was about to say "Yeah" when he changed his mind. Why bother lying?

"No," he said. "Have you?"

"Not truly," answered Guthrie. "I've had them in my sack but never in my heart."

Hackermeyer stared at him with hostile eyes. "What's so great about that?" he muttered.

"What's so great about what, Hackermeyer?"

Hackermeyer swallowed.

"Sex," he said bitterly.

Guthrie blew out smoke. "What's so great about sex? you inquire," he said. He stuck out his lower lip and nodded. "You're right," he said. "What *is* so great about it?"

Hackermeyer pulled a hard candy from his pocket and peeled off the cellophane wrapper.

"Well, for one thing," said Guthrie, "we soldiers are interested in sex because we are seeking, you see, to create lives to replace those we have destroyed. I read that somewhere." He yawned. "I believe I would like to create a life right now," he said. "With a 38 D-cup."

He inhaled hard, burning off a quarter-inch of tobacco, then expelled the smoke. "Love, too, is war," he intoned, imitating Roosevelt. "In both pursuits, one moves upon one's objective— and conquers same. Man in the battle—and man in the bed—is one and the same personality." He looked at Hackermeyer gravely. "The answer," he said, "is homosexuality."

Hackermeyer felt himself stiffen.

"Only joking, Hackermeyer," said Guthrie, raising his hand. "What's the matter, don't you like queers?"

"Do you?"

"Oh, I say love and let love."

Hackermeyer felt his stomach muscles ridging as fear and anger mounted in him. If Guthrie tried anything . . .

Guthrie chuckled. "Hackermeyer," he said. "If you could but see your face."

"Never mind."

"Fear not, Hackermeyer. I like ladies."

"Yeah?"

"*Yeah*," snarled Guthrie, a momentary wild look on his face. He stretched out his legs. "Well, I won't shock you anymore," he said. He started yawning widely. "Oh, God, wake up, Guthrie, the world needs you." Reaching into an inside pocket, he drew out a paper and unfolded it. Hackermeyer glanced at its headline. *Pounce on Platter Pirates*, it read; *AFM Trails Air Check Racket*.

"Fascinating?" asked Guthrie.

Hackermeyer averted his eyes. After a moment, he looked back. "What's that?" he asked.

"*Variety*, Hackermeyer. Voice of the entertainment industry."

Hackermeyer pointed brusquely at the story. "What's that?" he asked.

"I will try to explain," said Guthrie, yawning, "if I can manage to stop yawning for five seconds. You see, the jukebox operators are re-recording records played on the radio, then playing the new records on their jukeboxes without paying any money for the privilege. Isn't that despicable?"

Hackermeyer hissed. "Stupid," he muttered.

"Perhaps so," said Guthrie, turning the page. "Ah, *Chatter*," he said, pursing his lips. "Mmm-hmmm. Robert Paige has trained in from the East and Bradford Ropes is en route to New York for a brief holiday. Good show, Bradford. Laraine Day, on the other hand, is conquering flu while, at the same time, Tallulah Bankhead has recovered from laryngitis. Oh, I tell you, Hackermeyer, it's good to be in touch with the news of the day." He puffed on his cigarette. "And, lo and behold, here is dear old daddy," he said. "*Gerald Guthrie assigned by Metro to screenplay 'Man of Action.'* Yes, that's dear old daddy."

"Why isn't he in the war?"

"The army can't afford him," said Guthrie, skimming through the pages. Hackermeyer watched him, wondering if Guthrie hated his father.

"I see that the exhibitors are worried that the opening of Hollywood Park will make a further crimp in the box office," Guthrie said. He clucked worriedly. "Poor exhibitors," he said. "And *Twentieth Calls Twenty Moppets*," he read. "And *Cugat's Pic Chore*—that's a clever play on words, you see. *Xavier Cugat and Ork yesterday pre-recorded for Metro's 'Weekend at the Waldorf.'* Yowza."

Yawning, Guthrie tossed the copy of *Variety* across his shoulder. "The world goes on, Hackermeyer," he said. "Life prevails." He dropped his head back into his helmet liner. "Two points," he said. He took the cigarette from between his lips and tossed it aside. "And, as Tiny Tim said"—he muttered, yawning; his voice went falsetto—"Scrooge, you're a lousy old bastard!"

HACKERMEYER LAY ON his side, listening to the endless crashing detonations of the mortars. He couldn't sleep. His eyes felt hot and tight and when he closed them he experienced a rush of dizzying blackness like a tangible pressure on his brain. But the tidal darkness never swept him into sleep. Now his eyes were open again.

If I knew what was wrong, he thought. He'd been thinking it for hours now. He was exhausted and he wanted to sleep but his mind wouldn't stop. It kept returning to the past. By now, he was far beyond his relationships with Cooley and the squad members, living and dead.

He was deep in his childhood, remembered scenes drifting past one another, uncontrolled. Him walking in Prospect Park with his father, who was angry with him for sulking because he couldn't have a bag of peanuts. Him in his room on a summer night talking in secret whispers to the little girl across the alley until his uncle came in for the third time, spanked him hard and shut the window. Him taking home a grimy dog he'd found and letting it sleep on the living-room sofa, then crying and brooding because his Cousin Clara wouldn't let it stay. Him, angry, ripping two pages from his uncle's photo album, hiding them beneath a chair and not telling anyone about it. Him going into the garage of a neighborhood boy and looking at pornographic cartoon books the boy had taken from his father's bureau; pocketing one of them and taking it home. Endless, pointless memories of guilt.

When, finally, he slept, his mind kept spinning out threads of thought, now twisted and hideous. He dreamed that his father was trying to get into the cave, offering the fishing rod if Hackermeyer would let him in. He hit his father with the rod and screamed at him, *You can't come in!* There was gunfire and, looking out, he saw that his father had been shot down by a German patrol. He crawled to his father and tried to block the gushing wounds with his hands. He cried, *I'm sorry, Papa! Papa, I'm sorry! Can you hear me? I'm sorry! I'm sorry!*

Then the Germans came rushing at him, firing their weapons, and he jolted awake, so hard that he struck his head against the stone-packed ceiling of the cave. Whimpering with pain, he sat hunched over, shaking violently, palms pressed against his aching skull. I want to be dead, he thought. I want to be dead; oh, God, I want to be dead!

DECEMBER 17, 1944

HACKERMEYER JERKED OPEN his eyes. Someone was pulling his leg.

"Cut it out," he mumbled.

"Hack, damn it, wake up!"

Hackermeyer struggled up on one elbow and looked dully toward the cave entrance. It was still dark.

"Will you get out of there?" snapped Cooley. He sounded angry.

Heart laboring, Hackermeyer collected his gear and crawled from the cave, shivering as he stood. It was incredibly cold.

"I been looking for you half an hour, damn it," Cooley told him.

"Oh. I—" Hackermeyer broke off woodenly.

"Why the hell didn't you let me know last night where you were?"

Hackermeyer swallowed. The cold air seemed to freeze the inside of his mouth. "I—I couldn't find you," he said.

"Yeah. All right, look, we're moving out. You know where everybody is?"

"Well—"

Cooley made an irritated sound. "Who ain't you sure about?" he asked.

"Well, I—"

"Come on, Hack, come on. There's no time."

"Tremont."

"He was with me; he's over there," said Cooley, pointing. "What about the others?"

"I know where they are."

"All right, then, get them and take them over that hill there."

"Yeah?"

"Well, look where I'm pointing, for Christ's sake."

Hackermeyer clenched his teeth, sucking at the air. He turned his head and looked. "Yeah?" he said.

"Take them over it. The kitchen truck's there. Get them some chow, then bring them back here. We move out in—" Cooley checked his watch. "Oh, Christ," he said. "You have twenty-five minutes. Come on, let's go."

"Okay."

Cooley grunted. "I'll meet you here," he said. "I have to see the captain." He looked at Hackermeyer in the darkness. "All right?" he asked.

Hackermeyer shuddered. "Yeah."

Cooley turned away and Hackermeyer watched him leaving as he clipped on his cartridge belt. "—hell's the matter with him?" he muttered. "Think I tried to get lost or something."

Hissing out breath, he stepped over to the cave, tore down the blanket, and kicked at the bottom of Guthrie's right overshoe. Guthrie yelped in surprise. "Get up!" snarled Hackermeyer, slinging aside the blanket. "We have twenty-five minutes to eat and get back here!"

"Tell room service I'll have breakfast in bed," muttered Guthrie.

"Oh, you stink!" said Hackermeyer, stamping away from the cave. The hell with Guthrie; let the bastard starve! He looked around through slitted, venomous eyes. Where the hell were Fearfeather and MacFarland?

He found them dug in against a bank, both asleep. As he came up to the foxhole, Hackermeyer heard grass crackling icily beneath his tread. Squatting down, he pounded on one of the helmets with his fist.

"What the hell!" MacFarland cried.

"Wake up!"

"What are you—nuts?" squawled MacFarland.

Hackermeyer spoke through his teeth. "We move out in twenty-five—in twenty minutes," he said. "If you want to eat, follow me. If you don't, forget it."

"What's the matter, Hackermeyer?" Fearfeather asked in a sleep-drugged voice.

Hackermeyer stalked over to a tree. He leaned against it, then pushed away and waited restlessly, stamping his overshoes on the frozen ground. Who does he think he is anyway? he thought. Let him get somebody else for assistant squad-leader. I didn't ask for the Goddamn job. Screw it! Who wanted it? He hawked up phlegm and spat it out. Damn stupid job anyway. He looked around murderously. Go to his lousy ranch? The hell with that! I wouldn't go if Cooley paid me!

Hackermeyer shivered convulsively and bit his lower lip so hard it hurt. He felt a tingling looseness around his eyes and fought it off in agonized fury.

"Leave me alone," he muttered. The querulous tremble of his voice made him angrier yet.

COOLEY GESTURED, PALMS down, and they all hit the ground. Hackermeyer stared bleakly at the frost-covered soil, the grass tufts frozen into greenish-white blades. There was an iced-over puddle in front of him and, reaching forward, he broke in the ice with his rifle butt.

"Hack."

He looked up and saw that Cooley wanted him to come forward. He started to rise, then fell again as Cooley gestured agitatedly for him to remain prone. A spasm of anger shook him as he crawled forward, gaze fixed to the ground.

"Look out there," Cooley told him, pointing.

All Hackermeyer could see was a fenced-in clearing about forty yards ahead, on its far side a low hill niveous with frost.

"You know what it is?" asked Cooley.

"What?"

"A pillbox."

Hackermeyer shuddered, then forced back the irritation. "Why aren't they shooting, then?" he asked.

"See that bush?" asked Cooley. "The dark one?"

Hackermeyer felt his heartbeat quicken uncontrollably. A pillbox. He would have walked right up to it if Cooley hadn't stopped him.

"See that opening behind the bush?" asked Cooley.

Hackermeyer squinted. "Yeah?"

"That's the embrasure." Cooley glanced around. "Stay here," he said.

"Where you going?" The question popped out before Hackermeyer could restrain it.

"To get some fire on it," Cooley answered. "Don't move now."

Cooley started crawling away. Abruptly, there was a rattle of machine-gun fire from the center of the hill, and bullets whistled overhead, bouncing off the trees. Hackermeyer fell flat, then scrabbled around to see if Cooley were hit. He watched the sergeant move rapidly across the ground. A geyser of dirt shot up near Cooley's leg.

"Put some fire on it!" Cooley yelled just before the machine gun stopped firing.

Hackermeyer turned back, then called across his shoulder, "Sarge?"

Cooley glanced at him and Hackermeyer pointed at the bazooka. Cooley shrugged. "Try a couple if you want," he said, dubiously.

Before Hackermeyer could call for him, MacFarland dashed over and dropped beside him. "Hello, joyboy," said MacFarland.

"What?"

"Oh . . . Jesus, forget it," said MacFarland, slipping a rocket shell from its canister. "Let's hope this bastard is working."

Hackermeyer put down his M1 and worked the bazooka off his back. While he aimed, he felt the back of the tube jiggle as MacFarland slid in the rocket shell and connected it. All around, the squad and platoon were firing at the pillbox embrasure. When the target wasn't human, no one withheld their fire, Hackermeyer thought.

MacFarland crawled beside him. "Right," he said. Hackermeyer glanced at him and saw how vividly white the scar on MacFarland's chin was.

"Where'd you get the scar?" he asked without thinking.

"Baseball bat," said MacFarland. "Come on; fire."

Hackermeyer turned back front, pressing his cheek against the bazooka sight. "Anyone behind?" he asked.

"If there is, he's going to get his ass fried."

"Damn it—!"

"No! There isn't," said MacFarland. "Jesus, what makes you so happy?"

Hackermeyer braced himself and aimed at the dark slit behind the bush. He sucked in slowly at the freezing air, then held his breath and pulled the trigger. There was no recoil but, instantly, a liquid roar sounded behind them. A moment later, a sharp explosion detonated on the hill. Hackermeyer stared at the spot where the slit was. Smoke was pouring off it. Had he hit the right place?

They both fell on their faces as machine-gun fire blazed from the slit, lashing bullets back and forth above them.

"Great shot!" said MacFarland.

"Go to hell!" yelled Hackermeyer.

Now, the lane of German fire lowered sharply and started tearing up the hard turf. It passed in front of them and Hackermeyer felt a stinging spray of dirt across his neck.

"Let's get out of here!" said MacFarland.

"Cooley said—"

Cooley's voice broke over them. "Pull back!" MacFarland shoved up and raced toward the thicker part of the woods. Hackermeyer glanced back and saw him slam to the ground as the line of machine-gun fire came ripping back. He's hit, he thought. But, as the jet of bullets passed, MacFarland was up and running along with Fearfeather and Tremont. Hackermeyer looked around, conscious of a worried pang. Where was Guthrie?

"Shall we retire to the locker room, Hackermeyer?" Guthrie's voice inquired.

Hackermeyer whirled and saw Guthrie to his right, lying behind a fallen tree. Turning away, Hackermeyer looked toward the pillbox again. On impulse, he put down the bazooka and pressed the M1 to his shoulder. Aiming carefully, he fired at the slit. Immediately, the machine gun faltered, then stopped. He heard his bullets ricocheting off concrete.

"Hack!"

He looked around.

"I said pull back!" ordered Cooley.

"Yeah, yeah." Hackermeyer started up, then flopped down clumsily as the machine gun started firing again. Crawling from cover to cover, he moved back to Cooley.

"When I say pull back that's what I mean," said Cooley.

"I was just—" Hackermeyer broke off, aggravated by the thought that he was acting as Linstrom had when Cooley had bawled him out for risking his life over a barbed-wire pole.

"Just what?" demanded Cooley.

"Nothing."

Cooley stared at him a moment, then turned away. "Get down," he said.

"Sure," said Hackermeyer. He sat behind a tree and thrust aside the M1 and bazooka. Why bother? he thought. When the explosions sounded, he looked around the tree. Mortar shells were detonating on the pillbox.

He turned back as Guthrie sat beside him.

"Sounds like the surf at Malibu," said Guthrie.

Hackermeyer scowled. Why didn't Guthrie leave him alone?

What was he trying to do, play up to him? Hackermeyer felt a sudden, fierce desire for Guthrie to try something so he could smash in his face with his rifle butt.

He closed his eyes and shivered. What the hell was wrong with him? Why was he becoming so bloodthirsty? No matter what the problem was, the only solution he could think of was violence. He tried to reason away the disturbance. He was in a war; it was his job. Except he knew that, somehow, it had become more than a job to him.

"Get ready."

Hackermeyer glanced around and saw Cooley squatting nearby.

"The mortar boys will drop smoke shells in a few seconds," Cooley told the squad. "We'll move in right after them. Use your grenades on the slit. Hack, we may have to use the bazooka on the back door."

Hackermeyer grunted.

"Here we go again," said Guthrie. "Boy Scouts of America on the attack." He was up in a crouch, the BAR resting across his legs.

Hackermeyer rose to one knee and slung the bazooka diagonally across his back. He picked up his M1 and checked it. There were two cartridges left inside. He took them out and inserted a full clip. He wouldn't think about killing Germans. If it happened, it happened. Otherwise—

The explosions ended.

"Go!" cried Cooley.

Hackermeyer lurched to his feet and started running. Ahead, the hill and clearing were obscured by heavy, phosphorous smoke.

The machine gun opened up as they reached the fence. Hackermeyer and Guthrie hit the ground together. Guthrie snapped down the bipod legs of his BAR and started firing into the smoke. Hackermeyer shot blindly in the same direction. German machine-gun fire swept the area, chewing apart the fence rail as it passed, spewing clouds of splinters into the air.

Ten minutes later, they were back in the woods. An artillery

observer came forward and called down fire on the pillbox.
When the barrage had lifted, the company advanced under a
second screen of smoke. After sixteen minutes, the machine-gun
fire drove them back again.

"Now what?" muttered Hackermeyer as he slumped down behind the tree.

"How's that, sonny?" Guthrie asked, cupping a hand behind
his ear like a trumpet for the deaf.

Hackermeyer was going to ignore him when he felt a twinge
of guilt for the way he'd treated Guthrie that morning. For all
his idiocies, Guthrie was an efficient soldier. He advanced quickly
on the order and didn't have to be prodded into firing on enemy
positions.

"I said, Now what?" he answered.

Guthrie shrugged. "God knows," he said. "What we need is
a Gerald Guthrie script. He'd figure it out."

They both turned quickly at the crackling roar. A flame-
thrower was being fired at the pillbox. The phosphorus smoke
had drifted from the clearing and Hackermeyer could see the jets
of flaming gasoline shoot across the clearing, burning everything
in their path and plunging brightly into the embrasure. Abruptly,
he glanced to the left and saw two men approaching the blind
side of the pillbox carrying a long, clumsy-looking pole with a
bulky weight on one end of it.

"What's that?" he asked.

"Pole charge," Guthrie answered.

Hackermeyer watched the two engineers advancing toward
the pillbox, carrying the heavy pole. They kept moving, now
walking in a crouch, now crawling. Hackermeyer saw bullets
spewing up dirt around them and wondered where the shots were
coming from.

"Fire at those trees out there!" yelled Cooley.

Hackermeyer started firing, wishing that there was a definite
target to aim at. There were probably snipers out there but how
could you tell? Then again, it might be another defensive position, it occurred to him. For several moments, he had a stulti-

fying vision of one German stronghold after another blocking their way to Saarbach.

He looked back at the engineers. One of them was writhing on the ground, clutching at his left side. The other one was going on alone, pushing the heavy pole charge. He moved very slowly; without progress, it seemed to Hackermeyer. But then, the flame-thrower had stopped and the man had pushed the pole close to the embrasure. Now he was running away and diving to the ground. "Cease fire!" Cooley ordered.

A heavy silence cloaked the area. Seconds passed; half a minute. Guthrie snickered.

"What's wrong?" asked Hackermeyer.

"The charge is probably wet," said Guthrie. He shook his head. "Daddy would never have written it this way."

They watched the wounded engineer being dragged off by his comrade. Then the artillery observer came forward again. "Assume the position, kiddies," said Guthrie, stretching out.

The barrage lasted eighteen minutes, the last round White Phosphorus. Just after it landed, Cooley was on his feet, ordering them forward on the double. Ears ringing, Hackermeyer pushed up and started running toward the pillbox. This time there was no machine-gun fire to stop them. Hackermeyer scraped over the top fence rail and started across the clearing, dodging shell holes. As he ran, he pulled a grenade from his belt and held it ready. Behind him, in the swirling smoke, he heard other soldiers running. The unexpected silence was eerie; no gunfire or explosions, only the rapid crunching of overshoes on the ground.

The hill appeared in front of Hackermeyer. He started up the side of it, twitching as a soldier loomed in front of him. The soldier glanced back and he saw that it was Guthrie. Then he noticed the dark bush Cooley had pointed out and saw, behind it, the embrasure and the dark machine-gun barrel protruding. Guthrie underhanded a grenade through the slit and lunged to the side, knocking Hackermeyer down. Struggling to his feet, Hackermeyer lurched upward, holding tightly to the grenade. The explosion inside the pillbox sounded muffled and flat. He kept on climbing until he reached the peak of the hill.

His muscles jerked convulsively. Below, he saw a line of Germans pouring from the back entrance of the pillbox. The tape was off his grenade before he was conscious of it. He tossed it down among the Germans and dropped instinctively. Before the blast had left his ears, he was firing his M1 at the survivors, picking them off intently. He saw one raise his arms. He fired and the German fell backward with a startled look. Hackermeyer shifted the barrel end and aimed again.

An overshoe kicked aside his M1. He twisted around and glared up into Cooley's face.

"Can't you see they're surrendering?" demanded Cooley.

Hackermeyer's teeth began to chatter. He clamped them together, staring up in mute derangement. Cooley looked at him another moment, then lunged down the steep bank. Hackermeyer lay there trembling, watching him go. Other soldiers were descending the bank too, their weapons pointed at the Germans. Hackermeyer wanted to stand but he felt drained and impotent.

Sudden machine-gun fire blazed from the distant trees and Hackermeyer saw the Germans, scythed by bullets, crumpling to the ground. He saw Cooley dropping with the other American soldiers, lying motionless. Darkness flooded up behind his eyes and, with a hoarse cry, he reared up and started down the bank, firing his rifle from the hip. He bolted through the clumps of fallen Germans, unconscious of his feet and legs. He seemed to float in pulsing blackness.

Something clamped on his ankle and he slammed against the ground. Gasping, he jerked his foot free and started up again. A body plunged across him, pinning him. He thrashed beneath it wildly.

"Stop it!" Cooley shouted in his ear.

Hackermeyer felt himself go limp. He lay, shivering, under Cooley's weight, barely conscious of the mortar shells exploding up ahead.

When the machine-gun fire stopped, Cooley rose to one knee cautiously, looking toward the trees. After several moments, he turned to Hackermeyer.

"What are you trying to do, win the war all by yourself?" he asked.

Hackermeyer couldn't move his tongue. He shook his head in small, bewildered movements. Cooley gestured toward the pillbox.

"Go on inside with Guthrie. See that everybody's out," he said.

Hackermeyer pushed up and stumbled toward the pillbox, feeling Cooley's eyes on him. He glanced down at his rifle and saw that the bolt was retracted. Fumbling for a cartridge clip, he dropped it, kept on going, pulled another clip from his web belt and shoved it into the M1, jerking his thumb free as the bolt slammed shut. He felt as if every muscle in his body were made of quivering gelatin. He stepped through the doorway and jarred down into the gloomy chamber.

Dead Germans lay sprawled across the concrete floor. Hackermeyer stepped over one whose throat was ripped apart and gushing blood. The odor of the room curled into his brain and he fell against the table, shoved it over violently. He kicked aside one chair, then another.

"Tem-per," Guthrie's voice rebuked him banteringly.

Hackermeyer whirled and Guthrie ducked back startledly. "For Christ's sake!" Guthrie told him. "Point that elsewhere."

Hackermeyer lowered the M1 barrel with a shuddering breath.

"Any Germans here?" he asked then, voice dry and rasping.

Guthrie gestured toward the floor, his eyes never leaving Hackermeyer's.

"*Live* ones?" Hackermeyer said.

Guthrie stared at him.

"No, Hackermeyer," he said.

They looked at each other a moment longer. Then Hackermeyer twisted around and headed for the door, almost tripping over one of the bodies. Catching his balance, he heard something crunch beneath his heel. Glancing back, he saw that he had broken one of the German's fingers.

He stumbled from the pillbox, squinting at the whitely frosted ground, nearly colliding with Cooley.

"Nothing," he said. He started past Cooley but the sergeant held him back. "Come here," said Cooley.

Hackermeyer walked beside him stiffly, noticing Fearfeather and MacFarland looking at him. Nosy bastards, he thought.

Cooley stopped beneath the shadow of a pine tree. "Sit down," he said.

"—not tired."

"Sit." Cooley pressed on his shoulders and Hackermeyer slipped down awkwardly. Cooley squatted beside him. "Take a deep breath," Cooley told him. "Take two; they're free."

Hackermeyer sucked at the air. He coughed, then sneezed.

"All right?" asked Cooley.

"Nothing wrong with me," said Hackermeyer.

"Yes, there is."

Hackermeyer dropped his gaze and stared at the ground. It seemed to ripple and he closed his eyes. He started, opening them quickly, as Cooley sat beside him.

"You don't smoke?" said Cooley.

Hackermeyer swallowed. "No."

Cooley put his hand on Hackermeyer's leg. "What's the matter, son?" he asked.

"Nothing's—" Hackermeyer broke off, fuming. "Nothing."

"Why'd you shoot that Kraut?" asked Cooley. "He had his hands up."

"I didn't see him."

Cooley grunted. "Okay, we'll give you the benefit of that," he said. "Long as you understand that a soldier can get—mixed up in combat."

Hackermeyer leaned against the tree. Just leave me alone, he thought.

"Feeling better?" Cooley asked.

"I'm all right."

"I get on your nerves this morning?"

Hackermeyer swallowed. "No." He fumbled at his canteen holder but couldn't get it loose. Glancing at it wrathfully, he jerked off a glove and pulled it open, withdrawing the canteen so fast that he dropped it. He avoided Cooley's eyes as he picked it up and unscrewed the cap with shaking fingers. Water spilled across his chin. He wiped it off brusquely. Cooley didn't speak.

Hackermeyer put away the canteen. "We staying here?" he asked.

"Regrouping," Cooley said. He paused. "Look, Hack," he said. "I know I told you it's your job to kill Krauts. It is—and you're doing a hell of a job. But . . . well, you got to watch out you don't get so—fired up about it you can't stop. It's a job, Hack, not a . . . way of life, if you know what I mean."

Cooley spat to one side. "Let's face it, son," he said. "When we kill, we ain't men, we're animals—and that ain't giving much to the animals. Uncle Sam says, Okay, boys, kill all the Krauts you like. Enjoy yourself."

Hackermeyer glanced aside covertly.

"It's no secret, Hack," said Cooley. "We all know killing can be fun. Hell, it's exciting. But the excitement goes fast, Hack— real fast. And, if you get too wrapped up in it, it'll wind up making you sick. It can turn you into so much an animal you'll never get back from it. I know; believe me, I know. I've seen it happen. I don't know what your . . . background is, really. I guess, from what you told me the other day, it was pretty rough. But don't let it carry over into what we're doing here. Don't let this war become part of"—Cooley gestured vaguely with his hands— "whatever war's going on inside of you."

Hackermeyer drew in a long breath and let it waver out. "I'm not," he said.

Cooley was silent.

"You know what you were doing the other day?" he asked then. "On the slope? While the Krauts were rushing us?"

Hackermeyer tensed.

"You were screaming," said Cooley.

Hackermeyer shuddered. So what? asked the voice.

"Hack, I'm not bawling you out or . . . taking back what I said about killing Krauts. I'm just—passing on a little free advice because I like you."

The hell you do! the voice exploded savagely in Hackermeyer's mind.

"The trouble with killing—wholesale," Cooley said, "is—well, the guy who does it hurts himself more than the Krauts he's knocking off. Maybe I should've said this before. I guess I just didn't think about it. But a guy who kills for a living, Hack—and that's what we're doing here, ain't it? Killing for a living?—A guy who does that . . . he don't feel like he wants friends. He sticks to himself. He don't want anybody around. Maybe I'm wrong but . . . I got a hunch you sort of been like that all your life anyway. And—Well, maybe killing's making it worse. That's why I want you to watch it."

Is that all? asked the voice sarcastically.

"You want friends, I know that," Cooley said. "Everybody does. Except a killer. Oh, I'm not saying you're anywhere near being a killer, son. Christ's sake, you're just a kid. But it can happen. I've seen it happen. Used to be a guy in the squad turned killer. Hack, he got so fouled up, he used to hang around me asking, When are we moving out? When am I going on patrol?"

Hackermeyer shivered.

"All the poor bastard wanted to do was knock off Krauts," said Cooley. "He didn't want to eat or sleep or talk or—Christ, he didn't want to take time out for a crap. Spent part of the time cleaning his weapon, the rest of it on my back asking me to let him go on patrols. After a while, Hack, he got to looking like a zombie. I would've sent him back but we were so short I couldn't. Besides, he was good. He was awful good."

Cooley gestured with his hands.

"He got it finally," he said. "The way you almost got it, before—a machine gun. He started running at it, firing his rifle, screaming like a—friggin' banshee." Cooley's voice trailed off. He blew out breath. "Slugs almost cut him in half," he said.

They sat quietly.

"I'm not bawling you out, son," Cooley said at last.

"Yeah."

"Let's go!" someone called.

Cooley patted Hackermeyer's arm. "Here we go, son," he said, standing. "Easy does it now."

Hackermeyer pushed to his feet and walked away from Cooley. Guthrie joined him as the squad moved out.

"Sergeant telling you the facts of death?" he asked.

Hackermeyer stared ahead. "Horatio was just telling me—" He broke off nervously.

"Who?"

Hackermeyer crimped his lips, his face like stone.

"Horatio?" Guthrie looked incredulous. "You're not telling me that Cooley's first name is—No, no, you jest, Hackermeyer."

Hackermeyer felt sick to his stomach. He saw himself vividly—stripped of all pretense—hitting back at Cooley with a cheap kid trick. He hated himself completely.

HALFWAY UP THE ridge, two aid men were descending with a litter. Hackermeyer noticed the red crosses on the fronts and sides of their helmets; on the bands they wore on each arm. As the litter was carried past the five of them, he looked at the teenage soldier lying on it. The boy appeared withdrawn from reaction to his head injury—as though he hoped that, by ignoring the gravity of the wound, he could limit its impairment. The faces of the aid men were, equally, expressionless. As though they were avoiding any emotional proximity to the boy. As though they chose to remain aloof from any aura of potential death lest it, also, claim them for its victims. As they moved away, Hackermeyer saw that there were red crosses on the backs of their helmets too.

"Don't you fret now," Fearfeather called to the wounded boy. "You're going to be fine."

The boy did not respond. He lay, immobile, staring at the iron-gray sky.

"Poor fellow," said Fearfeather. He slipped off his glasses and began to clean them.

"He's out of it anyway," said MacFarland.

"He may well be out of everything," Fearfeather answered.

Hackermeyer looked at the lean Missouri boy. What was Fearfeather thinking? That, shortly, the wounded boy would be rejoining his loved ones on the other side?

"Wonder how long the war's going to last," said Tremont faintly.

MacFarland belched. "Heard some guy say that Lloyds of London is betting twenty to one it'll be over by Christmas."

"Yeah?" said Tremont eagerly.

Guthrie snickered.

"So?" challenged MacFarland.

"If Lloyds of London bet on the war as often as I've heard they did," said Guthrie, "they wouldn't have time to sell insurance."

"You don't think it's true?" said MacFarland.

"I don't think it's true," said Guthrie.

"Well, I don't believe that we should look to rumor for our comfort anyway," said Fearfeather, slipping his glasses back on.

MacFarland looked sour and they ate in silence for a while. Guthrie drew a pamphlet from his overcoat pocket and leafed through it. Hackermeyer read its title: *French Phrase Book*.

Guthrie clucked. "Just when I get some of this down cold," he said, "we move into Germany. Now I'll have to learn all over how to ask, 'Where is the bathroom?' "

Fearfeather chuckled. "That's very comical," he said.

"I'm a very comical fellow," said Guthrie.

"Sure you are," said MacFarland.

Hackermeyer turned away from them and stared into the distance. In his ears, their voices sank to a rhythmic murmur.

He had avoided thoughts of it all day. That had been simple enough; they had been moving constantly since they'd left the pillbox. But now they were stopped and Cooley had said they might be getting a long break. He could no longer avoid thinking of it. It was like a boil in his mind. Either he tried to drain it or the pressuring ache might grow unbearable.

Don't let this war become part of whatever war's going on inside of you.

Was that what he was doing? Was that the reason he'd been feeling so nervous—so guilty about everything he said and did? He thought about shooting the German soldier. Had the man really been surrendering? Had he seen that the man was surrendering and shot him anyway? He couldn't remember. He was pretty sure he'd seen the German raise his arms—but had that registered in his mind as surrender? Mightn't he have thought that the German was about to throw a grenade? Maybe there was nothing wrong, after all. If he'd only been overexcited and failed to recognize the man's gesture for what it was, then all that lecturing by Cooley had been so much hot air. He'd never done it before, had he? When he'd killed those other Germans, there had always been a reason. He ran back through the list, wincing as the total mounted. Had there been that many? And he couldn't begin to tabulate the number he might have shot during that counterattack.

Well, the hell with it! snapped the voice. What did Cooley expect? Either you killed or you didn't. If you had to make all kinds of distinctions, you might as well forget the whole thing. In combat, there wasn't time for weighing possibilities. You pulled the trigger fast or you got killed. Cooley knew that. What was wrong with him? One minute he talked about medals, the next minute he bawled you out.

Hackermeyer felt a hot discomfort in his stomach that made the food he'd eaten feel like lead. He couldn't justify criticism of Cooley anymore. He needed Cooley's approval. He didn't like the feeling but there it was. The way he'd gotten so fouled up that morning because of Cooley's disapproval made it pretty clear that—

Maybe that was it. Maybe it was because Cooley's censure had upset him that he'd gotten mixed up and fired on the surrendering German. Maybe he just hadn't been thinking, that was all.

Hackermeyer stared bleakly toward the distant trees, knowing that he hadn't found the answer. All he knew for sure was that he'd displeased Cooley. Maybe if he gave up his life, Cooley would think well of him. Somehow, it seemed the only answer; a terrible, yet logical, solution. Maybe that was why he'd rushed at that machine gun before; to make up for his blunder so Cooley would like him again.

Hackermeyer visualized himself falling on a German grenade

and, shielding the explosion with his body, saving the others. He saw himself assaulting a machine-gun emplacement that was picking off the squad. He saw himself throwing a grenade among the Germans, then bayoneting them even as he died. He saw himself destroying a pillbox that was holding up the entire American advance on Saarbach. Almost dreamily, he saw himself lying dead, Cooley kneeling beside him, looking at his still, white face. He saw a tear on Cooley's cheek. *So long, Hack*, the sergeant whispered. . . .

Hackermeyer twitched and reached up, startledly, to touch the tingling looseness underneath his eyes. You'll never make me cry! he thought, enraged. Suddenly, irrationally, he thought about his teeth. He hadn't cleaned them since he'd lost his brush. If he didn't do it soon, they'd get cavities and—

The hell with it! The skin grew taut across his cheekbones. Let them get cavities! Let them look like Swiss cheese for all he cared! He wasn't going to eat all his food, either! He was going to throw the damn stuff away!

"Oh, my God," said Guthrie, stunned.

"What's wrong, Guthrie?" asked Fearfeather.

"What's today's date?" asked Guthrie.

"I believe it's the . . . my heavens, what day *is* it?" Fearfeather looked amused. "One certainly loses track of time up here."

"It's the—sixteenth, isn't it?" asked Tremont.

"Seventeenth," said MacFarland. Hackermeyer stared at his scar, visualizing a baseball bat hitting MacFarland's chin and splitting open the flesh. He winced, imagining how it had felt.

"By God, it's my nineteenth birthday," said Guthrie.

"It is?" said Fearfeather in surprise. "Well, many happy returns of the day, old man."

"Just don't say many more of the same," said Guthrie.

Fearfeather chuckled. "I see your point."

"Sorry I didn't get a chance to bake a cake," said MacFarland flatly.

"Who needs cake when there's dog biscuits?" said Guthrie, biting into one of his ration crackers.

"So you're nineteen," said Fearfeather, smiling. "Well, here's your birthday present." He handed over the two-cigarette pack from his ration.

"You shouldn't have," said Guthrie.

"The best is none too good for you, sir."

"Speech," drawled MacFarland.

"My friends," said Guthrie, spreading his arms in benediction. "One day, whilst engaged in that gripping period known as basic training, we were ordered to dig foxholes. I, with a curious fit of energy, began to sprinkle topsoil about the edges of my foxhole so that enemy aircraft—which might, at that moment, happen to be flying across Georgia—would not spy my position, you see. Whilst engaged in this laudable activity, a full colonel came striding across the ridge—"

"And you shot him," said MacFarland.

"No. No, I didn't shoot him because I knew that he had come, you see, to inspect the bastion. And so he had. He came directly to my foxhole and he said to me, he said, 'Soldier,' he said, 'that's *good*.' Well, I tell you, men, the tears filled my eyes as I watched his sturdy figure moving off—he was three feet tall. He had filled my heart with song, you see. He had given me hope and courage. Inspiration. Since then, everything's been downhill."

Fearfeather applauded.

"Guthrie, you're a humorist," he said.

"No, I'm not, I'm an escapist," said Guthrie. "I crouch behind a breastwork of jocularity. I'm sure I've said that before."

"I'm sure you have," said MacFarland.

"Well, if that's being an escapist," said Fearfeather, "I would enjoy being one as well."

"No, no, you're the spiritual type," said Guthrie. He raised a mollifying hand. "No offense meant," he said. "I, truly, believe you get a sort of metaphysical jolt from combat. Right?"

"Well," said Fearfeather, "I believe in what we're doing, surely." He smiled. "I don't know as I, exactly, get a jolt from combat, as you say but . . . well, I won't contradict you. If you, sincerely, think of me as the spiritual type, that's high praise indeed so far as I'm concerned."

"What type am I?" challenged MacFarland.

"Vell, ledz zee," said Guthrie, blinking at him as if through inch-thick lenses. "I vould zay you are zee—ah, eggs-draverted dype. Ja, ja, devinitely eggs-draverted. To you, var is—adwenture! You rezpond in your zkin, not in your heart!"

"Horse shit," said MacFarland.

"As you zay—horze zhit," said Guthrie, nodding.

"And Tremont here?" asked Fearfeather. "How would you classify him, Professor?"

"Oh, he's the he-rrro type!" Guthrie rolled his *r*s violently. "He vill beat us all to Berrrlin."

Tremont snickered and looked pleased.

"And Hackermeyer?" asked Fearfeather.

"Oh, dere's a caze vor you," said Guthrie. "Vow. Crrrazy like a bedbug!" He peered into Hackermeyer's face. "Don't zhoot me now, Hackermeyer."

Hackermeyer lowered his head so they wouldn't see him swallow.

"He's only joking, Hackermeyer," said Fearfeather. He lit his small corncob pipe and blew out smoke. "I imagine everybody's different from everybody else," he said. "That's why life has the great variety it does. We're all individuals."

"Not us," said Guthrie. "We're just a bunch of Goddamn kids."

"Now, Guthrie," Fearfeather rebuked him mildly.

"Yeah, what's with this sergeant anyway?" asked MacFarland. "How come he thinks teenage soldiers are no good?"

Hackermeyer looked at him. He didn't like him talking about Cooley like this.

"Oh, I'm sure it's not that bad," said Fearfeather.

"Sure it is," said Guthrie. "We're Goddamn kids."

"Now, Guthrie, you shouldn't take the Lord's name in vain so casually."

"Small *g* in goddamn," said Guthrie.

"I'm sure the sergeant has his reasons for believing that we're not the best of soldiers," said Fearfeather.

"Well, he's full of it," said MacFarland. "Any war book'll tell him we make the best soldiers. We have no ties and we're in better shape."

"Well, as to that, I wouldn't say we have no ties," said Fearfeather. "Personally, I feel quite attached to my daddy and my mother."

"Sure, but you don't worry about them all the time. Like an older man worries about his wife and kids."

"He's right," said Guthrie. "I hate to admit it but he's right." He shrank back in mock fright as MacFarland raised his hand as though to backhand him. "I don't know why our poor, misguided sergeant says these things, because he probably knows he's wrong."

Should he stop them? Hackermeyer wondered. He was still the assistant squad-leader. He could tell them to knock it off.

"Teenage soldiers exist primarily in the present," said Guthrie, "which is the only time in which a soldier should exist."

What about me? thought Hackermeyer vengefully. Do I exist in the present?

"Then, too," continued Guthrie, "as our good Doctor MacFarland has pointed out, there is the high order of the teenager's reflexes. Further, if war means anything to the teenager, it's as some sort of—crazy game. At the same time, they're highly idealistic about concepts which an older man would question. Like *Mom* . . . *America* . . . *Democracy* . . . *Liberty*. Teenagers accept these generalities on trust. They can be fired into a rage by them."

"What do you mean, generalities?" demanded MacFarland.

"See?" said Guthrie. "Already fired into a rage."

"Go screw yourself," said MacFarland.

"Teenagers make good soldiers because they're unthinking machines," said Guthrie. "Smoothly operating machines. They do not brood, neither do they contemplate. I am, of course, referring to normal teenagers, not us mangy misfits."

Fearfeather grunted in amusement. "You do like to put on as being the world's number one cynic, don't you, Guthrie?"

"Indeed I do," said Guthrie.

"He's a riot," said MacFarland.

"Well, I believe that, basically, your analysis is correct," said Fearfeather. "It's only when a young man reaches his maturity that he starts to thinking about such things as the meaning of war."

They all grew silent as if the weight of the discussion had crushed response.

"Course the thing is," said Guthrie, after a few moments, "if you kill off all the teenagers, who's going to be left to reach maturity?"

They turned as Cooley approached.

"Dig in, boys," he said. "We're staying for a while."

"Oh, goody, we get to dig again," said Guthrie.

Cooley looked at him balefully.

"We must be extra kind to Guthrie today, Sergeant," said Fearfeather. "He's the birthday child."

Cooley grunted. "Birthday child, uh?" he said. "How old are you, Guthrie, ten?"

"Eleven," said Guthrie proudly.

"You should be ready for knickers soon," said Cooley. He spat to one side. "Happy birthday," he said. "Dig in."

Hackermeyer watched the sergeant moving off with Tremont. Shouldn't the assistant squad-leader be dug in with the squad leader? He pushed the thought aside. What difference did it make?

He and Guthrie began to dig.

"He wishes me a happy birthday," said Guthrie, tossing aside a clump of dark, wet earth. "I laugh up my sleeve."

"Go ahead," said Hackermeyer glumly.

Guthrie raised his left arm and held the sleeve end to his lips. "Ha ha," he said. He grunted. "Tickles," he said.

"That's very comical," said Hackermeyer.

Guthrie looked over in surprise. "Satire from *you*, Hackermeyer?" he asked.

Hackermeyer kept digging.

"You're so humorless," said Guthrie. "So stunningly humorless. Do you realize I've never seen you laugh? Laugh? I've never even seen you smile."

"At what?"

"True—at what?" said Guthrie. "There *is* nothing. You have to make up things. Otherwise, your sense of humor will dry up and blow away. Then you won't be able to laugh at all and if you can't laugh, you're through."

"Dig," said Hackermeyer.

"Dig," echoed Guthrie. He plunged his spade into the viscid ground and wrestled loose a clod. "Still angry with Horatio, are you? That's not really his name, is it?"

"Dig," said Hackermeyer.

"Angry?"

"*No.*"

"You sound it," said Guthrie. "What did he bawl you out for, popping off that German?"

Hackermeyer shuddered. Guthrie had seen it, then. How many of the others had, also, seen? The uncertainty chilled him.

"I don't know what he's grousing about," said Guthrie. "It happens all the time. I've done the same thing myself."

Hackermeyer turned in amazement.

"You have?"

"Sure. Christ, you get all worked up, you can't stop pulling the trigger just like that."

Hackermeyer tightened. Then Cooley was picking at him for no good reason except that he didn't like him. He forced away the knowledge that, in his case, it had been more than just an inability to stop pulling the trigger because of excitement.

"You know, that Fearfeather's a strange one," said Guthrie as he dug. "Never met anyone like him. So tolerant it's unbelievable. He must have wonderful parents."

Hackermeyer wondered if he should mention Fearfeather's devoted pride in his father.

"It's important, God knows," said Guthrie. He straightened for a moment's breather. "I don't know what I'd have done without my mother."

Hackermeyer kept digging.

"What about your mother, Hackermeyer?" asked Guthrie.

Hackermeyer clenched his teeth. "I never had one," he said.

"She die when you were born?" asked Guthrie.

Hackermeyer dug. Why had he said it, why had he spoken at all?

"Did she, Hackermeyer?"

"*Yes.*"

"What about your father? Were you happy with him?"

"Were you happy with your father?"

"Like that, huh?" Guthrie lit a cigarette and started digging again. "No, I wasn't happy with my father. If I hadn't had my mother till I was ten, I'd have probably—" He blew out smoke. "Who knows?" he said.

"What happened to her?"

"She drowned, Hackermeyer," Guthrie answered. "One night she just—walked into the ocean and drowned."

Hackermeyer stopped digging and looked at Guthrie. "You mean . . . ?"

"I mean," said Guthrie.

Hackermeyer kept staring at him. Suddenly, Guthrie was different to him. Suddenly, it seemed as if he understood why Guthrie called himself an escapist. It was eerie to see someone become so modified by a few words. He could not recall ever being conscious of such a transfiguration. It was like a light flashing in his mind, showing him that Guthrie was more than just a fool; that Guthrie, too, had troubles.

MINUTES LATER, THEY finished digging and settled down with their equipment. Hackermeyer checked his watch. It was just past three-thirty. He stared at the watch hands for a while before looking up.

"You think . . . not having a mother is"—he gestured awkwardly—"important?"

Guthrie smiled dolefully. "Take it from the birthday child," he said, lighting a second cigarette with the stub of the first. "It's easy enough to break away, physically, from a mother's influence.

Emotionally—" He clucked. "Another story, Hackermeyer."

"What if you—never had one at all?"

"Then there's nothing to break away from," said Guthrie, blowing up blue-white smoke. "Except," he added, "you've sort of missed something."

"What?" He couldn't take his eyes off Guthrie.

"Oh . . . security," answered Guthrie. He paused. "Love," he said.

Hackermeyer lowered his gaze. Love, he thought.

"American boys are lucky in that respect," said Guthrie. "They get lots of love. Not enough discipline but lots of love."

Hackermeyer stared at his knees. Lots of love, he thought. He had the impression that there was some deep meaning in the words. Suddenly, he thought of Foley. Foley must have been given lots of love—and not too much discipline. Linstrom must have been given lots of love. Yes, he was sure that Linstrom had been given much more love than discipline. And Fearfeather? He must have received a good deal of both.

He stared, absorbed, into his thoughts. Was it an answer? Did it explain things? Like Foley's pleasant nature yet inability to be a first-rate soldier? Like Linstrom's concern for the rabbit and the bird and, at the same time, his abject failure in combat? Did it explain Guthrie's escapist wit? Fearfeather's tolerant strength? Most of all—oh, God, most of all—did it explain *him*?

"You think—" he started.

"What?"

Hackermeyer looked confused. "You think—it's the answer?"

"What?"

Hackermeyer hesitated.

"Love," he said finally.

"The answer to what?"

Hackermeyer looked more confused. "I don't know," he said.

"Peace of mind?" suggested Guthrie.

Hackermeyer nodded; vaguely, then decisively. "Yeah," he said. That was it exactly.

Guthrie thought about it; nodded. "Yeah," he said. He stuck out his lower lip. "Yeah, it probably is the answer, Hackermeyer.

It probably is." He grunted ruefully. "It's sure as hell a better answer than hate, anyway."

He stretched and yawned. "Oh, who can understand anything?" he said. "Especially right in the middle of the—biggest Goddamn enigma of all; namely, war."

He took off his helmet and put it down.

"Funny," he said. "There was this church in Metz. Beautiful place, what was left of it. We were billeted there a couple of days. One afternoon I was sitting in a pew cleaning this—cruddy weapon here. Upstairs, in the loft, some guy was playing the organ. Crazy. Cleaning a weapon of destruction while listening to hymns in the house of the Lord." Guthrie hissed. "Jesus," he said, "I can't even understand that."

Hackermeyer looked at him in concern. "Guthrie?" he asked.

"Mmmm?"

Hackermeyer cleared his throat.

"Do you . . . really think I'm—crazy?"

Guthrie laughed quietly. "Why do you ask that?"

"You said so before."

"Oh." Guthrie smiled. "I was only joking, Hackermeyer. Don't you know that?"

"You don't think I am?"

"If you are, we all are," Guthrie answered.

Hackermeyer started to reach for his M1, then withdrew his hand. He'd clean it later. He jiggled the ration box in his palms. After a while, he drew out the two-cigarette pack and looked at it. He ran a finger over it. Abruptly, he held it out to Guthrie.

"Happy birthday," he said.

"HALT, WHO GOES there?"

"Hackermeyer."

Fearfeather released a wheezing breath. "Right you are," he murmured. Hackermeyer edged forward in the heavy blackness until his shoe touched the rampart of the outpost foxhole. As he squatted, he wondered if he should tell Fearfeather that he'd failed to demand the password. He decided against it.

"How's it going?" he asked.

"All right so far. You gave me a turn there."

"I'm sorry." Hackermeyer had an urge to pat Fearfeather on the shoulder. He felt a warm glow of affection for the Missouri boy. It was a melancholy feeling, yet, somehow, pleasant to him.

"My time's not up already, is it?" whispered Fearfeather.

"No, not for—" Hackermeyer checked his watch. "Twenty-five minutes yet."

"How come you're not resting?" scolded Fearfeather.

Hackermeyer smiled. He felt very old and resolute; like some watchful patriarch moving among his children. "I'm not sleepy," he said. He wanted to reach down and pat Fearfeather's head like a father patting the head of his son. He wanted to say something comforting and wise.

"It's a nice night," he said. He frowned; that sounded stupid.

"Well, I—guess you could say that," said Fearfeather politely.

Hackermeyer almost chuckled. "I'm just talking," he said. "It's a lousy night." He shivered as the damp cold seemed to penetrate his flesh and settle like a dew around his bones. Hot coffee would taste good right now. He wished he had some to share.

"Feels like snow," said Fearfeather.

"Yes, it does," agreed Hackermeyer, getting a momentary vision of Fearfeather's amiable face. His hand twitched as he repressed the desire to pat Fearfeather's shoulder. He had a fleeting urge to go to each of the squad members and pat their shoulders, speak to them comfortingly before . . .

He blinked, perplexed. Before what?

"Well, I guess we'll be—moving on that town tomorrow morning," said Fearfeather.

"Saarbach? Yes, so Cooley says." Unconscious of it, Hackermeyer spoke measuredly, as Fearfeather did. And tomorrow night we may be meeting on the other side, he thought. He was going to say it, then decided that it might upset Fearfeather to have death mentioned on the eve of a big assault. He wracked his brain for some cheering remark. He considered telling Fearfeather about Cooley's first name. No, that would be pointless.

"I trust there are enough men left to make the assault tomorrow," said Fearfeather.

Hackermeyer felt a stir of vague surprise. Fearfeather, actually, sounded frightened.

"There will be," he assured. Somehow, it was even more satisfying to think that he was less afraid than Fearfeather. He took a deep breath and felt a sense of peace inside him. Peace of mind, he thought. How wonderfully it had come upon him. He basked in its quietude.

"What we were talking about before," he said. "About Sergeant Cooley and teenage soldiers?"

"Yes?" said Fearfeather.

"The reason he feels like he does is that he lost a son on Guadalcanal," Hackermeyer explained. "He has nothing against teenagers. It's just that . . . well, he doesn't like to see us here."

"I see," said Fearfeather, and Hackermeyer felt a marvelous contentment at having made him understand. Cooley would like that.

"Yes, I see," said Fearfeather. "I can, surely, understand that. Poor man."

"That's right," said Hackermeyer placidly. "It's just a matter of—"

The rifle shot made him flinch so violently that his unstrapped helmet tilted off and bounced across his shoulder. He looked around in shock, head moving in quick, erratic jerks, the sense of peace immediately stripped from him. He twitched again as, high above, there was a popping sound and a flare ignited blindingly.

"*Oh, my good Lord,*" said Fearfeather just before rifle and machine-gun fire tore apart the silence.

The clearing below was thick with German soldiers, some running, some prone and firing. Hackermeyer squatted frozenly, gaping at them. He was barely conscious of the bullets whistling past him.

He lost his balance and fell as Fearfeather jerked at the skirt of his coat. He lay on his side, staring at the mass of German soldiers. All around him, the defensive fire was growing heavier as more of the company members awoke.

"Hackermeyer, get down here!"

He turned, and was surprised to see a look of panic on Fearfeather's face. Mechanically, he slid across the rampart and jarred to the bottom of the foxhole, once more staring at the rush of infiltrating Germans. He couldn't understand where they had come from. He felt dazed and stupid.

"Where's your rifle?" shouted Fearfeather.

Hackermeyer turned to him again.

"Take mine!" Fearfeather thrust out his M1 and Hackermeyer looked at it. "Take it, Hackermeyer!" Fearfeather stared at him in terrified dismay, then, abruptly twisted around, the light reflecting on his glasses. Overhead, more flares burst into shimmering luminescence. Hackermeyer watched Fearfeather lunging out and dragging back his M1. Fearfeather pushed it against him. "Shoot!" he cried.

Suddenly, Hackermeyer realized that Fearfeather was one of the soldiers who couldn't fire at enemy soldiers. He looked dumbly at the Missouri boy. The awesome flickering light, the din of gunfire, made him feel immersed in some incredible dream.

"Hackermeyer!"

Taking his rifle, Hackermeyer leaned across the rampart. All right, he thought. He felt the flooding of emotion in himself again. All right, I'll help you, son, he thought, and bent over to aim.

He began to tremble. He couldn't fire. He stared at the attacking Germans and knew that he was incapable of shooting them. He stood up, wavering, trying hard to think. He was conscious of Fearfeather screaming his name but he couldn't answer. He felt wooden, mute, completely helpless. Breath fluttered from his lips.

"For God's sake, Hackermeyer!"

He blinked his eyes and saw two Germans charging them like figures seen through lighted water.

"Hackermeyer!"

He became aware of Fearfeather clutching at his arm, trying

to hold him back. He pulled away. You don't understand, he thought. He fell against the foxhole wall and started climbing out. Fearfeather caught his leg.

"What are you doing?" Fearfeather cried.

Hackermeyer kicked himself free. He was out now, pushing to his feet and moving off. He had no weapon; he needed none. He stumbled toward the two Germans. I'll save you, he thought. Don't be afraid, I'll save you. His plunging stride was broken as one of the Germans toppled over. The remaining one kept charging him, a bloated, shapeless form. Hackermeyer stared at the German's glittering bayonet. Now, he thought; now!

Fearfeather rushed past him so quickly that he staggered to a halt and stood, transfixed.

The German lunged. Fearfeather cried out horribly and fell, pulling the rifle from the German's hands. The German screamed, and Hackermeyer saw a hole appear in his twisted face. Dark liquid spouted from the hole; the German fell.

Hackermeyer's legs gave way. Suddenly, he was on the ground, crawling over to Fearfeather. The Missouri boy lay staring at the fiery sky, his hands clutched around the handle of the bayonet driven deep into his chest. He looked more bewilderedly affronted than in pain. Hackermeyer gaped at him. Darkness pulsed and ebbed before his eyes. *No*, he thought. He blinked lethargically, leaned closer, squinted.

Fearfeather was smiling at him.

Aghast, he saw Fearfeather's right hand loosen from the bayonet handle and flutter upward. Hackermeyer's breath congealed as the hand flopped against his face. He felt the glove palm patting feebly at his cheek. Fearfeather said something, but he couldn't hear the words. He bent over and put his ear to Fearfeather's moving lips.

"You be—careful—now—Hacker—"

Hackermeyer waited. There was no more. He straightened up a little. Fearfeather had stopped talking, but his mouth was still open. Hackermeyer waited for him to continue. He felt himself waiting. "Yeah?" he muttered.

Then he realized that Fearfeather's hand lay motionless

against his cheek and, with a gagging noise, he shrank away. The hand fell limply to the ground.

"Fearfeather?" he said. He couldn't hear his voice above the crashing gunfire. No, he thought. Somehow, he was unimpressed. He couldn't believe that Fearfeather was dead. In his mind, Fearfeather was fully alive. He looked down fixedly at the lean, unmoving features. Fearfeather's skin glowed whitely in the radiant light.

Sudden darkness pressed against his eyes and Hackermeyer shuddered. He kept staring downward as if he could still see Fearfeather.

The first explosion made his limbs twitch spastically. Looking up, he saw the night erupting with vivid bursts of light. He stared at them, unable to budge. Suddenly, it seemed as if a part of him were in his uncle's house again, the darkness being ripped asunder by a storm. Petrified, he watched the lightning, listened to the thunder. During every lurid flash, he caught a glimpse of Fearfeather lying in front of him, the German rifle angling up acutely from his chest. And he was paralyzed, a helpless casualty of the savage, timeless war within himself—the war for which there was no peace and never could be; the war from which he never could escape except to darkness and to death.

DECEMBER 18, 1944

HACKERMEYER LAY SLEEPING on the bottom of the foxhole, legs pulled high, hands clutched beneath his chin, his narrow face drawn into a mask of apprehension. His breath was thin and faltering as he drifted just below the level of awareness. The instant he was touched, his eyes sprang open, staring. He looked at Guthrie as if he'd never seen him before.

"Time to go," said Guthrie.

Hackermeyer kept staring at him, his face like stone. Then he pushed to his feet. "Where?" he muttered.

"What do you mean, where?"

Hackermeyer looked around. In the dim, gray light, men were gathering together their equipment. Overhead, there was a scouring of shells, in the distance, a constant rumble of explosions.

"Coffee?"

Hackermeyer looked at the canteen cup Guthrie was holding out. He shook his head.

"Why didn't you wake me?" he mumbled.

"What?"

Hackermeyer looked around again. "Where is he?" he asked.

"Who?"

"Fearfeather."

Guthrie didn't answer. Shuddering from the intense, biting cold, Hackermeyer turned back. "Well?" he asked.

"He's dead, Hackermeyer."

"I know he's dead! Where is he?"

"They took him away."

Hackermeyer swallowed. "Say so," he muttered. He kept looking around. "Should have woke me."

"Cooley said to let you sleep."

He turned on Guthrie. "Yeah?"

"Yeah," said Guthrie.

Hackermeyer glowered at him. Suddenly, he looked around for his rifle. He saw the bazooka and picked it up. "Oh," he said, appalled.

"What's the matter?"

Hackermeyer picked up the bazooka sight and looked at it dumbly.

"What did it do, break off?" asked Guthrie.

Hackermeyer grunted.

"Jesus," said Guthrie. "That's what I call cold."

Hackermeyer pressed the sight against the bazooka as if trying to seal it back in place. It dismayed him that equipment that had been entrusted to him had broken.

"You all right?"

Hackermeyer twitched and looked around. Bitterly, he flung aside the broken sight and picked up his rifle. He almost groaned

aloud. It was caked with mud and there were rust flecks everywhere. And they were moving out; he wouldn't have a chance to
clean it.

"Why didn't you wake me?" he demanded.

"I told you, Hackermeyer."

"Sure. Sure." Hackermeyer shivered so hard that he dropped
the bazooka. Bending over to retrieve it, he dropped the M1. He
sucked intensely at the air.

"Hackermeyer, are you all right?"

"Oh, shut up." Hackermeyer grabbed the M1 and rubbed the
palm of his right glove across the bolt top. It did no good. He
rubbed harder but the rust remained. He looked around nervously to see if there were time to strip the rifle. "Is there . . . ?"

"What?"

Hackermeyer held himself tightly. "My rifle's dirty," he said.

"They all are."

Hackermeyer looked at the BAR. "Yours isn't," he said.

"Sure it is."

"It isn't! You can take time to clean your gun, can't you?"

"Oh, for Christ's sake, Hackermeyer."

"Not me, though!" He looked at Guthrie in a trembling fury,
then, abruptly, turned away. "Forget it," he snapped.

"Oh, Gawd," said Guthrie.

Hackermeyer glared across his shoulder, then looked around
for the bazooka sight. He shouldn't have thrown it away. There
might be welding equipment somewhere nearby. He imagined
an officer looking at him with accusing eyes. . . . "You threw away
the sight?" said the officer. "Did it ever occur to you that we
might repair it?" The officer turned away, disgusted. "Well, it's
too late now, soldier," he said. "There's nothing we can do now,
so you might as well forget it. Thanks a lot! You're doing a great
job!"

Hackermeyer tightened with resentment at the officer. Can I
help it? he thought. He looked uneasily for the sight. He had to
find it.

"You boys ready?"

Hackermeyer whirled and looked at Cooley.

"How you feeling, son?" Cooley asked him as he handed down the boxes of grenades.

"Fine." Hackermeyer turned away and dumped the grenade boxes on the ground. As he looked for the bazooka sight, he imagined that Guthrie and Cooley were exchanging glances about his behavior. He looked back quickly to trap them but only Cooley was gazing at him.

"What are you looking for?" asked Cooley.

"The—the—" Suddenly, his mind was blank.

"The bazooka sight broke off from the cold," said Guthrie. Hackermeyer glared at him for interrupting.

"Forget it," said Cooley. "We can't glue it back on. Get ready, we're taking off any minute now."

Hackermeyer's lips flexed back as he watched Cooley moving away. What if there's welding equipment somewhere? he almost shouted. He turned away in a rage. The hell with it, then! Why should he worry about their Goddamn stupid equipment if they didn't even care about it themselves?

He shivered guiltily. The bazooka had been put in his care and he'd let its sight break off. Cooley must be disgusted with him. Now that he thought about it, Cooley's voice had been tinged with disgust. He wouldn't be assistant squad-leader much longer, that was certain.

"Sure you don't want any coffee?" Guthrie asked.

"*No, I don't want any coffee.*" Hackermeyer started jerking the grenades from their boxes.

Guthrie moaned. "Oh, you're in good shape," he said.

"Oh . . . shut your mouth." Hackermeyer taped down the grenade arms with tense, angry movements and slipped them over his web belt. From the corners of his eyes, he saw Guthrie take another drink from the canteen cup, then pour out the rest of the coffee and put the cup away. He felt guilty for talking to Guthrie like that. He pushed aside the feeling irritably, glancing at his watch. Six-fifteen.

As he gathered his equipment, he glanced down the slope. The infiltration had failed; dead Germans lay everywhere. He remembered kneeling by Fearfeather during the attack; remembered how the rifle had angled up from Fearfeather's chest, held by the bayonet. It was all he remembered. Breath faltered in his lungs. He was a murderer. He'd tried to kill himself and had killed Fearfeather instead. Nothing he did came out right—and now he was a murderer. Well, he'd pay. He nodded quickly to himself. He'd pay, with his life, for killing Fearfeather. But what if he wasn't killed? He might go on and on, and . . .

His legs began to tremble. He couldn't seem to breathe. Fearfeather had been so kind, so generous. In his mind, he could still see Fearfeather's smiling face. He couldn't visualize Fearfeather accusing him even now. That was the most hideous part of it. Even dying, Fearfeather had patted his cheek and told him to take care of himself.

Hackermeyer sucked in fitfully at the air. He'd failed to save Lazzo. He'd driven Linstrom to his death. He'd helped kill Foley. He'd waited too long to help Wendt; Wendt was probably dead. He'd told everybody that his father was dead when his father was alive. He'd even helped to kill his father. God, what a monster he was! Why didn't he die, why didn't someone kill him?

The earth seemed to reel around him darkly.

"Hackermeyer?"

"I'm all right . . . !" He grabbed his rifle and bazooka and stumbled away. Just leave me alone, he thought. Leave me alone and I'll die and get it over with. He stopped walking and stared down the slope. Today he'd die like those Germans down there. Again, he nodded to himself. Today they were going into Saarbach and he'd die. He felt some relief at the knowledge. Death seemed beautifully inviting—yes, even with the possibility of going on afterward. Anything to get away from this.

He twitched as someone tapped him on the shoulder. Jerking around, he saw Guthrie pointing. He looked in that direction and saw Cooley standing with Tremont and MacFarland. Drawing in a deep, quavering breath, he followed Guthrie to where the others waited.

"All right, boys," Cooley told them. "Here's the scoop. Our orders are simple—take Saarbach by today."

Hackermeyer pressed his lips together. Good, he thought.

"You might be interested to know why the Krauts are putting up such a scrap," Cooley said. "It ain't only because they're defending their own soil. They've broken through up north and it's given the Krauts down here a shot in the arm. We'll probably be needed up there soon, so that's another reason we got to wind this up."

He turned his head and spat tobacco juice.

"After last night's attack, company strength is down to sixty-five," he said. "I'm telling you because I think it's better you know what the score is. Course the Krauts probably ain't in any too good a shape either. But whether they are or not, we're going into Saarbach today. We should make the edge of the forest by noon. Recon patrols say there's only a few scattered positions to knock out before we get there. Then it's across a plain—a thousand yards or so. As you can hear, artillery's throwing everything they have into Saarbach—105s, 155s, 240s, the works. We might even get some air force support before we move in on the town."

Cooley looked them over.

"I want you all to know you're doing a good job," he said. "I know I been—making noises about kid soldiers and all that. That's all they were, boys—noises. I'm proud of all of you and I know you're going to do a hell of a job today." He paused. "Questions?"

No one spoke.

"Tremont, you'll stick with Guthrie," said Cooley. "Hack, you and MacFarland buddy up. There ain't going to be any replacements, it'll just be the five of us." He smiled at them. "Right?"

"Right," said Tremont fervently, then blushed. Cooley patted his arm.

"Stay on your toes now, boys," he said. "Keep your eyes open and maybe we'll all see Christmas together."

A minute later, they were moving through the woods. Hackermeyer paid no attention to where he walked. He sauntered carelessly, knowing that, at any moment, he might set off a booby trap or be picked off by a sniper. He didn't care. He moved with a vengeful assurance, anticipating the end. He deserved and wanted death. Accordingly, he sought it in whatever violent guise it might appear. Everything seemed complete, the past all wrapped and sealed and put aside—only the momentary future to be dealt with.

He began remembering the ten days he had been with the squad. In retrospect, it seemed a lifetime. He went over every detail he could recall, examining them like someone adding up his life. It satisfied him to do so; his sense of fatalism was complete. No matter what he did, he was going to die. It was in the cards; the percentages had run out. Today, he would be killed.

"Hack."

He stopped and looked around. Cooley moved up to him.

"Take it easy, son," the sergeant told him mildly. "Watch where you're going. We ain't on a picnic, you know."

"I know." Hackermeyer spoke docilely. There was no resentment in him, only resignation. For a moment, he was conscious of how erratic his moods had been in the last day. Then it slipped away and he was calm again; tranquil in the knowledge that his trials were finished. He returned Cooley's gaze without a tremor.

"Try the bazooka on the first Kraut position we come to," Cooley told him. "If it hasn't any accuracy, ditch it."

Hackermeyer nodded.

"You're looking pretty vague, Hack," Cooley said. "You all right?"

He nodded again. Cooley looked at him a moment more, then clucked. "Okay," he said, but didn't sound convinced. He started away, then stopped and looked back over his shoulder.

"No one-man shows today," he said.

Hackermeyer shook his head. The sensation he'd had the night before was, partially, back—that comforting, idyllic prescience of death. Shortly, he would pay for all the terrible things he had done. The assurance soothed him as he started forward again, walking as though he were taking a stroll in the park. It was very close now. At any moment, the end would come with swift, inviolable justice.

When the machine gun opened up, the noise came almost expectedly. Hackermeyer stopped and listened to the staccato rattle of it. He didn't move. Trembling slightly, he waited. Now, he thought. He felt the hunger mounting in him. Now. The feeling surged and billowed. Death was near. His dark eyes searched for its inexorable coming.

He saw it then—a chain of miniature geysers spattering across the earth. He stared at it in fascination, his face twitching as bullets bounced and scraped off tree trunks.

"Hack!"

That would be Cooley. Hackermeyer didn't turn. He felt his legs begin to vibrate. Why didn't it come? He stood ready, waiting. Where was it? He hovered in the maelstrom of bullets but was untouched. Panic rose up, gorging. *Where was it?*

"Down!" screamed Cooley.

Hackermeyer cried out in fright. It seemed as if his body worked apart from him. Horrified, he watched the trees spinning around him, felt the earth crash up against his body. Abruptly, he was lying on his back, breath gone, staring up through foliage at the leaden sky. It didn't work, he thought. There was no pain, no darkness, no conclusion. He heard his mind cry out, afflicted: It didn't work! Breath grated in his throat. He looked around with unbelieving eyes. A sob broke in his chest. He flopped over on his chest and stared into the woods. Oh, God, it didn't work!

"Fire!" Cooley yelled. Hackermeyer picked up his M1 listlessly and put it to his shoulder, then lowered it again. He stared at the rifle. He couldn't believe that he had ever fired it; that he had, actually, killed Germans with it.

"Guthrie, Tremont, go!" cried Cooley.

Hackermeyer glanced aside and saw them pushing up, running several yards, then dropping, breaking the fall with their rifle butts and landing on their chests. They looked, to him, like figures in a dream. He watched Guthrie slam a fresh clip into his BAR and open fire in bursts of two and three. He saw Tremont lying close behind Guthrie, back rising and falling heavily in breath.

He twitched and looked around. Cooley had shouted something else. He caught a flash of movement to his right and, looking over, saw MacFarland sprinting across the ground, his face taut with concentration.

He started as someone crashed beside him.

"Go, for Christ's sake!" Cooley shouted in his ear.

Hackermeyer pushed up dizzily.

"The bazooka!" Cooley yelled. Hackermeyer looked down and saw it lying on the ground. He bent over sluggishly to pick it up. Cooley grabbed his ankle and flung him on his back.

"What the hell's the matter with you?" demanded Cooley.

Hackermeyer stared at him.

"You sick?" asked Cooley.

Hackermeyer muttered something.

"What?" asked Cooley.

"No."

"Well, Jesus, boy, wake up, then!" Cooley raised his carbine and squeezed off four rounds. They blurred together deafeningly in Hackermeyer's ears. He struggled to a sitting position and took hold of the bazooka.

"Go!" yelled Cooley, firing again.

Hackermeyer shoved up and started running. "God!" he heard. He jolted to a halt and looked around. He'd run directly into Cooley's line of fire.

"Will you . . ." Cooley looked apoplectic. ". . . Get down, for Christ's sake!" he roared.

Hackermeyer turned and, stumbling to the side, slammed to the ground. He lay, gasping, staring at the trees. The machine gun opened up again. He heard the strident buzz of it, the whistling rush of bullets overhead. If he stood, he'd get it. No; he shook his head. He wouldn't. If he stood, the gun would stop. Nothing he did worked out.

Cooley landed beside him again. "Fire!" he ordered.

Hackermeyer picked up his M1 and pointed it in the direction of the machine-gun emplacement. He couldn't pull the trigger. He couldn't even sight. He lay there, helpless, wondering what to do. He twitched as Cooley lunged across his back and pulled the M1's trigger. The rifle bucked against his shoulder once, twice, the bullets shooting up into the treetops.

"Damn it, *fire!*" raged Cooley. He grabbed the bazooka. "MacFarland! Shells!" he shouted.

Hackermeyer aimed at the barricade of fallen trees and pulled the trigger. The rifle jarred against his shoulder. Grimacing, he closed his eyes and pulled the trigger a second time. That was better. He braced himself and jerked the trigger again, again, surrounded by the ringing blasts, his nostrils filling with the acrid powder fumes.

As the M1 ejected its clip, Hackermeyer turned and saw MacFarland nearby, jerking a rocket shell from its container. Shifting his gaze, he saw Cooley trying to aim the bazooka without its sight.

"Keep firing!" Cooley told him.

Hackermeyer twisted around and pulled open a compartment of his web belt, worked loose a cartridge clip.

"Hurry!" ordered Cooley.

Hackermeyer glared at him. Suddenly he thought, That's *my* bazooka.

"I said *hurry!*" Cooley shouted at him.

"That's *my* bazooka."

"What?"

"That's my bazooka!" Hackermeyer yelled, infuriated.

Cooley's jaw went slack. For several moments, he gaped at Hackermeyer. Then, incredulous, he turned away. "Ready?" he demanded.

MacFarland crawled beside him. "Yeah!"

Shaking, Hackermeyer watched Cooley raise and lower the front end of the bazooka. He twitched as the flame rushed out behind it; he turned his head instinctively. The shell exploded in the trees beyond the barricade.

Cooley growled. "Again!" he shouted. He glanced aside and Hackermeyer averted his gaze, pressing the clip into his rifle. He closed his eyes again and fired off eight shots in rapid succession. The clip popped out. "Another!" he heard. He looked around and saw MacFarland disconnect the rocket shell, jerk it loose and sling it aside, shove in another one, connect it. He turned back front.

The roaring backfire sounded and the shell exploded on the ground ten yards in front of the emplacement. With a curse, Cooley shoved aside the bazooka. Hackermeyer watched it roll across the ground and stop against a bush.

"Keep firing, damn it!" Cooley shouted, reloading his carbine.

Up ahead, there was a booming detonation as a rifle grenade hit the barricade. The machine gun stopped.

"Bingo!" yelled Cooley. He rose to a crouch, eyeing the emplacement warily. Everyone held their fire. Cooley waited several more moments, then reared up. "Guthrie, Tremont, go!" he shouted. Hackermeyer watched them dashing forward, dropping.

"Go on," said Cooley.

Hackermeyer stood and ran, MacFarland beside him. Cooley followed, shouting, "Guthrie! Tremont!" They got up and were the first to reach the barricade. They started climbing up the side of it. Hackermeyer saw Tremont, straddling the top log, look into the emplacement with astonishment. Tremont whirled.

"It's empty!" he cried.

A rush of sights and sounds. The rattle of a German burp gun; Tremont crying out and toppling off the barricade; Cooley dashing to the right, firing his carbine. Hackermeyer spun and saw a German soldier shooting at them. Cooley went crashing to the ground. Without thinking, Hackermeyer jerked up his M1 and pulled the trigger. The snapping noise made his head swell violently against his helmet liner. He'd forgotten to reload! A cloud of darkness rushed at him. He fought against it, saw the German falling.

Cooley jumped up and started toward the body. Hackermeyer jolted in shock as a German officer jumped out from behind a tree, a Luger in his hand. He saw Cooley raise his carbine to shoot the German. Then he gaped, leaned forward, as the officer, instead of firing at Cooley, shoved the Luger barrel into his mouth and pulled the trigger. His head erupted in a spray of bloody flesh and bone.

Hackermeyer stumbled over dazedly and stared down at the officer. MacFarland joined him.

"Why'd he do that?" MacFarland asked, looking sick.

"They're crazy, that's why," said Cooley. "They'd rather die than lose." He strode over several feet and picked up the end of a length of heavy twine. Hackermeyer followed its quivering rise over to the barricade.

"Bastards," Cooley muttered. He dropped the twine. "I should have known."

"What is it?" asked MacFarland.

"They connect it to the machine gun," answered Cooley. "You waste all your time and ammo on the emplacement, then, when you overrun it, they pick you off from their real position."

"Oh, Christ," said MacFarland, wincing.

Cooley turned away. "Tremont!" he called.

Tremont sat up and looked over, his face chalk-white.

"You all right?" asked Cooley.

"S-s-sure," said Tremont.

A smile flitted across Cooley's lips. Hackermeyer watched him walk to the barricade. They'd rather die than lose, he thought. The words kept echoing in his mind.

THEY WERE WATCHING Saarbach being shelled.

From dozens of ranges and directions, the waves of missiles flooded in on the town; it rocked beneath the onslaught of explosions. Clouds of dark smoke ballooned above it. Bright fire tongues licked upward from its shattered rooftops and the air around it seemed to quiver luminously.

Hackermeyer slumped, motionless, against a shrapnel-pocked tree, unconscious of the icy wind that blew across his face; only partially aware of the distant barrage. He was wondering if it was true that he had wanted to die rather than lose. Cooley was right. A war was going on inside of him; *he was fighting himself*. Was some part of him so afraid of losing that fight that death had seemed preferable? Hackermeyer closed his eyes. It was so hard to understand, much less accept. Ideas never existing for him forced themselves on his attention. Clearly, he was not the same person he had been ten days before. Yet he had no idea what he had become. All he knew was that the texture of his life had changed. All he sensed was that he either faced those changes or they could destroy him.

He opened his eyes as Guthrie sat beside him. "How do," said Guthrie. A cigarette was dangling from the left-hand corner of his mouth.

Hackermeyer looked at him as if to find an answer in his face.

"Still discombobulated?" asked Guthrie.

Hackermeyer turned away. "I can't do anything," he said.

"What do you mean?"

"I can't—shoot my rifle. I can't—" He shrugged helplessly.

"Function?"

Hackermeyer nodded. "Yeah," he murmured.

"It'll pass," said Guthrie.

Hackermeyer looked back at him.

"What if it doesn't?" he asked.

"It will."

"What if I'm killed first?"

"Then you won't have anything to worry about," said Guthrie.

Hackermeyer turned away and stared across the plain toward Saarbach. Several yards ahead of him, the ground sheered away so precipitously that he could almost imagine he was sitting in the sky.

"Fearfeather couldn't shoot his gun," he said. "And he's dead." He couldn't add, I killed him.

"Fearfeather *wouldn't* shoot his gun," said Guthrie.

Hackermeyer turned back quickly. "What?"

"War was a sort of—mystic experience to him," said Guthrie. "A crusade against the forces of evil. He didn't want to kill." Guthrie grunted speculatively. "Hell, he wanted to be killed."

"You're crazy."

"No, that's right," said Guthrie. "To give his life in a—holy cause. That was his ambition."

"He wanted to work with his father."

"Not as much as he wanted to die nobly."

"How do you know?"

"He told me." Guthrie tossed away his cigarette. "I wouldn't be upset by his death if I were you. I'd give odds he died happy."

Hackermeyer stared at him. Was it possible?

Abruptly, he remembered that, while Fearfeather was helping to dig that foxhole the day before the counterattack, he'd called the war a crusade. *The Godless versus the God-fearing*—those were his very words. Hackermeyer drew in labored breath. Fearfeather had always seemed so well adjusted to him. Wasn't anybody adjusted?

"Then—" he started.

"What?"

Hackermeyer shivered. "I—didn't kill him," he said.

"Who said you did?"

"Well . . ." His face tightened. "He died saving me."

"He did?"

"Yeah."

Guthrie grunted. "Then he got exactly what he wanted," he said.

"What?"

"To give up his life for a fellow creature," Guthrie said. "That was his ideal, Hackermeyer. He told me so, a dozen times." He shook his head. "Christ, don't feel bad about him," he said. "His dream came true. He probably died smiling."

Hackermeyer's breath stopped.

"He did," he murmured.

Guthrie looked surprised. "Really?"

"Yeah."

Guthrie rubbed his eyes tiredly. "You know," he said, "I almost envy him."

Something welled up in Hackermeyer. All this time he'd been thinking of Fearfeather as some motiveless puppet he'd maneuvered to destruction. It hadn't been that way at all. Fearfeather had possessed a will of his own. He'd sacrificed himself because he'd chosen to do so.

Suddenly, Hackermeyer realized that the same thing must be true of the others too. They'd been individuals, not pawns. Linstrom had broken not because of anything Hackermeyer had done to him but because of what Linstrom had been. The same was true of Foley—of Wendt—of all of them.

By God, it was true of him too! There wasn't any ring in his nose. *He could do what he wanted.*

Guthrie peered loweringly into his face. Hackermeyer drew back. "What's the matter?" he asked.

"I thought, for one incredible moment, I saw a smile on your—" Guthrie broke off, shook his head. "No, no, I was only dreaming," he said. "Obviously, I—" His mouth slipped open. "Oh, my God," he said. "Another one." He touched Hackermeyer's cheeks with trembling fingertips. "And they didn't crack," he said.

Hackermeyer turned away with convulsive breath.

"You all right?" asked Guthrie.

"Yeah," he answered. There was tension in him but it didn't bother him. It wasn't the same kind of tension he'd felt before.

"Come on," said Guthrie.

"Huh?"

"Cooley wants us."

"Yeah." He pushed up and walked beside Guthrie. He could live with Cooley! The thought was like a burst of joy in him.

Cooley had drawn an outline of Saarbach in the mud.

"This is where the platoon goes in," he told them, pointing. "We move two blocks to this building and take it. They think it's an artillery post. I don't know what we'll come up against before we get there but that's our objective."

We'll take it, Hackermeyer thought. He looked at Cooley intently. He wanted to prove to the sergeant that he hadn't lost all his combat ability. Somehow, this strange new feeling centered on Cooley.

"As for getting to the town from here . . ." Cooley was saying. "The field down there is too exposed for minesweeping. We're going to have to cross it cold. We'll move in behind tanks fitted with exploder disks. If the tanks get stuck, we keep moving anyway. There'll be a cover of smoke to hide us. In case the tanks do get stuck—and they probably will—watch out for Schu mines; the ground is peppered with them. Avoid humps in the ground, any spot that looks wrong to you. Maybe you won't have to worry about them—let's hope so—but keep it in mind. That's pretty thick mud down there."

He pointed at the ground sketch with his bayonet. "There are, at least, two pillboxes on the outskirts of town," he said. "Approximately here"—he scratched an X on the ground—"and here. You see, we'll probably have to pass one of them."

He made another X on the ground, about ten inches from the edge of the town.

"Here's where we are now, on the heights," he said. "Down below, by the side of this road, right about—here—is a covered statue of Christ. Just beyond it is assault position. From there on you can expect anything. Keep moving—with or without the tanks. Don't stay put or you're finished. I can't emphasize that enough, boys: *Keep moving*. Fire your weapons and don't stop for anything. If you have to fall, okay, fall. But get right up and start moving again. We're almost to the finish line now—we can end it today. Let's not foul out now."

Hackermeyer clenched his teeth. We won't, he thought.

"Any questions?" asked Cooley.

Guthrie cleared his throat.

"Who do I see about getting a discharge?" he asked.

IT HAD BEGUN to snow. Scattered flurries of it blew across the slope and plain. The shelling of Saarbach had been going on now for an hour and a half. Hackermeyer stood waiting for the order to move out, his gaze fixed on the town. It was starting to disappear behind the veils of snow.

He turned anxiously as Cooley spoke his name.

"How you doing?" Cooley asked.

Hackermeyer cleared his throat. "Okay," he said.

"What was bothering you before?"

"Well . . ." Hackermeyer gestured slightly. "Mostly—Fear-feather, I think," he said.

Cooley grunted. "He was a nice boy," he said. "You can't brood about it, though. You never did before."

I'm not the same as I was before, Hackermeyer thought.

"You sure that's all?" asked Cooley.

Hackermeyer didn't answer.

"You're going to have to pay attention on this one," Cooley told him, inclining his head toward Saarbach.

Hackermeyer nodded. "I will."

"Okay," said Cooley.

"When are we moving out?"

"Pretty soon."

"Uh-huh." Hackermeyer's shoulders hitched forward as he shivered.

"You sure you're all right?" asked Cooley.

"Yeah." Hackermeyer nodded. "I'm all right."

"Okay, son." Cooley looked at him appraisingly. "I hope so. This is going to be one hell of a battle. I wouldn't like to see you going into it not ready."

"I'm ready."

"Right." Cooley started to reach out, then dropped his hand. "Guess I don't have to check your gear," he said. "You're a pro now."

Hackermeyer repressed the nervous smile.

"Keep an eye on MacFarland," Cooley told him.

"I will."

"He's all right, I think," said Cooley. "Tremont's the only one I'm worried about."

"He'll be all right."

"Let's hope so." Cooley turned his head to spit, then reached up and withdrew the tobacco plug from his mouth, tossing it aside. "Better not take a chance on swallowing it," he said. Hackermeyer grunted with amusement.

They stood, shoulder to shoulder, looking across the plain.

"Will this snow hurt us?" asked Hackermeyer.

"I don't think so," said Cooley. "Anything that fouls up their observation is good for us."

"Yeah. That's right." Hackermeyer blinked as a snowflake landed on his right eyelid. "It's—been a long time, hasn't it?" he said, not knowing exactly what he meant. "I mean—it seems long."

"What does?"

"Oh—" Hackermeyer shrugged. "Being with the squad," he said. "I guess it doesn't seem so long to you. You've been with it so long. You've seen so many soldiers."

"A lot of men," said Cooley. "Not too many soldiers."

Am I one? Hackermeyer almost asked. He shuddered. That would be a dumb thing to ask.

"Sarge?" he said.

"Uh?"

"What you—said that day."

"When was that, son?"

"When we were in that cave. You know?"

"What'd I say?"

"Well, you really said it after, when we left it."

"Said what?"

Hackermeyer braced himself. "About me—coming to—you know, stay with you?" he said.

"You're welcome to," said Cooley. "Any time."

"Well—" Hackermeyer cleared his throat laboredly. "I—I think I'd like that."

"Good," said Cooley. "Plan on it, then."

"What's it like out—?" Hackermeyer broke off as the sergeant patted his shoulder and said, "I think we're going. Hold on."

Hackermeyer watched him moving toward a knot of officers. I can do it, he thought, almost dazed. Cooley hadn't been just talking; he'd meant it. He could go and live with Cooley when the war was over. Any time.

Breath wavered in his lungs. He had to make it today. They both had to make it today—and tomorrow and every day until the war was over. The thought of losing that future on Cooley's ranch was terrifying to him.

He blinked and looked around confusedly. He unslung his rifle, then put it back again. Not time for shooting yet. He wondered if he'd be able to fire the M1 now. He thought he would but the uncertainty disturbed him. He mustn't fail Cooley. He watched the sergeant, saw him nod to one of the officers, then turn away from them.

"Keep it scattered on the way down," he told the squad. "Guthrie, Tremont, over there. MacFarland, Hack, here, here. Get ready."

They all stood motionless as Cooley raised his arm. Hackermeyer watched the sergeant's hand waver in the air and felt himself leaning forward in anticipation. I'm ready, he thought.

Cooley's arm dropped. "Here we go," he said. "Remember what I said and keep your eyes open."

They started down the slope. It was so sheer that it reminded Hackermeyer of the one on which the company had been fired on by camouflaged tanks. He shuddered uncontrollably. This was different, he assured himself. There were no concealing woods below and the Germans were disabled by artillery fire. Still, he could not dispel the rising dread. For the first time since he'd joined the squad, he had a reason for not wanting to be killed; he had a future that mattered to him. Would that make him a better soldier? Or a worse one?

Hackermeyer blinked his eyes, newly aware of his skidding, clambering descent. He had to pay attention. He wanted to survive. Keep your eyes open. He repeated the words until they drove away all other thoughts.

"Schnickelfritz, we are upon you," he heard. He glanced aside and saw Guthrie working his way down the slope a few yards away. He hoped Guthrie wasn't killed today.

He looked to both sides. As far as he could see in either direction the slope was thick with moving soldiers. He glanced across his shoulder. More and more troops were appearing on the ridge and starting downward. They must be using everybody, he thought. They weren't fooling anymore; the stalemate was ended.

He sucked in apprehensively at the glacial air, eyes squinted against the wind-scored buffeting of snow. It was coming down more heavily now. He wasn't sure whether he liked that or not. True, it would conceal them—but it would, also, conceal their targets. He shook off the thought. It didn't matter. Snow or not, the assault was launched. No point in worrying about it now.

Keep moving. Cooley's order rose up in his mind. He'd follow it. Nothing else mattered.

He looked toward the town and felt a twinge of shock. It appeared to have moved away from them. Several moments passed before he realized that, from the heights, Saarbach would look closer. He lowered his gaze. A thousand yards, he thought. The six miles Foley had spoken of were, finally, traversed; yard by yard, sometimes two and three times over. Now only a thousand yards stood between them and victory. The shiver of excitement faded as he realized that these thousand yards were going to be more deadly than all the rest combined.

A sound of heavy engines reached his ears. Peering through the snow, he saw the tanks lined up along the edge of the broad field, their engines revving at maximum. He saw the exploder disks attached to the fronts of the tanks; they looked, to him, like two gigantic tires axled close together. They couldn't be rubber, he thought. Rubber wouldn't explode a deeply buried mine, would it?

He forced away the question, once more contracting all thought to the single unit of himself. His job was to advance on Saarbach, following a tank or, if the tank got bogged, moving by himself—never stopping, falling prone if need be but advancing always. He'd concentrate on that, excluding from attention all other considerations. *Move*, he started a chanting in his mind. *Move—move—move—move—*

He froze as, farther down the slope, a flower of explosion blossomed. What was that? To his right, another explosion crashed. Suddenly, he realized that the Germans were firing on them. The idea startled him. He'd taken it for granted that the Germans were pinned down by the tremendous barrage being lowered on them. It was difficult to imagine their aiming and firing their cannons in the midst of that murderous deluge.

He clenched his teeth and forcibly shut down his mind. It didn't matter. He had only one concern and that was to keep moving. Tensed against the warning shriek of approaching shells, he started downward again, overshoes plowing through the sticky mud. They were almost to the bottom now. He could see men scuttling toward the tanks, the tanks beginning their beetlelike crawl across the plain.

He ducked instinctively as a piercing whistle sounded overhead. Up on the slope, an explosion thundered. Hackermeyer reached up and fingered the cotton deeper into his ears. *Move,* he thought. A thin rain of mud spattered down on him but he ignored it, kept on moving. Orange torches of explosions walked across the slope. Hackermeyer lunged downward several yards, then slowed himself. He looked around and picked out the forms of Cooley and Tremont, then that of MacFarland. Where was Guthrie? His eyes squinted into the curtaining snow until he saw Guthrie waiting for them on the level ground below.

They reached the bottom of the slope.

"On the double!" Cooley ordered. "Follow that tank over there! Stay behind it! Go!"

Hackermeyer started running with the others, gasping at the cold, wet air. Snowflakes landed in his eyes, they blew into his mouth. Ahead, he saw the tank grinding across the field. His stride faltered as an explosion roared close behind them and the ground shook. Shrapnel howled above him but he kept on running, gaze fixed on the almost constant flashes of explosion beneath the churning tank disks.

Something loomed in front of him; a dark pole with a structure built on top of it. As he drew nearer, he saw that it was the roofed-over statue of Christ that Cooley had mentioned. Passing it, he caught a glimpse of the weather-worn face and body on the cross.

Then it was behind him and he was running in the plowed-up wake of the tank. Breath fell heatedly from his lips; the beginning of a stitch needled up his left side. He stopped running and walked as rapidly as he could, noticing that he held his M1 at high port, wondering when he'd unslung it. Keep moving. The order flared automatically. He strode on quickly, skirting a shell hole. Glancing to the right, he saw what looked like dozens of hummocks on the whitening earth. Schu mines, he thought. Without the tank in front of them, they'd never make it.

He grunted in surprise as dense, white smoke came boiling

over the ground at him. Suddenly, he was walking in it. Smoke screen, he thought. He hadn't even seen it fall. He moved steadily through the roiling acrid-smelling mist. Now, between the smoke and snow, visibility was limited to several feet around.

"Don't leave the tank path!" Cooley's shout came from behind. Hackermeyer glanced down and felt a burst of panic as he saw that he was angling across the edge of the broad track. He moved in toward the center of it, overtaking Guthrie. They started on, then both stopped simultaneously as the blasts came rushing at them.

"Hit it!" Cooley shouted.

In an instant, both of them were prone, surrounded by the deafening bursts, the wail of shrapnel, the waves of battering concussion. Hackermeyer clung to the spasmed earth with talon-shaped fingers, eyes tightly closed, mouth yawning, body palsied. No! the voice screamed out in terror. Please, God, please, please, please! He realized that he was praying but he couldn't stop.

The explosions moved off to their left. "Go!" yelled Cooley. Hackermeyer pushed up on trembling legs and started forward. Guthrie moved beside him.

"You know what?" said Guthrie in a wavering voice. "War *is* hell."

They both jumped as the tank gun started firing, then continued on, their faces frozen into hard, twisted masks. Hackermeyer felt swallowed by the noise—the thunderclaps of shell explosions, the crashing reports of the tank cannon, the Schu mines detonating underneath the turning disks.

He and Guthrie stopped when the tank appeared in front of them. A cluster of soldiers stood around it, looking at one another fearfully. Hackermeyer saw that the tank was listing to the right, its treads clawing ineffectually at the mud. A man had popped up from the turret and was looking at the ground, his lips moving as if he were cursing. His tank was hopelessly mired. The labored grinding of its treads only pulled it deeper into the slime.

Abruptly, they stopped moving altogether.

Hackermeyer turned as Cooley flat-handed him on the shoulder. "Let's go!" Cooley hurried forward, gesturing for the other soldiers to move on. They looked at him fearfully as he pushed them away from the tank. Hackermeyer and Guthrie followed. As they passed the gigantic exploder disks, Hackermeyer saw that these were made of metal.

Everyone moved slowly and deliberately now, eyes fixed to the ground in front of them, apparently oblivious to the shell explosions all around. Everyone seemed to hold back, waiting for someone else to go ahead.

"Come on!" yelled Cooley, leading the procession. "Keep moving!"

"You go if you want to!" someone shouted angrily.

"Can't you see I am!" retorted Cooley. "Come on, let's go!"

Hackermeyer watched him, terrified. The sergeant was moving backward, hardly looking at the ground, urging on the other soldiers. Don't, thought Hackermeyer. He raised his right hand as if to signal Cooley.

Suddenly, all of them were statues as a sharp explosion flared nearby. Hackermeyer jerked his head around and saw a soldier flopping on the mud. The man began to scream.

"Go!" roared Cooley.

Hackermeyer shuffled on, his stomach muscles fluttering. He tried not to look at the soldier but, as the man stopped screaming, he had to glance aside. His stomach walls convulsed. The man was only twitching now and Hackermeyer could see that both his legs were blown off to the thighs; blood was gushing from the ragged stumps. Hackermeyer saw its brightness rivering off, then turned his head away, gagging.

Another explosion blasted to his left. Another soldier screamed out in sudden horror of annihilation. Hackermeyer kept moving, trying not to see the second legless body thrashing in the mud or hear the screams of witless agony. A voice kept murmuring, begging, in his mind: No, no, no. He didn't want to die; oh God, he didn't want to die.

Behind them, shell explosions jarred across the field like giant bootfalls. Everyone flung themselves forward and, for several minutes, Hackermeyer was isolated in his casing of resistance, eyes shut, body twitching, rigidly. When it ended, Cooley ordered them to "Go" and Hackermeyer pushed up, feeling limp and ponderous. As he started on, he glanced back and saw the tank afire, black smoke curdling from its turret.

"Watch your ground!" yelled Cooley.

Hackermeyer whirled back looking downward. There was a Schu mine right in front of him. The earth seemed to rock beneath his feet. The snow flew blindingly into his eyes. Breathing hard, he stared down at the mound of earth with the sprinkling of snow across it. He couldn't budge.

"Walk around it, son," said Cooley, taking hold of his arm. "Come on." Hackermeyer stumbled beside the sergeant, unable to take his eyes from the mine.

"There's another one," said Cooley, pointing. He let go of Hackermeyer's arm and moved away. Don't leave me! Hackermeyer almost cried, freezing in his tracks. *Keep moving*, parroted his mind. He swallowed hard and took a forward step. Every muscle tensed, he circuited the Schu mine slowly. Cooley was right, the realization managed to pierce his dread; the mines were easy to spot. There were so many of them and the Germans had made little attempt at camouflage. Hackermeyer kept moving, every step becoming more assured. Whenever anyone around him stepped on a mine, he forced blinders on his sight and kept on going. It seemed to him as if the thousand yards had been extended to a million. No matter how far they went, all he could see, ahead, was snow and smoke.

Another battering of shell explosions. Hackermeyer pressed against the bucking earth, eyes shut, mouth open.

"Names!" roared Cooley.

Hackermeyer twisted his head aside and yelled his name.

"Guthrie!"

"MacFarland!"

"Kelly!"

Hackermeyer looked up blankly. Kelly? He realized, then, that one of the men from another squad had answered without thinking.

"Tremont?" Cooley shouted.

"He-ere!" cried Tremont.

Shells exploded all around. They rocked the earth and detonated Schu mines, jetted murky clouds of mud into the snow-filled air. Razor-edged cleavers of shrapnel shot in all directions, walls of concussion slammed against them. Hackermeyer trembled, helpless, cleaving to the mud as if gravity had lost its hold and he resisted being sucked into the sky. Thought was gone again. He was a mindless clump of flesh and bone, welded to the floundering earth.

The shelling passed and Cooley shouted, "Go!" Ears ringing, Hackermeyer strained up and started forward giddily. His head felt as if it were filled with heated sand that shifted with his every step, threatening his balance. He almost trod squarely on a mine. Eyes forced wide and staring, he walked around the hummock slowly, holding his breath.

"Tank ditch!" Cooley shouted. "Cross it!"

Just ahead, Hackermeyer saw the wide, deep trench. Men were jumping into it, appearing on the other side, and clambering out laboriously. Hackermeyer hesitated on the edge before he jumped, bracing himself as he saw that he was going to land in muddy water. Splashing down, he lost balance and fell, his left hand sinking into mud beneath a foot of icy water. He pushed up with a gasp and staggered to the opposite side of the ditch. He lunged up the steep wall, failed to catch hold and slithered back again. He jumped a second time, a third, clawing at the muddy wall and slipping back. Up above, Cooley moved along the edge, grabbing soldier after soldier and hauling them up.

"We're through the mines now!" he was yelling. "You can take the lead out! Skirmish line! Let's go!" He grabbed Hackermeyer's wrist and jerked him to the surface. Hackermeyer saw Guthrie to his right and, behind, just landing in the ditch water, Tremont and MacFarland.

"Come on!" he shouted as he broke into a lumbering run.

Machine-gun fire drove them to the ground. Hackermeyer raised his head enough to squint toward Saarbach. The smoke was drifting off and, through the haze of snow, he could just make out the outskirts of the town. They were closer than he'd thought. He wondered when the American barrage was going to let up.

"Fire!" Cooley shouted. "Keep it heavy! Fire! Fire!"

Hackermeyer heard the burst of Guthrie's BAR and, raising his M1 automatically, he started firing. It doesn't matter if you see a thing, he thought, imagining himself lecturing Tremont and MacFarland; fire volume counts as much as accuracy! The M1 jarred against his flesh, the clip popped out. Hastily, he reloaded.

The American barrage was lifted.

"Hackermeyer, MacFarland, go!" yelled Cooley.

Hackermeyer shoved up and started running in zigzag lines. After seven yards, he hit the ground and started firing. Behind him, Cooley shouted forward Guthrie and Tremont. All around, squad leaders were moving up their men in short rushes. The smoke screen had almost dissipated now, and Hackermeyer could see a clump of burning cottages ahead. From one of them, a German machine gun was firing. The orange beads of tracer bullets skimmed out at them, flashing back and forth across the area.

"Hackermeyer, MacFarland, go!" yelled Cooley.

Hackermeyer pushed to his feet again and ran crashing down almost immediately as the line of machine-gun fire swept back toward him. He raised his M1 shakily and started firing. To his right and left, Guthrie and Tremont appeared, slapping down in the mud. Guthrie opened fire. Tremont only goggled toward the town, his eyes all whites. Nearby, MacFarland fired steadily.

An endless void of running and falling, of firing toward the cottages . . . Now Hackermeyer was rushing crookedly, his M1 raised to high port. Now he was dropping, catching his weight on the rifle butt, slamming to his chest. Now he was shooting, the M1 jolting at his shoulder, the acrid smoke fumes in his nostrils. Now he was prone and rigid, sweating out an eighty-eight barrage, the snowflakes tickling coldly at his neck, the smell of cordite choking him. Now he was running again, now falling again, now firing—locked in an inertia of repeated movements while the town drew closer . . . while men fell dead around him, doubled over by the lashing drive of bullets, cut apart by scaling metal, pounded to oblivion by shock waves. Running, falling, firing, running, falling, firing—all in a mindless trance; never conscious of individual movements, only of the total motion forward, of the din, the burning ache of muscles driven beyond their strength. Bundles of dead and wounded everywhere . . . He ran among them drunkenly, locked in a daze of instinctive locomotion. Only as they reached the edge of town did it occur to him that they had bypassed the pillboxes.

As though awakening from a dream, Hackermeyer found himself behind a hedge, the leafless twigs of it hung with strips of flesh and uniform. He stared at them, then flattened as a blast of machine-gun fire tore away the hedge above him. He glanced up and saw a soldier dashing toward the cottage, stopping to pitch a grenade. Abruptly, the soldier hitched backward from the rending impact of bullets, tilted to the left and sprawled, lifeless, on the ground. The grenade bounced off the cottage wall and exploded uselessly. Hackermeyer raised his M1 and fired it empty at the cottage window. To his left, Guthrie did the same. The air was filled with a transverse hail of bullets.

Another grenade exploded by the house, geysering a puff of white smoke that diffused, in seconds, to a heavy cloud. To his left, Hackermeyer saw a soldier rearing up and sprinting toward the cottage, a blur of dark motion in the falling whiteness. The man threw one grenade, another. The two explosions blasted close together, the machine gun stopped. The soldier plunged into the smoke, firing his sub-machine gun.

"Rush it!" Cooley shouted.

Hackermeyer scrambled up and started running toward the cottage. He heard the rattle of the sub-machine gun, then a third grenade explosion. Suddenly, the cottage was in front of him, the soldier looking through the window. As Hackermeyer came running up, the man turned quickly. "That's *it!*" he cried, and raced away. Hackermeyer watched him disappear, then looked around for the squad. MacFarland ran up, then Tremont, finally Guthrie and Cooley.

"Let's go!" shouted Cooley.

The five of them rushed around the corner of the cottage into an alley littered with piles of stone and masonry. Walls yawned on either side of them, revealing the structures behind them. A debris of broken furniture lay scattered everywhere. The nostril-searing reek of cordite filled the air.

"On the double!" Cooley yelled.

They reached a cross street and, after checking, Cooley sent them, one by one, around the corner—Guthrie first, followed by MacFarland, Hackermeyer, Tremont; Cooley last. Crouching slightly, Hackermeyer moved along the sides of burning houses, trying to see through the snow and rubble-hazed air. All along the cobblestone street, American soldiers were advancing, firing constantly at cellar windows, attics, rooftops. Spandau fire seemed to blaze from everywhere. Hackermeyer saw a German soldier rush into the street, firing his burp gun empty. The German threw his weapon to the pavement and flung his arms up, shouting, *"Kamerad!"* Bullets hit him as he spoke and sent him crashing back onto the street.

"Keep moving!" Cooley told them.

Hackermeyer started off again, eyes searching warily. A bullet snapped past his head, chipping off a scrap of masonry. Jerking his head back, he saw a flashing muzzle blast at the second-story window of a house across the street. Before he could raise his rifle, several soldiers from the other squads, along with Guthrie, poured fire through the window and the rifle barrel pulled back out of sight. Hackermeyer saw Guthrie standing, legs akimbo, the BAR slung at his hip. Guthrie snatched a clip from Tremont's hand and shoved it up into his weapon with a blur of movement.

"Keep it going!" Cooley ordered.

Hackermeyer walked unevenly along the cratered street, trying to look in every direction at once. His gaze jumped to a house half fallen over; to another house split open, outside wall sheared off, its furniture perched on the edges of floors; to a splintered tavern sign swaying in the wind; to the rotted body of a cat beneath a stone. He lunged across the foot of an alley, catching a glimpse of a fallen horse, its body bloated, its head smashed to a formless pulp. He jumped across a shell hole filled with muddy, snow-sprinkled water, skidded and almost fell.

Something banged down in the middle of the street and started rolling in a circle. Hackermeyer's body acted faster than his mind, and suddenly he was lying on the muddy pavement. The explosion of the grenade was thunderous in the narrow thoroughfare. Hackermeyer felt shrapnel buzzing past him, a fragment of it gashing across his helmet. Behind him, he heard the blasting chatter of an automatic gun and pushed up in time to see a German soldier toppling from a roof. The German landed with a heavy thud, his dark helmet flying off and flopping crazily on the pavement.

"Go!" said Cooley.

Hackermeyer stood on wavering legs and moved forward again. He started past the shrapnel-pocked door of a huge garage, his overshoes crunching on a litter of broken glass. He looked around, trying to maintain alertness, but his mind kept drifting; there was too much to follow. In the distance, he caught sight of a gas station and was startled to see the word Esso on it. There were Esso stations in Brooklyn!

He stopped abruptly. Up ahead, Guthrie had halted at the end of the garage and was peering around the corner. Hackermeyer twitched as Cooley hurried past him and joined Guthrie. He watched them talking together, wondering if he should be with them. He reached up and raised his coat-collar to keep the snow-flakes from landing on the back of his neck.

After several moments, Cooley waved them on and, one by one, they jogged across the rubble-strewn intersection like a line of bears. Hackermeyer saw wires hanging down from telephone poles in dark, tangled strands that undulated in the wind. He saw a shopwindow covered with wire netting. Trying to see inside it, he failed to notice the brick in his path. He stumbled on its edge and lost his balance, lurching against the fire-blackened wall of a building. Through its window he could see a charred debris of fallen beams and brick and metal all piled high in jagged, smoking heaps.

Pushing away, he hobbled onward down the street behind MacFarland. Across the way, he saw a tireless Volkswagen lying on its side, its roof caved in as though by some gigantic kick. He moved on, wondering how soon the town would fall. Now that they were actually in Saarbach, this part seemed, somehow, frighteningly anticlimactic.

Up ahead, a German machine gun began its dry, rattling fire and he ducked into a doorway, wincing at the ear-piercing ring of bullets ricocheting off brick walls and paving. Peering around the edge of the doorframe, he saw that everyone had taken cover. Cooley stood in another doorway with MacFarland. Guthrie lay behind a block of masonry, firing his BAR in rapid bursts. Hackermeyer followed the line of his fire to a second-story window overlooking the length of the street from above a narrow archway. Through the curtains of snow, he could just make out the gun muzzle protruding from the glassless cavity.

He started to raise the M1 when his gaze was arrested by the movement of an American soldier who had detached himself from the shadow of a building across the way. The soldier ran into the center of the street, firing a sub-machine gun toward the window above the archway. Hackermeyer saw that it was the same man who had knocked out the machine-gun emplacement in the cottage. He watched in awe as the man advanced on the archway, firing steadily. He saw bullets chipping up the pavement all around the man. In an instant, they had knocked the man's legs out from under him and he was on his side as if he'd just been tackled. Hackermeyer's mouth slipped open as he saw the man continue moving toward the archway, firing his weapon with one hand, pulling himself along with the other, leaving a scarlet trail in the snow.

Hackermeyer's head jerked up as a sharp explosion burst inside the window where the German machine gun was. He saw part of the wall buckle outward, showering bricks and mortar to the street below. Looking around, Hackermeyer saw a man fitting a second grenade to his rifle launcher. He looked at the soldier lying in the street. Two men were approaching him, their eyes fixed on the archway window, their rifles pointing toward it.

"Let's go!" said Cooley.

As he passed the wounded soldier, Hackermeyer saw that he was talking excitedly to his friends. The man started to get up as if he didn't realize that he was hit, then fell back, gasping. Both his legs were pumping blood from various holes, staining the snow with vivid, widening blotches. The two men held the soldier down and one of them looked around, yelling for a stretcher bearer.

"The hell with that!" Hackermeyer heard the wounded man say angrily. "Ain't nobody else can lead my squad!"

Hackermeyer turned away, a tremor sucking at his stomach muscles. He didn't want to think about sergeants getting hit. He walked off quickly, trying, in vain, to concentrate on his job. Somewhere, he had lost all mental focus. He couldn't zero in his mind on anything. The present moment seemed, to him, an inscrutable chaos. Men moved everywhere, apparently without direction or goal. They ducked into doorways. They were seen at first- and second-story windows. They disappeared into shadowy alleys. They skulked along the sides of buildings. They fired their weapons at an enemy who was everywhere and nowhere. What targets appeared were gone so rapidly that he was unable to raise his M1 before they disappeared or were destroyed. He realized, with a pang of guilt, that he hadn't fired his rifle once since they had entered Saarbach—and the more time that passed, the less could he imagine firing it. Yet he was required to do so. It didn't make sense. He remembered Foley saying that. He was beginning to appreciate the feeling that Foley had been trying to express.

He refocused his eyes and looked ahead. Guthrie and Mac-Farland were lying behind the rubble of a fallen building, firing into an open area. Hackermeyer saw Cooley gesturing to him and started forward, then stopped and looked around.

"Tremont?" he called.

Tremont's head appeared, poking through a window frame. "Yeah?" he inquired tremulously.

"Come on!" Hackermeyer waited for him and they both moved forward, crawling in beside the others.

"There's your target," Cooley told them, pointing. Hackermeyer raised his eyes above the top of the rubble and looked.

The building stood in the center of a wide square. It was three stories high, its stone face cracked and scarred by explosions. The platoon was pouring fire into it. Hackermeyer saw hundreds of tracer bullets flashing out like orange-white beads on strings that bounced off walls or disappeared through window openings. To their left, at another street entrance to the square, a heavy machine-gun crew had set up their weapon and was raking the building with continuous fire. There seemed to be no counterfire from the Germans.

"Start shooting, boys," said Cooley.

Hackermeyer knocked a chunk of masonry forward with his rifle butt. Resting the M1 across a brick, he started firing at the building. A mortar shell exploded in the square. A series of explosions followed, moving slowly toward the building until they started blowing off sections of the roof. Hackermeyer fired until the empty clip popped out. As he reloaded, he noticed Cooley talking to Tremont. After several moments, Tremont fired at the building once.

"Go on," said Cooley. Tremont fired a second time, pulling the trigger as if it had a razor edge. "Keep shooting, boy," said Cooley. "You ain't being charged for bullets."

With a faint smile, Hackermeyer squinted through the rear sight and opened fire again. Poor kid, he thought. He fired his rifle empty and reloaded it. It was easier shooting at a building than a person, he realized. He still didn't know how he'd react if his target were a German soldier.

He was aiming again when Cooley shouted, "Here we go! Let's pour it on!"

Hackermeyer looked around and saw that, from three sides of the square, men were dashing out into the snow-veiled open, zigzagging forward several yards, then falling prone and firing while other men ran out to join them.

"Guthrie, Tremont, get ready," Cooley said.

Hackermeyer glanced aside. Tremont was looking at the sergeant fearfully. "Keep firing," Cooley told him, and Tremont squeezed off another diffident shot.

Hackermeyer turned his gaze to the building and emptied his rifle into one of the second-story windows.

He was pressing down a new clip when Cooley ordered, "Guthrie, Tremont, go! Hack, MacFarland, heavy fire!"

Hackermeyer jerked his thumb free of the closing bolt and aimed. A snowflake landed on his right eyelid, making him blink.

"Fire!" Cooley shouted.

Hackermeyer started shooting as Guthrie and Tremont ran around the rubble heap and into the square, picking up impetus as they ran. He noticed that Tremont kept his eyes on Guthrie. The moment Guthrie buckled his knees and fell, Tremont did the same. Guthrie started firing at the building; Tremont lay shivering in the snow.

"Hack, MacFarland, go!" yelled Cooley.

Sucking in breath, Hackermeyer shoved up and lumbered around the pile of debris. He started running toward the building.

He was barely into the open when the German tank appeared. He staggered to a halt, gaping at the giant, square-hulled vehicle as it came grinding around the corner of the three-story building, treads rasping on the rubbled pavement, shooting out sprays of pulverized debris. The massive cannon jerked back, its detonation crashing in the air. Smoke swirled around the tank; the pavement shook. In an instant, the shell blew out the side of a house across the square. Hackermeyer fell.

The attack seemed to disintegrate with the tank's appearance. Hackermeyer saw men rushing back toward the side streets, many of them without their weapons. He pushed up shakily, looking around. Everywhere he turned, men were being cut down by the tank's machine gun and by shrapnel from the shell explosions. He stood on wavering legs and started moving backward, staring at the tank. It had stopped moving now and was raking the square with machine-gun fire. Hackermeyer dropped and heard the bullets clanging off the pavement. He buried his face in his arms and lay there, trembling.

Cooley jerked him brutally to his feet. He spun Hackermeyer around and shoved him toward the street from which they'd come. "Go!" he shouted.

Hackermeyer started running clumsily. The tank cannon blasted deafeningly, a shell flashed across the square, destroying the side of another house. Hackermeyer kept running. He scrabbled to the top of the rubble heap and skidded down the opposite side, grunting loudly as he hit the ground. Guthrie was already there, lying on his back, eyes closed, a trickle of blood on his right cheek. As Hackermeyer stared at him, Guthrie opened his eyes and returned the look. Neither of them could speak. They both ducked, wincing, as machine-gun bullets ripped across the top of the rubble, showering them with abraded stone.

Cooley and MacFarland came dashing from the square. "Come on!" yelled Cooley.

Hackermeyer struggled up and started after them, feeling as if he were caught in one of those dreams in which he couldn't run no matter how desperately he tried. His legs felt like solid blocks of stone. Ahead of him, he saw Cooley rake around, face twisted by a fierce grimace. "Let's go!" roared Cooley. Hackermeyer clenched his teeth and ran a little faster.

They all stopped running at the same time. "Jesus!" Guthrie cried.

A second German tank was waiting at the foot of the street. Its machine guns opened up on them.

"In there!" cried Cooley, shoving them toward the doorway of a nearby house.

Hackermeyer lunged into its dim-lit interior and staggered to a halt in the center of the moldy-smelling room. We're trapped, he thought. He stared incredulously at the pile of soggy newspapers on the floor, the litter of rusty cans, the broken crockery, the sagging, legless sofa.

"In there!" Cooley shouted. Hackermeyer whirled and saw the sergeant still outside, directing other members of the platoon from the bullet-raked street. Get in here! he thought. He started for the door, then stopped as Cooley rushed inside. "Guthrie, Hack, upstairs!" he ordered. "Cover the windows!"

Hackermeyer looked around for the stairs, feeling dizzy and unreal. "Here!" said Guthrie. Hackermeyer kept turning until he saw Guthrie standing at the bottom of a narrow flight of steps, then, coughing, he scuttled across the squeaky floor and trailed Guthrie up the stairs. His legs began to wobble and he grabbed at the railing. It started to crack and he let go hastily, pitching himself toward the wall. Pushing away from it, he climbed the rest of the stairs and stumbled through a narrow doorway. Guthrie was, already, at one of the windows. Hackermeyer limped over to him.

"Well, we've had it," Guthrie muttered.

"Huh?"

"Look! Look!" said Guthrie, pointing out the window.

Hackermeyer leaned out and shuddered. The German tank was moving up the street. He pulled back quickly.

"What do we do?" he asked.

Guthrie shook his head. "We've had it," he said. "This Goddamn town will never fall." He kept shaking his head. "Oh, Christ," he said. "What a waste of time. What a stupid, Goddamn waste of time!"

"What are we going to *do?*"

"We're going to die, that's what we're going to do!" flared Guthrie. "Oh . . . Christ!" He slammed the metal butt of his BAR against the wall, knocking loose a clod of plaster. "What a stupid, Goddamn way to run a war!" he raged. He slumped to the floor and leaned against the wall exhaustedly. "Oh, boy," he said. "Oh, boy, oh, boy, oh, boy."

Hackermeyer started to speak when there was a clatter of footsteps on the stairs and two men burst into the room. One of them was carrying a bazooka.

"Goddamn it, on your feet!" he yelled at Guthrie. "Cover that window, damn it!" Rushing to the other window, he leaned out, then jerked back in, grimacing. "Jesus, there it comes!" he cried. He lay the bazooka across his shoulder hastily. "Load it!" he shouted.

Hackermeyer watched the other man load the bazooka with shaking fingers. From the corners of his eyes, he saw Guthrie standing at the window. "Better hurry," Guthrie said, sounding almost amused. The man with the bazooka glared at him, then started peering through the bazooka sight as the other man connected the wires.

Suddenly, all of them were diving to the floor as machine-gun bullets thudded across the outside wall and through the windows. The man who had loaded the bazooka cried out shrilly and lunged to his feet, a horrified expression on his face. "Don't let me fall!" he cried. "Keep walking me!" Hackermeyer saw his face go white. The man took several rolling strides across the room, then collapsed. He drew his legs up high and kicked out violently as he died.

The other man, with a sobbing curse, crawled to the window and stood up quickly. He had just begun to aim when the bullets caught him in the face and knocked him backward like a club blow. Hackermeyer saw the man's eyes staring at the ceiling. The rest of his face was a torn, blood-spouting pulp. The bazooka rocked back and forth on the floorboards.

At the other window, Guthrie started firing his BAR. Hackermeyer heard the bullets bouncing off the tank with the sound of rivets being hammered in.

"Hack!" yelled Guthrie, pointing toward the bazooka, then firing again.

Catching his breath, Hackermeyer crawled across the floor and grabbed the bazooka. Sitting up, he worked his way to the window and waited, panting. When the line of machine-gun fire was lowered to the first floor, he pushed to his knees, twisted around and slid the bazooka across the sill.

He couldn't miss. The giant tank was only twenty yards away. Pulling in a quick breath, he held himself rigid and drew back on the trigger. The shell struck instantly. The tank shuddered and there was a muffled explosion inside it. In seconds, bright fire jetted from the turret openings, then sank quickly to smaller, bluer flames. Black smoke started roiling up in greasy billows.

"Beautiful!" yelled Guthrie, savagely delighted.

No one tried to leave the burning tank. Hackermeyer felt sick as he imagined what was going on inside it. He sank down into a half-lying, half-sitting position against the wall and stared at the man who had cursed Guthrie. One moment, the man had been vitally alive, furious, preparing to fire his bazooka at the tank. The next moment, he was dead, stripped of all action and reaction. Hackermeyer couldn't understand it.

There were hurried footsteps in the hall and Cooley dashed in. "Man, you really—" he started, breaking off, startledly, as he saw the two men crumpled on the floor. He looked at Hackermeyer.

"Did *you* knock out the tank?" he asked.

Hackermeyer nodded feebly.

"Good shot." Cooley looked at the dead men again, then back at Hackermeyer. "You saved lots of lives," he said.

They all hit the floor as the first shell detonated on the roof. "Now what?" shouted Guthrie.

A second shell exploded overhead and part of the ceiling caved in. Cooley disappeared in a shower of debris. Another shell knocked a hole in one wall and crashed out through the opposite wall without exploding. Lath and plaster rained on Hackermeyer. He felt a burning pain across the back of his neck and reached up, gasping, his glove fingers coming away red. He glanced up as Cooley stumbled over, clothes and features leprous with a coating of plaster dust.

"All right?" gasped Cooley.

"My neck."

Cooley dropped beside him and bent Hackermeyer's head forward. "Just a scratch," he said. He spat out plaster dust. "You're all right." He looked across the room. "Hey, Guthrie!"

"What?"

"All right?"

"Yeah! Sure! I'm happy as a lark!"

Cooley made a snorting noise. Then his head snapped around and he was looking grimly toward the window.

Another tank was coming down the street.

"Well, it's a cinch it ain't ours," said Cooley. "Let's get that bazooka loaded." Grabbing one of the containers, he jerked off its cap and slid out the rocket shell. Hackermeyer held the bazooka across his shoulder while Cooley slid in the shell and connected wires. He patted Hackermeyer's shoulder.

"Knock him dead," he said.

"Don't you want to—?"

"Hell, no, you're Deadeye Dick," said Cooley. "Go on." He grabbed Hackermeyer's arm. "Might as well use the new window," he said, pointing to the jagged hole the shell had torn out of the east wall. Hackermeyer walked over to it, Cooley beside him. Out in the street, the noise of the approaching tank was very loud. Hackermeyer looked past the roof of the adjoining house. About forty yards away, a Panther tank was grinding and squeaking toward them, its machine guns firing straight ahead.

"Get him," said Cooley.

Hackermeyer raised the bazooka and aimed. He glanced back to make sure Guthrie wasn't behind him. "He's all right," said Cooley. Hackermeyer turned and aimed again. Just as the tank cannon started firing, the bazooka shuddered in his grip and he saw the shell bounce off the turret, disappear.

He looked across his shoulder worriedly. Cooley was pushing in another shell. Hackermeyer swallowed but couldn't dislodge the obstruction in his throat. His teeth started chattering and he clamped them together, turning back to the hole. The tank was very close now. He saw a spray of hand grenades bouncing off its hull, all of them exploding without effect. He saw the snout of the tank cannon wheeling toward the house.

"They're going to—" he began.

His voice was lost beneath the deafening roar. The house seemed to stagger, flinging him against the wall. He bounced off and landed on his back, staring up through the hole in the roof. The tank cannon roared again, the house shuddering as the shell exploded down below. Hackermeyer slid a yard across the floor and shoved up on an elbow, looking around dizzily. He saw Cooley stumbling to the shell hole in the wall. The sergeant started firing his carbine.

"Guthrie!" he shouted. "Shoot into the cannon!"

Hackermeyer struggled to his feet and weaved to Cooley's side. The tank had stopped and was tilting to its left. He saw the cannon pointing at a house across the street, then firing. Magically, a ragged hole appeared in the side of the house. Smoke and debris came shooting out through the lower windows as the shell exploded.

"The bazooka!" Cooley shouted.

Hackermeyer picked it up. Shoving the end of it through the hole, he aimed at the tank and pulled the trigger. Fire belched out behind him, the shell bounced off the turret and shot up into the sky. Hackermeyer looked at Cooley helplessly. The sergeant was already sliding another rocket shell from its container.

"One of the bastards has to work!" said Cooley.

There was a muffled explosion outside, and they both looked through the hole. Smoke was gushing from the turret of the tank; the cannon end drooped silently. Abruptly, tongues of flame began to lick upward from the hatch. The tank shuddered with a violent, interior explosion, then another. A bursting shell tore out one side of the hull and Hackermeyer saw a burning man topple out onto the street. He turned away, then realized that someone was shouting at them from below.

"What?" yelled Cooley.

"Orders to withdraw!" said the voice. "Let's go! On the double!"

Cooley squinted toward the hall, a dumbfounded expression on his face. Hackermeyer watched Guthrie reeling for the doorway. "Yes, sir," Guthrie muttered tensely, staring straight ahead. "Yes, sir, folks."

"Oh . . . shit!" Cooley gestured savagely toward the hall. "Come on, let's go," he said.

Hackermeyer slung on his M1 and they moved into the hall and down the stairs. As they reached the first floor, Hackermeyer saw three soldiers lying dead. The walls were cracked and one of them was almost gone.

"All right, now listen," said the lieutenant, breathing hard. "We're going out through that opening over there. We're going back to where we entered town and regroup. Got it? All right, you, you, you, and you!" He pointed stabbingly at a group of soldiers, Guthrie and Hackermeyer among them. "Cover these windows! Cooley, watch them. I'll take out the first bunch."

Hackermeyer tottered to one of the front windows and, leaning the bazooka against the wall, unslung his rifle. The tank he'd
hit was just outside, burning quietly, a pall of black smoke curling
up from it. The odor of it filled his nostrils. As he drank some
water from his canteen, he wondered what was going to happen
next. He shook his head in tiny, fitful movements. There was no
way of knowing. Everything was in such a jumble.

Outside, a German machine gun opened fire and he jerked
back from the window. Looking around, he saw the first group
starting to climb through the hole in the wall. He watched them
running, one by one, across the rubble-strewn ruins behind the
house. One of them got hit and tumbled over on his side. He
crawled several feet, then was hit again and stopped moving.

"Get that bastard gun!" yelled someone.

Hackermeyer turned and looked out through the window, trying to pick out the gun's location. He ducked back instinctively
as a line of bullets ripped across the outside wall.

"Get ready," Cooley said. Hackermeyer turned and saw the
sergeant gesturing for them to assemble. He slung the bazooka
on his back and walked across the room, overshoes crunching on
the carpet of glass, plaster, and wood.

"Take off." Cooley patted the shoulder of a man Hackermeyer
had never seen before. The man clambered through the opening,
hesitated momentarily, then zigzagged across the ruins, pursued
by the geysering pound of machine-gun bullets. He dashed behind a distant brick wall and disappeared. Cooley sent out a second man. MacFarland went next, followed by Guthrie. They all
dashed crookedly across the open area and lunged behind the
wall, unhurt.

"All right, Hack," said Cooley.

Sucking in breath, Hackermeyer climbed through the hole
and started running in erratic lines toward the wall. Somewhere,
behind and above him, the machine gun opened fire again. He
heard the whistling hail of bullets, the clanging howl of ricochets,
the noise of stone and mortar being chewed away. Then the wall

was ahead of him and he ran behind it. Rocking to a halt, he leaned against the wet brick, gasping for breath. After several moments, he glanced around the edge of the wall. Cooley was just emerging from the house. Hackermeyer's muscles twitched empathically as the sergeant started across the open ground.

Suddenly, Cooley was hit. He staggered beneath the impact of bullets, picked up speed again, then lost his balance and crashed down clumsily in the rubble. Hackermeyer gaped at him in mute, incredulous horror. Cooley lay twisted and immobile. Unaware of it, Hackermeyer took a faltering step away from the wall.

"Get back here," ordered a voice.

Hackermeyer started running.

"Get back here, soldier!" cried the voice. Hackermeyer didn't listen. He ran as fast as he could toward Cooley, barely conscious of the bullets snapping around him. All he could see was the sergeant's body lying in the snow-coated rubble.

He reached Cooley and dropped beside him, groaning as he saw the sergeant's left shoulder and back running blood.

"Sarge?" he said. He couldn't hear his voice above the rattle of the machine gun. He reached down and touched the sergeant's cheek. Cooley's eyes fluttered open.

"Get out of here!" he gasped.

Hackermeyer felt a surge of relief. Suddenly, he was conscious of the bullets flashing past him. Grabbing hold of Cooley's web belt, he started to drag the sergeant toward the house. A fleck of bullet-struck mortar raked across his nose, making him gasp.

"Stop it!" Cooley cried weakly. "Get out of here!"

Hackermeyer didn't answer. Breath hissing through clenched teeth, he kept dragging Cooley through the bullet-pierced area, trying not to look back at the trail of blood.

"Hack, stop!" said Cooley.

Shut up! cried the voice. Hackermeyer kept towing desperately. He tried to pull the sergeant faster but Cooley seemed to be made of lead. Suddenly his hand slipped off the web belt and he crashed to the ground. Nearby lay the dead soldier, staring at him. Pushing up with a frightened gasp, Hackermeyer forced his fingers underneath the belt again and started hauling as quickly as he could. *Please, please, please*, he begged.

The house loomed up in front of them. Hackermeyer dragged Cooley through the opening in the wall, then, panting in exhaustion, muscles aching, he sank to the floor and stared at Cooley's back and shoulder. What was he going to do? He should have taken Cooley to the brick wall instead of back to the house. I couldn't have, he thought: the house was closer. He shuddered and looked around. What was he going to do?

Impulsively, he started to unbutton Cooley's overcoat. He had to get to the wound, he told himself. He had to bandage it so it wouldn't bleed so much.

"Hack."

He glanced at Cooley's pain-contorted face.

"Hack, get the hell out of here," said Cooley. He could hardly speak.

Hackermeyer grunted noncommittally.

"Hack—"

Hackermeyer pressed his shaking lips together. I'm not leaving, answered his mind. He tried to pull the sleeve off Cooley's left arm and Cooley gasped in pain. Hackermeyer bit his lip. "I'm sorry," he said. "I didn't mean to."

Cooley gritted his teeth and forced a grimacing smile.

"Hack." He swallowed. "Go away, son."

"No." Hackermeyer's voice was drowned out by the roar of an explosion in the street.

The skin tensed on Cooley's cheeks. "Hack, Goddamn it . . ."

"No!" He almost shouted it. With an angry motion, he jerked the sleeve from Cooley's arm. The sergeant's face went white. Hackermeyer shuddered. I didn't mean to, he thought. I have to stop the bleeding, don't I? He stared at the blood on his hands.

Abruptly, he looked around. "Stretcher bearer!" he shouted.

"Hack, for God's sake—"

"*No!*" Hackermeyer blinked away the obscuring shimmer of tears. "Stretcher bearer!" he yelled. He bit his teeth together till they hurt. "Goddamn . . ." he muttered, fumbling with his first-aid kit. He couldn't get it open and he sobbed with fury.

"Take it easy, son," said Cooley.

"No," he mumbled, as if Cooley were still telling him to leave. He helped Cooley swallow the pill, then sprinkled sulfa powder on the bloody, flesh-ripped wound. There was no time to remove the sergeant's field jacket. Pulling off his glove, Hackermeyer tried to pick shreds of the jacket material from the blood-pulsing slash. Rage exploded in him suddenly. *Goddamn, lousy Germans! He'd kill them all!* He rubbed a shaking hand across his lips as terror gripped him. What good was a little powder? What good was a pill? The blood still pumped from Cooley's body. Hackermeyer looked around in panic.

"Stretcher bearer!" he screamed. "Medics! Stretcher bearer! Medic!"

When he turned back, Cooley's eyes were shut.

"No." He bent over quickly, face twisted with fear. "Sarge?"

Cooley opened his eyes.

"Oh, for—" Hackermeyer started bandaging the compress over Cooley's wound. "Keep your eyes open," he muttered brokenly.

Cooley looked at him through slitted eyes. "Hack, for Christ's sake, will you get out of here?"

"Just keep your eyes open!" Hackermeyer cut him off.

He ran out of gauze strip and opened Cooley's first-aid kit. As he went on bandaging, he realized that he was crying, his chest hitching with sobs, tears rolling endlessly down his cheeks. The hell with it, he thought.

"Hack . . ."

He glanced at Cooley's face. The sergeant was smiling at him.

"I'll be all right now, son," Cooley murmured. "Why don't you go?"

Hackermeyer swallowed, tasting the salt of his tears. "No," he said, "I'm not—"

He whirled at the noise and jolted with shock. Out in the street, a German soldier had just gone running past the house. For a moment, Hackermeyer couldn't move. Then, he lunged for his rifle and jerked it off the floor. Flicking off the safety catch, he waited tensely, gaze darting from window to door to window and back again, the beating of his heart like knife-thrusts in his chest. He glanced at Cooley.

"Krauts?" the sergeant whispered.

Hackermeyer nodded, swallowing. "Krauts," he said.

In the street, another German trooper hurried past, equipment rattling. Suddenly, Hackermeyer drew back the Mr bolt. There was a clip inside. As he raised his head, he saw that Cooley was trying to sit up. He leaned over and pressed on Cooley's shoulder.

"Stay there," he whispered.

His head jerked around, a flash of movement catching his eye. For an instant, he and the German soldier looked at each other. Then Hackermeyer jerked up his rifle. Before he could fire, the German bolted out of sight. Hackermeyer lunged to his feet and rushed to the window. He saw the soldier rearing back to hurl a grenade through the other window and, flinging the M1 to his shoulder, he fired twice. The German toppled backward and fell, the grenade rolling from his fingers and exploding just as Hackermeyer ducked beneath the level of the window sill. Shrapnel thudded off the door.

Rearing up, Hackermeyer leaned across the sill and looked toward the square. He jerked back, startled. Dozens of advancing Germans lined the street. Hackermeyer stood frozen, wondering what to do. He started to take a grenade off his belt, then let go of it. It wouldn't be enough. He backed off slowly, the M1 level at his waist. Reaching Cooley, he knelt and, with shaking fingers, pulled cartridge clips from his belt, laying them out on the floor.

"What's up?" asked Cooley.

"Nothing. Just—" Hackermeyer glanced around for Cooley's carbine, then realized it was still outside where Cooley had fallen. He started up to retrieve it, changed his mind. No time. He wondered if he could get Cooley behind the house before the Germans got there. No, there was no time. The Germans would catch them moving and there wouldn't be a chance. Their only chance was that the passing Germans wouldn't look in through the windows. Even as he thought it, Hackermeyer knew it was impossible. One of them was sure to look.

Hastily, he jerked the grenades from his belt and put them on the floor. He was ready now. A momentary calm swept over him. He had a strange desire to smile. For some incredible reason, he wasn't afraid.

He looked down at Cooley. The sergeant's eyes were closed again. Hackermeyer started to speak, then decided that it was better if Cooley did keep his eyes shut; better if he didn't see what was about to happen. Hackermeyer smiled at him. He felt tears welling hotly to his eyes.

"It's all right," he whispered. "I'll take care of you. I'll—"

He stopped and glanced up in surprise. There was something in the sky. It grew in volume: a hissing, oscillating noise like that of a giant ax blade whirling. Closer and closer it came. Hackermeyer stared dumbly at the ceiling. What's that? he thought.

Then the world exploded. A roaring sea of darkness flooded over him. The last thing he was conscious of was throwing himself across Cooley to protect him. Then it was night.

HACKERMEYER OPENED HIS eyes and stared up at the chandelier. There was a mumbling of voices around him; footsteps, the sound of someone moaning faintly. Hackermeyer struggled up on an elbow, wincing at the stab of pain in his head. He looked around dizzily.

He was lying in a hotel lobby. Everywhere he turned, men were stretched out on folded blankets, medics and doctors moving among them. Hackermeyer squinted, trying to understand what had happened. At first his mind was clouded. Then, suddenly, he caught his breath.

"Sarge," he mumbled.

As he sat up, the pain exploded in his head. Hissing convulsively, he pressed both hands against his skull and bent over double, feeling as if he were about to vomit. He remained stiffly motionless for more than two minutes before attempting to raise his head again.

Nearby, a doctor was giving an injection to a wounded soldier. Hackermeyer watched until the doctor moved away, then turned and looked at the soldier lying to his left. The man was either dead or sleeping; Hackermeyer couldn't tell which. He turned his head and looked at the soldier on his right. The man was gazing fixedly at the ceiling, a bitter expression on his face. Hackermeyer's stomach heaved as he saw that the man's right leg was gone.

He stood up carefully, holding to the wall for support. His legs felt hot and aching. They began to quiver under him and he leaned against the wall. I have to walk, he thought; I have to find Sergeant Cooley. Straightening, he moved unsteadily to the aisle, which ran between the rows of prostrate soldiers. He started along the aisle, walking with studied care. He wanted to lie down and rest, but he willed himself on. He had to find Cooley. As he shuffled inchingly across the lobby floor, his gaze moved from side to side. He had to keep blinking to force away the darkness lapping at his feet.

A doctor passed him, muttering, "Latrine's outside, soldier." Hackermeyer kept limping toward a sofa at the end of the aisle. A man was sitting on it, smoking a cigarette. The man's right arm had been amputated just below the elbow; blood drops leaked from the bandage. He looked up as Hackermeyer reached the sofa. "Hi," he said, gesturing with his remaining hand. Ashes powdered from the cigarette and flecked across his lap.

Hackermeyer swallowed laboredly. "Have you . . . seen a—a sergeant?" he asked. His tongue felt thick and heavy.

The man snickered. "Seen lots of 'em," he said.

Hackermeyer cleared his throat, his eyes slitting as the pain in his temples grew worse.

"What happened to you?" asked the soldier.

Hackermeyer looked confused. "I—I don't know," he said. He looked around dazedly. "I better . . ."

He turned away and hobbled past the lobby entrance. Outside, in the darkness, several ambulances were backed up to the door. Two medics came inside.

"Hey, kid, you want to lend us a hand?" one of them said to Hackermeyer.

"Forget it, Charlie," said the other one. "He wouldn't be any use to us."

"Say . . ." Hackermeyer spoke as they hurried past him.

"What?" the one named Charlie asked across his shoulder.

"Is there a—sergeant in here?"

"Plenty of 'em. Take your choice."

"No," said Hackermeyer. "His name is—"

He watched the two medics moving off. Suddenly, he felt very weak and dizzy; the floor appeared to undulate beneath him. He closed his eyes and felt himself weaving back and forth in the darkness, then jerked them open again, thinking he was about to fall. Holding himself tensely, he started for the clerk's desk. A medic was sitting behind it, drinking from a paper cup.

"Say," said Hackermeyer.

The man looked up. His eyes were bloodshot, rimmed by wrinkled, shadowy skin. "Uh?" he mumbled.

"You . . . seen a sergeant. Cooley?"

The man coughed weakly.

"He's in . . . Company C," said Hackermeyer, leaning on the desk.

The man shook his head. "Christ's sake, I don't know," he answered, slurring the words. "There's a million guys in here, for Christ's sake."

Hackermeyer stared at him. The man's hand flopped on the desk as he gestured toward a box of paper cups, a collection of bottles, and a kitchen pot. "Have some gin and grapefruit juice," he said thickly. "Do you good."

Hackermeyer turned away and stumbled across the lobby toward an archway leading to what looked like a ballroom. As he moved, he saw another archway opening on what once might have been a dining room. Both rooms looked immense and both were crammed with wounded soldiers. Hackermeyer moaned softly as he visualized the job of finding Cooley. What if he's dead? he thought. He forced the idea away with an angry shudder. He's not, he told himself.

He stopped and rubbed the palm of his right hand across his sweating brow. He looked at the back of his hand. The knuckles were scraped and raw, caked with a lacing of dried blood. He let the hand drop and started walking again, moving up and down the ballroom aisles, searching for Cooley. He saw a boy crying in a corner and thought it was Tremont. He looked closer and saw that it wasn't.

"Hey, get me a drink of water," a man demanded. Hacker-meyer glanced at him.

"I—I don't know where—" he started.

"Forget it!" snapped the man. "Go to hell, you son of a bitch!"

Hackermeyer turned away and continued down the aisle. The man had reminded him of Lazzo. He wondered if he should try to get the man a drink of water. No, he thought; he couldn't stop until he'd found Cooley.

He moved through the entire ballroom, peering into every face he passed. Whenever a doctor or a medic came near him, he tried to stop them and ask about Cooley. Most of them brushed by curtly, too busy to stop. Those who did stop had no idea who Cooley was, much less where he was located. Hack-ermeyer kept on going. He was afraid to lie down now, certain that, if he did, he wouldn't be able to get up again. His head pounded, his limbs felt hot and fluid as he shambled through the dining room. Cooley wasn't there either.

Hackermeyer sat limply at the bottom of the lobby staircase. He isn't dead, he kept telling himself. He's all right, I know he's all right. But the fear kept mounting.

"Watch it, soldier," someone said behind him.

Hackermeyer looked across his shoulder and saw a medic leading a wounded man down the stairs. He pulled himself up and watched the two men passing by, then his glazed eyes shifted and he looked up the staircase. There must be more up there, he thought. Bracing himself, he started up. Each step was a total effort for him. He wanted desperately to lie down and close his eyes but he wouldn't let himself. He's upstairs, he thought; Ser-geant Cooley's upstairs.

A doctor came down the steps.

"Sir . . . ?" said Hackermeyer.

The doctor glanced at him. "You better lie down, boy," he said.

"Are there—more upstairs?"

The doctor smiled grimly. "On every floor," he said. He patted Hackermeyer's arm. "You better go downstairs and get some rest."

"No, I have to look for—"

"Suit yourself, boy, suit yourself," the doctor interrupted gruffly. "You better get off your feet soon, though."

"Have you seen—?"

Hackermeyer broke off as the doctor left him. He saw the staircase start to waver darkly and, with a startled gasp, he caught at the banister. No! he thought; I can't! He stood there trembling, clutching at the banister. He should sit down for a while. He shook his head obdurately. No. He had to find Cooley first.

Gritting his teeth, he started up the stairs again. The staircase stretched on endlessly ahead of him, each step higher than the one below it. Hackermeyer mounted them infirmly, resting between each upward movement. His legs and ankles felt as though they were made of heavy, fragile glass that might shatter underneath his weight at any moment. Sweat rivuleted down his cheeks and dripped from his eyebrows. Just a little more, he told himself. A little more now and you're there. There it is. A little way; just a little way. One more step. One more.

When he, finally, reached the second-floor landing, he sagged against the wall; then, unable to stop himself, slid down into a heap. No, don't! he begged. He fought away the darkness frantically. If he fainted, they might take Cooley away without him knowing it.

He raised his head inertly, squinting down the corridor. As far as he could see, wounded men lay shoulder to shoulder on the floor, plasma bottles dangling over most of them. Coughing weakly, Hackermeyer pushed himself against the wall until he made his feet again. Bracing himself, he started walking.

He had just reached the doorway to the first room when a piercing scream burst over him. Turning with a gasp, he saw half a leg thump down on the floor. Bile rose, gagging, in his throat as he twisted away, the scene etched vividly on his mind—the young soldier on a table, trying to sit up, a look of pain and horror on his face; the aid-man holding him back; the gray-faced doctor straightening up, a bloody scalpel in his hand. Hackermeyer felt his stomach roiling hotly. Stumbling against the wall, he leaned his forehead against its rough coolness. Please, God, *please!*

"Hack?"

Hackermeyer jerked his head around.

"Over here, son."

Hackermeyer was unable to repress the sob. Cooley lay on his back several yards away, a plasma bottle hung above him. Hackermeyer staggered to him, slipping to his knees. The sergeant's face seemed to draw back into fluttering shadows.

"Easy, son," said Cooley.

Hackermeyer couldn't seem to see. He closed his eyes, then opened them again. As in a dream, he saw his right hand reaching out for Cooley. The sergeant raised his left hand and their fingers locked.

"I'm glad to see you, son," said Cooley.

Hackermeyer thought he laughed. He rubbed unconsciously at the tears. "Yeah." He sniffled happily. "Yeah," he said. "H-how are you?"

"I'll be all right, buddy. How are you?"

"Fine!"

Cooley grunted, smiling. "Fine, huh?" he said. "You look like something the cat dragged in. Here." Letting go of Hackermeyer's hand, he lifted up a corner of the blanket over him and patted at Hackermeyer's face. "You're pouring sweat," he said.

"I am?" Hackermeyer smiled distractedly. "I—I don't know what's wrong with me. I don't know why I'm here even."

"How come you're walking around?" asked Cooley.

"I was—" Hackermeyer gestured. "I was just—looking for you."

Cooley smiled at him affectionately.

"You saved my life," he said.

Hackermeyer shook his head. "I didn't do anything," he said.

"The hell you didn't." Cooley grinned at him. "What's more, you were going to face the whole damn Kraut Army to do it."

"Me?"

"I saw," said Cooley. "Your cartridge clips on the floor. Your grenades." He snorted softly. "What did you think you were going to do—fight them all off?"

Hackermeyer shrugged. "No," he answered. "I just—"

He stopped and shook his head. "No," he said quietly. "I knew I was going to die."

"You could have ducked out the back," said Cooley.

Hackermeyer shook his head again. "Not without you," he said.

They looked at each other in silence. Then Hackermeyer coughed embarrassedly. "Wh-what happened to us anyway?" he asked.

"Near as I can figure out," said Cooley, "a shell landed on the house. Probably exploded that tank."

"Oh." Hackermeyer grimaced. "Is—is everybody else all right?"

"Didn't you know Tremont was killed?"

Hackermeyer looked blank. "He was?" he murmured.

"Yeah, he got it in the square, poor kid."

"I didn't know."

"I don't know about Guthrie and MacFarland," said Cooley. "I been out cold all afternoon."

"Uh-huh." Hackermeyer managed a smile. "Well," he said, "I guess you got a—million-dollar wound, hanh?"

"Guess I have," said Cooley.

"You won't have to—"

Hackermeyer's voice broke as icy terror gripped him. *Cooley wouldn't be with the squad anymore.*

"What's the matter, son?" asked Cooley.

"Nothing." Hackermeyer lowered his head so Cooley wouldn't see the movement at his throat. He wished he could tell Cooley how he felt. "I—I guess you'll be going home, huh?" he asked faintly.

"I don't know, Hack."

"Yeah." Hackermeyer nodded. "Well," he said, "maybe I'll . . ." He shrugged. ". . . be—you know—seeing you again. Sometime."

"I hope so," Cooley answered.

"I mean . . ." Hackermeyer lowered his eyes, then raised them anxiously. Had Cooley forgotten?

"You come out whenever you're ready, son," Cooley told him.

Hackermeyer shivered. "Yeah," he said, "I—will."

There was a trudge of footsteps in the corridor. Hackermeyer glanced aside as a doctor and two litter bearers came up beside him.

"He goes," the doctor said, pointing at Cooley.

Hackermeyer felt a sudden, painful contraction in his heart. He watched dumbly as the two men lifted Cooley onto the stretcher. Take me too, he thought; please; take me too?

Cooley turned his head.

"Take care now, Hack," he said. "We'll be seeing each other."

"Yeah." Hackermeyer felt a heavy throbbing in his head as he watched the litter bearers carrying off the sergeant. Abruptly, he pushed to his feet and hobbled down the corridor, teeth clenched against the waves of pain inside his head. At the top of the staircase, he stopped and watched Cooley being carried across the lobby. Good-bye! called a voice in his mind.

"Good-bye," he said. He stood immobile as Cooley disappeared through the entranceway. Then it was as if a cape of lead were thrown across his shoulders. Sinking to the top step, he leaned his head against the banister. Good-bye, repeated the voice. I'll see you again. I'll come to your house and live with you, okay?

He didn't know how much time had elapsed when he pushed to his feet and walked slowly back along the corridor. Entering one of the less crowded rooms, he found an empty spot and lay down. His body seemed to run into the floorboards like melting wax. Only his mind remained active.

He started to think about living on Cooley's ranch. What would it be like? he wondered. Would Mrs. Cooley take to him?

Or would he remind her of the son she'd lost? Maybe he could replace Jimmy, he thought, then frowned to himself. Of course he couldn't; Mrs. Cooley would resent him if he tried. He had never replaced his aunt's son, had he?

Hackermeyer pressed his lips together resolutely. Never mind, he thought. He'd make her like him. He'd work so hard and be so polite that she'd have to like him. After all, didn't he save her husband's life? Hackermeyer smiled, imagining himself being introduced to her. This is the boy who saved my life, Cooley told her. She put her arms around Hackermeyer and kissed him on the cheek. You're welcome in this house, she said. You bet you are, said Cooley—son.

Hackermeyer's chest labored with agitated breath. I love him, he thought, the words suddenly in his mind. At first they startled and embarrassed him. Then he relaxed. So what? he thought. Why shouldn't he? You didn't save somebody's life because you hated him, did you? Christ's sake.

Hackermeyer furrowed his brow. Didn't Guthrie say that love was the answer? It occurred to him that love might have been the one strength that Linstrom had possessed. Maybe that was why Linstrom had always irritated him so.

Hackermeyer closed his eyes. Never mind, he thought. It was too complicated. Things weren't that easy to explain. All right, so love was the answer; he'd let it go at that. The notion pleased him and that was enough for now.

"Hey."

Hackermeyer opened his eyes and looked to his right. In the corner of the room, a soldier was lying on a stretcher. Almost entirely bandaged, he looked like a shapeless mummy. Hackermeyer gaped. He saw the mummy's eyes looking into his. Then the mummy's lips moved and a hollow, cracking voice emerged.

"Well, I'll never play the violin again," the mummy said.

Hackermeyer's mouth slipped open. "Guthrie?"

"The same," croaked Guthrie. "Don't worry, boys, it's only a flesh wound."

Hackermeyer rolled onto his side and pushed up on an elbow. "What happened to you?" he asked.

"A wall fell on me, that's what happened," answered Guthrie.

"A *wall?*"

"A whole Goddamn wall," said Guthrie, nodding his bandage-swathed head. "Where the hell were you?"

"Huh?"

"I was waiting for you," said Guthrie hoarsely. "When you went back into that house with Cooley, I told them I'd stay and cover you when you came out. Only you didn't come out. Then those damn shells started landing and there I was under a brick wall. What a hell of a way for a hero to go."

Hackermeyer didn't know what to say. He looked at Guthrie with a pained expression. "Are you . . . hurting?" he asked.

"No, I'm loaded with something or other," rasped Guthrie. "I can't feel a thing. Only aggravation."

"Gee, I'm sorry." Hackermeyer shook his head. "A wall," he said.

"What happened to you?" asked Guthrie.

"I got—caught in that house," Hackermeyer told him. "I guess it fell on me—and Cooley." He brightened. "I saw him just before," he said.

"Yeah? How is he?"

"Okay. They took him out. To a hospital, I guess."

Guthrie nodded. "Yeah." He coughed weakly. "What happened to MacFarland?"

"I don't know."

Guthrie clucked. "Last I saw of him, he was taking off with the others. I expect he's all right."

"You know Tremont's dead?"

"Yeah," said Guthrie. "I saw it happen."

"Oh." Hackermeyer nodded. "Well," he said, "I guess you'll be—going home."

"I guess," said Guthrie. He blew out breath. "Guess there's just no killing me. I might as well go on."

Hackermeyer looked at him intently.

"Did you want to get killed?" he asked.

The mummy sighed. "I don't know," said Guthrie. "I don't think I cared much." He grunted. "Although I sure got mad when we got stuck in that house, didn't I? I guess I don't want to die stupidly anyway. That's something."

Hackermeyer nodded. Everyone was going home but him, he thought.

"Where will you live?" he asked.

"If I'm discharged?"

"Yeah."

"Oh . . . I'll get me a place somewhere. Santa Monica, Malibu."

"You won't live with your father?"

"No; hell no. He just got hitched again. He doesn't want me around."

Hackermeyer grunted. It was strange, but, for the first time since they'd met, Guthrie seemed his age.

"I wish—" he started.

"What do you wish, Hackermeyer?" asked the mummy.

"Oh . . ." Hackermeyer hesitated. "I'm—going to live with Cooley," he said.

The mummy eyed him speculatively. "Are, huh?" it said.

"Yeah. Yeah, he said I could come live on his ranch in—I forget the name." Hackermeyer stiffened. "Oh, God, I forget the name! No, no, it's—it's Taos, Taos. That's New Mexico."

"Yeah, I know," said Guthrie. "I went there once."

"You did?"

"There's an artist's colony there," said Guthrie. "I went with my father to visit some screwball painter."

"But—"

"I'm sure there are ranches there too," said Guthrie.

"Oh. Uh-huh." Hackermeyer swallowed hard. "Well, that's where I am going," he said. "Too bad—" He broke off awkwardly. "I mean . . . Well, it's too bad you can't come too."

Guthrie chuckled. "Me living with Cooley," he said. "What a vision." The chuckle faded to a sigh. "Yeah, yeah," he said. "Too bad about Russell Guthrie. What will become of him?"

The mummy groaned.

"Tune in tomorrow," it said.

HACKERMEYER LAY ON his back, hands clasped behind his head. A few minutes before, he had put away his wallet after looking at the photograph of his mother. He'd put it away without the usual pang because, for the first time he could remember, the future seemed to promise something good and no longer did he have to dwell on what might have been.

He thought about his wanting to die during the last few days. He knew that he'd only been looking for an escape. He didn't want to die now. He wanted to face the challenge of living.

He frowned as doubts assailed him once more. Had he really changed so much? How could he have, in such a short time? He stared upward in distress until it occurred to him that it didn't matter how much he'd changed. He knew he *had* to change, that was what counted. There was still a long way to go; but at least he was on the path.

Hackermeyer closed his eyes and sighed. Good night, he thought, I'll see you in the morning, Hack.

He sneezed. This Goddamn cold.

DECEMBER 23, 1944

SERGEANT EVERETT HACKERMEYER stood looking at the snow-covered hills beyond Saarbach. An icy wind scoured across the square, whipping the canvas tops of the trucks backing into position beside the company: the trucks they were to ride to Belgium.

Hackermeyer turned and looked at his squad: MacFarland—who was his assistant—and the four replacements. Hackermeyer repressed a smile. Three of the replacements were eighteen-year-olds. It was odd how young they looked to him; how inexperienced. He felt like Regular Army compared to them.

He turned to watch the truck backing in toward the platoon. After several moments, his eyes drifted out of focus. *Maybe you'll see Christmas*, he thought. He smiled, remembering the times Cooley had spoken those words. He'd see Christmas, all right.

If he had to, he'd see the whole damn war to its finish. Then he'd go to New Mexico and live with Cooley. Nothing could keep him from it. And, in the meantime, he'd take good care of the squad. The way Cooley had taken care of it.

He refocused his eyes as the truck was braked, and one of the platoon officers shouted, "All right! Pile in!" Hackermeyer turned to the squad, lips parted as he sought the words for his first command. Then he grunted with amusement.

"All right," he said. "*Come* on, children."

He turned away with a smile. Funny, he thought. It was the first time he could remember trying to make a joke. Guthrie would be proud of him.

Hackermeyer started forward.